Outside

ROCK STARS, SURF AND SECOND CHANCES

MICHELLE MANKIN

AMAZON BESTSELLING AUTHOR

Copyright © 2015 by Michelle Mankin
Cover created by Michelle Preast of Indie Book Covers
(https://www.facebook.com/IndieBookCovers)
Copy editing by Dr. Diane Klein
Interior design and formatting by JT Formatting

Library of Congress Cataloging-in-Publication Data
First Paperback Edition: July 2015

Mankin, Michelle
Outside (a Rock Stars, Surf and Second Chances novel) — 1st edition
ISBN-13: 978-1514661000 | ISBN-10: 1514661004

The steady churn of the ocean was our music

—Lincoln Savage

Part One

Prologue

Simone

I stumbled almost falling as I took the stage, tottering precariously on my three inch platform heels. For a moment I thought I had seen...but that was crazy. I gave myself an internal shake. It had been years. He was never coming back to Ocean Beach. Never coming back to me. He would never come through on any of his promises to me.

I smoothed my fingers over my curves. Though an indulgence much too expensive given my budget, the Lilly Pulitzer original I wore *was* gorgeous with pearl buttons on the neckline, an elegant scalloped hem and an artfully arranged whisper blue Lilly pad pattern that made it appear sheer under the lights. I didn't return my gaze to the corner where a flash of flame had seemed to reveal the harsh lines and stubborn planes of the ruggedly handsome face that I had sworn years ago to forget.

Just my overactive imagination conjuring up old desires and not a few regrets.

I moved to the center microphone, years of practice on the small stage making my sashaying stride seem confident and self-assured when I was neither tonight. Still unsettled, I stalled taking a sip from a bottled water and making sure the musicians were set while scanning the crowd at the popular San Diego club. Packed as usual, dozens of regulars with their leathery tans but also a handful of sunburned newbies sprinkled in. They sipped their specialty cocktails, few seeming to acknowledge me as they chatted beneath the flashing neon lights waiting for the music to begin.

After years of singing every Thursday through Saturday nights at the Tiki Bar I had developed a significant and loyal following. They had their expectations. I wasn't about to let them down. But expectations were tricky things. They could turn on you fast enough to snap your neck.

Nerves worse than usual my palms were sweaty as I grabbed the mic and turned to nod at Stan, my drummer. He laid down the beat. I closed my eyes and went to a different place. Way back in time to another place and another stage when I had been even more nervous, back when he had still been there to comfort me…

"I can't do it." I gulped down oxygen in slow shallow sips trying not to hurl at just the thought of going out there and singing in front of all those people. Important people, media and industry types.

"You've got this, Mona. It's nothing you haven't done

before."

"At school. In musicals. That one time at the Deck Bar. But never when it counted so much."

"Relax, babe." He pulled me into his strong capable arms, his warm hands settling on the curve of my hips, his talented fingers rubbing tempting soothing circles into my skin. I drew in his familiar scent, the ocean and sunshine embedded in his skin from all of the hours he spent on his surfboard. Totally and uniquely him. "Listen to me. No one has a voice like you do. I get chills every time I hear it. There's no way they aren't going to fall in love with you the way I have." He eased back his clear blue eyes traveling the length of me, his lip curling in appreciation at what he saw. There wasn't much he couldn't see with my borrowed slinky dress revealing too much thigh and cleavage.

"I'm gonna be sick." I tried to shrug out of his grasp but he held me tightly. "Please, Linc. Let me go." I dropped my chin, staring at the silver heart pendent that contained our initials. "I just can't do it. I'm sorry."

"You can." He gently lifted my chin with his curled forefinger. The inexpensive silver skull ring I had bought for him from the vendor on the beach felt cold against my clammy skin. "I'll walk with you right to the stage."

I stilled taking a couple of deep breaths, wanting to make him proud. Always wanting to please him. Loving him so desperately with every fiber of my being. Never coming close to imagining how badly he would break me at the end.

"Simone?" Ron my guitarist hissed bringing me and my thoughts back to the present.

"Yeah, thanks." Unable to help myself after that flashback my gaze traveled again to that corner, illuminated by the flickering hurricane candle in the center of the pub table. Long legs sprawled out in front of whoever sat there but the brim of a ball cap completely shadowed his features. It couldn't really be him. My mind had to be playing tricks on me.

Linc wasn't the type of guy to slink around in some back corner. If he went to clubs at all anymore he would be there in the front row surrounded by security, crooking his finger at whatever babe he had chosen to spend the night.

I ripped my gaze away from the phantom, shutting my mind to the delusion that my time with Linc represented and channeled all of my jumbled emotions into a song I had written way back when I used to believe in love.

Believe in the promise of us
Hearts as one love's guarantee
A bond so strong we both can trust
To draw us close whatever may be

I just want you to
Take me
And shape me
Remake me
Baby, come on and
Save me.

Outside

Lies between us in the dark
Hearts divided you and me
Ties all broken we're apart
Drifting on an empty sea

Why can't you just
Take me
And shape me
Remake me
Baby, reach out and
Save me.

I don't need some perfect hero
All I really want is you
By my side today tomorrow
Tell me that you want me, too

Please come back and
Take me
And shape me
Remake me
I'm begging you to
Save me.

Chapter 1

Linc

T he bar fell silent as she finished. A round serving tray clutched tight to her chest, the bleach blonde who had been waiting on me stood as motionless as the Hula girl statue that adorned my table. My eyes glistened from the same poignant ache she was trying to hug away. The patrons were mesmerized. Even the jaded bartenders paused to shake off the melancholy mood her lyrics invoked before returning to complete their drink orders. I found myself leaning forward as if to close the physical distance between us, my grip so hard on the table top that my knuckles had turned white.

The song washed up a summer's worth of heart crushing memories. Simone was still just as breathtakingly gorgeous and talented as ever. She epitomized perfection. Pitch. Range. Interpretation. Moves. Beauty.

Unforgettable.

Her caramel colored hair didn't have quite as many sun

streaked highlights as it had back when she'd been mine, nor was her tan as deep. I wanted to believe she wasn't spending as much time sitting on the beach in a bikini mooning over some other guy out in the surf. But her olive toned skin was still sun kissed and her locks were still long, wavy and loose around her delicate shoulders. Her eyes were squeezed shut as if she weren't prepared to let go of the past, *our past*, and her hands, the ones that used to caress me bringing both my body and my soul to life, remained tightly woven together around the mic.

She had written that song for me, for us, a plaintive last plea that I had ignored. I sucked in a ragged breath. Hearing it was like a knife through my heart. But I didn't have one. Not anymore. Not since she had left me.

The inside of my hollow chest burned as I was crushed by the weight of those memories.

That first time I had seen her on the beach. So young. So shy. So incredibly beautiful.

That first time she had looked at me with more than just adoration in her striking, lit from within honey hued eyes. That perfect kiss which had followed.

And then there was that last time. That night I lost her. That night her life affirming love turned to scorn. That night the light had gone out of my life.

I never should have come back.

I should have let the lawyers handle it.

But I couldn't stay away.

Not anymore.

Not when I finally had a legitimate reason to see her.

Not knowing everything I knew now.

She started to sing again. This time it was a tune I

didn't recognize but I knew it must be an original. Her song crafting structure was more complicated now than it had been back then, but it was still poetically lyrical as rhythmic, bluesy and beautiful as she was.

She swayed side to side behind the mic pole. A sexy temptress, her dress a seduction that concealed more than it revealed, and me in my world of denial wanting to believe that I was still the only man in the room who knew all that lay beneath it.

Graceful. Sensual. The initial stiffness only I had probably noticed when she first took the stage was completely gone. No woman moved the way she did. No woman felt the way she did like warm satin beneath my fingertips. No woman so reminded me of the ocean at dawn wild and free and full of possibilities. No woman's scent was as sweet, like a crisp California breeze. No woman made love to me as if savoring every single stroke and caress.

No woman came close, other women only temporarily satisfied a physical need, nothing more. No one had ever met my spiritual needs the way she once had.

I watched her effortlessly drift through two more tunes as the club grew more and more crowded, the bodies packed together on the dance floor slowly shuffling to the sultry beat. The next round of applause included a thinly veiled sexual proposition from some guy in the crowd. My fingers curled tighter around the O'Doul's bottle that had grown warm in my hand. I was too busy slaking years of unquenchable thirst on the vision of her to bother with any cheap non-alcoholic substitute.

Simone lifted a bottled water to her perfect lips, her honeyed gaze straying back in my direction. She might as well have palmed me through my jeans.

I pulled my ball cap lower over my fevered eyes and shifted, trying to adjust myself without being obvious like some hormonal teenager.

"Last number before I take a break." She poured the words into the mic, her voice as rich and nuanced as the expensive bourbon I had been fond of in the past. The news of her imminent departure sent a rustle of disappointment through the mostly male crowd.

"Any requests?" she asked curling her lips into a ghost of a smile. It wasn't the smile that used to turn my world upside down but it was a seductive one nonetheless, and it engendered a few more ribald remarks.

She ignored their innuendos cocking her head to the side, a long tendril of light caramel curling around her right breast. My fingers flexed remembering the way she used to arch those luscious tits of hers into my worshiping hands.

"'Last Night of the World'." My voice was huskier than usual because of the direction of my thoughts and because of the memory that accompanied that particular tune.

Her head snapped my way, her skin paling as the blood seemed to drain completely away from her pretty face. I tipped the brim of my cap back and leaned forward into the light. Her gaze locked on mine. Her hand went to her throat.

"Linc."

I was sorry I had startled her but it was worth it just to hear my name flowing over her lips in a breathless whisper the way it once had so easily so long ago.

Chapter 2

Simone

*E*very single muscle every fiber of my being froze focused on the man who once had been the sun in my personal universe.

Linc was as handsome as he had ever been and any subtle differences I could make out only added to his allure. Not that I would ever admit it aloud. Leather jacket over a faded t-shirt. Worn jeans. Tall lean physique. Not the type of guy who spent every waking moment pressing weights, but definitely in shape and completely at ease within a body he knew how to move in the most pleasurable ways possible.

His hair color defied simple explanation. It was mostly the color of the wet sand along the shore and longer than it had been in the latest round of online photos. Waves of thick uneven layers curled into his ears and above them the ends flipped up around his collar. I recalled lying beside him late at night sifting my fingers through those layers and

5

tracing those golden highlights.

I sighed without meaning to and my bereft fingers flexed around the mic.

I noticed how tan he was and how his eyes were the same as I remembered, a crystal blue like the ocean past the breaking waves. Laugh lines around them and his irresistible lips seemed to be permanent rather than temporary now. I imagined he had regained his sense of humor after all of the years and years of success. Even though he had deeply hurt me I had always wanted to believe he was happy in the life he had chosen. I needed to believe one of us had repurposed the pain and moved beyond it.

Seeming to mistake my lingering perusal as an invitation, Linc smiled slowly, laugh lines deepening to bracket the mouth that used to curl my toes with devastating kisses. The multicolored club lights flashed their reflection in his eyes as he moved toward me. His lazy rolling stride that reminded me of the ocean he had once tamed on his board had only a slight barely noticeable hitch now.

When he reached the center of the dance floor, the murmurings started to rise becoming a chant as more than a few in the similarly aged crowd recognized him. But I couldn't let him get any closer.

"Hey, all you Tiki bar barflies." Eyes still linked to his, terrified by how little willpower I had to resist him, I leaned forward into the mic forcing my lips into a smile. "I'm sure by now you've noticed we have a celebrity in our midst. Help me welcome to the stage, the lead singer of the Dirt Dogs, OB's own. Mr. Lincoln Savage."

Clapping along with everyone else I stepped backward planning my escape. Linc's eyes narrowed as the crowd surrounded him, a surge of energy propelling him toward the stage accompanied by pleas to perform.

As he advanced, I retreated. One step, then two, my legs were as shaky now as they had been when I had first taken the stage. When he hit the stairs to come up, I hit the shadows whirling around on my heels nearly falling as I fled down the dark hall behind the platform.

I was grateful that everyone was busy fawning over him rather than gawking at me in my obvious panic. My hands trembled as I twisted the knob to the storage closet that also served as my dressing room. Once safely inside, I kicked off the high heels, stripped off the dress and hastily returned it to my hanging bag. Hopping around on the cold concrete floor on my bare feet, I shimmied into my jeans, threw on a top and stepped into a pair of flip flops. The whole process took less than two minutes. I had never changed so fast in my entire life.

Heart beating frantically in my chest, I popped open the door and peeked out into the hall exhaling with relief that it was deserted except for the club's bouncer.

"Early night, Miss Bianchi?" he asked from his position beside the entrance to the stage.

"Yeah, Paul." I cocked my head to the side, mind blanking as I heard Linc's voice. The song was old yet familiar. One birthed when I had still been a part of his life. I remembered it all. The rooftop club debut. The vintage van parked outside. All four band members and me all together in one motel room to save money. Ramon playing a complicated chord progression to warm up and then Linc adding in the words to transform the exercise into a song that would become both transcendent and timeless.

That was the final cut of the evening. I couldn't take any more. My knees went wonky beneath me. I grabbed the cool cinderblock wall for balance as the world seemed to tilt on its axis just as violently as it had back when I had first heard Linc crooning into a mic. Decadent. Dreamy. Breathy and utterly divine. Those same husky tones he used when making love to me. And seeing him and hearing him again after all this time was devastating to me because I had to face the fact that I still wasn't over him.

Tears burning behind my eyes, a sharp sob lodging in my throat that I was unable to speak around, I just shook my head at Paul and flew past him. Blasting out the backstage door and dashing through the alley I nearly dropped my hanging bag and purse several times in my zeal to escape, until I finally reached the brightly lit street lined with palm trees and crossed it to the club's parking lot on the other side.

My keys rattled in my shaking hand as I tried to locate the right one to open my car door. The key ring slipped out of my sweaty hand forcing me to kneel down on the asphalt in order to fish them out from beneath the undercarriage.

Standing again I made a mental note to skip the designer dresses for a couple of months so I could afford to get the power locks fixed on my aging Accord.

"Mona!"

"Shit," I exclaimed hand to my throat, spinning around, my wide eyed panicked gaze colliding with his. "You scared the crap out of me."

"Yeah?" A dark brown brow shot up and disappeared beneath his tumbled hair. "Serves you right for taking off on me like that. What did you expect?"

I straightened to my unimpressive full height. Five foot six to his six one. "Lurking in the shadows. Showing up without warning. How do you figure I've wronged you?"

Linc ran a hand through his hair while his gaze continued to travel the length of me making me feel stripped, naked and vulnerable. His perusal had always been intense. I resisted the urge to cross my arms to cover my breasts. The way my body still reacted to his gaze as if it were a physical caress was ridiculous.

"What do you want, Lincoln? Why did you come here? Why show up again after all this time?" I tossed my hair over my shoulder affecting nonchalance I did not at all feel.

His eyes were dark the way they'd used to be with desire when they lifted to meet mine. A trick of the light? He took a step toward me his expression entranced almost as if he didn't even consciously realize what he was doing. My rear hit the car door as I backed away. I had nowhere to go. But I couldn't let him touch me. I couldn't. He would know the power he still had over me. I lifted my chin.

"I don't know." His voice was low the words strained as if they had been hard for him to speak, making me believe they might actually be the truth. We had learned similar lessons in our childhoods that made it hard for either of us to share our truest feelings.

"I'm sure you have some idea." I arched a brow. "It's been years, Lincoln." His eyes narrowed. When I addressed him by his full name it usually meant I was angry. "How did you know where to find me?" I crossed my arms over my chest.

"Ash told me." I dropped my gaze. Ashland Keys. His cousin. The drummer of the Dirt Dogs. My friend and sometimes confidant. At one time almost something more.

Silence stretched uncomfortably between us. I could feel the weight of his stare on my bowed head. I was just about to tell him off and lifted my eyes to do so when I thought I saw something. Deep within his mesmerizing gaze. Something important. Something significant. Something I couldn't afford to believe anymore. Just a glimmer but it was gone so quickly I convinced myself I had only imagined it.

Another trick of the light.

What we had was over a long time ago.

Always a lie or a truth that had become a lie as other things had grown more important to him.

Guys like Lincoln Savage weren't for women like me. An equal. A former flame with expectations beyond just the night.

Guys like him wanted young temporary little things who were dazzled by their fame, didn't expect them to be sober and didn't protest when they woke up alone in the morning.

Chapter 3

Linc

"What do you want, Lincoln?" Her question echoed in my brain.

What I really wanted would send her running faster than she'd sprinted from out of the bar moments ago. The awareness, the attraction, the need, it was the same as it had always been between us. I wanted *her*. I wanted to dial back time to before I screwed everything up. I wanted her naked, her perfect rose tipped tits bouncing as I pounded into her so deep and so good she would never consider another. I wanted to taste her cherry flavored lips. I wanted her hair wrapped around my fist so she could never leave me again. I wanted…

"Well Ash should have kept quiet." She licked her lush lips and my mind went off on another tangent. Difficulty focusing was always a problem around her. "My business is none of yours anymore. You should have called first. I would have told you that I wasn't interested. That we'd said everything there was to say already a long time ago. Don't get me wrong, Linc. I wish you well, but I wish it for you well away from me."

She gave me her back fumbling again with her keys while I stared at her gut churning, hurt by her words and the memories. Frustrated by her reaction to me when I still wanted her so badly. Mad at myself for daring to hope that our reunion might have played out differently.

"Alright, Mona." My tone was terse. Her spine snapped straight. "Have it your way."

"Don't call me that anymore." She whirled around so fast her hair slapped her face. "It's just Simone now."

"Ash still calls you that." I frowned. I had overheard him on the phone to her periodically over the years on holidays or special occasions. Less since the funeral but every single time I caught their conversations I wished I hadn't. The memories were just too bitter. It always sent me into a shit spiral of self-pity.

"That's different." Her eyes flashed honeyed fire. "He's a friend."

"Dammit, Mona." I leaned in closer inhaling her sweet scent and nearly brought to my knees with desire. I wanted to have her. Right here. Right now. I had to curl my fingers into fists to keep from reaching out, grabbing her and reminding her how it used to be between us. Her lids lowered and her breathing turned ragged. Was she remembering, too, or trying to forget?

"Go away, Linc." Apparently the latter.

"Maybe I can't," I admitted my voice raspy with stripped down need. "Maybe I don't want to."

"Don't." She closed her eyes and her chin dropped.

"Don't do this to me." She wet her lips. They visibly trembled. Even though I knew I had upset her I still wanted to kiss them. "I'm not one of your groupies easily flattered by your bullshit. The fact that you're a big rock star doesn't impress me. I know who you really are Lincoln Savage. I've seen you at your best and I've survived you at your worst. So don't think you can come here and play games with me." Her chin came up and her eyes blazed anew.

She was so beautiful when angry. I wasn't playing games, not really, but it was obvious she wouldn't believe me. Wouldn't believe the truth if I had been brave enough to verbalize it in that moment. So I fell back on the pretense, my excuse for being here tonight.

"They want to use 'Save Me' in the new Donavon Blaine film." I finger raked my hair out of my eyes. "You sang it beautifully tonight by the way."

She shrugged always so quick to dismiss her talent.

"I could produce it and split the royalties with you fifty-fifty."

"You can take it. It's only really half mine anyway." Her expression was hard. "But take all of it." I felt the words she didn't speak…*the way you took everything from me.* "I don't want any part of it. I especially don't want or need anything from you. I don't need the aggravation."

"It has the potential to make a lot of money, Mona." My words were clipped, my tone terse. "The Blaine franchise is huge. He's America's James Bond, for God's sake. And their offer is very generous. It'll generate residual income for both of us for years to come."

"Be that as it may. I still don't want anything to do with it." She shook her head fiercely the sun lightened tips of her hair brushing the top of her tits that looked fantastic in her pink Roxy tee, but would look even better out of it. "Do you need me to sign something?" Her voice rose. She seemed panicky about the whole situation. "I'll sign it to over to you right now. I have a pen and paper in the car."

I got angry. I knew she was really rejecting me, not the money. My next words came unfettered and unkind. "Yeah I guessed you'd react this way." Stubborn. Proud. Beautiful. Why did I think she would ever give me the chance to be the hero again when she had already recast me as the villain? "Once a sheltered rich girl, always one. What's a couple of hundred thousand to you anyway? Right?"

"Not a girl anymore." She turned her head. "Far from sheltered. Certainly not rich." She muttered something additional under her breath but I didn't catch it with the noise of the traffic behind us and her face turned away. She got the door unlocked and I stepped back as she swung it open. My thoughts scattered as she bent over and I recalled another time when she'd been in that position for me. I squeezed my eyes shut but it was too late. Blood rushed south so fast I got light headed.

"Here." She snapped something in front of me. "Take it." I opened my eyes taking the paper she thrust at me my fingers brushing hers in the process. Close proximity to her and my imagination were making things difficult, like trying to get a fix on a wave set on an uncharted beach. Touching her reawakened my body *and* my soul. The latter had been dormant for years.

My eyes continued to burn intently as I stared at her. So much of who she was seemed to be locked away now. I couldn't read her the way I once had. I didn't know a lot. I had told her the truth when I had admitted that. But one thing I *did* know. I cared for her like no other woman since and I wasn't going to walk away from her. Not this time.

"The lawyers won't accept this." I crushed the paper in my hand. Pure embellishment. "They'll need to draw up something official. I'll get them to do that. Then I'll bring the documents to you."

"No." She shook her head. "Have them fax it to me."

"No electronic signatures. Those don't stand up in court." More misdirection. "Why are you making this so difficult, Simone? What are you afraid of?" I pressed but she didn't respond. "I'll bring the papers to you tomorrow." I pretended to give in. "The sooner this is taken care of, the sooner you can get me out of your life again. That's what you want, right?"

Chapter 4

Simone

My view of the blue water of the Pacific was framed by the t-shaped one half mile long concrete Ocean Beach Municipal Pier on my left and the rocks of the South Channel Jetty in the distance on my right. I sat on my blanket on the beach cradling the warm mug in my hands as I listened to the waves. Even with the sun barely awake the morning after my run-in with Lincoln, there were already several surfers standing on their boards their fins stirring up trails of foam behind them.

My thoughts drifted back to last night churning the way the sand did within the tide.

"...that's what you want. Right?"

I couldn't afford for him to find out just how wrong his supposition had been. Seeing him again after all the years had jarred me out of my comfortable drifting on the periphery groove. It had taken me a long time to get this far, too ridiculously long to smooth the waters after all that had happened. I needed to right the course. Only ridding myself of him once again would allow me to do that.

Chulo's squeaky bark broke the cycle of my musings, like rubber soled sneakers on a gym floor. My diminutive Havanese was the only male I allowed to have access to my heart anymore. His black and white pom pom ears flopped in the breeze, his curly plumed tail wagged behind him as he bounded back and forth on the beach, stopping periodically to rear back on his three and a half inch hind legs to pounce on crabs who dared to encroach upon his beach domain.

I looked up as a shadow fell over me blocking out the sun's early morning rays.

"Hey, Simone." Recognizing the interloper Chulo abandoned the crabs, raced over and pranced happily around the dripping surfer. He flashed a smile as my Havanese hopped around on his back legs like a miniature dancing bear.

"Morning, Patrick." I set my mug of coffee to the side, gathered Chulo to my chest, buried my face in his cloud of fluffy fur and smothered his cute face with kisses before setting him back down.

"Mind if I sit here with you for a bit?" Patrick asked.

"Not at all." I scooted to the side to make room while he used his long zipper string to pull off his hood. He shook out his dark glossy mane of hair before he plopped down on the blanket beside me. I offered him one of my doughnuts but he made a face and waved a hand in refusal. Patrick was very particular about what he put into his body. Me not so much. And it should probably be noted that Patrick's body was every bit as alluring as his hair. Surfing was a good all-around workout. Patrick in his wet suit gave testament to that fact much as Linc had when similarly attired in the days when I used to sit on this very same beach to watch him carve up the waves.

"You're here late this morning."

"Uh huh." Distracted I reached for my cup surprised to discover it empty. I set it aside sighing as I watched Chulo scare a flock of seagulls into flight.

"Chulo seems happy enough. So what's eating you?"

I turned to look at him. His grey as the Southern California fog eyes were steady on mine. "What makes you think I'm upset?"

"Your forehead is all scrunched up. It gets like that at the first of every month whenever the bills are due." Patrick was more observant than I gave him credit for. I shouldn't have been surprised that he read my mood so easily. We'd been friends long enough for me to know that he had a keen mind to go along with his quirky sense of humor and startling good looks. He was every woman's dream but for some reason enjoyed spending most of his time with me. "Do you need any help in the store today?"

"No thanks. Not today." When we were busy or I had somewhere else to be during business hours Patrick was always willing to lend a hand. But it hadn't been busy this month. I couldn't afford the help and his comment about the bills reminded me that I had more pressing problems than what to do about my ex.

Reluctantly I stood and called for Chulo. He came running right away his thick fluff flying back from his masked face.

"You can talk to me, Simone." Patrick rose, too, towering over me. "I might be able to help."

Doubtful. Patrick meant well but he was just a kid about the same age as I had been all those years ago with Linc. Well, no need for my thoughts to go there. I put my hand on his arm pasting on a smile. "You working at Hodad's today?"

"Yeah. I've got the four to nine shift." He looked at me as if he wanted to say something more but decided against it. "I can bring you a burger during my break." The surfer staffed restaurant was just a couple of businesses down the main drag from mine.

"That would be really nice. Thank you." I hadn't bothered with grocery shopping the night before even though supplies were as lean as my bank account. It had been all I could manage to get home from downtown without having a car accident along the way. Lincoln Savage was not easily dismissed. Then or now.

Patrick nodded and loped off. A group of young bikini clad teens sitting with their legs dangling over the beach wall turned their heads to track him as he scooped his board out of the sand and jogged up the wide concrete steps to the street level. He took the sidewalk past them toward a nondescript paint peeling down to the bare concrete three story apartment building beside the pier where he shared a one bedroom unit with three other guys on the top floor. Looks and condition aside, rent with a view was expensive in Ocean Beach.

Patrick waved at me before he crossed under the pier. I waved back before shaking out the sand from my blanket, folding it and tucking it under my arm.

I still didn't know what I was going to do about Lincoln but I couldn't afford to waste anymore headspace on him. I had work to do.

I clipped on Chulo's leash and took the same steps Patrick had to the street level on my way to work. As I passed the public parking lot I waved and returned greetings from other early morning surfers donning wetsuits from the backs of their vehicles.

Palm tree lined Newport Avenue started at the beach and led to downtown OB 's eclectic mix of shops. From ice cream to bars to psychedelic themed international hostels to tattoo shops, we had it all. The wide range of colors and shapes was unusual in California where most town zoning was uniform and strict. But we weren't a conventional SoCal town. We had too many free spirited, thumb your nose at the system types to be one of those. But we looked out for each other as though we were one big family. That was one of the reasons I had returned.

The bell to the shop jingled as I pushed the glass door with my name etched on it to let myself in. I flipped on the lights and surveyed the small retail space that I had painstakingly arranged, though admittedly not as artfully as the previous owner. The girl's Roxy section was mostly pink, orange and black attire and swimsuits, while the other half of the shop was for the guys and featured lots of grey and black, with Volcom, Hurley and Quicksilver gear featured. I didn't have any surfboards but I had all the smaller accessories to support the lifestyle. Leashes. Surf wax. Booties. And an entire rack of rash guards.

I loved the shop I had purchased from Karen at a steal, but I knew the inventory was getting a little tired. I also knew that I wasn't going to survive another month on the income from it. I needed a second job. Actually a third if I counted the weekend gig at the Tiki Bar.

I put my blanket and mug behind the counter and removed Chulo's leash. He was the official ambassador of the shop. He found a slice of sunshine from the large exterior window to nap in while I got busy. If not like new I could at least make what I did have in the store look presentable.

Hours of rearranging current inventory and only a handful of paying customers later I lamented having too much free time on my hands. It meant money wasn't coming in and that I had plenty of time to think, which wasn't a good thing at the moment. I worked and reworked the figures with a pad of paper, a pencil and a calculator before sagging against the counter.

The numbers didn't lie. There was no way I was going to make a profit this month.

I felt two insistent taps on my lower leg. Grateful for the distraction from my full on fret mode over the budget, I glanced down at my Havanese. Chulo danced on his back legs his expression making his irritation evident before he tapped his paws against me once more. "Sorry fluffy face. It's time for your walk, isn't it?"

He seemed to smile indulgently. His expressive green and gold flecked eyes seemed to say, 'I only put up with you and your shortcomings because I love you, human."

"I love you, too." I scooped him into my arms and was just about to turn the shop sign to closed when my cell rang. I frowned at it. The plan for the damn thing was too expensive but I couldn't go without it. It wouldn't be safe and I used it as my business number anyway.

"Mona's Surf Shop. This is Simone. How can I help you?"

There was a long pause on the other end and then his voice.

Lincoln's.

"Simone, what is this? Some kind of joke? Tell me you don't really have a surf shop named *Mona's*?"

"Um." *Shit.* I forgot that I had given him this number to call me when he had the papers ready. As if I had any other number I could have given him. It was just that I had planned on being able to recognize his caller ID. But I had been too distracted and it was my habit to answer with the shop greeting. Too late now. I would just have to brazen it on out. "Yes, this is the right number and yes I named it Mona's because Simone sounded too French." I twisted my hair around my finger, a nervous habit. Hopefully, he would buy all that and not realize that the shop name was mostly just a nod to the fact that I was far from over him. "Did you get the stuff back from the lawyers already?"

"Yes and no." He sighed and even his sigh sounded sexy to me. I tried not to imagine what he was wearing or not wearing. I suppressed a shiver. "Yeah I have the documents but well...I'm hoping I can convince you to reconsider. Maybe you don't need the money, and I can understand why you don't want to work with me, but having your name on a project like this is a really big deal. I wanted to ask if maybe you'd let me take you out to dinner so we can discuss it further."

"That's not really a good idea." But even as I spoke the words of refusal I glanced around at the shop and remembered that big pile of unpaid bills. A fat royalty check

would probably go a long way towards solving my problems.

I scooped Chulo into my arms. He licked my face and
it tickled. "Stop that, baby." My voice was husky with love
and amusement. I giggled.

"What the hell's going on?" Lincoln queried sounding
irate for some reason. "Is there someone with you?"

As if.

But I smacked Chulo loudly, a big muhwah just to give
Lincoln something to think about, a slight deception that
might keep him from flirting with me. I didn't need that
temptation. I looked at my pooch and he gazed back at me
as if he were reading my thoughts. Taking an extra job
would mean I would have less time for him and the beach,
both of which kept me sane.

Chulo seemed to nod in furry agreement.

I could suck it up and work with Linc on this. Swallow
my pride just a bit. For me, Chulo and my shop.

"Nothing's going on. But I've changed my mind. I
think I will listen to your pitch. I'm having dinner with a
friend at Hodad's. Why don't you swing by and join us?"

Surely it wouldn't be that hard to deal with Lincoln for
the brief amount of time it would take to finalize things.
Meeting him in a busy place surrounded by my friends
would keep me out of real trouble.

That was all I needed to do. Keep my focus on the end
result. What I had in my life was good and I had everything
that I wanted. Well, except the money. But I certainly
didn't need Lincoln or the heartache that went along with
him.

Chapter 5

Linc

I lucked out and got a spot right next to the popular hamburger joint. I wondered why she had suggested it. Was she trying to send me a message by having us meet in the center of town where it had all started for us?

I cut the ignition on the rental and threw my arms over the wheel trying to find the peace that had eluded me since last night. Hell since fifteen years ago if I was being honest with myself. And I had been even more tense and irritated since I got off the phone with her. Sure I was getting to see her which is what I wanted, but knowing there was another guy in her life made me more than a little crazy. Realistically I knew she had to have moved on. But in my heart I liked to remember the way things had been and dreamed she was still waiting on me to come back so we could patch things up and move forward together. The way I had always wanted. The way it should have always been.

I twisted my watch band around and checked the time.

I was five minutes early. I looked out the driver's window and saw the ocean at the end of the street. I swallowed heavily. So many memories. When I returned my gaze to the restaurant I saw her, standing just outside the entrance with a guy who was young and tall enough to be on the LA Lakers. From his body language it was obvious that he was way into her, leaning over her with his hand on the wall above her head. Whatever he was saying made her entire face light up. The way it used to for me. Her gold eyes sparkled beautifully in the setting sun.

My gut twisted and jealousy set it aflame. I gripped the steering wheel so hard the metal seemed to groan. So this was the guy. The competition. I stared at both of them till my eyes burned before blinking.

So be it. He might be younger and he might be able to make her happy the way I once had, but I had at least one thing on him. She had been mine first.

I got out of the jeep pocketing the key as I made my way up the wide sidewalk past several different storefronts all connected together. Some I recognized. Some were different. Diagonal parking spaces and the two way street with a yellow stripe down the center reflected the layout of a typical old fashioned downtown, except that the rerouting of the Five around the area cut OB off from more traditional and in my opinion more boring commercial ventures.

He saw me first. His eyes narrowed slightly before he said something to her. She turned around, amusement draining from her face and wariness replacing it.

My determined stride faltered but I recovered quickly giving her a leisurely head to toe scan. The one I had perfected over the years on women who didn't matter. "Hey,

Mona. You look smokin' hot," I drawled suggestively. "Who's your friend?" I smiled but there was not a trace of amusement in it. It was more of a territorial flashing of my teeth. A message between him and me. A guy thing to let him know the score up front.

Mona was mine.

"Patrick Donegal." He stepped away from her grinning widely as he held out his hand. Was he dense? Had he not gotten the message? Or did he think I didn't rank as competition?

If I were in his place I would have pulled her into me and kissed her. Flexed my biceps. Something.

"Simone was just telling me a little bit about you," he explained.

She had never mentioned me to him before? That was interesting. I wondered if that was a good or a bad thing.

"She says you're a musician." His tone made his words a question instead of a statement.

I nodded feeling Simone watching me closely.

"Cool. What instrument do you play?"

"A little guitar now. Some piano." How old was this guy anyway? I knew the Dogs weren't as relevant with the younger crowd. Edgier groups like Tempest were pushing us older hard rocking band aside. But to tell the truth I didn't really care all that much anymore. Fame had become a long, lonely, mostly dissatisfying road.

"He sings, too." The corner of Simone's very kissable lips twitched. I found myself mesmerized by the sight. I wanted to taste the inadvertent amusement my evasiveness had caused.

"Really?" Patrick cocked his head to the side the end

of his stubby ponytail poking through the venting in the backwards no shoes, no shirt no problem Hodad's ball cap he wore. A matching Hodad's t-shirt with the same slogan and a white bar towel hung from the back pocket of his shorts.

Why hadn't I noticed the work duds before? I knew why. I was too busy looking at Simone and seeing red because she had been talking to him. I wondered if I might be wrong about their relationship. She didn't say anything about her friend *working* at Hodad's. God, I hoped they weren't together. The guy reminded me of myself at that age. He probably surfed, too. I reluctantly found myself kind of identifying with him.

"Yeah, I'm in a band. The Dirt Dogs. Maybe you've heard of them?"

"Sorry." He shook his head, and I had to smile. It actually felt good to meet someone and not have to deal with any preconceived expectations. "I've got a band, too. We're just starting to make a name for ourselves. We play local gigs mostly. But we're actually playing at the Del this Saturday night. You should come. Bring Simone with you. She says it's too far for her old beater to make it."

"That sounds like a great idea." I touched Simone's shoulder. A flash of heated awareness rushed through me. I had wanted to touch her since I first got a glimpse of her sexy body in the crisscross botanical print halter and earth toned drawstring pants that skimmed her perfect ass. Her skin felt warm even through the layer of soft fabric. Her eyes dropped to my hand as if to say, 'Back off'. I kept it where it was and even applied a little pressure. Her lips parted as she sucked in a sudden breath and my dick jumped in approval. Excellent. She wasn't completely immune to me. I could see her pulse beating rapidly in her neck. Mine was beating just as fast. "What do you say, Mona?"

Looking a little bewildered, she licked her lips. "Huh?"

"I've got the rental. I could take you to see Patrick and his band. I think he'd like it if you went. Right, Patrick?"

"Yeah. She's always making excuses but the guys and I invite her all the time."

"Sure. I want to go." She gave me a subtle look that I knew meant retribution was coming later for backing her into a difficult spot. "But are you sure you're going to still be in town?"

"I'm sure." I wasn't going anywhere. We had a show at Humphrey's on Friday but after that the tour was over. We were taking a break. An extended one while we, mainly me, decided if we wanted to continue doing the rock band thing anymore.

"Let's go inside." I put my hand on the center of Simone's back a little lower than was proper but I had to feel the bare skin her cropped top left exposed. See if it was as satiny soft as I remembered. I was pleased to discover that it was. I leaned in close and lowered my voice. "I'm suddenly starving."

Chapter 6

Simone

Dipping beneath the red Hodad's awning Linc and I entered the restaurant through the open door-way. Loud rock music and the aroma of sizzling meat and onions hit me immediately. I noticed nearly every seat was filled from the VW bus that had been repurposed to seat two diners to the long surfboard shaped table that spanned the entire length of the interior. My stomach grumbled as I scanned for a spot. Meanwhile Linc began to rub seductive circles into my skin with his thumb.

His touch was infinitely more devastating in its present position that it had been on my shoulder. Nerve endings flared with heat as he widened the circles under the pre-tense of guiding me toward an empty blue painted booth in the back. Murmuring an excuse about having to get back to work, Patrick waved over his shoulder as he moved away.

"Thanks for not using the intimidating celebrity angle on him." I motioned with my eyes toward where Patrick was clearing a table as I scooted onto the bench. His brow creasing Linc stared at me for a long beat before he eventually nodded once and moved onto the bench opposite. Had he been contemplating sitting on the same side?

"I'm curious as to why you think I would?" His clear blue eyes searched mine while his fingers drummed on the polished wood table top.

"Hmmm." I arched a brow. "Maybe because of that guy thing you pulled out on the sidewalk. "Hey, Mona." I made my voice as low as I could to mimic him. "You look smokin' hot."

"Nice impersonation." He laughed and his gorgeous eyes glittered with amusement.

Hands folded on the table in front of me I waited for him to explain. I had answered his question. It was his turn to answer.

"The celebrity shit isn't a big deal to me, Mona." He covered my hands with his. My gaze dropped to where we were joined and I was reminded of the first time he had touched me. My body had reacted much the same. Immediate attraction. A rush of heated desire that made my pulse pound hard. Lightheadedness. "Definitely not something I feel I need to mention when first meeting someone. It's refreshing to just get to know people as a regular guy without all that." He squeezed my fingers and withdrew his hand but my flesh burned where he'd touched me. My gaze fluttered up to his face. His sexy lips wore a slight frown. "I heard your stomach growling when we came in. What would you like to eat? I'll go up to the counter and place an order."

I told him and when I insisted on having my own order of fries he lifted a querying brow. "What?" I scowled at him. He had to remember I loved fast food. I had always been the most excited about trying out each new greasy spoon as we had traveled up the coast all those years ago.

"These portions look pretty big, babe." He scanned me again, his gaze lingering on my eyes delving deep for truths I didn't want him to discover.

"Yeah? What's your point? I missed lunch and I'm hungry." I could feel myself getting defensive.

"That's not like you. Skipping meals."

"Ok first off you don't know me well enough anymore to make a definitive statement like that." I was working toward more than a little peeved now. "And I resent the fact that you think you do. Fifteen years is a long time. People change."

"You're right. They do." I got the idea he meant more than just their eating habits. He didn't say anything else for another tense moment and I could tell he was a little angry, too. His jaw was clenched and his eyes were a darker blue.

"I got busy at work," I admitted, immediately regretful for my previous tirade and wanting to smooth things over. I didn't want to be at odds. It wouldn't serve any purpose for both of us to lose our tempers. "I didn't have time for lunch."

"Fair enough." His face lightened. He knocked on the table twice. But I think we need to talk about that when I get back." He sauntered away beneath the surfboard that dangled from the ceiling weaving his way through the crowd made up of mostly locals dressed in casual worn beach wear like me. The menu of burgers on the dry erase board wasn't complicated but they were delish. The shakes were legendary, big scoops of ice cream overflowing the silver mixing cups they were served in. They always came with extra spoons, too.

But even more enticing than the menu was the walking away view of Lincoln. So sexy with his wide shoulders and lean torso encased in a navy half button hoodie and his tight ass outlined in dark indigo Buffalo jeans. The navy color made his eyes look even more hypnotic and made my heart beat even faster. I tore my eyes away from the temptation and dropped my head into my hands. I felt a headache coming on and rubbed my aching temples.

Keeping my mind on the end goal and not on him was going to be a lot harder than I had initially anticipated.

"What's wrong?" Linc asked when he returned folding his leanly muscled frame into the booth on my side, scooting so close to me that his hard thigh touched mine. A memory resurfaced that I swept aside as quickly as I shifted away from him. His arm over the back of the bench. His beckoning heat. His enticing scent. I tried not to hyperventilate as I pressed closer to the wall. If only the physical distance I'd created between us would be all it took to overcome my weakness for him.

"What the hell, Mona?" Linc frowned. "Why do you keep acting all panicked around me?"

I tensed grinding my teeth together as I glared. Needing a moment to measure my words, I took my time and then some before responding. He drummed the table as he waited. "Stop it." I squashed his fingers flat. "And stop pushing me. Stop touching me. Stop flirting with me. Just stop it, alright." My stupid eyes filled the way they often did when I got angry. I squeezed them shut and pulled in a deep breath to collect myself before opening them again. He was staring at me and what I thought I'd seen in the parking lot the night before was right there blazing steadily inside his eyes. Warmth. Caring. Regret.

Two of the three I'd seen there before but the regret was new. And I knew in that moment that putting a world of distance between Lincoln and me wasn't going to make a bit of difference, not when he looked at me that way. Startled by the realization my eyes got wide.

"I'm sorry, Mona." He spoke softly almost as if he were afraid that if he spoke louder I would bolt. He was probably right. "Sorry that I screwed up with you. You were the best thing that ever happened to me. I miss you. Not a day goes by that I don't think about you and what we had." I blinked at him stunned completely silent by his words. "I know we can't go back. I know it's over for you. I can't change the mistakes of the past. But I'm here and you're here right now. Could you at least give me a chance to get to know you again?"

I nodded. I couldn't possibly form words. There were too many random thoughts running through my head and too much emotion clogging my throat.

"Good." He tapped the spot beside him. "Stop hugging the wall. You can sit closer. I won't promise I won't flirt. You're a beautiful woman. I'm a man. It goes with the territory. I'm sure you're used to it by now. Own it. Accept it. You don't seem to mind when Patrick does it."

"What? He doesn't, and I don't," I sputtered. "You're wrong. He doesn't think of me that way." My eyes drifted to Patrick who seemed to be watching the two of us closely.

He smiled when he caught me looking, waved and lumbered over with our order and a large shake I didn't remember requesting.

"I brought you a vanilla shake. I know how much you love them." Patrick shrugged as if his observation and thoughtfulness wasn't a big deal. The casual movement made his toned muscles flex beneath his Hodads' t-shirt.

Lincoln lifted a brow as if to say, 'See, I told you so.'

"You're right I do. Thank you, Patrick." I busied myself taking things off the tray and arranging them on the table. I avoided looking at both of them as I dug into my burger. The extra sauce dribbled down my chin. Lincoln handed me a napkin.

"I like a woman who can enjoy her food. Who has enough of a figure that there's something to hold onto besides bones when I've got her in my arms. Wouldn't you agree?" he turned his intense speculative gaze on Patrick.

"Sure," Patrick replied readily while looking at me and I caught the definite gleam of interest in his eyes that I had never noticed before. My brow creased. Knowing Patrick had a crush on me was going to make things awkward between us. "But she doesn't eat enough."

"Yeah?" Lincoln popped a French fry into his mouth, chewed and swallowed. "Why's that do you think?"

Patrick glanced at me and shrugged keeping my secrets.

Grateful, I beamed at him.

His gaze traveling back and forth between us, Lincoln frowned.

I knew Lincoln didn't like being shut out but he would just have to deal. Accept the boundaries that I set for him. I had to maintain the barriers between us or else I was afraid I was going to give him whatever he wanted.

Chapter 7

Linc

I watched her carefully out of the corner of my eyes while we ate. I caught her watching me every bit as cautiously. I had hoped my words would have made her relax more around me. I guess I'd been wrong. I finished my last bite, crumpled the waxy paper, wiped my mouth with a napkin and set my jaw determined to try harder.

"How's your shake?" I asked.

"Good." She scooped a spoonful and offered it to me. Her expression was so expectant I couldn't refuse. I leaned in my eyes on hers and opened my mouth. She seemed to realize her tactical error immediately. If she was trying to maintain a distance between us offering to feed me from her own hand wasn't the way to go about it.

She tipped the spoon in and I wrapped my lips around it, my gaze conveying the message that I was imagining them around something infinitely sweeter. She pulled in a sharp breath that she didn't immediately let back out. I added in a, "mmm," before sitting back. She got even more flustered turning away and messing with her growing pile of discarded napkins.

"I didn't remember you liking sweets."

"Not usually," I replied, "but I could be convinced. Could you give me another bite?"

"Help yourself." She slid the shake toward me.

"Not what I had in mind, babe."

"That's all you're gonna get, Linc."

"Fair enough." I grinned.

She tried not to smile. Held it off pretty well but her lips twitched. "Ass," she muttered with her eyes twinkling beautifully. She wasn't one to ever hold onto a pique long except understandably at the end of us. I was glad to discover that trait of hers hadn't changed.

"You finished?" I gestured toward her empty plate.

"Yeah." She pushed back from the table and smoothed a hand over her stomach. "I eat anymore and I'll pop."

"I wouldn't want that." I had lots of questions I wanted answered but it wasn't going to be easy to get them. I had noticed the look that had passed between her and Patrick. She was wary about sharing with me. I understood her reticence. We had carved more than an inch out of each other fifteen years ago. But though I remembered the pain, lately I remembered the love better. I was willing to take on the risk to have her back.

"Maybe it would help if we walked it off." I was scooping our trash back onto the tray to throw it away when Patrick suddenly reappeared to take it from me.

"You heading out?" he asked Simone. She glanced at

me then back at him as if she were looking for an excuse to ditch me.

No way, I thought. She wasn't going to get away that easily. I played my trump card. "We still have things to discuss," I reminded her.

Not looking too happy about that fact, she nodded, slid out of the booth and put her hand on Patrick's arm. "I'll see you later at the beach."

I gritted my teeth and shoved my fists into my pockets so I wasn't tempted to go all primal and rip the guy's arms out of their sockets.

"Let's go." She lifted her chin and headed toward the door. I followed and the spike of anger turned into something else as I watched her sexy ass sway in those linen pants.

Outside, she drew in a deep breath of air. "I love this time of day. The salt from the ocean smells so good. I don't know how you stay away."

How indeed? I turned away from the vision that was her and started down the hill to the beach. I semi offered her my hand as we strolled but she acted as if she hadn't noticed. That was ok. I could bide my time. For a little while.

"So what all is involved with this royalty deal?" she asked, the rise and fall of her tits as she breathed making it extremely difficult for me to concentrate.

"Not a whole lot," I hedged. "We'll draw up a contract. Get the song produced. Split the royalties and residuals fifty-fifty." I shrugged.

"Yes but what do I need to do?" She didn't seem surprised that I hadn't tried to lower her percentage of the deal. Either she had some measure of trust in me or she didn't know how underhanded things like that usually went in the entertainment world. An unknown like her versus someone in the business like me? In most cases she'd be lucky to get anything beyond a meager one time payoff.

We reached the parking lot and for once I got distracted not by her but by my other love, the ocean. The sun had already set but the stars hadn't yet come out. There was still enough light to see the waves curling in the distance. I pulled in my first deep breath. Moist and salty. My ears feasted on the siren's roar of the surf. I closed my eyes imagining running into it with my fingers wrapped around the rails of my board.

"Do you still miss it?" she asked softly.

I turned away from one temptation and looked at another. Her hair swirled around her beautiful face and slim shoulders. She understood what it had cost me to give up the ocean but I avoided answering that question directly. She and the surf were so intertwined for me. I couldn't tell her that it had been easier to get over losing it than her because that wasn't strictly true. I had *never* gotten over her.

"Sure. I've actually taken it up again just recently." Short runs. Shallow waves. Safer waters.

Her eyes brightened. "That's fantastic."

I nodded. It was but being with her was better.

"I'm so glad, Linc." She touched my arm. "So, so glad."

I covered her hand with my own to hold her to me as we strolled along the firmer sand near the water. "How about you, Mona? I can't believe you have a surf shop. That's not at all what I pictured you doing. Where is it located?"

"Here," she admitted while twisting a wayward strand of her caramel hair. "In OB. It was Karen's first but she sold it to me. She couldn't bear to stay in town after..." She trailed off but I didn't need her to finish. I knew and I understood. Memories had kept me from returning though mine weren't nearly as devastating. So much had happened to all of us. But I was pleased that Simone seemed to be more comfortable sharing with me now. Had my revelation opened up things a little between us? I certainly hoped it had. "I only went away for a while. It didn't stick. This is my home now. I live in my parents' place."

I stopped and turned her to face me. I didn't like the idea of her living there at all. "With your mom and dad?"

"No." She pulled away taking a few steps to distance herself before turning back to face me while walking backward. "Just me now. My mom got the house in the divorce. My dad sold the business and moved away. She got sick with stomach cancer five years ago. He didn't even come to her funeral. Not that I would want him to. I haven't seen him in years."

Holy shit. There was a lot there to assimilate, a lot that she had gone through without me. Guilt and regret churned heavily in my gut. "I'm sorry, Mona."

"It's ok." But I got the idea that it wasn't. Far from it. Looking lonely and distracted, she moved toward the water skimming her feet along the bubbles of foam. She'd had an awkward relationship with her mother but the one with her old man had been a twisted hateful thing. It was one of the reasons why I believed she didn't have as much self-confidence as she should. But even though he wasn't around anymore, I could tell that he was still hurting her.

"I'd like to see your shop." I measured my steps to match hers so I could walk along beside her but didn't pry anymore. I had issues of my own with my father that made me feel vulnerable. I hated it for her as much as I did for myself.

"Yeah. Sure. Maybe." She stopped. "This is probably far enough. I'm going to just walk home from here." She pointed over my shoulder. I hadn't realized we had been walking that long. "I should go in. I'm still tired from last night."

"Alright," I allowed though the last thing I wanted to do was say goodbye to her. Spending time with her sharing a meal, walking and talking…it was more than just making love to her that I'd missed. My life was incomplete without her.

"Is this Blaine thing for real," she queried out of the blue.

"Yes, absolutely." My features tightened with consternation. "Why wouldn't you think it is?"

"I don't know. I guess I feel like there's something you're not telling me. Something you think I won't like. I don't understand why you didn't let your lawyers handle the details in the first place. And I don't know why you didn't just ask me to sign something at dinner." Looking like she wanted to cry, she turned away and tipped her face into the breeze. "What are you doing, Linc? What's going on? Why are you really here?"

So smart. So intuitive. So different from all the other women I had known. The ones that followed the band around couldn't give a flip about me. The last one had tried to snap a nude pic of me with her cell when I turned over to peel off the condom.

I was going to have to give Simone at least a partial truth.

"You're right. There is more. There are papers to sign. Sure." I finger combed my hair out of my eyes. "But they'll want you to sign those at the studio. I gave them the video that Zenith recorded of you at Huntington Beach. The Blaine people loved it of course, but they want us to do the song together.

Chapter 8

Simone

"Hey land lubber." Vassel gave me his usual morning greeting before popping the last bite of his English muffin into his mouth, crumpling the waxy paper and tossing it into the open hatch of Tasha's Outback.

"Hey, asshole." The diminutive blonde protested while fastening her purple streaked hair into a ponytail. She retrieved the wrapper and shoved it back at Vassel. "Throw your stinky trash in a trash can."

"Don't be so testy, Tater Tot." Only Vassel and her other band mates could get away with using that nickname without getting maimed. Tasha was tiny but tough. She held her own with all the guys on and off her surfboard which I admired. But she had always disliked me for some reason.

She hopped off the tailgate, grabbed her board and threw a ring of car keys at Patrick who had been watching the exchange with an amused smile on his handsome face. "Lock up before you hit the water, Donegal."

He dipped his chin to acknowledge her command and then smiled at me. "Where's your shadow?"

For a minute I thought he meant Lincoln. Probably because he had been on my mind constantly. Even more so since his revelation last night. A duet with Lincoln? Could I? We had fallen back to our easy way of just being together. Would it be wise when I was still so susceptible to his charm? I sighed. I didn't know what I was going to do about my former flame but I could answer Patrick's question.

"Chulo's getting de-fluffed at the groomer." I smiled despite my inner turmoil. "He'll be depressed. He's so much smaller without all that fur. He'll give me a look like I betrayed him. Like how could I let them take away his mojo."

Patrick laughed sliding my folded blanket out from under my arm. "Here, let me help you get your pallet set up. Princess of the Shore."

"Thank you, kind Sir." I stood back rubbing the chill bumps from my bare shoulders. It was a little cold to be in a tank and cut offs before the sun came up all the way.

"You coming, loser?" Dylan, Vassel's half- brother, asked Patrick pushing away from the wagon where he had been leaning. His thick brown curls were almost as sigh worthy as Patrick's inky locks. Both the half- brothers were head turners. Their mother had been a fashion model who liked handsome men. Obviously. Vassel's father a Greek exchange student, Dylan's the son of a French diplomat. If one were in the business of comparing, it would be hard to pick who was better looking, Dylan with his classical looks like Michelangelo's David, or Vassel with his shaved head, expressive brows and his always there dark stubble.

As the only girl in the band Tasha stood out among the exceptionally good looking all male crowd.

"In a minute." Patrick tossed him the keys. "I need to talk to Simone first."

"Alright." Dylan threw his friend a knowing look I didn't understand.

"What do we need to talk about?" I asked, my head tilted to the side. Without thinking about it I reached for a lock of hair that had fallen into Patrick's eyes and moved it aside. He grabbed my wrist, slid his fingers down my arm and caught my hand.

"What are you doing?"

"Something I should have done a long time ago apparently."

"Hey, Patrick. How's it going?" Another surfer, a pretty young brunette with her wet suit half unzipped to reveal a sexy bikini top she more than adequately filled, strolled past us tossing him a flirty smile.

"Hey, Reese." He turned quickly away dismissing her. Looking irritated he tugged on my hand and pulled me toward the concrete pillars beneath the pier mumbling something about too many distractions.

"I'll tell you what I'm doing," he said releasing me once we hit the shadows, "when you tell me what's going on with you and that guy you were with last night. You're a helluva lot more than just old friends."

"Nothing's going on. Not anymore. Lincoln and I were together a long time ago, not that it's any of your business."

"How long is long exactly?" His eyes narrowed.

"Fifteen years ago if it's that important."

"I figured it was something like. It doesn't seem to me that he got the message that it's over, though."

"You're totally wrong about that."

"That's good to know, Simone." His gaze dipped to my mouth for a moment before returning to my eyes. "Because I gotta tell you I'm more than a little territorial where you're concerned." His grey eyes glittered fiercely. "In case you haven't noticed, I'm the one who's been here at your side for the past two years. It's me who makes you smile whenever that haunted look crosses your eyes. It's me who talks you down whenever you feel overwhelmed. It was me that convinced you to try out for that gig at the Tiki Bar that you love doing so much. Not him. Where the fucking hell was he? Not here. That's for damn sure. The guy must be a complete idiot to have let you go."

He stalked toward me walking me backward till my back hit one of the cold damp pillars. He lifted me, pressed me into it and then moved between my legs. *Holy shit.* I hadn't even had a second cup of coffee yet and I was dealing with decisions involving two hot guys. Feeling dazed I just blinked at him.

"Simone, I don't know what went down between you and him but I can tell he hurt you. Everyone who knows you can see the evidence of that. Any guy who gets close, any guy who shows any interest you shut down." His piercing gaze cut through all my apparently penetrable defenses. "I hope to God you're not still in love with him." I tried to look away so he couldn't see the truth but he captured my face and framed it in his warm hands. "Fifteen years,

Simone. That's crazy. I can't even wrap my brain around it. Did he ever call? Ever visit you? Ever attempt to make whatever went wrong right between you?"

Tears pricked my eyes. I didn't speak but had nowhere to hide from his cutting but accurate perception. "I didn't think so." His eyes softened, his handsome face moving closer to me. "You're in love with a ghost, Simone. A romantic image of a guy from the past who doesn't exist. He's old fucking news." He rocked his body between my legs as if to make sure I remembered he was there, as if I could forget with his breath bathing my lips. "But I'm right here. I'll always be right here if you'll let me. It's time for you to move on. Time to start living again. Get off the shore. Get off your safe little blanket. Stop watching life pass you by and start experiencing it again."

And then Patrick kissed me, his hot tongue spearing between my parted lips. The ten year age difference melted away. The only thing that mattered was the heat, the chemistry and the connection I had ignored but that I realized had always been there between us.

Chapter 9

Linc

C ell in my tight grip, I paced the length of the hotel suite that suddenly seemed way too small. She wasn't returning my calls this morning. I had left one message, gone for a run along the waterfront, had breakfast, waited an hour then called again.

Nothing.

The silence was drowning my hope. I felt like a fish flopping around on the line not yet resigned to its fate. I had a sinking feeling that the longer I let this silence stretch on between us the further away she'd drift until I wouldn't have a prayer of reaching her.

I tagged my car keys from the coffee table and headed for the door.

Fuck this.

She *would* talk to me. An ocean of time had already passed. I wasn't wasting any more of it.

So I drove a little too fast. I made it from Shelter Island

where I was staying to OB in half the time it should have taken. I slowed it down only when I hit the main drag, my eyes peeled for her surf shop.

It was easy to find. Nothing fancy, just a wooden plaque with palm trees on either end and the nickname I had given her sandwiched between those two. Pride and something much more significant unfurled brightly within my chest knowing what it probably meant to her to have gone a different direction from what her old man had always wanted for her.

I parked the jeep outside, clicked the locks and entered the shop holding open the door for a young woman leaving with her arms full of packages.

I noticed a bell jingling softly over my head but mostly what I noticed was Simone and the wounded look in her eyes when she realized it was me.

"You shouldn't be here, Linc," she said to her chest since her chin was tucked into it, a long wave of sun streaked hair spilling forward, a makeshift curtain to hide behind.

"What does that even mean?" Who the hell knew with that very ambiguous statement? I shouldn't be back in her life or maybe it was just about me being at the shop. She'd been noticeably vague when I had mentioned wanting to see it.

She didn't answer right away and I took advantage of her momentary lapse to look around. Instantly I knew why she hadn't wanted me to come. It wasn't the merchandise which was trendy and well selected. It was the photos, blown up and lining the walls of the shop. Pictures she had taken back when we had been a couple on that mini tour that had launched the band. Not pictures of us but of the beaches we had been on together. Seeing them and remembering rocked me back in my Vans.

"I mean you shouldn't have come back to OB," she said her tone edged with weariness. "There's nothing here for you anymore."

Shit. Tension stiffened my arms and my hands involuntarily curled into fists as if I could grab hold of those memories and relive them. Wishing I had done something, *anything,* to have changed the outcome back then.

"That's where you're wrong." I disagreed turning to face her. She had moved out from behind the counter that had been done up to look like a tropical bar.

"No, Linc." She shook her head. Her chin wasn't down anymore. It was slightly lifted and her jaw was set into a determined line that I knew didn't bode well for me and my plans.

"Mona," I protested reaching for her but she took a step backward. I swallowed gesturing around the shop at those photos. "You're not over me anymore than I'm over you. How can you..." My voice broke and my eyes burned with determination as I took another step forward grabbing hold of her, my fingers curling around her upper arms, my grip not strong enough to hurt but strong enough that she couldn't get away from me. Not this time. This time we were having the conversation I had been avoiding, the one I'd been dancing around because I had no idea how she'd respond.

"How can you stand it?" My voice was husky when I started again. "Looking at them every day." I had gotten rid of all but that one from Huntington Beach after I had made love to her the last time and she had bought me the ring I never wore anymore but still kept in my possession. "All those memories." I pointed with my head keeping my grip firm on her. Were my eyes as glassy as hers? My expression as panic stricken?

San Clemente. Newport Beach. Huntington Beach. Shorelines we had explored. Places where we had explored each other. "Doesn't it hurt too much to look at them?"

She shook her head and matching tears escaped from her golden hued eyes.

"It hurts me," I told her honestly. "Knowing how it was. How happy we were when you took those pictures makes the pain of what happened after seem a thousand times greater."

"At first maybe," she admitted dropping her gaze. "But not after a while." She licked her lips and swallowed. "Before I hung them in the shop I used to allow myself one picture and one memory a day. I would take the photos out as if each were a treasure and recreated the details in my mind. What we had been doing. How the air tasted. How you looked. How you sounded. Every word of our conversations. My feelings. Yours," she whispered while I reeled from her admission.

When she focused on me again her eyes were clear and no longer swimming in wetness. "Then I hung the best of them on the wall and put away the rest. To me they're just two dimensional images now. They don't have any power over me anymore and neither do you." Something flittered across her gaze when she finished but before I could analyze she continued gutting me some more. "Go away, Lincoln. I have my life now. *My* life." She struggled to loosen my grip but I held her firmly. She had taken her shot and I had absorbed it. I deserved worse probably. She deserved so much better than I had given her back then. This time I was going to man up and give it to her the way I should have before. "There's no place for you with me anymore," she whispered.

"So you say, but I'm here to say you're wrong. You say those memories are just photos to you now. I say that's a lie, Mona. I was there. I remember. I think you do, too. How could you ever forget? The passion we shared. The longing that won't go away. The ache. The sense of completion we found with each other." I slid my hands to her arms going slowly, holding her gaze, making my intention clear because I wanted her surrender and she needed to know she was giving it freely to me.

Stepping closer my thighs brushing the shapely tanned legs her cutoffs left bare, my metal belt buckle to her stomach, her tantalizing breasts in that thin top seeming to swell where they pressed against my chest.

I tunneled my fingers deep into her silky hair swearing I could feel her nipples becoming erect points even through her shirt and mine. "I'm going to kiss you, Mona. Afterward you can tell me if you still think it's over."

She slowly blinked, her eyes no longer bright honey but darkened with that passion she tried to deny. I lowered my head gaze dropping to her lips waiting until she wet them for me. "Thank you, babe. That's beautiful. You're beautiful."

Then I brushed my mouth over hers and a bolt of desire I didn't try to deny made my body shudder. I wanted to savor the feel of her soft satiny lips but I couldn't. I dipped her backward over my arm slanting my mouth hungrily over hers, my tongue between her lips, the desire I always felt with her becoming a roaring blaze within me. Once things got this far with her I never had any control. It was all about taking her, having her and making her mine.

Again.

Chapter 10

Simone

I was lying when I told him that the past no longer held any power over me. Still potent Lincoln wielded that power expertly as he kissed me. My memories paled in comparison to the reality. My heart pounded, my knees weakened and I clutched handfuls of his cotton t-shirt in order to stay upright. The passion. The longing. The ache. He was right. They were all still there and they crashed over me like a will crushing wave.

"Linc," I moaned the moment he tore his mouth from mine, not to beg him to end his ravenous assault but to plead for him to continue it. I arched my neck to the side to give him better access for the torrent of hot open mouthed kisses that followed. My restless fingers were as active as his were, his shaping my breasts and molding them to his hands while mine reclaimed the hard masculine contours of his chest.

"Mona," he breathed my name with eyes that were on

fire before his lips crashed onto mine again. Heat erupted between us followed by a flurry of mutually desperate movements.

Shirts were hastily discarded. I'd never been more grateful for a built in bra in my life. Going up on my toes, I gripped his taut biceps for balance and pressed my swollen aching breasts to his bare chest my nipples tightening to points that I rubbed shamelessly against his hot skin. He traced the contours of my spine pressing me closer to help but still I wanted more and needed to be closer.

"Mona." He lifted my chin so I had to look at him and the hard lines of his passion ravaged face. "I love you." I froze. "I need you to know." His hands returned to my forearms fingers tightening around them as if he sensed my immediate unease. "I never stopped. I wouldn't even know how to."

"Let go of me," I spat harshly while twisting to get free.

"Babe," he cautioned as if I were one of his groupies he needed to calm down when he'd given her the 'Hey, hit the highway' speech.

"Don't babe me, Lincoln Savage." I yanked one arm free and then the other, immediately crossing them over my breasts, furious with myself that I still ached for his touch, my seesawing breath a telling reminder of how dangerously close I had come to succumbing.

"How could you do this to me?"

"Do what exactly?" His expression changed from indulgence to anger.

"Come back here." I shook my head to express my irritation since I couldn't use my arms to gesticulate wildly to match the way I felt inside. "Mess around with me. Throw around words like those like I'm supposed to believe them."

"Maybe because they are the truth." Each word was clipped.

"Then you must have forgotten everything you said you remembered." I shook my head dismissively. The pressure to cry was there but I refused to release the flood. "So many times we talked about what love meant to us. What we meant to each other. And you think you can just come back here after all this time, after taking the heart I gave you and ripping it to shreds and then leaving me to pick up the pieces." I backed away from him as if he were a physical threat, hugging my arms tighter around my torso trying to ward off the outer chill and the inner one that was spreading inside of me.

His own arms folded over his chest, he stood in front of me in just his dark indigo jeans and all those lean sexy muscles that played havoc with my senses. He stared at me in shock, as if *I* had somehow wounded *him*.

"I want you to get out." I pointed with my eyes toward the door. Swallowing nervously as I realized that anybody could have come in and could still come in while I stood there in the middle of my shop half naked and completely vulnerable.

Frowning he tagged his shirt from the floor and shrugged it on. I hastily retrieved and replaced my own feeling marginally better to at least have those barriers back in place between us.

Gaze hardening, he took a purposeful step toward me. Unlike before I stood my ground.

Outside

He needed to know this ended now.

"I'm leaving," he announced dipping his chin before his eyes lifted to regard me. I felt a hurtful tug in my chest but quashed it. There was a steady resolve in his gaze that frightened me almost as much as that kiss had. "But I'm not going far. I'm sticking around for as long as it takes." He took a couple of steps toward the door turning to face me again just as I was beginning to dissect those words. "You're wrong. I haven't forgotten. I can't forget any of it."

Chapter 11

Simone

After Linc left, I closed up the shop early. I needed to clear my head. I had been in a man drought for years then suddenly I'd been kissed by two on the same day. One sexy like an easy Pacific breeze, the other a gale force blown in from my past on some ill karmic wind.

I swung by the groomer on my way home to pick up Chulo. Without all the extra fur he was half his regular size. I smothered him with kisses but my heart wasn't into it. He was as sullen and withdrawn as I was. I knew from experience he would perk up by tomorrow. Whether or not I would was still in question.

Usually when I felt this way I would head down to the ocean seeking its solace but not today. I wasn't ready to face Patrick. Instead I stayed on the straight and narrow following the sidewalk home.

Inside the two story place where I had grown up, I stepped out of my flip flops leaving them in the entryway.

Outside

Chulo trotted off in front of me, less bounce in his paws than usual on his way to the laundry room and the solitude of his kennel.

I padded across the hardwood floors and entered the nineteen forties kitchen that had never been completely redone. It was a hodge podge of eras. The new stainless steel refrigerator I had purchased after inheriting the house looked out of place alongside the old porcelain sink and a refurbished mint green oven and stovetop.

Unable to summon the energy to whip up anything fancy, I popped open a Longfin Lager and grabbed a pre-packaged salad mix. Balancing my bounty I relocated back into the living room I had passed through a moment earlier. Perched on the edge of my tired old sofa, I set down my beer and started in on the greens, flipping through the channels with the remote as I ate but nothing could hold my attention. Before I realized it my dinner was gone but my thoughts were still completely unsettled.

I took my empties back to the kitchen, throwing the beer bottle into the recycling bin and washing out my bowl before setting it on the drying rack next to the sink. I stared out the window watching Mrs. Kowalski's grandchildren bouncing on the trampoline in her backyard, a sharp pang piercing my heart.

Mrs. Kowalski had been my mother's only friend. Before my mom got sick I would listen to them in this same kitchen drinking tea together and dreaming about the day when they'd both have grandkids to spoil. Well that dream never came true for my mother. I missed her despite the issues that had strained our relationship. We had grown to understand each other after I had come back home the second time. We had never been close enough for her to give me advice until near the end, but I could have used some of her wisdom right now.

I knew Patrick had said a lot of things that were spot on this morning. I was letting my life pass me by. I had missed several opportunities to move on with other interested guys over the years. None had measured up, not even coming close to the standard Lincoln had set, so I had just given up dating. One year faded into the next until here I was fifteen years later with a failing surf shop and a bunch of broken dreams.

I touched my fingers to my lips remembering Patrick's kiss. There was a definite spark between us even though he was ten years younger. But if I was going to venture outside my comfort zone was he the guy I wanted to take a chance on?

And what about Linc? The ghost had returned. No longer haunting my thoughts but trying to possess me completely.

His kiss hit more than just a spark. It reignited the blazing fire of our past with soul consuming flames.

I took a long bubble bath upstairs soaking in the water until it turned cold. I allowed myself one glass of white wine. I needed my thoughts clear of alcohol's persuasive haze.

Patrick's honest observations and Linc's passionate revelations were all tangled up inside my head, but with one common thread. Withdrawing as long as I had wasn't normal. The time had come for me to let go of the past. But to move forward I would have to make peace with it first.

After donning a comfortable pair of capri sweats and a

Outside

'Surfing is my Life' top, I dropped down onto the center of my white ruffled, quilt covered bed inside a room that sadly had changed as little as I had over the past fifteen years, though at least I had removed the original Dirt Dog's band posters from my pegboard.

I ran my fingers reverentially over the outside of the worn picture album that I had retrieved from the trunk at the head of my bed where it had sat barely touched for years.

Cracking it open made my heart race.

There was more than just images of Lincoln and me within its pages.

Part Two
2000

Chapter 12

Simone

"He's gonna be really mad," Karen said, a look of concern clouding her pretty features. "You sure you're gonna be ok?" Her sundress swirled softly around her slender calves in the ocean breeze.

"Yeah. I just wanna watch the sunrise then I'll go home and face his wrath."

Chewing on the end of her blonde French braid, Karen focused her hazel eyes on the Pacific, its surface nearly completely flat in the grey predawn, only making a gentle gurgle where it capped against the rocks at the shore. The tropical storm had temporarily calmed the usual swells after it had blown through the night before.

When she glanced back at me, her expression remained uncertain. "I could stay and then go with you. Your dad…"

"I'll be alright." Dealing with him was my burden to bear. I had become accustomed to it and it was embarrassing to me to have others witnessing the way he treated me.

As a hostess at the restaurant Karen had seen his abuse firsthand before she went off to college. She had gotten a full scholarship to a prestigious college on the east coast. Something my father never failed to point out. My grades had only been good enough to gain admission to SDSU a dozen miles up the road.

"Ok, Simone." She grabbed my hand from my slack arm and squeezed it. "Good luck then. Call me later and let me know how it went."

"Sure," I replied dully, but I knew that I probably wouldn't. We both had difficult fathers who didn't understand us but the tight bond that had developed between us hadn't survived the first semester given the physical distance and the heavy course demands of our freshman years. Coming back home for the summer after having been away was proving to be more difficult than I had thought it would be for many reasons.

Karen jogged up the steep stairs to Narragansett Avenue. My street was nearly three stories above the sea. She would have to pass by my house on her way on to hers on Santa Cruz Avenue several blocks south. I turned back to the ocean dropping down on my rear on the dew damp sandstone, tucking my legs underneath me and arranging my skirt around them. Breathing in deep gulps of delicious salty air, I watched the sun peek over the horizon, gorgeous orange, yellow and red streaks of color christening the sky.

I tried not to think about how angry my dad would be about me staying out all night. College had been my declaration of liberation from him. I had changed. I no longer cowered every single time he ranted. He wasn't coping with the changes in me very well.

Outside

Lost in my thoughts I watched the seagulls flying around the pier, breathed in deep breaths of moist salty air, closed my eyes and tipped my face into the breeze.

College was great. Even though San Diego State University was only fifteen minutes away it felt like another world. I loved the challenge of my classes and loved the freedom to be my own person where I wasn't known as Alberto Bianchi's daughter.

Leaning forward hands clasped together, I was feeling at peace with my decision to finally speak to him about changing my major. I started to hum at first then began to sing exuberantly the way I always did when I didn't have to worry about pleasing an audience.

"Fuck! Who the hell is that singing?" A sleepy irritated deep masculine voice complained.

I abruptly stopped after the words 'nothing seems real' and jumped to my feet but stumbled on my deadened legs. I rubbed my calves frantically silently praying for them to wake up. Mortified and a bit frightened by the unexpected interruption, I was poised to flee but stilled when a man emerged from around a deep niche in the cliff.

Finger combing his thick waves of sandy blond hair and tucking a tee back into his frayed jeans, he stopped and stared at me. For a long moment we held each other's eyes. His were clear blue like my ocean though a little bloodshot around the edges. They widened slightly and for a moment it almost seemed as though he was just as stunned by my appearance as I was by his.

A warm shimmer of recognition rolled through me. I had seen him around town. A professional surfer who was visiting for the summer. The women in town gravitated toward him like he was the moon and they the ocean tide. He was good looking in an effortless kind of way. Confident demeanor. Strong jaw. Compelling smile that he flashed often though I had only seen him do so from a distance.

I could certainly understand the appeal.

"Lincoln what's going on?" A red head with tangled hair and pink stubble abraded skin stepped into view. Our eyes widened as we regarded each other.

"Kit," I said.

"Simone," she acknowledged glancing away quickly. She was a waitress at Napoli's Seaside. My father only hired locally and practically everyone had worked at our place at one time or another. It was the only fancy restaurant in OB, so popular the tourists from downtown San Diego even made the trek to sample my father's famous mussels.

Not only did I know who Kit was, I also knew that she was married.

"I'll see you around," Kit told Lincoln avoiding my eyes as she skirted around me and hit the same stairs Karen had used earlier.

I followed her for a moment with my eyes.

"What were you singing just now?"

"Huh?" I turned back to look at Lincoln. He wasn't watching Kit. Gaze appraising and maybe even appreciative, he was staring at me still, his light eyes sparkling like the surface of the ocean.

"The song," he explained his tone reflecting his amusement. "It sounded familiar." His sexy lips curved up at the corners as I continued to be confused. "It's driving me nuts. I just can't seem to place it."

"Oh." My cheeks flamed. That explained his keen interest. It wasn't me he was interested in. It was the song. "It's 'Last Night of the World' from the musical Miss Saigon."

"Really?" Brows darker than his hair rose. "Well that's cool I guess." His bemused smile widened and a slight dimple creased one cheek. "You usually out here giving impromptu performances at dawn?"

I smoothed my skirt before peering up at him through my lashes. "You usually out here on the tidal flats carrying on with married ladies?"

The smile and the sparkle of amusement vanished. I had meant the comeback to be coy but he apparently received it differently. "Don't be so quick to be judge and jury for all that you see, Simone. Especially when you're not privy to all the facts."

I bowed up a bit at his high and mighty tone, but then nodded. He was right and anyway what business was it of mine? He seemed surprised by my reaction to his scolding but then he didn't know me. It would take harsher words than those to upset me.

"I gotta go," I muttered and turned away moving toward the stairs. This whole scene had gotten weird and a little awkward.

"Ok," he agreed readily. "Only Simone."

"Yes." Fingers curled around the rough wood railing, I turned to look back. He was a solitary compelling figure, his hands plunged deep into his pockets, his broad shoulders looking tense as the wind rippled across the loose cotton of his shirt giving an enticing hint of the impressive musculature that lay beneath.

"If you get in the mood to come down to this spot again, I'm usually here early most mornings." He regarded me steadily something in his gaze that I couldn't identify piercing me deeply. "Oh, and I really enjoyed hearing your song."

Chapter 13

Linc

"What's going on with you tonight?" Ash bumped my shoulder. Hard. Almost knocking me over. My cousin was built like a Charger linebacker but he didn't seem to realize his strength.

"Nothing." I tipped back my beer chugging it and draining it dry before tossing it aside. "I've just got a lot on my mind."

"Yeah," he smiled and lifted a platinum brow. He was much more the typical blond blue eyed So Cal surfer than I was. If I wasn't in the sun every day my hair tended to revert to boring brown.

"I bet. Kit is smokin'."

"She's alright." I didn't usually reveal anything at all about the chicks I slept with but Ash and I were cousins. Practically brothers truth be told given the amount of time I had spent at his house over the years instead of at my own with my old man always on some drunken bender. "Nothing special."

He dipped his chin to acknowledge my words and we went back to staring at the dancing flames inside the pit.

"You ever heard of a girl named Simone? Long light brown hair with pretty highlights. Honey colored eyes. Sings like a siren."

"Simone Bianchi?" He glanced at me sharply. "Sure. Her family owns Napoli's Seaside. I didn't know she sang. But she's got a figure…" He trailed off using both his hands as if tracing her delectable curves that I couldn't help but notice. I would've been dead not to. "Where'd you run into her?"

"At the beach this morning." I shrugged indifferently but Ash wasn't buying it. He knew me too well.

"She's not your usual type." His steady gaze was assessing and I knew he saw the obvious interest I hadn't been able to hide. I had been thinking about her while getting churned in the disappointing surf all day. Her captivating voice and equally captivating body. Her pretty face. But there had been something else, something beyond those things, a mystery within those striking eyes of hers that seemed familiar and that intrigued me.

"She's out of your league, dude." He rubbed his fingers together. "Her family is loaded. Besides, her dad keeps a real tight leash on her. And he *hates* surfers. You wouldn't get past the front door."

Maybe, I thought. I would need an unconventional approach. I wasn't willing to let it go and I refused to leave seeing her again up to chance.

I stood brushing the crumbs from the tortilla chips we had been munching on earlier onto the cracked concrete patio and tilted my head toward the backyard gate. "I'm gonna go for a walk. You wanna come?"

"No thanks. I gotta head over to Ramon's place in a bit."

"Band practice," I guessed. "Again?"

"Even the Dirt Dogs the most popular band in OB needs repetition to get better."

"I can't believe you let your dad name your band." Uncle Gene was a big Red Sox fan from before he moved to San Diego and liked the nickname the fans gave to scrappy hardworking players.

Ash shrugged. "We've got a gig coming up at the Deck Bar."

"Where Dominic's dad works?"

"Yeah and that's probably part of the reason we got the job since I mostly suck as lead singer, but otherwise I don't think we're half bad. Even better whenever you step in and sing with us. You ought to swing by after your walk. Join us for a song or two."

"I might," I replied noncommittally. I loved music but I wasn't as serious about it as Ash and the others were. I was proud of them for the success they had, but tonight I had a much more pressing curiosity to satisfy. Besides I really wasn't feeling like listening to Ramon's crap. The band's guitarist tended to be long winded about the latest chick he was into.

Once outside the gate, I hooked a sharp right my feet automatically leading in the direction my heart wanted to go.

I had to see her again.

Chapter 14

Simone

I sat in my booth headphones over my ears listening to Rihanna's new CD and trying to project calm as I waited for my father's inevitable lecture. I'd lucked out when I was able to sneak into the house after the beach. My mother had been passed out cold on the living room sofa, an empty bottle of wine on the end table beside her, and when I'd tiptoed upstairs past my parent's bedroom it had been empty.

My dad hadn't come home at all last night as far as I could tell. Apparently things had gotten even worse between them after I left for college.

I took another sip of my sparkling water as a blur of movement outside the restaurant window caught my attention. I turned in time to see Lincoln enter through the main door. Dinner was in full swing, the white tablecloths draped over tables, roses in vases, candles flickering and the patrons dressed in their usual finery. Heads turned and censuring stares ensued as Lincoln waited in front of the hostess stand sandy hair windblown, wearing the same casual clothes he'd had on at the beach.

I couldn't figure out why he kept hanging around. Didn't Ava the hostess on duty tell him Kit wasn't working tonight?

Chin lifted, Lincoln's defiant stance said 'fuck you if you don't think I belong here', an attitude I definitely admired but could never pull off myself. The only sign that he was affected by the stares was the slight tick in his cheek from his clenched jaw and for some reason that hint of vulnerability drew me in more than his obvious attributes.

Without consciously meaning to, I got up and was on my way to intervene when I brushed into one of our bow tied waiters. After murmuring an apology to him, I found that Ava had met me halfway.

"That guy's asking for you." Ava tipped her chin toward Lincoln. "He's really cute." Her eyes twinkled with interest.

"Ok, thanks." I replied.

He was here for me and not Kit. *Why?* I wondered.

That knowledge made me feel flustered and my voice was a little breathless when I reached him. "Hey," I greeted Lincoln while passing on a grateful smile to the patron who scooted around us tying up Ava's attention. Lincoln's light blue eyes latched onto me as if I were a life preserver in an uncharted sea. "Ava said you were looking for me?" My tone indicated my surprise and my heart thudded against my ribs as I waited for him to reveal his purpose for being here. Plus now I could feel all those stares on me, too. I hoped my father remained in the kitchen.

"Who else?" His dismissive gaze swept the room. "Don't see anyone but you."

I smiled wider than I should have at his interest. His gaze dipped to my mouth briefly before returning to my eyes, his glittering dangerously as if my smile had pleased him. His warm fingers curled around my elbow and he leaned in close.

"Come outside and talk to me a minute." His voice was deep and tempting. "I want to ask you something." The warmth of his breath tickled against my skin making me shiver.

"I can't." I shook my head wondering why my denial made him look so angry. "My dad's in the kitchen." I nervously twirled a lock of my hair. "I'm in trouble with him already and I don't want more. He specifically told me to stay here and wait for him." I pleaded with my eyes for him to understand. Even though I had just met him I didn't want him to think that my obedience to my father was a weakness. Sometimes being strong meant doing what you had to do instead of what you wanted.

"I don't really get it," he drew out his words and that strong jaw of his tensed again. "It's not like I'm asking you to run away with me. I just want a moment with you alone."

"Ok," I agreed ignoring the loud bell of caution clanging in my ears and Lincoln's widening eyes because I was too caught up in the idea that I could be a girl who didn't always have to fall in line with her father's wishes.

"Simone, what's going on here?" His familiar booming voice stopped me cold.

I spun around taking in my father's red mottled face

76

and his flashing dark eyes. My gaze immediately dropped to the black and white hexagon tiles. One glance had told me what I needed to know. Time to deflect, appease and escape.

"Nothing's going on, Daddy,' I said softly but distinctly. He didn't like it when I mumbled. "Nothing at all. I was just..." I faltered for a believable explanation.

"I came by to apply for a job, Sir." That was news to me, but if that were really the case why had he wanted to talk to me alone? Was this just a ploy to cover for me to keep me out of trouble with my dad? He had gotten worse over the years and I bore the brunt of most of his displeasure. No one stuck their neck out for me with him anymore. Not even my mother. "Simone was just..."

"Miss Bianchi," my father cut him off. "My daughter is Miss Bianchi to you. Mr..."

"Savage. Lincoln Savage." My chest was tight with anxiety but my heart went a little fluttery hearing his full name for the first time.

"Mr. Savage. You happen to be in luck. A position just opened up. I need a busser and a washer. Do you have any experience?"

"Yes, actually. Not here in OB, but in San Diego I worked at an In-N-Out Burger two summers in a row."

"Fine. Follow me to the kitchen. Edgar will show you where everything is and we'll see how you do this evening before I make a final determination."

"The pier," Lincoln whispered low as he passed by me giving me a quick purposeful look I couldn't begin to decipher. "I want to see you again. Come to the pier tomorrow."

Linc

I washed dishes, cleared tables and I listened. What I suspected from witnessing that one brief encounter between Simone and her father was almost immediately confirmed. It wasn't just his daughter who feared Alberto Bianchi's wrath, it was the entire staff.

The man ran the restaurant like a prisoner of war camp. Cooks, servers, busboys, bartenders. They all jumped at a word from him and kept their eyes to the ground when being reprimanded like Simone had done. With a different upbringing I might not have picked up on what was going on so fast but my old man was a sorry ass drunk with a heavy hand. I recognized a tyrant when I saw one.

Simone was employing deflecting techniques where she sat in the booth with him right at the moment. Her head bowed to his authority as he gesticulated, her pretty hair formed a shimmery curtain for her to hide behind. Sweet, beautiful and in obvious need of a champion. Gut churning I took more time than was necessary to clean table thirteen so I could keep an eye on her.

"Don't worry about Simone," a soft feminine voice said low.

Startled I nearly dropped a wine glass as I spun around to see who had spoken to me. A beautiful middle aged woman with eyes so heavily lidded I could barely see their honey color, lifted a half full tumbler of something to her berry stained lips and polished it off before continuing. "She has her plan." She slurred a little too loudly and slapped a manicured hand on the bar for a refill. "Three years. When she has her degree she can be free of him. Of us. May the Blessed Virgin Mary grant that it would be so." She clumsily twirled a tendril of dark brown hair around her finger. That was when I made the connection. This was Simone's mother.

I thought it best not to acknowledge any of what she had revealed or that I'd been watching Simone in the first place. I knew from experience that drunks were not good at keeping secrets. I slid my bucket of dirty dishes from the booth and headed back to the kitchen.

Chapter 15

Simone

My eyes were a little puffy but they were dry now. I had silently cried alone in my room with the door locked after having been reprimanded and having my phone confiscated. Letting my dad know he'd gotten to me was never a good thing. I'd learned from a pretty young age that he seemed to derive a warped degree of satisfaction from upsetting people, my mother and me in particular.

Not wanting to waste my time on the beach being sad about things I couldn't change, I tipped my face to the warmth of the rising sun and filled my lungs with the fresh ocean air. It was later in the morning than I had planned to come but erring on the side of caution I had waited until my dad had left the house.

When I refocused my sunglass shaded gaze back on the ocean, I saw Lincoln enter the water beside the pier confidently wading through it up to his waist with another surfer beside him. Even with his full wet suit on and his sandy hair covered I recognized him. His handsome profile. The confident efficient way he moved. I had certainly watched him enough last night as he bussed tables before I'd gone home and retreated to the sanctuary of my room.

I don't think he noticed me. I was sitting in front of the rocks behind the lifeguard stand. I was a full fifty yards away from him and the pier but close enough to see him flash a carefree smile at the guy next to him before they both hopped on their boards and paddled out.

The cry of the gulls, the roar of the crashing waves and the occasional voices of the early rising surfers soothed me, though they were too far away for me to actually make out what they were saying.

Eyes fastened on Lincoln, I watched him bobbing on the flats, watching the set pattern and waiting for the perfect wave. So much of surfing seemed to be patience and timing. Sleepy in the sun I leaned back. Using one of the rocks as a pillow, I rested my eyes, dozing off.

Suddenly appreciative hoots and hollers snapped me from my slumber. I turned my head and focused my gaze where I'd last seen Lincoln. He wasn't sitting on his board anymore. He was up in a regular left foot forward crouch, arms out for balance using his hips and knees to turn as he shredded a sweet wave. I watched him harness its power taking it all the way in and dry docking it before popping off his board. Steadying the board he placed his other hand over his eyes to shield them from the sun as he nonchalantly scanned the shore.

I knew who he was looking for and I felt it, the moment he found me. He went completely still and so did I, the force of his captivating personality palpable across the space separating us.

He smiled and waved. I smiled back wishing I was closer so I could have a better view of the dimple that I knew had appeared. He tucked his striped board under his arm and waded out. I stood and moved to meet him. He unlatched the Velcro fastener from around his ankle. It had a cord that tethered him to his board and was his lifeline while in the surf. He set the surfboard down on the sand, unzipped and peeled off the top of his wet suit shaking out his hair and revealing a toned muscular torso that made my heart stumble for a couple of beats. Even through my shades I felt the weight of his perusal.

"Hey," I said lifting my sunglasses up on top of my head when he got close. I tried not to blush as his gaze ran the entire length of me head to bare feet. "You looked good on that wave."

"Yeah?" His lids lowered and so did his voice. "I was just showing off for you."

Had he seen me there all along?

"You're the one who looks good." He looked me over carefully almost as if checking for bruises before smiling slowly seeming to appreciate the simple white cotton blouse with the cap sleeves and the khaki shorts that I wore, as well as the way I filled them out. "Although..." He trailed off and took a step closer. So close I could feel the contrasts between the cold of his lower body in the wet suit and the warmth of his naked chest. "You've got a little drool left over from your nap." My cheeks flamed as he stroked the pad of his thumb across the lower corner of my mouth. The motion of his thumb parted my lips and my heart started beating so fast I was afraid I was going to go into cardiac arrest. My entire body woke up and took notice the instant he had touched me. I desperately wanted him to kiss me.

"Did you get it all?" I whispered even though no one was around to hear me. My eyes locked on his.

He held my gaze while his thumb traced the line of my jaw and softly skimmed the shell of my ear. A shiver rolled through me. I swayed toward him. "Yeah." His voice was even deeper than before.

I blinked up at him. I couldn't even remember what we had been talking about. I felt hot, feverish and tingly all over as he stared at my lips, his eyes darkening. He leaned in, his hands curling around my upper arms and gathered me closer. I held my breath as his head lowered and his mouth came closer to mine.

"Hey, Linc!" A male voice shouted.

Startled, I sucked in a sharp breath and stepped back while Lincoln turned looking irritated about the interruption.

A plethora of appreciative whistles accompanying their approach, three surfers strode toward us walking together in a row, their wet suits half unzipped to reveal bodies almost as ripped as Lincoln's. Their forms cast shadows in the sand as they raked their curious yet wary gazes over me as if they were Lincoln's posse and I might pose some sort of threat to him.

Maybe it was time to lay off watching the old black and white westerns my father favored.

The tall, dark and tatted one broke off from the others and gave me a long leering look. "Well, well, well. Look who Linc's got on the line now." He was Hispanic with eyes so dark they were nearly black and he spoke with a slight accent. "Simone Bianchi, I haven't seen you since high school." Grinning he leaned toward me and I side stepped closer to Lincoln. "She smells as good as she looks, like flowers or something *muy delicioso*. Pretty high toned company for you, eh *amigo?*" he said to Lincoln before his gaze shifted to me. "But if you're lowering your expectations, Simone, I'd be happy to accommodate you."

"Back off, Ramon," Lincoln growled. "She's not the type of girl to be interested in your shit."

The silver blond blue eyed surfer next to Ramon was silent but his speculative gaze was active swinging back and forth between Lincoln and Ramon.

"Aren't you gonna introduce us?" The dark haired surfer with the short haircut and the light green eyes asked Lincoln while his gaze remained on me. Without waiting for Lincoln to decide, he offered me his hand and I took it liking him and his wide friendly smile right away. "Dominic Campo. I've seen you around town. Your family owns Napoli's Seaside. Right?"

I nodded.

"Dominic's his given name but we call him Patch." Lincoln threw his arm across my shoulders and pulled me closer. Almost as if he wanted to give his friends the impression that we were a couple.

"Why?" I asked.

"Because dude's always tinkering and fixing things," Ramon explained.

"I'm Ashland Keys." The platinum haired blond finally spoke up, his gaze narrowing slightly seeming to be stuck on the spot where Lincoln and I were connected. He didn't seem too happy about it.

"Simone. It's nice to meet you," I said softly feeling a little uncertain. I didn't understand why he seemed displeased with me and had just belatedly realized that he was the surfer Lincoln had been with earlier.

"Ash is my cousin but he's more like a brother," Lincoln said. "His mom and mine were adopted sisters."

"Were?" I queried before stopping to consider that we might have stumbled into a painful subject. I covered my mouth while mumbling an apology.

"It's ok, babe." Lincoln's arm tightened around me before I could even think about pulling away. "My mom died before I could remember. Ash's mom, my Aunt Maggie, is the only mom I've ever really known. She's great. I'd love for you to meet her."

Ash frowned. He didn't seem to like that idea.

"Your aunt and uncle are coming to see our show tonight." The wind ruffled the short layers of Dominic's inky hair as he spoke. "Why don't you come and bring Simone with you?"

"Oh, no. That's ok." I was smiling as I worked out my refusal because Dominic was being so friendly. "I'm sure Lincoln has other plans and I have to work."

"Lincoln." Ramon snickered. "It's so damn cute how formal you are with him."

I flinched. The sarcasm in his tone wasn't complimentary.

"Everyone calls him Linc," Dominic explained.

Embarrassed I nodded but dropped my gaze digging my pink frosted tipped toes into the sand.

"I think it's an excellent idea. What do you say, Simone?" Lincoln asked and I lifted my eyes to look at him. The way the breeze combed through the thick layers of his sun streaked hair was distracting. I wished I could do it with my fingers instead.

"I don't know." I shrugged.

"I wish you would. They don't go on until ten. Napoli's closes at nine thirty. That's enough time for both of us to finish work and walk over together."

"Alright," I agreed after only a token moment of hesitation. I wanted to do it. I would worry about the risks later. "I'd love to go. Thanks for inviting me." It would be a little tricky figuring out a way to hide where I was going and who I was going with from my dad but it wouldn't be impossible.

Lincoln made me feel so many things I'd never felt before with another guy. It was worth any risk to find out what might happen between us if his friends weren't there.

Chapter 16

Linc

*C*autious and making sure no one was shadowing me, I turned the corner to the shallow back hallway where all the dry goods for Napoli's were stored and where I'd seen Simone going a moment earlier. After another night of watching her from the periphery, this time while she played hostess smiling warmly, listening attentively and gliding gracefully to each table to make the diners feel welcome, I was near crazy with the desire to touch her again, to put my lips to hers the way I had almost done there on the beach.

Hearing her father's raised voice put an immediate cabash on that plan and all the other heated fantasies I'd indulged in over the evening. That long slit in her skirt had given me all sorts of ideas.

I hadn't seen him all evening but he was definitely here now and laying into her. From my position behind a stack of boxes I could clearly see them. She had her back to the wall and he was looming over her. My gut churned and my hands curled into impotent fists.

"Table eight said their mussels were served cold."

"I know, Daddy. I took care of it. I already replaced the entrée, apologized and comped their meal." Her voice was soft and conciliatory.

His wasn't. "It shouldn't have happened in the first place. You need to be more on top of things when I'm away. You seem to have forgotten everything I taught you while you were off at college. Head in the clouds spending way too much time on those inconsequential theater classes."

"I can't be the manager and the hostess at the same time." Her words were reasonable as was her tone but I could hear the slight edge of panic in it. "Without you here we were short staffed."

"Excuses, Simone. Poor ones. I won't tolerate you turning out all flighty like your mother."

"She's not...She wouldn't be if you would...I'm not..." Her face turned to the side. She saw me, her eyes widening slightly within her pale face and I saw her jaw tightening with the effort it cost me to control my anger.

"Another night like tonight and I'm warning you that I'll change my mind about paying for those electives you seem to have grown so fond of. You need to remember you're at SDSU to earn a business degree."

"Yes, Daddy." Her voice was dull, lifeless, resigned. I didn't like it.

He turned away from her and I ducked back the other way stepping into the kitchen just as he came around the corner behind me.

I washed and I scrubbed out pots and pans trying to work out my frustration. Steam billowed up from the commercial dishwasher beside me but my thoughts were much hotter. I was furiously angry about the way he treated her when she was such a dutiful daughter. He seemed intent on destroying her spirit, the part of her that made her eyes sparkle, the part of her that seemed to come alive near the ocean, the part of her that unashamedly belted out show tunes at dawn.

After closing, I jogged home, showered, changed into a white button down and clean jeans and jogged back to the beach pacing back and forth above the stairs where we'd first met and where we'd agreed to meet again tonight.

Had it only been a couple of days?

It felt like much longer.

Maybe because her golden eyes were all I thought about when I went to bed at night.

Maybe because my fingertips buzzed with the compulsion to touch her soft skin again, to learn and trace every single curve of her body.

Maybe because I knew she was different.

That I had to have her but knew deep down that once I did there would be no going back to the way my life had been before.

Even surfing and qualifying points had been pushed into the background inside my mind.

"Sorry I'm late." Her voice was huskier than usual. Had she rushed like I had? She certainly sounded out of breath. I got that way too when I turned around and looked at her.

She'd showered and changed. Waves of her flowery

scent assailed me. Tendrils of her hair were still wet. I shut down the immediate thought of her naked in the shower. I'd never make it through tonight without doing something crazy and way too soon if I allowed my mind to go there.

"You look beautiful." I ran a hand across my heated neck. "I mean you looked beautiful earlier at work, too, but now…" Fuck. I was acting like a nervous guy on a first date. I had a stray thought that maybe that was because this mattered. *She* mattered and it had never been like that with me and other chicks. Ever.

She preened under my compliment. The cautious look in her eyes becoming that pretty sparkle that made her honey hued eyes glow in the illumination of the street lamp.

I took a step toward her, fingers feeling bereft until I had them on her soft skin again. Nearly shuddering I traced one arm, bare like most of her body in the short strapless white dress she was wearing. We both dipped our heads to watch my hand glide over her golden skin all the way down until I reached her fingers and intertwined them with mine.

I swallowed hard. My mouth seemed suddenly devoid of moisture. When I lifted my gaze her eyes were even brighter than they'd been before.

"Linc." She stared into my eyes and breathed my name making it sound as if she were stunned by what she saw. God, I hoped so. I was definitely knocked off my board by her.

"I wanna kiss you, Mona. So bad. But not here, not now, not with you looking so perfectly beautiful." My fingers tightened on hers. "I already told my aunt I was bringing you, and she wants to meet you. But my first priority after that is going to be finding someplace private because

Outside

then I am going to kiss you. And I'm going to kiss you hard. And I won't be able to stop after just one."

Chapter 17

Simone

I was nervous even before he said those things and called me Mona, like no one ever had before but I loved it that he had. Now I was practically panicked. Sure I was delighted that he wanted to kiss me, but Lincoln wasn't like the boys I had gone out with in college. He wouldn't fumble. He definitely wouldn't make me wish I had said no instead of yes. And that scared me because I didn't want to disappoint him.

The short walk to the Deck Bar was a blur. Even though the ocean was right there on my left, even though the moon sparkled romantically on its surface and even though Linc's hand was warm on mine, I couldn't enjoy it the way I should.

"Hey," he told me gently turning me to face him at the base of the wooden steps that led up to the second story where the open air bar was located. "Where'd you disappear to?"

He was too perceptive. "I don't know what you're talking about." I tried to deflect him.

"Don't." His expression hardened. "Tell me the truth. Don't tell me what you think I want to hear. You don't have to hide from me. I don't know who you think I am but I'm not like you're father."

"I know that." My stomach tangled into a knot. I knew he'd seen my father dressing me down, seen the shrinking violet I became, had to become, around him. My chin came up. "Don't you dare feel sorry for me, Lincoln." I tried to tug my hand free but he wouldn't let me so I gesticulated irritably with the other one. "I don't know what this is all about with you but I'm going home now. I don't need anyone's pity." I felt the prick of angry stupid tears behind my eyes. "So what if my father's an asshole and my mother's a drunk? So what if my home life sucks? I have a plan. He thinks he's the one who controls me but maybe it's the other way around. Maybe you don't know everything you think you know. Maybe you're the one who's being too quick to judge without having all the facts." My chest heaving with the force of my passion I had to stop to catch a breath and that's when I noticed Lincoln's expression had changed. His eyes were no longer glittering with anger. They were glittering but with something else now, something significant, something I could get more addicted to than his smooth as silk voice, his handsome face, his gorgeous body, or his elusive dimple which suddenly made a surprise appearance.

"Damn, you're fucking phenomenal when you're pissed off." He stepped closer releasing my hand not to let me go but so he could frame my face with both of his. He stared deeply into my eyes that still burned brightly from the pressure of holding back my impassioned tears. "I'm falling for you Simone Bianchi. Just so you know upfront what's going on. I didn't take the job at Napoli's because I was desperate for the money. I've got tour sponsors since I turned pro and living with my aunt and uncle keeps my expenses low so I'm pretty much set through the next year if I'm careful. Not that I don't appreciate having some extra cash to spend until the next qualifying event. I got that job because of you, to be near you. What I feel for you has got *nothing* to do with pity. You're one of the most gorgeous women I've ever seen. The most gorgeous when you light up like this. When you get that dreamy spark in your eyes and then look at me like you just did just a couple of minutes ago when I almost kissed you." He exhaled heavily his minty breath fanning my face. "Fuck the waiting."

He lowered his head. My heart started pounding wildly. My lids fluttered closed and his warm lips touched mine. I was prepared for an assault, for the hard kiss he had warned me about, but not for this one. The gentle persuasion, the back and forth feather light brushing of his firm masculine mouth against my lips decimated my senses. The kiss was so divine, so magical and so sweet that I sighed as soon as he lifted his head. My lids fluttered open and my sight was filled with the vision of his gorgeous face. His eyes were completely dark and his expression was so fiercely possessive that my pulse pounded even harder. No man had ever looked at me with such intense desire before. And because it was Lincoln and because I was falling for him every bit as over the falls hard as he was falling for me, I suddenly felt as beautiful as he'd said I was to him.

Outside

I smiled and went up on my toes feet sliding completely out of my flip flops.

And
then
I
kissed
him.

Linc

S
he totally changed, completely transformed after I
laid it all out for her. I was still reeling from her
pressing her ripe luscious lips to mine. Simone
made me as dizzy as when I got on my board and did a full
turn reverse. Currently laughing and smiling, she was
charming my aunt and uncle with her effervescent personality and drawing the attention of every single male inside
the packed club, all of them moths to her irresistible flame.

"Linc tells us that your family owns Napoli's?" My
aunt had to practically shout to be heard over the heavy
bass thump of the recorded music. My Aunt Maggie might
not be as striking as Simone's mother but she had platinum
hair just like Ash and blue eyes similar to mine and my uncle certainly treated her as if she were a rare beauty. He
sifted through her shoulder length hair while she grilled
Simone for personal details I had mostly already given her.

"That's right." A shadow crossed Simone's pretty face at the mention of the restaurant. My aunt must have noticed and smoothly changed the subject.

"Are you looking forward to going back to SDSU in the fall?"

"Yes." A curt nod accompanied that answer and she tucked her delectable body closer into my side. I liked that being close to me seemed to make her feel more comfortable but I wondered why my aunt's innocent questions were making her feel awkward.

"What are you studying?"

"Officially?" she blurted out then covered her lips as if she hadn't meant to be that candid.

"Yes." My aunt smiled. I had the same problem around her. She was one of those people who were easy to talk to. "I promise not to tell." She elbowed my Uncle Gene who looked out of place in coastal California since he resembled a mountain man with his imposing build and thick beard.

He pretended to be serious locking his lips with an imaginary key but his coppery brown eyes danced beneath bushy brows near the same color.

"I want to get a degree in theatre arts," Simone admitted. "I love singing and acting on stage. Maybe if I'm really lucky I'll get a chance to perform on Broadway someday. I actually got the part of Kim in Miss Saigon on a campus production this fall."

"That's the title role isn't it?" My aunt guessed as I looked at Simone completely floored by that revelation. "That's a big deal."

Simone nodded. "Don't say anything to anyone else. Please. For real. My dad isn't at all supportive." She looked down at her feet, her internal light dimming further. "I haven't told him yet." I wondered if she ever really planned to.

My aunt touched her arm. Simone looked up, her eyes shimmering, reflecting the twinkling lights woven through the rafters of the open air bar that sat on stilts and hung over the water. "I won't tell a single soul."

"Neither will I," my uncle chimed in.

God, I loved them. My dad certainly was no prize, but I'd hit the jackpot having both of them and Ash solidly in my corner throughout the years.

The recorded music screeched to a stop and the overhead lights flashed a couple of times. Like everyone else, I turned to look at the stage and watched my surfing slash sometimes rocker buddies take it. Ash as usual looked a little green as he took his seat behind his drum kit and tapped on his snare beginning the song without any lead in. Ramon looked confident popping along with the guitar chords that launched the band straight into a cover of the Foo Fighters' 'Gimme Stitches'.

They had come a long way from their modest beginnings. They were actually pretty damn good. Dominic was exceptional on the bass. Ramon was no slouch on the guitar, though their sound would have been fuller with a second guitar and someone to harmonize with Ash.

My aunt and uncle found their table and motioned for us to join them but I shook my head, taking Simone's hand and leading her out to the empty space in front of the stage that served as the dance floor.

I didn't care that we were the only two people on it.

I didn't care that it wasn't really a slow song.

I didn't even care that I was going to get an earful of teasing from the guys later.

I just wanted to hold her.

Chapter 18

Simone

I reminded myself to breathe and tried to do it slowly, though the proximity to Lincoln and my racing heart made it difficult to do. His hands resting on my lower back seemed to scald my skin through the cotton of my dress and even though he kept a respectable distance between our bodies as we swayed in time to the music, I was imagining us being much closer.

What would it be like to have a man like Lincoln Savage make love to me?

My hands glided across his broad shoulders. Taut. Lean. Warm. And so very tempting.

How would it feel to test and learn every masculine curve and contour of his muscular body, to have his weight on top of me, to feel him inside of me?

My cheeks grew hot. I laid my head against the rock hard wall of his chest to hide them.

"You ok?" he whispered, his breath stirring the wispy

tendrils of hair near my ear.

"I'm fine." I willed my heated cheeks to cool before looking at him. "Better than fine," I admitted peering at him through my lashes and boldly reaching up to trace the whisker roughened planes of his handsome face. His eyes darkened, the direction of his gaze dipping to my lips. Seemed we might be having similar thoughts.

"We'll stay until their set is done. If I don't I'll never hear the end of it from the guys or my aunt and uncle. But then we're going for a walk down on the beach. Just you and me."

I nodded wondering if the surface of my eyes glittered with as much passion as his did. Maybe, but surely mine didn't glow like the Pacific on a cloudless day. I closed my eyes, swayed closer and dreamed about Lincoln being mine.

Ash introduced the next number. "RHCP's 'Otherside' for the couples in the audience." I cracked open my eyes. I felt out of it as if Lincoln's ocean fresh scent had been a drug I'd been mainlining. We weren't alone anymore. A dozen or more couples had joined us on the dance floor. Seemed we might have started something.

When the song ended, Linc pressed his warm lips firm-ly to my temple. I sighed contentedly.

"I don't know if they're through but it's getting late and I don't want you getting too tired." He took my hand and led me closer to the raised stage. "I just wanna let Ash know we're heading out then we'll split."

Ash had other plans. "Seems my brother has a pretty songstress on his arm tonight. Simone," his gaze and his words snagged me, "Come up here and sing something for us. Surely you know some Rihanna."

"I'm sorry." I felt Lincoln's tension on my behalf. "I told him about your singing right after I first met you. I didn't realize that it was something that needed to be keep secret." He spoke over the heavy bass drum beat intro for 'We All Want Love'. "Listen, you can do this, Mona. It's just a short tune and it'll be bigger news if you refuse."

I nodded numbly.

He whispered more encouragement. I must have processed it because my feet started forward. I stepped up onto the small stage and took the mic someone handed me. Somehow I did it. Staring into Lincoln's warm gaze, pretending it was just the two of us I sang a song about needing something, about needing someone, about needing love.

And it didn't feel at all like a stretch to sing those words to him.

Chapter 19

Linc

Ash was starting to piss me off. I couldn't figure out what his problem was with Simone. It was almost like he was jealous of her which made absolutely no sense. She on the other hand had blown me completely out of the water with her singing. Her voice on the beach had been one thing with the ocean and the wind dispelling its power and range. But here in the club with the microphone and the speakers it had given me chills.

I wasn't the only one impressed. A line had formed after my aunt and uncle had complimented her. I don't think that was the result Ash had been going for but I was glad she had gotten it. She deserved to be affirmed openly and often. She was positively beaming by the time the well-wishers dispersed and she caught my eye.

I uncrossed my arms and went to her. She passed her mic to Dominic, put her hands on my shoulders and I helped her down from the stage waving to the guys without speaking a word. I was done with talking and done with sharing her.

"You stole the show." I took her hand after we stepped outside into the humid air. The steady churn of the ocean was our music now. I curled my fingers tighter around hers and led her down the stairs.

"I did, didn't I?" She turned to look at me and her smile widened. She swung our arms as we walked along the sidewalk almost as if jazzed on the energy of performing and I hoped also because she was with me. Without consciously making the decision to do so I led us in the direction of the pier. I believed the water called to her the same way it did to me.

We both popped off our shoes when our feet hit the sand. "Leave 'em," I insisted when she started to reach for hers. "We'll come back for them later."

"Alright," she agreed pressing her body closer to my side as we strolled along the water's edge a full moon illuminating our path. Hand in hand we were silent for a while but it wasn't an uncomfortable silence. It was one of the most comfortable nights of my life. I glanced at her. It was her, not the peaceful setting. She was the part I had been missing in my life. The solace I'd always lacked even in my aunt and uncle's home.

As if sensing the weight of my heavy thoughts she stopped walking and turned to look at me. I stared back at her wanting to memorize every single detail. Her pretty expectant face. The breeze tossing her hair around it. The moonlight caressing her sexy body and giving it an almost ethereal glow. The way her toes unconsciously dug into the sand as if she wanted to become one with the beach.

"Come here." I tugged her hand to pull her into me and she came willingly resting her slender fingers against the center of my chest. I wrapped my arms tightly around her enfolding her into me. I forced myself to be patient, to savor, to just enjoy the feel of her soft curves, the ultimate counterpart to my hardness.

But every muscle in my body was drawn taut and on high alert. Just like when I was in the final round of a competition and time was running out on the clock and I knew that I was getting ready to pop up into my stance and catch the perfect wave to the perfect score.

I reveled in the thump of her heart beat.

At the silky texture of her hair as it swirled around both of us in the steady ocean breeze.

I tipped her chin up. Her eyes were alight like the moon. She smiled at me in a way that told me she was marveling in the moment, too.

I loved her. I knew it to be true but it was too soon to speak the words aloud. So I decided to show her. Soft at first like the last time, I touched my lips to hers to declare my intention to cherish her. But I wouldn't be able to keep them there because I lost all focus when she was near me, because I had wanted her from the start, because she was a fever surging through my blood, because her lips were the catalyst that quickened my madness.

"Linc," she breathed. Her eyes were seductively lowered, the lush warmth of her mouth spilling over mine and her fingers moving restlessly on the front of my shirt as if she didn't know what to do with all of the need coursing through her.

I knew she wasn't experienced. All the signs were

there but that wasn't a turn off. The opposite. It meant no man had ever tempted her to cross the line. It meant she was all mine. And that was good because from this moment on I was all hers, too.

"Put your hands on my skin. Under my shirt, babe." I adjusted my stance to more fully align the part of me that pulsed for her with the part of her that melted for me.

She complied immediately and I hissed in a breath as her fingers touched me. A bolt of desire rocked me and I didn't hold back anymore. I crushed my mouth to hers. Her fingers glided from my abdomen to my back and she kneaded the muscles there as if encouraging me to deepen the kiss. So I did. My firm demanding lips overs her soft ones that gave me entry. I slanted my head and tunneled my fingers into her silky hair to cradle the base of her skull in my hands. Tongue thrusting inside I drank deeply from her sugary nectar, feasting on her sweet taste while my hips mimicked my mouth's movements.

Low needful sounds bubbled up from the back of her throat and exploded like champagne bubbles on my tongue. I groaned as she rolled her core over me. I swore I could feel her damp beckoning heat even through her dress and my boxers and jeans. I nearly threw her to the sand and took her in the shallow surf like some scene from an old movie.

But I couldn't.

Not her.

I reined in my desire like a blow tail in reverse, ripped my lips from hers, untangled my fingers from her hair and took a big step back nearly stumbling because my feet had sunk into the wet sand.

Moonbeams glowing in her hair, she opened her eyes and swayed unsteadily. Her expression grew confused as her passion cooled. "What's wrong?" She touched her kiss swollen lips with fingers that trembled. "Did I do something wrong?"

"No, Mona." My voice was low, the strain within it evident as I wrestled against this insane desire for her. "I've never had a kiss more perfect or a woman in my arms who felt more right than you."

Chapter 20

Simone

"Are you only taking prerequisite classes for your business major?" Karen asked.

"No." I shook my head.

"Good. I hope you're taking advantage of some of the arts offerings. I still remember all the plays you did in high school. I'll never forget the last one where you were the prostitute and sang that song before you died."

"'Someone Like You' from *Jekyll and Hyde*."

"You gave me goosebumps." She nodded reflectively. "I've always hoped you'd go on to do something with that, fly, like the girl dreams about in the song." She tipped her shaded eyes my way. "Have you tried out for anything at SDSU?"

The sound of the surf was punctuated intermittently by the laughter of children building a sandcastle on the beach next to us. I tipped my face up into the warm sun and considered my next answer carefully. "Yes I have," I said

107

vaguely. "But enough about me, what do you want to do once college is over?"

"I don't know. I didn't even want to go to Yale in the first place. It's a whole other world. I like it better here. If it were up to me, I'd come back to OB. Open up a surf shop. Hang at the beach as much as I could. Do my own thing, have a family of my own someday." She sighed wistfully turning her head to watch the kids.

This was nice. I had missed talking to her. Maybe we hadn't grown so far apart. Maybe the distance just made it feel that way. I liked that we were sharing again.

"That sounds like a really good plan." I brushed sand off my beach towel and peeked once more at the spot on the ocean where Lincoln was floating on his board alongside Ash, Ramon and Dominic.

I didn't want to appear too eager or too into him. Even though we had shared a kiss that had rearranged my world. Even though he had walked me home after and given me another one that had rocked me every bit as much as the first. Even though he'd cleverly gotten around the fact that I didn't have a cell and had passed me a note written on a Napoli's coaster asking me to come to the beach to meet him.

Even with all of that proof that he was interested, in the back of my mind I worried that what was going on between us was just some kind of fluke. An experienced guy like him would quickly lose interest in a girl like me. Maybe that was why things hadn't gone any further with him the night before.

"He's staring over here at you," Karen huffed from her blanket beside me. "Again."

Outside

My heart sped up and my lips curled into a pleased smile. "Could you get my back for me?" I passed the bottle of Coppertone to her. "It feels hot. I'm afraid I might have missed a spot."

"Alright." She frowned as she popped it open and poured some of the coconut scented lotion into her palm. "But don't think I don't know what you're doing, Simone." She gestured for me to turn around. I moved my ponytail to the front as she started to spread the sun warmed liquid onto my heated skin. We had been on the beach in our bikinis for a while. "You've deflected every single question I've asked you about him." She pouted her lips. "It's not fair. Everyone's talking about you and him being at the Deck Bar together and you haven't told me a thing. You always would tell me when you liked a guy."

She tapped my shoulder to let me know she was through and handed me the bottle. When I turned back around, she was leaning forward arms over her knees staring out at the ocean. "I'm sorry. Things are different now. My dad is even less tolerant than he was before." I sighed. "I can't afford to do anything that would upset him."

She shifted to look at me. I could see the narrowing of her eyes behind her opaque tinted shades. "Why does he hate surfers so much anyway?"

That I couldn't answer, though I knew. I just shrugged.

"Oh, oh, oh!" she exclaimed suddenly. "Linc's coming out of the water." She squeezed my knee. "They all are and they're heading this way."

"How do I look?" My heart fluttered around inside my chest.

"Hours in the sun," she mused, lifting her glasses onto

her braided hair and tucking a few loose tendrils of mine behind my ears. "Barely mussed. You look beautiful. I hate you."

"Give me a break, beauty queen." I rolled my eyes as she returned her shades to their original position. "It's not me who wore a homecoming *and* a prom queen crown."

"Mona." His shadow fell over me and his deep voice gave me a shiver. But the sun was so bright even with the shades I had to cover my eyes to look up at him.

"Linc." I smiled giddily my stomach flip-flopping when he smiled back, his dimple winking at me within his tanned gorgeous face.

"And who's this?" Ramon asked while cocking his hip forward and rolling his gaze slowly over my stunning friend to check her out.

"I'm Karen." She smiled confidently. "Who are you Mr. McCool? You look familiar."

"Ramon," he replied like his name should mean something to her.

She slapped her thigh. "Ramon Martinez?"

He nodded, his mane of thick black curls sliding forward across his forehead.

"Gonzalo's little brother?" she queried.

He stilled. "Nothing little about me, *chica*," he rallied.

She snorted. "You graduated a year after Simone and I did."

He nodded. "So did Ash and Dominic." He hooked a thumb at the two surfers who flanked him.

"You look hot." Ramon wiggled his dark brows. "Why don't we go for a swim so you can get cooled off?"

"Sure thing, Romeo," she teased. "But only if Simone

comes, too."

I nodded my agreement. I was ready to cool off. I peered over at Linc to see what he thought of the idea. He was unzipping and removing his wet suit. He apparently approved. My mouth went dry as he tossed it aside.

Sure I'd seen Linc in only his board shorts before but it was from a distance and that had been before I'd had my hands on him and all those lean contoured muscles current- ly on dazzlingly display.

He offered me his hand and I took it readily but sud- denly felt shy and kept my lashes lowered. "Simone and I are heading to the pier," he informed everyone while drap- ing his arm over my shoulder. "That work for you, Mona?"

I nodded, my heart doing summersaults within my chest as Linc began tracing random soft circles on my skin just above the slope of my right breast. I could feel my muscles tightening in response to what he was doing and where he was doing it.

"I don't want you around Ramon in a bikini," Linc said low as he steered us along the water's edge. He sounded kind of angry. I didn't get it but I was grateful he wasn't looking at me. I skimmed my toes through the water em- barrassed by my body's obvious reaction to his touch. If he noticed that my nipples were peaked and jutting against my top, I hoped he'd attribute it to the coolness of the ocean instead of his touch and my desire for him to widen those circles and…

"He's a friend." Linc stopped and gently turned me to face him, his long capable fingers curling around my shoulders. "But I don't trust him around you with you look- ing like this." His gaze dipped and fingers tightened.

"Damn, Simone," he growled his voice even deeper than before as he rested his forehead against mine. "All I can think about is pulling those strings so I can get you naked. I want to see, touch, and taste every single incredible inch of your body."

Chapter 21

Linc

The awkward first date feeling was nothing compared to the maelstrom of my emotions now. After having held her in my arms, after having sampled her lips, after having *those* types of dreams starring her, I had scarcely been able to form a coherent sentence. Let alone do anything but go all caveman when first seeing her in that barely there bikini.

Hello Sport's Illustrated, my vote for your next swimsuit edition is right in front of me here in Ocean Beach.

I had alternated between wanting to cover her with her beach towel and throwing her over my shoulder to find someplace private where I could remove the tiny scraps of material and have my way with her.

"Linc, are you sure about this?" I blinked rapidly several times totally having lost track for a moment of where we were and what we were doing. Straddling my board while I walked her out into deeper water Simone looked uncertain. If her fingers hadn't been curled around the rails of my board she probably would've been twirling that long ponytail of caramel.

"About what?" I asked gliding the pads of my fingers across the smooth golden skin of her thigh under the pretense of guiding her on my board further into the surf.

She swallowed before answering and I wondered if maybe the puckered nipples I hadn't failed to notice were caused by me instead of the cooler temperature of the water. I hoped it was me. She was certainly driving me insane. My every fantasy brought to life. Breasts that would overflow my hands, curvy hips just right to sink my fingers into.

"About me riding on your board." Her golden eyes reflected the ocean's sparkle. "I thought a surfer's board was sacrosanct."

"It is, babe." I was having difficulty keeping up with the conversation. I was still tripping on the image that came to mind when she mentioned riding. "To the surfer and his girl."

As she slowly smiled her even beautiful white teeth left impressions on her ripe berry flavored lips. Apparently she liked the idea of being my girl as much as I did.

The water was to my waist now, finally deep enough for us to paddle out past the breakers. I drew myself onto the board and turned to look at her over my shoulder. "Tow is over. Get to work back there, Mona." It was good that I was in front, seeing her bending over to paddle with those tits of hers spilling out of her top would make me entertain more thoughts of laying her out on my board and taking her on it. Here in the middle of the day knowing everyone could see us it wasn't an option, but at night, if sharks weren't a concern I would have given that particularly tempting fantasy some serious consideration.

I shifted to make room for my growing erection. My cock and I would've loved to fulfill a few different fantasies with her right then. *Soon,* had become my internal mantra.

I leaned forward and dug into the surf with hands cupped into paddles trying to get a grip, focusing on the fighter jet roaring overhead to distract myself from Simone.

Once we slipped into the gentle swells, I swiveled around to face her. "Come here. We're far enough away from the shore to be safe from prying eyes and I want to kiss you."

She shimmied forward, tits swaying and lips curled seductively like some kind of erotic water nymph from my dreams come to life.

Eyes focused on hers, I leaned forward the moment her knees touched mine placing my palms on her sexy thighs. Her hands wrapped around my forearms her fingers gripping so hard her nails nearly pierced my skin. I skimmed my hands an inch higher up her leg. She gasped and I took advantage pressing my lips to hers and dipping my tongue between the parted seam. Slow slick glides of my tongue to hers with languid swirls I deepened and deepened the kiss that I never wanted to end.

I felt the sun on my skin and the water lapping my lower legs but mostly what I felt was turned completely on and inside out by her. "Mona." I lifted my mouth from her lips and skimmed them across her jaw. Her eyes remained closed. Her lashes formed dark fans on her cheeks as she arched forward seeming to lean into each stamp of my lips against her creamy soft skin. "Mona," I tried again.

"Mmm." She sighed, lids fluttering open, her eyes dark and unfocused.

"I gotta go in. I have to take a phone call from my sponsor, but I wanna see you again." I needed to. I hated the thought of being even a single moment without her. I wasn't just a caveman with her; I was a jealous and possessive one. "Patch is having a party at his house. Nothing special just some beers and burgers." I suspected it was another excuse for them to get out their instruments and play in front of an audience. "I'd like you to go with me."

"I can't, Linc." Her hands going back to the rails of my board, she frowned. "I want to, but I have to work."

"It's your parent's place." I tried to hide my disappointment. "Can't you get someone to cover for you so you can take the night off?"

She shook her head.

"Is your dad always that unreasonable?" I had tried to convince myself that the way he treated her was mostly a work related thing.

She closed her eyes briefly. When she reopened them, she was still sitting in the same position but I could tell she had withdrawn from me disappearing behind that shield she always had up at the restaurant.

Frowning, too, I squeezed her knee. "He doesn't..." I choked on the mere thought. My drunk old man and me was one thing. She was his daughter. I could barely speak the words. "He doesn't hurt you does he?"

"No." Her honeyed gaze flared with denial. "Of course not. It's just that the business is important to him and it's important to him that I'm there and do my part to make it successful." Her brow creased and she started to mess with the end of her ponytail. "It's all tangled up together. I'm sorry I can't go. He pays for my school, Lincoln. I can't afford to make him any angrier with me than he already is."

Chapter 22

Simone

I shuffled around the restaurant like a mindless zombie, the minutes magnified into hours and the hours into an eternity. I hadn't realized how much faster time passed when Lincoln was around. Even though I wasn't free to talk to him at work, his presence soothed me, almost as much as the ever present ocean always had.

He was quickly becoming the center of my existence. He was already the focus of my thoughts.

That probably wasn't a good thing.

I had my goals and whatever this was between us, we only had the summer to figure it out. He had his competitions to go to and I had my responsibilities at Napoli's. If tonight was any indication I didn't think compromise was going to be easy. He hadn't been very happy about me turning him down.

Plus he was already popular here in OB and probably just as in demand at those qualifying events.

Outside

We had only shared a couple of kisses. Body melting, mind blowing, life changing ones. But we didn't have anything exclusive. Though this felt very serious to me, could it possibly mean as much to him?

Or was he even now at the party with someone new?

"Simone!" I jumped at the sound of my father's voice.

"Yes, Daddy." I hurried over to the bar where he was rearranging the glassware. It had been an unexpectedly slow night.

"You've been out of it all night. Messed up six tickets already. Go on home. Get some rest so you can be better focused tomorrow. I can close by myself tonight."

My slumbering heart stirred in my chest. "Alright." I tried not to let my inner excitement bleed through into my tone. There was still time. I was going to go to Dominic's party. My father hadn't specifically forbidden me from going out when he'd taken my cell phone. Feeling my mood completely altering, I impulsively kissed his stubbly cheek. He looked at me funny but smiled.

I don't think my feet touched the sidewalk all the way home. I flew up to my room and had six or seven rejected outfits on the bed when my mom knocked on my door and pushed it open, a full to the brim goblet of wine in her hand.

"Going out again?" She looked at the bed and then at me in my old robe, my hair in a clip high on my head. "Seems like tonight's important to you, Simone, honey." She only slightly slurred her words. It was still early enough in the evening for her to be coherent. It was sometimes nice to talk to her. I knew she loved me the best she could. But tonight I was in a rush.

"Did you need something?" I prompted irritation swirling when she moved further into the room and wandered to my closet perusing the selection, running her fingers over the clothes in much the same manner I had earlier.

"This one always looks good on you." She removed a sleek silver mid-thigh length dress.

"It's perfect." The over one shoulder was sexy and the two large embroidered black flowers on the bodice and hem kept it from being too formal. I hugged her and she returned it with her one free arm still clutching her precious wine with the other.

She didn't seem to be in a hurry to leave so I shrugged out of my robe and slipped the dress on opting for a pair of flat sandals with big fake diamonds. I was letting down my hair and fluffing it with my fingers when she came up behind me. Our eyes met in my dresser mirror, hers the same color as my own. Growing up I'd always thought she was so beautiful but I had never noticed how alike in looks we had become. Funny, I didn't really favor my father at all except for my skin tone.

"You've met a boy haven't you?" She gently turned me around by my shoulders finger curling a tendril close to my temple.

I went still but didn't say anything in confirmation or denial. I loved my mother but she had a loose tongue, especially when she had been drinking.

Her lips flattened as she continued studying me, fingers running softly over my hair. "I'm sorry I haven't always been there for you." Her eyes filled. She was feeling overly emotional. She'd obviously had more to drink than I thought.

Outside

I squeezed her hand, the empty one. "It's ok, mom." Why did I always feel like the grown up with her? I had ever since she turned into the ghost, floating through life at the house or the restaurant, only a faded image of the vibrant woman she'd once been. "I'm probably going to be late." I kissed her cheek avoiding looking into her sad eyes and refusing to feel guilty about shutting her out. "I won't be out all night." No way did I want a repeat of my father's wrath. "Don't wait up for me."

I didn't know for sure what I'd find at the party. I just hoped Karen was there. She'd been invited, too. I'd called and left a message on her cell. I hadn't heard back from her yet. I snagged the clutch from my bed. I might be over-dressed for burgers and beer, but I wanted to look my best. I needed the confidence boost.

Chapter 23

Linc

"How many beers is that, dude?" Ash asked loudly over the music and party chatter. He folded his arms over his chest and gave me a parental look. That disapproving buzz killing one.

"Not enough," I muttered.

"She's just working." He frowned. "Lighten up about it already. It's not like she's with another guy. And anyway, you only just met her. You need to give her some space."

All that was true but Ash didn't realize I'd fallen for her. It sounded crazy but she was my moon, in total control of the ebb and flow of my moods now.

I shrugged noncommittally. My feelings for Simone were too new and raw for me to discuss even with my best friend. "What about you and Karen?" I lifted my chin toward where Simone's friend sat on a lawn chair surrounded by a legion of admirers. "She keeps looking this way. I think she's into you, man."

"Nah, not a girl like her." Ash followed the direction of my gaze and shook his head. "She can have her pick. I think she's just spying on you for Simone."

"Really?" I cocked my head. "Why would she do that?"

"Are you really that dense?" His blue eyes danced with amusement at my expense. "Because Simone's into you, as dopey over you as you seem to be over her. Anyone can see it." I froze solid soaking up that possibility, hoping he was right.

"Hey, you ready, Ash?" Dominic bumped fists with my cousin and me.

"Sure," Ash replied after a moment's hesitation, a green sheen suddenly misting his skin.

"You guys are certainly pushing hard with this Dirt Dogs shit," I guessed glancing at the makeshift stage on the concrete patio where Ash's drum kit and the rest of the instruments and equipment were set up.

"Yeah." Dominic lifted a shoulder and dropped it. "We gotta pursue other options. Most of us can't make a living surfing."

Not that great of a living, I thought. The call with the Billabong rep hadn't gone all that well. Lots of surfers and not enough sponsor money to go around. It was a good thing I'd saved up every dime of my winnings so far this year and that I had the extra income from Napoli's. I was going to need it in order to pay for my flight out to the event in Fiji.

"Why don't you join us for a song?" Ash asked.

"Why not?" Dominic interjected apparently on board

with the idea.

"You did a kickass job on 'Better Man' when we were messing around the other day."

"Yeah and I could really use the backup on vocals tonight," Ash said. "My throat's feeling a little sore." Now that he mentioned it I had noticed his voice sounded a little more gravelly than usual.

"Sure. Alright." I slapped him on the shoulder. I was familiar enough with their set list to help out. Plus I could use the distraction from my obsessing over Mona.

Simone

I entered through the backyard gate tagging along with a late arriving set of couples. The music was loud and compelling drawing in curious stragglers from the In-N-Out Burger a couple of doors down from Dominic's house.

There were too many people in front of me for me to see the band but they sounded different than the night before.

I wondered why.

Then I realized.

Lincoln.

Belting out lead vocals on Pearl Jam's "Better Man". No tired Eddie Vedder imitator, his interpretation was undeniably appealing. His singing voice was much like his speaking one only richer mic'ed up. And extra sexy without a doubt.

I pressed in sidestepping and apologizing profusely as I made my way toward him, the last guitar fading out just as I broke through. Ash clapped him on the shoulder. Girls with glittering eyes surrounded the two of them, Dominic and Romeo smiling big with their own impressive entourage. Lincoln hadn't noticed me yet.

Hands clasped tightly together on the handle of my clutch, my eyes were shining with pride for him. He'd been so fantastic. Everyone else obviously thought so, too. It wasn't just on the ocean that he excelled. I shook my head brushing off a guy who offered me a solo cup filled with beer. I wasn't interested in anyone or anything else. I just wanted Lincoln.

"Hey." Looking pretty in a mint colored top and jeans, Karen smiled and handed me an uncapped bottled water. "I didn't know you were coming."

"I guess you didn't hear me trying to call you earlier." I grinned goofily.

"Guess not. The music's pretty loud. Couldn't stay away, huh?" She surmised.

I shook my head. "He's something. Isn't he?"

"Yeah. Sure. If you're into that whole hot bohemian surfer god rock star thing, but..." She trailed off her eyes widening slightly.

I shifted to follow the direction of her gaze.

I went utterly still, my anticipatory smile fading away as a million tiny knives stabbed me in the center of my chest as I watched Kit put her hand on Lincoln's arm. He turned toward her. She went up on her toes kissing the lips I'd tasted just hours ago. All of the knives coalesced into one dagger right though my heart.

"I've gotta go." I spun around and pushed back through the crowd I'd just expended so much effort pressing though before. Every single person seemed intent on hindering my progress. Anguish clenched my stomach making me feel like I might hurl. Tears blurred my eyes. I stumbled and my sandals skidded on an empty paper plate someone had discarded on the grass.

I righted myself on the gate poised to flee when I heard someone call my name. Ash. He caught up to me studying me with a steady assessing gaze. "It's not what you think."

"Yeah." I snorted my disbelief. "Sure. Look, it doesn't really matter, alright?" I turned to leave but he grabbed my arm. I looked down at his fingers on my skin then back up to his face. There was something in his eyes that I didn't understand, something that said he was well familiar with the pain I was feeling in that moment, but it wasn't something I would begin to understand until I reflected on it years later.

"Let me walk you home," he offered softly.

The pressure of unshed tears behind my eyes, it was on the tip of my tongue to refuse, but it was late. I was dressed in a way that invited attention that I didn't want anymore. It would be safer to have an escort and I didn't know where Karen was. There was no way in hell I was going back into the party to find her.

"Thank you, Ash." I curled my fingers around his corded bicep, leaning heavily on him accepting the offer of his strength and protection but sadly still pining for another's.

Chapter 24

Linc

"**Y**ou're a fuckin' prick, Lincoln Savage," Karen spit the words at me, her hazel eyes flashing her ire. "Simone's too sweet to tell you to your face, but I'm so the hell not. I can't believe you! Why did you even invite her here tonight if you had plans to be with someone else?" My gut became a heavy lodestone as I felt Kit scooting into me. I quickly pieced the puzzle together realizing Simone must have been at the party, seen me with Kit and reached the wrong conclusion.

"Simone Bianchi?" Kit hissed. "You and Simone." Her brows rose. "But she's just a girl."

I nodded sheepishly. I thought it probably wouldn't help to point out that Simone was only a year younger than me. "Kit," I said low when I realized Karen wasn't going anywhere. Ramon had joined us with a 'what the hell is going on' look on his face. He apparently thought Karen needed backup. "I'm sorry if I gave you the wrong idea

128

about us."

"If she's with you," her face twisted into something ugly, "then why'd she leave with your cousin?"

Simone and Ash. I didn't want to believe it. Not for a minute. Just the thought of her with someone else made me insane. "Is that true?" I managed to ask Karen.

She shrugged. She wasn't going to comfort me. She was sticking to the role of Simone's protector. If I wasn't so freaked about the situation, I would've been glad that Simone had someone looking out for her in that way.

"Patch," I called grabbing his arm as he drifted past. Looking addled, he stumbled a bit as he rounded to face me, a chick with him, overfilled cups slopping beer from their unsteady hands. Karen's eyes narrowed as she watched him sway. "Where's Ash?"

"He left a minute ago. With your girl." He grinned stupidly. "She looked hot as shit. Short dress with those legs of hers. Hard to miss."

Only I had. Because of Kit. *Fuck.* I slid out my cell. I couldn't call her since her dad had taken hers away. I hit Ash's number instead, my heart slamming with irrational jealousy.

Simone

"**Y**our phone's ringing," I told Ash. We had both been quiet as he escorted me home, each lost in our own thoughts. Still I'd been grateful for his company. There had been more than a few leering looks from the drunks downtown before we turned down the suburban side street into my neighborhood.

"Oh yeah." Slowing his pace, his eyes met mine as he slid his cell out of his front jeans pocket. I got the idea he'd been deliberately ignoring the call. "Hello." He frowned and I could feel his eyes on me as he listened. We were getting close to my house and the closer we got the more frayed my control over my emotions was becoming with Ash watching me so intently. "Yes she is. I didn't want her walking home alone...She's pretty upset. Maybe you should talk to her yourself." Ash offered me the phone. "It's Linc."

"No." I backed away from the cell as if it were a poisonous viper.

Lips pressed together, Ash withdrew his outstretched arm. "She doesn't want to talk, dude. Do you wanna...No, not yet." An extremely long pause as Ash listened. "I don't know. I'll ask her."

"Mona," he spoke so softly I had to lean in to hear him. He seemed afraid I would bolt. I was seriously considering it. I just wanted to go to my room to be alone. "Linc wants you to know he's not with Kit. That he didn't know she was going to be at the party, and that he hasn't been with her since the morning you two met. He also wants to know if you'll let me walk you back to where he is so he can explain in person."

My heart wanted to latch onto those words, to go to him and let him explain away what had happened. My brain told me facts were facts. I'd seen him with her. He hadn't tried to avoid the kiss. I should never have let him charm me in the first place. Better to put an end to it now. Why delay the inevitable?

I shook my head. "Tell him no explanations are necessary." Thinking about him just made my chest ache. "I need to go home." I pointed to the two story house with the porch light blazing. "That's it right there. Thanks for walking me. You don't have to come any further."

I spun around ignoring Ash's attempts to call me back. My hurried strides made his voice quickly fade into the background. If only my attachment to Lincoln could be as easy to sever.

The tears I'd held off flooded my eyes. Blindly, I jogged up the porch steps, unlocked the door with my key and entered the foyer.

"Simone." My father awaited wearing an ominous expression. My mother was behind him concern in her eyes. My father put his cell back to his ear while motioning me into the living room. I complied sitting on the edge of the couch. "Yes she just came in. Thank for calling."

Dread knitted my muscles into knots.

"That was Kit." My eyes grew wide.

"She was concerned about you. Says you've been hanging around an older boy with a bad reputation. One of our busboys. A surfer."

Each of his words ratcheted the tension within me

131

higher. All true facts that I couldn't deny.

"Simone, I can't begin to express how disappointed I am in you."

I nodded, dropping my gaze. I had left the house with such high hopes but returned deflated. I knew my father. He wasn't going to let this go. I was going to lose more than just my cell after this perceived infraction. I was about to lose my freedom.

Chapter 25

Linc

"Yeah that was her father," I confirmed to Ash. "Asshole just shit canned me." Predictably, though I doubted Simone had told him anything. I was pretty sure the breadcrumb trail of blame led straight to Kit. She hadn't tried very hard to hide her jealousy and I hadn't reacted very well to her second attempt to try to reconcile with me at the party.

By that point I wasn't in the mood to sugar coat. Separated from her abusive husband or not, I wasn't interest in Kit anymore.

I just wanted Simone.

And I needed to see her.

I knew I could make her understand and it was eating me up inside that she refused to speak to me. At the restaurant I could have found a way to make her listen but now that I'd been fired that was no longer an option.

"I don't know what to do." I eyed my cousin across the

small space that separated our twin beds.

Expression sympathetic, he leaned forward and patted my shoulder. "Maybe you could appeal to her through Karen."

"No." I shook my head toeing out of my Vans and scooting backward in my bed, resting my shoulders against the wall. "She's made up her mind about me. I don't think she was a big fan of how I treated Kit, either. I don't think there's much chance at all of her being my advocate." I closed my eyes and leaned my head back. "Do you think that she'd listen to you?"

"I doubt it. When two girlfriends close ranks that usually puts us guys on the outside."

"This sucks." I sighed. Silence descended. It was nearly two in the morning. My aunt and uncle had been asleep when we came in. Their bedroom just across the hall was quiet, their home in a peaceful neighborhood far from the noisy main drag of town. The only sound at the moment besides my heavy defeated breathing was the swish of Ash's jeans and the jingle of his belt and buckle hitting the floor on his side of the room.

"I'm sorry, Linc." He switched off his lamp. I opened my eyes to almost complete darkness. His mattress springs squeaked as he settled underneath his covers. "I realize now she means a lot to you. We'll put our heads together in the morning and figure something out. It's not like she lives in another country. Her house is just a couple of blocks over." His shadow moved as he punched his pillow and flopped back down. "Have you and she…"

"Nah, man. It's not like that. I mean sure I want to go there." It was all I thought about, but there was something much more to it than just that. I knew how I felt and I was more and more certain every day. But that was something I wanted her to be the first to know and it panicked the hell out of me that I might not get the chance to tell her now. "I've never felt like this before," I admitted low not sure if Ash heard me. There was no response on his side of the room. "It's almost like I can't breathe right when we're apart."

I didn't fall asleep until the morning. When I woke up Ash was gone and my way forward with Simone wasn't any clearer with the birds chirping than it had in the dead of the night.

Ditching the clothes I'd slept in, I slid on a pair of Hurley's, grabbed a package of chocolate Pop Tarts and my board and wet suit from the hooks in the garage before heading to the beach. I thought better on the water and since she seemed to be a lot like me in that regard I hoped maybe she might find her way there, too.

She wasn't there but the rest of the gang was zipping up and fastening their ankle tethers.

"Where's Ash?" I asked donning my own wetsuit.

"Dunno," Dominic replied. "Haven't seen him since last night." He straightened and moaned. "My head hurts."

"Told you not to mix beer and hard liquor," Ramon told him before scooping his board off the sand and heading into the surf.

"You work things out with Simone?" Dominic asked me as we followed Ramon out.

I shook my head. "She won't talk to me."

"Bummer," he accented the second syllable.

I nodded. It was that for sure.

Once beyond the break point, we separated each waiting for our wave. We were out early as we were most days and had the ocean to ourselves. I popped into my stance when I spotted a wave with good height. I got some real good air on a full round house, linked the flat to another wave and milked that till it disappeared. I heard the guys cheering and I acknowledged them with a wave, going back out to wait for another one, but my heart wasn't in it and that wasn't a good thing. I had Fiji coming up. I needed the points. Half the qualifying year was gone already. If I didn't place in the next event it was going to be hard to make the championship cutoff.

I forced myself through the motions riding wave after wave until I was exhausted. When I finally waded out, Ash had shown up and he was pacing the shore.

"Where have you been?" I raised a curious brow wondering why his hair was slicked back and he was wearing a button down and khakis instead of swim trunks.

"At a job interview." He grinned. "I heard a position just opened up at Napoli's. So I got it."

Chapter 26

Simone

I discovered it was harder to face the morning knowing Lincoln Savage's smile wasn't going to be on the other side of the night. Infinitely harder knowing that it might never be. Oh and the fact that my life was on complete lockdown.

No phones.

No friends.

No free time.

No beach.

Resigned I went to work earlier than usual with my dad. We took inventory and went to the discount warehouse to purchase supplies to restock the kitchen after the busy weekend. On the way back to Napoli's we drove past the ocean. Unable to stop myself I scanned the shoreline for his familiar form.

I saw a lone surfer on his board in the water.

My heart wanted to believe it was Lincoln but logic

said that it was unlikely. He was always with his friends.

"I really don't understand what the fascination is." My dad's voice rattled the fragile silence between us. He'd been watching me. His gaze returned to the front windshield, his fingers wrapping tighter around the steering wheel as we turned into the alley behind the restaurant. "They're bums. Marijuana smokers. Street people with suntans. Why you would want to waste your time on one I'll never understand. I always thought you were the steady practical one. The one with ambition and drive. I'd hate to find out that you have your head as high in the clouds as your mother."

I kept silent, gaze straight ahead, hands clasped together in my lap, the dutiful daughter.

"Am I making myself clear, Simone?"

"Yes, Daddy." Dutiful, reprimanded daughter.

"Good. It's about time you showed some sense." He turned off the ignition and removed the keys. "Grab a couple of the bread bags, run in and tell Edgar to send some of the guys to help me unload."

"Yes, Daddy." I unlatched my belt and popped open my door.

"Oh and Simone." I turned to look back at him. "I hired a new busboy this morning to replace your surfer." My throat closed as my mind flashed with a memory of Lincoln, his black Napoli's work shirt snug around his toned torso, his biceps flexing and his eyes twinkling as he cleared a table and caught me watching him.

"I want you to cross train him," he continued. "He seems like a good kid. His mom's on the city council. His dad works as an adjuster. He has experience waiting tables at the Deck Bar. I'll start him in the kitchen, but my plan is to move him into service."

"Sure, Daddy." Plastic bread bag handles threaded three deep on each arm, flip flops slapping against the concrete, I pulled open the heavy steel door and entered the building. The short hallway was still dark and the only activity in the restaurant this early was in the kitchen.

I threw my shoulder into the two way door and pushed it open. The blast of warmer air was pleasantly layered with garlic and basil. The trays of hand rolled meatballs lined the counters awaiting their turn inside the large commercial oven that dominated one side of the kitchen.

I almost didn't notice him at first, a cloud of steam semi-concealing him, his toned arms up to the elbows in suds and a teetering skyscraper of dirty dishes from the night before waiting to be washed beside him.

I went completely dormant. Feet rooted to the floor. Edgar said something to me but he had to call my name twice and repeat his request for it to register. The busboy, his platinum hair tucked into a backwards Napoli's ball cap, turned his head toward me. Eyes a darker blue than Lincoln's locked with mine for a moment before he looked away.

Ashland Keys was the new hire?

I blinked, my brain coming back into focus as Edgar removed the bread bags from my arm. "My dad's in the alley. He says to send the guys back to unload."

Edgar barked instructions in both English and Spanish and the prep chefs moved past me on their way to the Suburban. Ash turned off the water and dried his hands before following. His eyes slid to me again as he casually bumped into me. I felt him press something into my hands. "Sorry, Miss Bianchi," he apologized. "I slipped on the mopped floor."

"It's ok," I managed casting my gaze furtively toward Edgar to make sure he hadn't noticed anything to report to my dad. He hadn't. He was busy loading meatballs into the oven.

I had no idea what was going on but I knew I didn't want to give my father any more reasons to sanction me.

I backed out of the kitchen glancing down at my hand once I was in the dark hallway. It held a greeting card sized envelope with Mona scrawled on the front.

Nerves on edge, I jumped and tucked the contraband behind my back as the rear door reopened, light streaming inside like an interrogator's spotlight. The crew marched back inside their arms laden with groceries. My dad led, followed by the two prep chefs, then Ash. He leaned down and whispered in my ear. "Read it. Don't throw it away."

Numbly I watched him catch up to the others. When I was alone again, I stared down at the envelope.

Reason clamored loudly. *The plan. Remember the plan. There's no place for Lincoln and the heartache that comes with him.*

But my fingers seemed to be governed by my heart. They slid open the lightly glued seam. There were several photographs and a note inside. Linc's face was on the first photograph only he wasn't smiling. My chest got so tight I couldn't breathe. I staggered backward ducking into the storage room.

What would it hurt to take a peek at the rest?

I could return it. Who would know if I looked?

Outside

My secret. My choice.

I suddenly felt less trapped inside my life. Linc had that effect on me even when he wasn't physically present. Breathing a little easier, I went through the contents. The next picture was the pier and the final one was of Linc on his board. I wondered if Ash had taken it. Tears pricked my eyes. I could almost hear the familiar soothing roar of the ocean and feel the warmth of the sun that was sparkling on it.

Good morning, Mona, Linc wrote and I could hear his perfect voice in my mind. *The beach is not the same without you here to share it with me.*

Chapter 27

Linc

"Tell me everything she said. Everything she did," I grilled Ash the minute he got off work. Dude looked exhausted. First the early morning interview after the late night talking. Then being on your feet all day, not even a minute to breathe. I knew what it was like working for Alberto Bianchi. But it had been worth it to me just to be near her. Knowing Ash had taken the job for my benefit meant the world. I told him so. Repeatedly.

He dropped onto his bed flopping backward, forearm over his eyes. He didn't even bother taking his shoes off. "She didn't say anything. Her father hardly lets her out of his sight. It's weird."

"Did she read the note?" I leaned forward elbows on my knees.

"I'm not sure, Linc." He removed his arm. "I gave it to her. She slipped the envelope back to me right before we closed. I can't really tell if she opened it and she didn't say anything about it."

Shit. My gaze dropped to my bare feet on the rug. I heard the rustle from Ash's side of the room and knew he'd sat up.

"Hey," he called, tapping my knee with his fist. I looked up to see eyes like my Aunt Maggie's brimming with empathy. "Number sixteen and the best small wave surfer on the qualifying circuit doesn't give up when the ocean looks flat. You need to be patient. Winds change. You know she's not immune to your charms. But you hurt her, so she withdrew. Right now she's probably wondering whether loving you is worth the risk of getting burned."

My eyes widened at his insight and at his use of that particular word.

"C'mon, Linc." He noticed. "I love you like a brother. You think I can't see how it is with you and her?"

I didn't confirm or deny it.

"Do another one. I'll pass it on. Don't press about the Kit thing. You said your bit about it. She'll either believe you or she won't. Just show her how you feel with the pictures and tell her with words. She needs to know why she should put herself out there for you."

I mulled that advice over finally leaving Ash alone. Honestly he fell back on his bed and crashed the minute I stopped pimping him for details about Simone.

I left the house, my mind playing the final part of our conversation as I wandered by the restaurant Hurley cap and hooded sweatshirt shadowing my features hoping to catch a glimpse of her.

I remembered the first time I had seen her there. How she'd looked at me as if she really saw me, as if she admired me, maybe even needed me in her life.

Ash had mentioned that she seemed different to him.

"How so?" I had prompted.

He had shrugged a far off look in his eyes. "Conflict-ed," he had finally admitted. "At a loss." He had gotten quiet and I had thought he was finished when he added, "Like maybe she's got all these intense feelings rumbling around inside of her that she doesn't know how to express." His voice was low as if the words vibrated from somewhere deep inside his chest. "Feelings that maybe she's never felt before. Maybe she's afraid to unleash them because maybe they won't be reciprocated and she'll lose the things she has for just a chance to have the one thing she's always dreamed about."

Simone

I moved from table to table checking the salt and pep-per shakers and refilling the sugar and artificial sweeteners that were running low, tasks that the serv-ers performed but that I was doing today because I needed an excuse to be busy and because I was hoping to run into Ash before my father returned from his errands.

A week had passed since Ash had started working at Napoli's.

A week of deliveries from Linc.

Outside

A week for my resolve to be chipped away.

After all, what good was a plan for escaping this life when I might miss out on a man I was pretty sure I wanted to share it with me?

It was all so wickedly seductive.

My beach. Him on it.

Telling me how he felt about me in a lyrical fashion. I had memorized every word.

I watch the sunrise
The dark transforming to soft grey then lavender
I hear the ocean's steady roar
But my souls a lonely island.

The pure gold of your eyes
Is more beautiful than the blue water
Your smile had more allure
Than the ebb and flow of the tide
If only you were here.

Your laughter refreshes
Renews
And energizes.

The shore
The sea breeze
The rip and curl of the perfect wave
Nothing is as it should be without you here.

I sighed then jumped as Ash's voice sounded behind me. I hadn't heard him come in.

"Hey, Mona," he greeted. "You're here early today. Waiting for me?" He leaned close. I could smell the ocean on him the same as Lincoln. "Or maybe just the postman?"

I spun around. His eyes were glinting with teasing humor but there was something else in them lately, something that seemed a little sad. I hadn't said anything about the envelopes though I readily took them every time he offered, perusing the contents over and over again any time I could get a minute alone until the end of his shift when I returned them to him seemingly unopened. But I was pretty sure my fingerprints were all over everything.

Could the sadness he hid so well have something to do with Lincoln?

Did he think I was going to end up hurting someone he obviously cared so much about?

"You missed a table," he said meaningfully setting his cell on the linen draped surface.

I immediately covered it with my hand and slid it into my pocket.

"Don't leave him hanging much longer." His eyes met mine, his expression all serious now. "He won't say anything but it's tearing him up. He's off to the beach every morning by himself, staring off into space. Waiting." He frowned. "Make a decision." He stalked away his shoulders stiff, his movements abrupt.

I had never seen him so worked up. But he was right. The summer was slipping away. Soon I would have to return to college.

I ducked into the ladies restroom, clicked the latch closed on the stall and remembered the last note. Tears burned my eyes and fear surged in my heart. I knew what I was going to do.

I found his number on Ash's Nokia and called it.

"Ash. What's going on? Has anything happened?"

Hearing his voice and the eagerness in it almost brought me to my knees. Only the fact that it was the public restroom and the restaurant kept me from doing it. Leaning heavily into the partition, I cleared my throat and spoke. "Linc. It's me. Simone."

"Mona," he exhaled and I heard the sound of running water being turned off. Was he getting ready to take a shower? My throat went even drier than before.

"Where are you? How are you? It's so good to hear your voice."

"Yours, too," I admitted. "Listen I'm at work." I didn't want to tell him I was in the women's restroom. "I can't talk long. I just wanted to say that the things you wrote... that you..." I trailed off realizing there was no way I could manage this over the phone. Woman up, Mona. I straightened from the wall. "I need to see you." Touch you. Feel you. "Can you meet me at the beach? The stairs where we met the first time?"

"Sure. Absolutely. The sooner the better."

I told him a time and he agreed. My hands were trembling when I ended the call. I only hoped it would be late enough. That my mom would be passed out. That my dad would choose to remain home this evening instead of returning at dawn.

I had good reasons to be afraid.

My father would probably find out that I had defied him once again. Even if he didn't, I might very well get my heart broken in the end.

I knew those were both legitimate possibilities but I didn't care. Not really. Not anymore. Not as much as I cared about Lincoln.

Chapter 28

Linc

I headed to the sandstone beach at the base of the stairs to her street an hour early.

She hadn't given me any indication about what she was thinking but I wasn't going to leave anything to chance. This was about choice. I had chosen her. Now I needed her to choose me.

I quickly quashed any thought that she might choose differently.

I went all out on the presentation.

And then she appeared. My water nymph, an other-worldly creature, the light blue gauzy dress clinging to her curves like sea foam. She had a silver band around her upper arm that I assumed had her house key on it and flat sandals strapped to her delicate feet.

Spellbound I stood at the bottom of the steps grateful I had my hand on the steel railing because I wasn't feeling all that steady on my bare feet all of a sudden.

She seemed hesitant as well until her eyes drifted past me to my preparations. She smiled brilliantly, that inner light of hers beaming out, warming my soul.

"Mona, you look incredible, but you've been too far away for too long. Won't you come closer and talk to me for a while?"

She bobbed her head in reply her eyes glassy. Happy tears I hoped. I couldn't help myself. As soon as her sandals hit the last step I swung her up into my arms and kissed her, just a touch, just for a heartbeat, my firm lips to her lush ones. A fleeting reminder of just how sweet it might be.

"You can put me down," she said when I lifted my head.

"No thanks. I like you right where you are." I hugged her tighter to my chest not thinking it could get any better but then it did as she placed her palm against my cheek. I leaned my face into her soft touch. Eyes full of wonder, their honeyed depths reflecting the glow of the hurricane candles I'd lit and arranged around the blanket, she stared up at me.

"This is so beautiful, so romantic. And the notes and photos took my breath away."

"You are my breath, Mona and you take it away from me every time you leave. But," I grinned to lighten the heavy, "don't tell anyone about the hearts and candles. Ash already knows how far gone I am for you. But I'd rather not give Dominic and Ramon any ammunition."

She giggled and I treasured the sound and sight of her happiness. I let her down once my feet hit the blanket but I did it slowly savoring the feel of her curves sliding down my body.

"Sit," I prompted when she didn't move and started to look uncertain. She lowered herself onto the edge of the blanket facing the ocean, tipping her chin into the ocean breeze the way she often did. I sank down beside her, tugging the hem of my tee that had ridden up from the waist of my Volcom cargo shorts all the while watching her, my body already mourning the loss of contact.

Now that I had her here I didn't know where to begin. Ash had cautioned me about mentioning Kit but I didn't like leaving that hanging between us.

"I missed this." She turned to look at me, her smile wistful and her eyes a little sad. "And you."

"I did, too." I scooted closer and took her hand curling my fingers around her. "Everything I said, everything I wrote is true."

"I know that now." Her eyes brightened. "I'm sorry for the way I reacted. Sorry for misjudging you. I've got no right…"

"You have every right," I cut in. "If I had seen another guy kiss you. When someone suggested that you and Ash might be…" My fingers tightened on hers. She winced and I brought our joined hands to my mouth and brushed my lips across her knuckles in apology. "I would have reacted the same way," I concluded.

Her lips parted as if in awe of what I had confessed. I reached for her, the surface of my palm skimming her soft cheek and my fingers threading in her silky hair.

"What do we do then, Linc?" Her voice was low and emotion filled. "I leave for school again soon and you leave for Fiji even sooner than that. I don't see how it can work for us. I'm not grounded anymore but my dad..." She trailed off and I filled in.

"It will work if we both want it to. It worked tonight."

Honeyed eyes wide, she nodded.

"So we'll be committed," I confirmed.

"We'll have to keep our relationship secret. You'll get tired of sneaking around. You said yourself that I'm not the type of girl you're used to. I'm not experienced. I've only been with two other guys." Out of excuses, she looked away withdrawing from my touch and untangling her hand from mine. I could see the sheen on her eyes. It wasn't the type of bright glaze I wanted them to have.

I moved placing myself in front of her so she had to look at me, had to see the sincerity blazing from my steady gaze. "I will *never* get tired of being with you." I thought it best to alleviate that concern first. "And I believe that what I actually said to Ramon was that you weren't the type of girl to be interested in his kind of shit. The temporary get laid without any emotional attachment type of crap. I'm glad that there have only been two other guys for you." That meant there were only two murders I had to plan. "Now that I've met you, I wish that there had been no others for me. I don't want my past to hurt you or come between us. I can promise you that there hasn't been anyone else since the day I met you and that there won't be anyone else as long as we're together. Honestly, I only want you, Mona."

I framed her face and her lids fluttered closed, the tension in her face relaxing as if my touch and my words soothed her. "I want all of you. I want to know everything about you. I want to make you smile. I want to hear you sing again." I brushed my mouth across her soft lips. Her eyes opened though they were a little hazy. "And I want you naked." My voice lowered an octave as I imagined it in my mind. "I want to caress every single sexy inch of you. And I want you to touch me, too. But that will come." My eyes burned with certainty. "I promise you."

Chapter 29

Simone

I wanted everything he did and then some. I opened my mouth to tell him but I think he already knew. He could taste the surrender on my lips as his slick tongue traced and glided between them. He could hear it in the soft moans he greedily swallowed slanting his head to deepen the kiss before feeding me a long hot male groan of his own. He could feel my need for him in the tensed arc of my body and the way my fingers explored every hard male contour I could reach while he rained warm showers of desperate kisses across the exposed surfaces of my skin on my cheek, my neck and collarbones.

His breath began to sound ragged matching my own. My breasts rose and fell with every one, the nipples tight points that ached for his touch.

"Mona, we need to stop." He drew back and framed my face again his thumbs stroking my cheeks his eyes as dark as the night beyond our island of candles on the sand.

"I want you. Right now. So badly. If you could feel how fast my heart is racing, if you knew how hard my cock is, you wouldn't even believe it."

Curious I moved my hands from his forearms. One palm I brought to the center of his chest and felt his rapid rhythm. The other I slid lower fingertips savoring each ridge of his abdomen holding my breath, biting my lip in anticipation as I went lower.

"Mona." He said my name on a shuddering breath. "Stop." He snagged the lower hand first then peeled the other one from the perspiration dampened cotton clinging to his chest. Covering mine with his own he brought them up to his lips and kissed each while staring at me. "Not to-night, babe. Soon like I promised. Not because I don't want to is the point I'm trying to make. Because I want to too much. You are special, Mona. More important than any other woman I've ever known. Worth waiting for."

He released my hands and laid back on the blanket, placing one arm behind his head for a pillow. "Come here." He crooked his fingers and gave me that charming one dimpled grin. "I want to hold you for as long as I can be-fore you have to go in."

"My sandals," I protested bending at the waist to un-clasp the straps. "I'll get grit all over the blanket."

"Leave them on," he commanded. "I don't care, and I don't want to waste the time it would take for you to get them off when I could already have you here by me." He raised a brow. "I don't want to waste any time that I have with you."

I turned and crawled toward him, the sandstone cool beneath the blanket but he was warm, a virtual inferno of heat as he drew me closer my body aligning to his. He threaded fingers into my hair cradling the base of my skull and bringing my head to rest against his chest.

"Tell me what you did this week."

"Didn't Ash tell you?"

"Sure. But I don't think he pays the same attention to the details as I would when it comes to you."

I grinned against his chest. I was pretty sure he could hear the smile in my voice as I began to share. No one had ever been as interested in the mundane details of my life. He not only told me how important I was to him, he was showing me. "I re-supplied inventory with my dad in the mornings, balanced the books at night. Hostessed some. Managed a bit."

"Sounds tiring."

"It is. It was." I yawned to prove it. "What did you do?"

I listened to the rhythmic rise and fall of the tide as he shared how much he looked forward to taking the pictures for me, finding the right words. How he had surfed. How he and Ash had spoken each evening about me.

Safe and secure in his arms I started to get sleepy and closed my eyes. I felt his body twist before he kissed the top of my head. His arms tightened around me. "Rest, Mona. Sleep a bit. I'll wake you before the sunrise."

Chapter 30

Linc

D awn was just starting to turn the world from black to grayish half-light as I walked her up the stairs and back toward her place kissing her once more before reluctantly letting her go.

I hated being parted from her.

From my position several houses down from hers, I watched her sexy hips sway as she continued on the sidewalk and climbed her porch steps. Key inserted in the front door she turned back to wave, her lips lifting in a melancholy smile.

I dipped my head to acknowledge it waiting as she entered, wanting to be sure that she was safe. The lights remained off in the foyer but I wasn't leaving until she made it to her room.

On the walk from the beach she had shared how she'd gotten caught after Dominic's party and it troubled me more than I let on how her father had treated her. It was more than just being separated from her that bothered me about bringing her home.

I couldn't protect her when she was in there and I was outside.

A soft glow illuminated the second story window on the side of the house. The blinds opened and I saw her silhouette in the frame.

Taking my cue to leave, my heart a tight lump in my chest, I turned away forcing my feet in the direction of my home, the ache of separation from her growing more painful with each step.

I was going to have to do some serious planning. She was right about the time we had together being short. I resented the daylight for stealing her away. I wanted each minute of it to go by faster so I could see her again, hold her again and maybe a bit more.

Day by Day.

Night by Night.

Hour by Hour.

I was determined to treasure every single moment that she was mine. The future was never certain. But that future was coming toward us as surely as the waves inevitably reached the shore.

Outside

Simone

I stood at my window watching him walk away, his strong shoulders hunched, his head bowed and his hands shoved deep into his cargo short pockets. A chill that felt a little like a premonition tiptoed up each individual vertebra of my spine. I wrapped my arms around myself to ward it off. I wasn't going to just hope for good things to happen with Lincoln. I was going to make certain they did.

I didn't like him being sad.

I knew I could make him happy.

I wanted to show him just how committed to us I was. So I held off sleeping or showering the residue of dew and sand from my skin. Instead hugging my arms around myself I replayed every word from our night together until the clock on my nightstand hit a less egregious hour.

Popping the cordless phone out of its charger I punched in Karen's number as I headed into my bathroom, locking the door. I took off my sandals with it cradled between my shoulder and ear.

For Linc and me to work with my father against us, we were going to need support.

Plus a little creativity.

After filling Karen in on the details of my night with Lincoln, she was more than willing to help. The cloak and dagger aspect of my relationship with him resonated with her for some reason. Plus she hadn't been totally out of the loop. I hadn't been grounded from talking with her on the house phone this past week. She had pretty much swung back to being pro-Lincoln after he had publicly brushed off Kit at the party and initiated the love note campaign.

After we coordinated our plans I jumped into the shower and feigned surprise when my mom yelled for me to pick up the phone as I was blow drying my hair. Karen went through the whole spiel just in case anyone was eavesdropping. The story was that she was heading to the community pool and was inviting me to join her. I held my hand over the receiver and obtained permission before agreeing to meet her there.

"Don't forget you need to come in early for your shift," my father reminded me at the base of the stairs. "I need you to start training Ash tonight."

"Sure, Daddy."

"He's a real hard worker. A nice boy." Ash was totally nonverbal at the restaurant besides the occasional whispered words to me and a consistent yes to everything my dad asked him to do. And no surfing talk. No wonder my dad liked him.

I shrugged. "He's alright."

"He's your age. He's taking classes at City College. Maybe you two could go out some time? Wednesdays are usually slow."

A night off with Ash as an alibi? Hallelujah the surf gods were shining their golden rays of approval on Linc and me.

"I'll think about it," I told him trying not to sound over-ly eager. I didn't want him to get suspicious. I twisted the latch and opened the door hefting my swim bag up higher while calling out over my shoulder. "See ya later, Dad"

Flip flops snapping excitedly against the pavement,

lips curved in anticipation of surprising Linc at the beach I headed to Karen's house a couple of street further from the coast than mine. We would do a U-turn and go the other way once we met up. It was a little extra walking, but whatever I had to do to facilitate the ruse.

Turns out he surprised me, instead.

Wearing only a pair of long black and white swim trunks and a black Volcom ball cap that was slightly askew, his arm draped over his surfboard, taking my breath away and my heart already though he didn't know it yet, Lincoln smiled his dimpled grin and my expression turned into something else entirely. Something he seemed to understand. Something that meant he was the only one for me and probably always would be.

"C'mon gorgeous," Lincoln picked up his surfboard and opened his other arm for me to step into. "I wanna teach you how to surf."

Chapter 31

Simone

At the beach we met up with the rest of the crew. Each had their own reactions to Linc and me. Karen seemed practically euphoric as if she had single-handedly orchestrated my reunion with him. Ash seemed reserved though pleased. Ramon only smiled. Dominic took it in stride as if things were how they were meant to be.

We threw our towels and bags in a pile and stacked the boards together. Karen and the others complained about the heat and decided to head into the surf for a swim. Lincoln had other plans for us. He began running me through the steps to pop up on the board while it rested on the shore.

Karen's laughter and a chorus of male shouts drifted back to me over the sound of the waves lapping the shore and my labored breathing. After what seemed like my hundredth attempt on the maneuver that was a lot like doing a pushup and then jumping to standing, Linc nodded his approval.

Finally.

I stood still toes sifting sand while Linc crouched beneath me fastening the tether from his board around my ankle. His masculine fingers lingered on my lower leg. His eyes were hot and I got that way, too, just looking at him.

My arms felt like lead and trembled with exhaustion as we paddled out together. We moved into a position on the other side of where the waves were breaking. Lincoln gave me some more advice and information about the sport that mostly went in one ear and out the other. I didn't really care at this point about any of that and I didn't care that I had been up all night either.

What I really cared about was him. I had been on a total high since the moment he had placed his warm fingers on my skin his hands practically spanning my waist plucking me out of the water and depositing me on his board.

Now I was laid out on my stomach in position ready to paddle and pop up while he bobbed in the water beside me. He shook out his mane of wet hair and the droplets cooled my sun heated skin. The blond highlights faded into a more uniform brown when drenched by the ocean water. We stared at each other as we floated both a little tipsy on one another it seemed.

"I could stare at you all day, gorgeous." Linc's sculpted lips curled. When I assured him I could do the same his dimple appeared to wink at me. "But if we do that," his expression turned stern, "you'll forget what I just taught you and we'll have to start all over again. You need to immediately put what you learned into practice." He nodded his head thoughtfully. "Trust me. I remember from when I was first starting out."

"Who taught you?"

"My old man." He frowned. "It's the one good thing he did for me. The only thing we ever had in common really. I practically killed myself learning new maneuvers hoping if I got good enough I might win his approval. And then maybe he'd quit drinking and knocking me around. But it was never enough."

I gasped tears filling my eyes as he so matter of factly shared the terrible details of his upbringing. Leaning toward him, I grabbed his hand and brought it to my chest near my heart that ached for him, for the boy who had tried so desperately to please an unloving father.

"Don't feel sorry for me." His gaze grew hard.

"I don't, Linc. I just..." My lip trembled. "I just wish things had been better for you, that's all. I'm so glad you have your aunt and uncle and Ash. I know..." I trailed off afraid to share.

"Tell me," he prompted.

"I'm not saying it's exactly the same but I think I understand just a little bit of how you must have felt. Things aren't so great with my parents, either," I began.

"I know, Mona." He squeezed my thigh.

"Everyone knows how they are," I whispered. "People feel sorry for me. I hate that. That's why college is so important to me. I have to get my degree so I can finally break free from all of that." I pleaded once again for him to understand what I'd never properly explained.

"I don't feel sorry for you." His clear blue eyes glistened like the surface of the water all around us. "The fact is I'm damn proud of you." His voice thickened. "Beautiful *and* brave. I'm falling for you hard. You know that. Right?"

I nodded though I wondered who was falling harder.

Chapter 32

Linc

I wanted to nix the surfing lesson, paddle us in and kiss her breathless. The only thing that kept me from doing so was knowing that I wouldn't be able to stop at just kissing, not when I so desperately wanted to take her and make her completely my own.

"Hand on the rails and get ready to pop into your stance." I tweaked her toes where they dangled in the water beneath my board.

She nodded and did as she was told. I nearly swallowed my tongue watching her tits nearly fall out of the tiny purple triangles that barely covered them.

"There's a good lump building behind us." Only years of practice and familiarity with this beach allowed me to focus on her and the set pattern at the same time. "Now!" I ordered.

She popped up weight balancing as I had shown her on the beach earlier and she managed it fluidly. Caught the decent sized wave, got the swell underneath her just right and even ducked into a crouch to take the curl for a couple of seconds until it collapsed on her.

Water nymph. Surf goddess. Otherwordly.

By the time she surfaced flipping her heavily saturated hair out of her eyes, I was there to claim her. "You were brilliant." She grinned nearly as big as me as she clung to the board. "Unbelievable for a first time. I think you're a natural. Let's do it again."

Her eyes darkening she shook her head. Vehemently.

"Babe, it takes a while to learn to read the waves well enough to exit at the end of a good barrel like that," I cautioned. She had no reason to be discouraged.

"Linc, I know you love surfing as much as I enjoy singing and I certainly love watching you. But I am done." She enunciated each word. "Totally wiped. My knees were shaking the entire time. I'd much rather be a spectator than a participant."

I couldn't fathom how anyone could quit after a ride like that. Since I had been a little grommet surfing had soothed my restless soul. But I could respect her wishes. "Sure. I'll take you in." I propped my elbows on the board to lean across and kiss her hard, licking the salt from her lips.

When she reopened her eyes she looked a little dazed, but she perked up by the time we waded in and all the guys congratulated her on her ride.

"Unbelievable." Ash shook his head.

"Freakin' unbelievable," Dominic clarified.

"Pretty sweet," Ramon said with his board under his arm and the surf surging around his ankles. "But why are you coming in?"

"I'm good with being one and done. It was fun but a little too scary."

Ramon and Ash both looked at her like she was crazy.

"Chicks," Dominic commented drolly as we all tossed our boards into the water and headed back out. "Go figure."

Chapter 33

Simone

With Karen sandwiched between Dominic and Ramon, the threesome led the way on the sidewalk ahead of us. Linc had his own board under his left arm and me tucked into his right, a place I very much liked being. Whistling under his breath Ash trailed along just behind us.

Even after hours of surfing, the guys were still full of energy. I had an even greater admiration for what they did after my one and only maiden voyage.

"How much further is it, Ash?" Karen threw the question over her shoulder. "I'm starving and my feet hurt," she complained.

"It's just up ahead, Q2." Dominic had coined the nickname for Karen the day he had discovered that she had been both homecoming and prom queen at our high school. "But I'd be happy to carry you, if it pleases your majesty," he teased reaching for her, but she shimmied away from him giggling.

"No. I'll do it," Ramon insisted. He frowned as he jostled the taller surfer.

Grinning Karen took off running across a closely cropped lawn. Both surfers dropped their boards and pursued her each tugging on one of her arms when they caught her.

"This is it," Ash explained tipping his head toward the one story white stucco home with its red clay Mission roof tiles and arched Mediterranean windows.

"Nice house," Karen observed bumping a hip against Dominic and Ramon in turn as she easily yanked her arms free. I agreed with the assessment, admiring the classy architectural notes and well-tended flower beds filled with thriving purple topped Kangaroo palms.

"Thanks," Ash responded before insisting that Dominic and Ramon pick up their board from where they'd discarded them earlier on the lawn.

"You and Linc seem pretty serious." Karen linked her arm with me while the guys went to store their boards in the garage.

I nodded.

"I'm happy for you, Simone." Her hazel eyes twinkled in the late afternoon sunlight. "But I'm gonna keep an eye on him just in case. I don't want him breaking your heart right before you go back to college."

I tensed at the mere thought that the end of Linc and me might come before we'd really even had a chance to begin.

"Hey." She touched my arm. "Don't disappear on me. I like this daring new version of you that he seems to bring out. I was just teasing." She studied me a beat as the guys came back around to the front of the house laughing and jostling each other as guys seem fond of doing.

Ash jogged up the concrete stairs and opened the front door leading the way inside. Linc followed close behind casting me a backward glance as he did. Our gazes locked and held as Karen completed her thought.

"I wouldn't worry," she said softly glancing back and forth between Linc and me as her bookends returned to her side. "The way he looks at you," she whispered, "the only way it's going to be over is if you want it to be."

We all followed Linc and Ash across a small tiled entryway through the corner of a casually decorated living room into a large kitchen. The Spanish style blue and red tiled counters were overflowing with boxes of snacks and bottled drinks. The glass paned cabinets were filled with brightly colored plates and bowls and mix matched glasses. It was easy to see that this well used kitchen was the heart of his aunt and uncle's home.

Linc

We must have scarfed down half of the food in Aunt Maggie's kitchen. Standing side by side at the tile counters the girls formed a sandwich assembly line with Ash adding pickles and chips to the plates while the rest of us had waited in our seats around the whitewashed table.

Chugging sodas and talking loudly while leaning against the counter, Ramon and Dominic were back to their usual positions flanking Karen and formulating plans for meeting up later. She was going to have to choose between those two soon or things were going to get ugly.

Ash was across from me seemingly lost in thought as he rearranged his discarded crusts on his plate. Simone was tracing the knuckles of my hand with her delicate fingers. Just that feather light touch alongside the titillating view of her in the mesh cover up that concealed next to nothing made my cock so hard I was having difficulty concentrating.

"You've got crumbs all over your lap." Looking up at me through lowered lashes Simone's gaze gave away little but she had to have seen the massive hard on in my shorts. "Maybe we should go out into the backyard to brush them off."

Hell yeah she'd seen. The low suggestive purr of her voice had me imagining all sorts of things we could do together in the back yard. I wanted to touch her so badly. I glanced at the clock above the sink. For this to work out between us, and I needed it to, I had to be responsible with her.

"What time do you have to be at work?" I asked while tucking a wispy strand of caramel hair behind the shell of her ear. She shivered and her nipples seemed to get even harder beneath the triangles of fabric that covered them. My cock twitched in approval.

She licked her lips before speaking. Was her mouth as

dry as mine?

"In less than an hour," she replied sadly a faint reflective crease appearing between her brows. "Sooner really because I have to walk to Karen's house first to keep up the pretense before heading over to the restaurant."

I frowned. I didn't like the reminder of how little time we had left today or how we had to keep that time together secret. I stood abruptly kicking back my chair. "Let me show you where the bathroom is. You can shower and change here."

I grabbed her hand and led her through the living room and into a hallway that led to the bedrooms and the one bath. Still holding her hand, reluctant to let her go I pushed open the door to the bathroom. "There's all kinds of shampoo and stuff in there." Tugging on her hand I drew her closer reveling in the feel of her soft body against mine. "I'll shower outside in the cabana. Make it fast, yeah? I want to spend as much time with you as I can."

I never got cleaned up so fast in my life. I shook my hair after toweling off and finger combing it leaving a wet footprint trail as I reentered the house. When I passed through the kitchen Karen and Dominic were conspicuously absent but Ash raised a brow and Ramon gave me a thumbs up.

"Five minutes, Linc," Ash warned. Not stopping I tucked the beach towel tighter around my waist and hit the back hallway just as the door to the bathroom popped open, a billow of steam heralding her appearance.

Sun kissed skin from her slim shoulders to delicate ankles swathed in a white bath towel, my sea nymph's hair was slicked back from her forehead and hung loosely down her back. Our eyes met, hers lifting from a survey of her own it seemed.

"Linc." Her lips parted on my name whether an invitation or a caution I didn't care. Every caress during the day had been too brief. Those trailing touches along creamy soft coconut scented skin only left me longing for more.

I snagged her swim bag from the floor outside the bathroom and grabbed her hand pulling her inside my bedroom and locking the door.

I tossed the bag on my unmade bed, the sheets still rumpled from the hours tossing sleeplessly before Karen had called. When I turned back to Simone her pretty honey hued eyes were wide with trepidation.

"Don't be afraid, babe." I closed the short distance between us quickly plunging my fingers into her wet hair and tilting her head back. "I just need to kiss you again." Taste you. Touch you. "Privately." I lowered my head and touched my mouth to hers, satisfaction roaring through me when her lips parted for my probing tongue and her hands skimmed seductively over the water droplets along my spine to bring me closer.

Again and again I thrust my tongue into the dark recesses of her mouth, her sweet flavor an addictive ambrosia. Moving her backward I rocked my hips between her thighs once I had her body pressed against the door.

She whimpered and I groaned deepening the kiss when she ground her pelvis over my cock seeking relief for the fire that burned within her core. Heat licked every single inch of my skin. Suddenly the towels were too much between us. I ripped my lips from hers.

"Linc." Her fingers dug into my shoulders. "Don't

stop."

"Not planning to, babe. But I need to touch you." I reached for the spot between her generous breasts where the towel was still knotted. Lifting my gaze to hers I silently sought her permission.

"Yes," she breathed.

That was the word I longed to hear. I whipped the towel aside and pulled in a sharp breath my heart slamming madly as I took her in. Sure I had seen her all day in that bikini but seeing her without a scrap of fabric to hinder my enjoyment was another thing entirely. Her full tits had dusky rose nipples so hard they begged to be sucked. Her hips were perfectly rounded and the thatch of dark curls nestled between her shapely legs called for my cock.

"Mona," I groaned appreciatively, my blood on fire and my heated gaze scalded by the sexy goddess before me all tanned skin but for the paler parts her bikini shielded from the sun. I covered her mouth with my own again no longer gentle but in full out possession mode.

I didn't care that we didn't have time. I didn't care that I hadn't yet told her exactly how I felt. I was going to show her.

She was mine.

I unclasped my towel, smashed my body into hers and crushed my hard lips to her soft ones. She met each thrust of my tongue with sweet slick slashes of her own. My heart raced and my mind blazed with only one purpose. She seemed to be with me. The low sexy sounds she made in the back of her throat told me so and made my already aroused cock as hard as steel.

Filling my hands with her tits I flicked the nipples with

my thumbs.

She moaned into my mouth and I groaned shifting my body, grabbing her thigh and positioning her leg around my waist so I could align my pulsing cock with her center.

"Linc." I felt the shudder that rolled through her as well as the damp heat between her thighs. I was just about to lift her in my arms and throw her on my bed so I could reach the supply of condoms in my nightstand when a sharp rapping on the door startled both of us breaking us apart. Simone's half-masted eyes widened.

"Linc!" Ash's shout sounded harsh after the soft feminine sighs I had been feasting on. "You and Simone need to get out of there. Fast. We gotta go. We're gonna be late for work."

Chapter 34

Simone

W armth flooding my cheeks I ducked my head into Linc's chest. I couldn't believe I'd almost made love to him while his cousin had been right there outside the door. Surely he had heard my moans. How would I ever look Ash in the eyes again?

Warm fingers curled around my chin and lifted it. Before I could get totally freaked out Linc's warm passion darkened visage filled my own. "Don't be embarrassed," he whispered. "Ash knows how I feel about you. I'm sorry I got so carried away. But only because we don't have time to finish what we started." His gaze intensified. "But we will. I promise you."

A louder knock than before bounced into my shoulders. "C'mon, man," Ash cajoled sounding exasperated.

"We'll be right out." Linc's tone was gruff. "Give us five minutes."

"We don't have five." Ash sighed heavily. "You know

how her dad is."

At the mention of my father the remaining passion smoldering in my body fizzled out. I slid my naked body along the wood of the door while looking for my bag, but he was too distracting. Even just out of the corner of my eye the view of Lincoln Savage naked was a view that demanded attention. Potent male. Fully gloriously aroused. Tanned skin everywhere except where board shorts would cover. Lean and sexy contoured muscles that my fingertips tingled with the urge to trace.

I licked my lips. Linc took advantage of my momentary indecision grabbing me firmly by my shoulders and turning me to look at him. He stroked the pad of his thumb across my cheekbone. That's all it took. I shivered feeling the heat of passion licking my skin once more.

He lowered his head and brushed three warm soft kisses across the path his thumb had taken. Without consciously deciding to I stepped closer pressing my body to his. His strong hands glided down the length of my spine coming to a stop on the curve of my rear. He turned his head. "We'll be right out," he shouted to his cousin before turning back to me. "It'll be ok," he asserted his tone low and soothing. "I'll help you get dressed. I won't be able to walk you now but Ash will make sure you get there in time. Promise. Ok?"

I nodded numbly my mind trailing behind him tripping on his words. What did he mean about helping me get dressed?

He stepped away and my gaze stalled on his pale tight ass. When he turned back around and caught me staring his lips curved into a seductive half smile. "Babe, you can't look at me like that. You gotta help me out." He opened my bag and sifted through the contents withdrawing a nude satin bra and a matching lace thong. "You wear things like this all the time?" His gaze was hot as it traveled the length of me.

"Yes." I swallowed, my throat suddenly dry as the desert. My undergarments in his masculine hands made for an erotic tableau. "My mother's French. She values fine lingerie and gives me a generous allowance to buy my own. I like the feel of them against my skin. They make me…"

"Damn sexy," he finished for me his voice a deep rasp. "Come here," he ordered in that insistent way of his that made my skin tingle. As I moved toward him toes skimming over the braided rug by his bed he slid the bra strap up his wrist where it dangled. He bent stretching my lace thong open between his thumbs. "Step in."

Resting my hands on his firm wide shoulders curling my fingers into his warm skin I did as I was told dipping one foot and leg inside and then the other. Long masculine fingers caressed my legs and then my hips as he slid the thong into place. Heat shot like an arrow straight to my sex as he lingered for a moment his grip tightening possessively his thumbs stroking lightly back and forth just inside the waistband scant inches from where I ached for them to be. If he would just delve a little deeper he would feel how hot I was for him, how much I needed him, how much I longed for him to make me his.

My breath hitched when he glided his strong hands over my hips and down slowly smoothing the small triangle of lace at the top of my behind.

He lifted his hooded gaze, dark blue eyes liquid with

passion capturing and holding mine. "Beautiful," he intoned reverentially as he leaned in touching his lips to mine and brushing a soft tantalizing kiss across my mouth while lovingly massaging the bared globes of my ass. When he straightened my breathing was uneven and he had my bra outstretched between his hands. I lowered my eyes to watch his masculine digits slide the delicate nude satin straps up my arms. His smooth purposeful motions and the contrast between us made me feel more feminine and pretty than the lingerie ever had.

"Turn around," he ordered and I did, though I did it in a daze as his capable hands arranged the silk cups over my breasts weighing and shaping them as he did so. My nipples jutted hard against the cool satin. "Fucking gorgeous," he whispered as he fastened the clasp. "Shame to cover all that beauty." He trailed warm fingers across my hot skin turning me back to face him.

I gulped as I took in the stark look of male hunger on his handsome face. He sank to the bed behind him and closed his eyes briefly as if to regain control. "Linc," I called stepping between his legs. I couldn't stand for him not to be touching me anymore. I ran my fingers through his thick wavy hair.

He made a low masculine sound of approval that seemed to rumble from deep inside his chest. "What are you doing to me, Simone?" He opened his eyes and the clear blue color was barely visible around the black of his enlarged pupils. "I can't catch my breath. It's like a massive wave has crashed over me and I can't find the surface. All I can think about is you." He reached for me. I felt the needful tremble in his arms as he brought me forward placing his stubble roughened cheek against my smooth abdomen.

"I feel exactly the same," I whispered as if we were sharing some deep dark secret. I sifted my fingers through the damp strands of his hair marveling at the contrasting colors of sandy brown, platinum and gold as well as feeling a little frightened by the intensity of emotion that just seemed to keep growing stronger and stronger between us.

He lifted his head twisting his trim waist as he reached for the rest of the things in my bag. "Let's get you covered quickly before I lose it." His gaze was darkly possessive, the message sent that even though I was standing over him he was still the one in control.

My slightly wrinkled cotton blouse was hastily buttoned. I let out a long shaky breath that I'd been holding as he stood still gloriously naked and still fully aroused as he ordered me to step into the skirt he held open for me. I did and he gently turned me around tucking in the hem of the blouse leaving shimmery trails in his wake wherever his fingers touched my skin. The heat between my legs still smoldered. I still ached for him. I was so temped to throw caution to the wind, to strip to my bare skin again and beg him to take me and make me his.

The words were on the tip of my tongue when he drew up the zipper and stood, his hands spanning my waist, his hard body pressed against the back of mine so tightly that I could feel the hot insistent thick length of him and answering desire pooled just as hot within me.

"Please, Linc." I reached back for him digging my fingers into his taut ass, pulling him more fully into me and turning to look at him over my shoulder.

"Soon, Mona," he promised his clear blue gaze seeming to penetrate to my soul. "Very soon."

Chapter 35

Simone

My calves burned as we power walked past the one and two story houses with well-tended lawns like Ash's until they gave way to commercial establishments the closer we got to Napoli's. Ash had been mostly silent since we had left his place. I had been, too. Linc and I had made plans to meet up on the beach again the next day but that was over fourteen hours away. The ache in my chest since he kissed me goodbye just wouldn't go away. The way he made me feel. The unexpected happiness he brought into my life. The group of friends I suddenly found myself a part of. It was all so seductive but unstable like the towering red and orange sandstone cliffs along the Point Loma peninsula that crumbled when too much pressure was put on them from above.

When we came to the intersection Ash grasped me by the elbow and escorted me across. I glanced at him discovering that his brow was still furrowed, his serious expression unchanged since leaving his house.

"What did Linc say to you before we left?" I asked.

"He told me to keep an eye on you for him." The crease in his brow deepened.

I frowned. "I can take care of myself."

"I bet you can." Ash's expression softened as he studied me. "But you shouldn't have to with your own father."

Jaw tightening, I glanced away. Suddenly I was even more reluctant to step inside Napoli's. I stopped beneath the awning at the back door, the shadow that fell over me matching my darkening thoughts.

"Hey." Ash touched my arm. "Don't be mad at Linc. He's just worried about you. He's very sensitive to your situation given his own past."

I nodded. A small frisson of doubt made my stomach knot. Surely the way Linc felt about me was motivated by more than just a desire to rescue me.

"You're very important to him, Simone."

I cocked my head to the side studying Ash the way he had a moment earlier. "You don't seem very happy about that."

"No." His lips flattened. "I guess I'm not." He ran his hand through his straight platinum strands and sighed heavily. "I'm afraid the two of you are destined for disaster."

Hurt by his words immediate hot tears stung the back of my eyes.

"It's not that I don't like you, Simone." His tone softened. "In fact I've grown very fond of you." He reached toward me gently tucking a stray strand of hair behind my ear. Instead of his kind words making me feel better they made me feel worse, his ominous prediction echoing my own unsettled thoughts. And just like Linc I was oversensitive about people feeling sorry for me.

"Maybe you're wrong." I stuck my chin up. "Maybe it'll work out great between us. Maybe we'll surprise you."

"Maybe," he allowed. "Only Simone." The somberness in his tone stopped me before I opened the door to go inside. I turned to look back at him. He was frowning again. "Linc's life has been tough. Tougher than he's probably let on. Lucky he got out of Logan Heights at all. You know surfing is his outlet. Like therapy. It's not an optional thing."

"I understand." Feeling defensive my fingers curled into my palms. "I would never do anything to jeopardize that for him." I couldn't believe Ash thought I would.

"Good." He nodded curtly. "I don't really think he would let you or anyone else come between him and his surfing anyway. Surfing is his true love, Simone. I'm not sure he has room for another."

I stumbled as I entered the building and his words sank in. My initial impression of Ash was right. He didn't want us together. He was just as protective of Linc as Linc was of me. But what Ash failed to realize was that we were really on the same team. We both loved Linc and wanted what was best for him.

Linc

"**H**ey, Karen." Simone sounded defeated on the other end of the line.

"No, it's me."

"Linc." She breathed my name like I was an answer to a prayer. She was definitely the answer to all of mine.

"Karen let me borrow her phone." She and Patch were so hot and heavy in the other room where we'd all been watching a movie that I didn't think my request had even really registered with her. "Ash says you can't come to the beach tomorrow."

"No." A short pause. "I'm sorry. My dad wants me to help supervise a deep cleaning of the kitchen."

"It's ok," I reassured. She sounded as disappointed as I was.

"I guess you could probably use the extra time to do some more surfing."

"Sure but I'd rather spend it with you."

A longer pause. "Maybe you shouldn't."

"Why the hell not?" I sat up straighter my fingers tightening around the cell.

"Your competition isn't far away. I don't want to be a distraction."

"Who the hell said you were a distraction?"

"Ash," she whispered.

"That interfering bastard." I let out a long breath. I appreciated where he was coming from. I was sure he thought he was helping me, but he and I were still going to have some serious words. "You are *not* a distraction. You are my inspiration. I want to win first place in Fiji just to make you proud of me."

"I am proud of you, Linc."

"Really? I'm glad. We're from different worlds you and me. College is never going to be an option for me. It's too damn expensive, even if I wanted it. I've got my whole future riding on this surfing thing."

"You're phenomenal. I'm sure you'll succeed." Her voice lowered. "I'll be thinking about you the entire time you're gone. I'll go to the church and light a candle for you."

"Thanks, babe." So sweet. Every word. Everything she did made me fall further under her spell. "Don't worry about tomorrow." My voice deepened reflecting the weight of my feelings. "I'll be thinking about you all day. And you have your fake date with Ash tomorrow evening. Right?" My cousin had apparently asked her out in front of her father before his shift started. I owed him big for that and for watching out for my girl for me.

Ash had quickly called in that favor. I was going to front the band at their Deck Bar gig. No way I would have done it otherwise. It was going to seriously cut into my date with Simone. And I had big plans for tomorrow evening. I had a promise to fulfill to her and to myself.

Chapter 36

Simone

My parents were both up in my room with me before my 'date'. Ash had so totally won my father over that he had uncharacteristically extended my curfew until two a.m.

When he left, my mom remained, a silent presence until the door clicked closed behind him.

"Are you sure you know what you're doing?" she asked from her position on the edge of my bed, wine glass in hand sounding surprisingly coherent considering the fact that I knew she was on her second bottle of wine.

"Sure, Mom." I smoothed the silky fabric of the short hem of my dress over my thighs and turned around to face her. "Why do you ask?"

"You just seemed so excited about that other boy and now," she pursed her full lips and tapped on them with a thoughtful finger, "you seem to have moved on rather quickly. That's not like you, Simone."

"I'm good, Mom." With Lincoln and what I hoped would happen later tonight. Beyond that I had tons of doubts but those were uncertainties I refused to dwell on.

"Ok, honey." She rose and swayed only a little bit when she crossed the room to kiss my cheek. "Have fun. And don't sacrifice your happiness just to please your father. It's not worth it."

The door clicked closed once more. I let out a breath knowing the words she had spoken were not just for me. I knew she was miserable and drank to escape but I couldn't fix things for her. All I could do was what I felt was right for me and my own life.

I grabbed a small clutch. Karen had helped me pack it before she had left. The square foil packet she had added had been accompanied by an admonishment for me to be safe.

I checked my reflection in the dresser mirror. Hair up for sophistication, lots of soft gardenia scented skin revealed by a daringly low corset style bodice that I'd covered up with a sweater. No way my dad would let me out of the house if he saw what was underneath. I slipped my bare frosty pink tipped toes into my rhinestone flip flops and withdrew a cherry flavored gloss from my clutch. I was just swiping the wand across my lips when the doorbell rang.

I popped open the door and heard Ash talking to my father downstairs. He looked up when I swept down the stairs making a big entrance as if this were a real date and Ash was my real beau.

His lips lifted slowly, appreciation and something else flashing in his eyes that passed too quickly for me to read. "You look stunning, Simone," he told me taking my free hand and pulling me toward him so he could kiss my cheek. "Linc's going to flip," he whispered in my ear and my heart summersaulted.

"You look very handsome," I said which was the truth. He looked sharp in a pair of khakis and a white button down that set off his platinum hair and accentuated his tan. Fingers tightening on his I turned to my parents. "I'll be in at two. I promise. You don't need to wait up for me."

Ash led me outside to the porch. He held my hand until we reached the waterfront, much longer than was probably necessary but I didn't complain. It was a little chilly and I was a bit nervous. I found the contact reassuring even though I knew he wasn't my biggest fan.

"I'm sorry about the things I said to you the other day." Ah, Lincoln must have said something to him.

"It's ok, Ash. You're entitled to your opinion. I'm sure you have Lincoln's best interest at heart but there's something you ought to know." I pulled in a breath for courage. "I love him, Ash. I plan to tell him tonight." And show him but that was more than Ash needed to know.

Eyes suddenly bright, he nodded once. It seemed as though he might have already known. "So we're good?" he asked after a moment in which he seemed deep in thought.

"We're good." I agreed.

"Then, c'mon, surfer's girl. Your man's waiting for you. And he's driving the rest of us all crazy."

When we reached the bar a couple of minutes later, I put my hand on the downstairs newel, glanced up at all the twinkling lights of the club and lost my courage for a moment. No matter what Linc had said I was still nervous and didn't want to disappoint him.

Outside

"Everything ok?" Ash asked me just as I heard Lincoln's voice over the sound system doing a sound check. His voice steadied me. This was right. In every way he was right for me.

"Yeah." I nodded my head and shook the last of my lingering doubts away. "My flip flop just slipped." I followed Ash up the stairs falling behind him as he bounded up them two at a time.

When I reached the top Linc was there waiting to meet me. His gaze swept me head to toe with something beyond just appreciation in his eyes. My heart fluttered in response.

"You look…" we both said at the same time and then we laughed unashamedly as if neither of us had a single care in the entire world. Maybe just this one night that could be true.

He swept me into his arms his warm lips pressing into my temple. I heard him inhale. "You smell as good as you look and you look like a goddess."

My lips pulled into a wide smile. He touched my nose softly when he leaned back, his clear blue eyes sparkling with joy I was sure reflected my own.

"If I'm a goddess then you're a god." I raised a brow trying to make my tone flippant and keep my expression playful. He looked divine in a faded but form fitting wine stripped button down and cargo shorts that were loosely belted to his narrow hips. "If you insist on putting me up on an unrealistic pedestal, then I'll put you on a higher one. So don't go there," I teased.

"Already have, gorgeous. And then some. So deal with it." He tugged my hand. "Come on. I saved you some seats up front. Apparently the place is sold out." He lowered his voice to a confidential level. "There's a rumor that Charles Morris, the head of Zenith Productions is stopping by to listen."

"You're kidding." My eyes widened. "How'd you find that out?"

"Patch's dad caught wind of it on his shift. Apparently the guy gets chatty when he's had a couple of extra strong drinks. He's been up and down the coast recently scouting for new talent. Soon as Ash found out he threw up...twice."

"Oh, no!" I glanced over at Ash. He was seated behind his drum kit, his features waxen. He caught me staring and rolled his eyes.

"On the stage, loser." He motioned with his sticks.

"I gotta go," Linc said. "But I have special plans for us later." He softly pressed his firm lips to mine.

After that kiss my body hummed. After those words my mind buzzed with even more anticipation.

I was really glad I'd worn my sexiest lingerie.

Linc

I watched her as the place filled. I wasn't really nervous about the singing thing. I was on edge for entirely different reasons. I wanted everything to be perfect. I wanted tonight to be one she would never forget. I wanted to show her that I was the only one for her.

Outside

The sound of her carefree laughter carried over the din loosening the tangle inside my chest. Her pretty eyes glittering she peeled off her sweater and draped it over the back of her chair. I nearly came unglued. She was practically falling out of the tight corset top. How was I going to keep guys away from her with her looking like that?

I put the mic back in the stand and started toward her.

"Whoa. Where are you going, man?" Patch pointed to his watch. "Show's starting in five. That producer guy is here, too. Didn't you see him come in?"

"I've got bigger issues." I shook my head and hiked a thumb toward Simone.

"Yeah, I can see that she does. I mean that you do." He grinned and slapped me on the back. "It's gonna be ok. She can handle herself. Look."

I turned my gaze back to her. Simone had her arms crossed over her chest giving some dude with a death wish the brushoff. She pointed over at me and he glanced my way. He smartly took the meaning of my 'get the hell outta here' stare.

Simone smiled at me, all white teeth and 'kiss me' glossy lips with her inner light on full glow. I beamed back at her.

Looking back and forth between the two of us, Patch groaned. "Let's get the damn show started before I gag."

Chapter 37

Simone

When the club lights dimmed to just the twinkling ones in the rafters and the spots shining on the stage, I reached for Karen's hand and clasped her fingers tightly. The energy within the packed club crackled like the air in a lightning storm.

Then Linc wrapped his fingers around the mic and embodied that energy. Song after song it radiated out from him rippling through the restive crowd.

Wide eyed with wonder I turned to Karen as rabid fans pressed toward the stage after the set, several feminine voices chanting Linc's name.

"Did you know he could sing like that?" she asked me.

I shook my head. "I only heard him the one time at Dominic's party." He'd been good then but tonight he seemed to be in his element. He must have been practicing every day with the guys during the week we had been apart. My gaze drifted back to the stage. Linc was signing bar napkins and chatting amiably with some of the patrons but he looked as if his mind were somewhere else as he glanced frequently at me.

I smiled to let him know that we were ok. It was just nine thirty. I hadn't told him yet about the extended curfew.

Karen and I were sipping our third round of diet cokes by the time the crowd finally thinned and a distinguished man with jet hair and piercing blue eyes approached Lincoln saying a few words to him that I couldn't hear. Afterward he pressed a business card into Linc's hand and turned away.

Linc passed it to Ash and hopped off the stage to where I waited, his body coiled with tension and his eyes intense.

"Who was that?" I asked taking the hand he offered me feeling the pop and sizzle of anticipation the instant we connected.

"Charles Morris. The Zenith guy." He shrugged. "He said he liked our sound."

Lincoln's sound, I thought but kept that inner observation to myself.

"You ready?" His gaze slid to Karen and then back to me.

"Yes, absolutely." Was that my voice? Did I really sound so smitten?

Linc's gaze dipped to my mouth and his eyes darkened.

"Don't worry about me," Karen said with a knowing smile. "Patch and I have plans of our own." She had shared briefly about her burgeoning relationship with Dominic. Seemed I wasn't the only one head over heels for a surfer.

His determined expression discouraging any additional devotees, Linc led me though the throng. I had to almost jog to keep up with his long strides.

"Let me catch my breath." I dug the soles of my flip flops into the concrete sidewalk outside.

"Never." His grin slashed possessively across his handsome face right before he spun me into his arms and his mouth crashed onto mine. Firm lips moved insistently parting mine and his tongue immediately swept into my mouth. I clutched his hard shoulders for balance in a world that suddenly tilted on its axis. His strong arms tightened around me. My breasts were pressed into his rock solid chest. Against my belly I felt the undeniable thickness of his arousal. Everything in me responded. My body bowed into his, my mouth widened and the hot ache between my legs became unbearable.

"Linc," I cried when he ripped his lips away. I was desperate for him. No longer afraid. So turned on that I started to tremble.

"Mona." His palms pressed into my lower back his fingers opening and closing bunching the fabric covering my rear. "I want you so badly." His breath blew damp heat across my face. His eyes were twin molten pools that reflected my desire. "Watching you from that stage. Not being able to touch you." He stopped speaking abruptly and released me, stepping back.

I swayed suddenly feeling terribly bereft without my body against his. He lifted his chin and pointed to an idling vehicle along the curb.

"Brent's a friend. He's gonna take us where we need to go."

"Where are we going?" I asked as he took my hand again helping me onto the middle bench seat of the old pickup truck.

"It's a surprise." His heated gaze stoked the embers of my desire. I licked my parched lips. His gaze dipped to my mouth. His eyes flared. I could feel the hot blazing combustible chemistry ready to ignite between us. I swallowed as he turned to Brent. "Drive," he ordered.

The main drag disappeared as we turned left onto Nimitz Boulevard and headed downhill toward San Diego. Lincoln put our joined hands on his thigh, his warm fingers drawing random circles on my skin making it difficult for me to concentrate. I sat up straighter as we turned and entered a marina.

"What are we doing here?" My brows drew together in confusion. Brent stopped the truck in front of a dock filled with spired catamarans and gleaming hulled power boats.

"You'll see." He leaned forward, slapping our taciturn driver on the shoulder and thanking him before popping open the rusty door, pulling me out and immediately sweeping me off my feet and into his arms.

"Linc!" I exclaimed breathlessly twining my arms around his neck as he strode purposefully across the pavement and onto the wooden planks of the dock that creaked under his feat. "Are we going on a boat?"

"I want tonight to be special for you." He dipped his head, waves of sandy brown shadowing his gaze briefly beneath the orange dock lighting. "I want to make love to you over and over again on the ocean that we both love so much."

I burrowed my face deeper into his chest feeling his

heart beat pounding beneath my cheek and pulling in deep lungfuls of his unique scent, reminiscent of a briny Pacific breeze brimming with limitless possibilities.

At the end of the dock he stepped onto the stern of a huge tri decked mega yacht. Ducking beneath an overhang he adjusted his hold on me so he could open a swing gate before he inserted a key to open the glass door that led inside.

Eyes wide at the luxurious interior my fingers dug into the soft cotton of his shirt. The living room we were in was bigger and fancier than the one at my house.

Wall to wall cream carpeting, gleaming cherry wood walls and loads of expensive furnishings lay beneath a soaring ceiling that opened to the deck above.

"This is incredible, Linc. It's so beautiful." My voice was thick.

"Yeah, it's amazing what five million can get you. It belongs to a wealthy friend of my aunt's." He sounded a little wistful. "I can't afford to buy you all this luxury, Simone. But I can certainly borrow it for my gorgeous goddess for a night."

"I don't care if you can't. I just care that you did all of this for me. I…"

"Hold this," Linc interrupted before I could finish the three words. He shifted to pick up a bucket from the granite bar. I kept one hand on his chest and took the handle of the bucket with the other, peering inside to see the sparkling cider and Ziploc of hulled strawberries it contained.

My heart rate kicked up even higher. Opulent surroundings fit for a queen with all of the accoutrements. Extravagantly romantic.

He took me past a large dining room table in two toned cherry, crossing a central hallway with a staircase and more gleaming wood that reflected the spot halogens that were scattered throughout the interior.

He finally set me down inside the master bedroom by a huge bed. Its luxurious cream comforter had been folded back in preparation for our arrival. My feet sank into the plush carpeting. Tears sparkled in my eyes as I took in all the thoughtful details.

When I turned back to him he extended a flute already filled with bubbly cider. Then I noticed something else, the music emanating from the boom box on the dresser beneath a shuttered window. Sweeping violins and lilting clarinet from an instrumental version of 'No One is Alive' from *Into the Woods*.

Every single detail seduced but none more so than the handsome man gazing back at me with the promise of passion such that I had never known gleaming from his bright eyes.

"Linc, I don't know what to say." My free hand fluttered in front of me. "This is so much. You're so much. And I'm just me."

"Drink your faux champagne." His eyes narrowed to slits as he slowly circled me. I could feel his intense perusal like a physical caress. My throat went dry. My body tingled and tightened as he regarded me with the grand music adding even more drama to the scene. I took deep sips. The refreshingly sweet beverage moistened my mouth.

Holding me captive with the power of his gaze, he lifted his glass to his sexy lips. I was spellbound watching his Adams apple move as he drained it dry as though he were just as parched as I was. "You are everything to me, Simone Bianchi. You overwhelm me." I had never heard his voice so deep.

"Linc." I blinked back the rush of tears from his words. "Please touch me." I stepped toward him.

"Be still." He held up a hand to stop me. "I'm not finished. And once I start touching you I'm not going to be able to stop. I very much doubt I'm going to be able to go slow, either." A wry grin lifted his lips. "At least not the first time."

A sheen of warmth cascaded through me at the idea of him making love to me again and again.

"I love you." My breath caught. "Almost from the first moment I met you. When I first saw you something clicked inside of me like when I saw the ocean for the first time. And then when I kissed you I knew for sure." He closed the distance between us and I lifted my chin to keep his gorgeous impassioned face in view. His hands wrapped around my elbows to draw me to him, his fingers curling into my flesh.

It felt so good, so right, that I sighed. His gaze dropped to my mouth and then his lips took mine in a searing kiss that I felt from the tips of my toes to my tingling scalp. His mouth was gentle but I could feel the cost of his restraint in the way his forearm muscles vibrated beneath my hands.

When he lifted his head and looked at me his eyes alight with adoration I did feel like the goddess he had named me. Boldly I spun in his arms lifting my hands to remove the pins that held my hair and peered at him over my shoulder. "Could you undo my zipper?"

His adoring eyes flared at the request. "I could." My

hair whispered to my bared shoulders and I drew in a sharp breath as the cool air within the room met the fevered skin along my spine. "You ok?" he asked his voice husky.

"Just cold," I explained.

"I can certainly fix that." He turned me, his grip on my shoulders gentle but purposeful. His gaze dipped to take in the sheer lace of my demi bra and the matching thong before it returned to my face, the look within his eyes darker than I had ever seen it. "Dammit, Simone. You are beyond anything that I have ever imagined." He traced a lock of my hair from over my ear to where it ended over my breast. His hand trembled. I shivered. Not from the cold this time. From desire.

"The way you treat me, Lincoln Savage. The things you say to me. You make me feel like anything is possible, as if I really am all those things to you."

"You are." He skimmed the pad of his thumb across my bottom lip parting the two. "You so are." He kissed me again. This time the kiss was wet and delectably deep. This time his mouth slanted first one way and then the other before his slick tongue glided between and touched my own.

When he broke the connection of our mouths and stepped back my hand went to my lips. They felt swollen and sensitive. I felt thoroughly claimed and now it was my body that vibrated with need.

His hands went to the buttons of his shirt.

"Please. Let me." My hands replacing his I stumbled a bit in my haste to have my tingling fingertips on his warm skin. Once the last button was undone, I glided my hands along the smooth contours of his wide shoulders reveling in the width of them. When I finally completed my task his shirt fluttered to the floor. A half-naked bronzed male god stood before me. Chiseled and strong. A warrior. A survivor. A surf god with a tempter's voice. I lifted my gaze. His eyes sparked and his handsome face was drawn tight with stark need.

"Babe, you're driving me crazy." His hands fell to my shoulders, warm and possessive as he turned me around then traced the length of my spine. Heat rushed to my throbbing core as he unclasped my bra, the lace an erotic whisper against tightened nipples that ached to receive his bold touch. The slide of the straps down my arms left a shimmery trail of awareness in their wake.

The scrap of black lace fell to the cream carpet without a sound. But my gasp turned into a moan when I felt Linc put his warm hands on my waist setting my aroused flesh ablaze as he slowly moved them higher and higher and higher.

Chapter 38

Linc

*H*er skin beneath my fingertips was the softest thing I had ever felt and I wanted to draw it out. But I didn't know how I could when everything within me screamed take her now and make her your own.

"Linc." She shuddered so hard when I palmed her luscious tits and softly flicked the tight rosy buds with my thumbs that I thought she might have already come. "Again." She lightly panted leaning back into me and arching into my hands. "Again. Do that again. Don't stop."

I did. Gladly. Being with her like this, looking at her sexy body, feeling her beneath my hands, watching the way she seemed to come apart every time I touched her, it was all even better than I had dreamed. "Babe, I could play with your tits for hours if my cock wasn't already so damn hard just from looking at you."

She spun in my arms feeling like warm liquid silk. Once facing me she tipped her head back to look at me and pressed her awesome rack into my chest. Her hard nipples scored my skin and made me feel even less controlled than I already was. I wanted her writhing beneath me taking my cock as I gave it to her hard.

I lowered my head and took her sexy mouth plunging my tongue between her cherry flavored lips. Deep, then shallow, then deep again, I repeated the pattern, the same one I planned to use with another part of my anatomy. Soon, it had to be soon or I was going to erupt inside my cargo shorts.

Sliding my palms a little lower, marveling at the perfection of her lush curves, reveling in the soft sounds of appreciation that she made, I hooked my thumbs into the waistband of her thong and dragged the flimsy lace over her sexy thighs and down her shapely calves before looking up at her and ordering, "Step out, babe."

Delicate hands on my shoulders she complied. I slowly rose trailing my nose over her sweetly scented skin, calves first then thighs until I reached the gentle swell of her abdomen where I nipped her before straightening all the way and taking her mouth again. Hard. Letting her know with each eager slash of my lips and every relentless stroke of my tongue that I sensed her arousal, that she drove me mad with desire and that she belonged to me.

"On the bed," I grunted walking her backward tugging my belt loose and removing my shorts and boxers as I followed her. Her naked bottom settling on the bed, she scooted to the middle. I caressed and parted her soft thighs before positioning my body between them. "Simone look at me." Lifting her gaze from where we were almost joined she blinked her dazed eyes. Balancing my weight on one hand the roar of my pulse in my ears nearly deafened me as she lifted her hips to bring her glorious mound closer to my hand. "You're a goddess. A temptress. My only love." I sifted through the gift she offered me finding her nub swollen and soaking wet. I swirled my thumb around it slowly and deliberately. "So beautiful." My tone was reverential my considered movements like those of a master artist creating on a pristine canvass. "So gorgeous. I couldn't have dreamed of someone more perfect for me."

"Linc." Skin flushed, her legs parted wider and her hips moved in response to my stimulation. I couldn't take anymore. I grabbed the packet from the mattress, ripped it open with my teeth, smoothed it on and plunged my sheathed cock into her hot perfect heat.

"You feel so good," I groaned. With my gaze on hers I began to move deep and shallow, deep and shallow.

She moaned softly and her lids started to close.

"Don't look away, Mona. I want to see the desire in your eyes."

Her hands went to my hips her fingernails digging into my ass as she lifted off the mattress to meet every one of my thrusts. Her hot fast rapid breaths let me know she was just as close to the summit as I was. "Yes, Linc," she canted as I circled and drove in deep. "Yes. Yes."

"Mona," I praised dipping my head, capturing one of her perfect tits to suck on and then the other. "You feel so good. So hot. So fuckin' fantastic."

I took her mouth again pulling her full bottom lip between my teeth before gorging myself on the sweet interior. Out of breath I ripped my mouth from hers. "Hard, Mona." I warned. "I'm gonna take you so hard."

Her rose tipped tits swayed as I dug my fingers into her lush ass yanking her closer thrusting inside once and then doing it again and again and again. Her lids fluttered closed but even without seeing her eyes I could read the ecstasy on her lovely face. Her back arching off the bed, she exhaled my name and let out a long low orgasmic moan.

"Mona," I groaned soaring over the other side of the wave with her and flooding her with my desire.

Chapter 39

Simone

"I love you," he breathed the words into my neck as he collapsed his deliciously sexy body on top of me. I pressed my lips to his stubble roughened cheek but held back from saying the same thing. I wanted so badly to echo his words, but irrational fear gripped me keeping me from telling him what I had already revealed to Ash.

Just as my breathing started to level out he pushed up on his arms and withdrew from me taking off the condom as he left the bed. "Take a shower with me." His eyes were heavy lidded and his voice was raspy in the aftermath of our shared passion.

"I shouldn't," I told him slanting a glance at the clock and noting how little time remained. "I can't go home with my hair too wet or smelling like a different shampoo. I'm afraid of what my father might do."

His jaw hardened. "Fair enough." He stared at me the

muscle in his jaw twitching. He looked like he wanted to say more on the matter but in the end he refrained. "You can use the tub while I get cleaned up."

I bobbed my head in agreement watching as he moved toward the bathroom. Taut ass. Long firm legs. Strong wide shoulders with tousled sandy hair kissing them. He was glorious to look at and beyond glorious as a lover. But what would happen when he left for Fiji? The summer was swiftly drawing to a close. My heart was already fully his even without me voicing those words. If things ended, *when* they ended my paranoid brain insisted, I was going to be devastated.

Totally.

Dully, I shuffled behind him unable to fully bask in the shimmery afterglow of our lovemaking. Once inside, I began to draw a bath. I heard the shower door close but waited until the water in the tub reached halfway up the sides before stepping in and lowering myself into the warm embrace.

Careful to keep my hair out of the water I washed off and regarded Linc as he showered. He started with a quick lathering of his thick mane of hair then followed with a chest to toes sudsy wash over all those perfectly contoured muscles I longed to trace more fully.

He shook his hair dry just like he did at the beach, stepped out of the shower and caught me staring. Totally mesmerized.

He grinned whipping the towel off the rack and fastening it around his trim waist. "Need some help slowpoke?" he teased stalking toward me his light blue eyes glittering in the bright vanity lights.

"Um, no." I dropped the bar of soap I'd been squeez-ing back into the dish and stood. His gaze dropped to my body and rose again only slowly as though he were reluc-tant to relinquish the view.

I stepped out onto the bathmat and started to stretch for a nearby towel but he beat me to it. He unfolded it and held it open for me to walk into.

"Come here," he ordered. I took the first step and he moved toward me enfolding me in the towel at the same time that his lips recaptured mine. His mouth was firm and delicious but he didn't give me a moment to savor before he licked between the seam in mine and slanted his head to deepen the kiss.

I arched into him, warm heady need and the pleasure I knew he could give engulfing my body. I wanted him. Again. I feared that the time we had was running out. Deep down I knew there was a part of me that was never going to recover when it inevitably did. That there was never going to be another man who could melt me with a single kiss.

Just when the current kiss was starting to get really good, when I'd gone completely pliable in his arms and had moaned my approval into his mouth, he ended it. I opened my eyes to find him studying me closely. "What's wrong, Simone?"

"Nothing," I lied. *A small deception,* I told myself. "I'm just tired."

"Hmm." He watched me a moment longer his nar-rowed gaze drifting across my features as if doubting the validity of my words. "You know you can tell me any-thing."

I nodded held captive by the intensity of his gaze.

He touched the tip of my nose and his expression lightened. "Come." He offered me his hand and I took it readily. Why ruin the limited time we had together worrying about things I couldn't control?

"I know you saw the strawberries. Maybe after you eat something you'll regain some energy." He stopped at the row of bookshelves across the room where he'd abandoned the bucket earlier and turned to face me.

Hands holding my own towel to my chest I watched him open the Ziploc. When he had one of the succulent berries in his hand he beckoned me closer. Drawn more by my hunger for him than by the chance to sample the delicacy I complied. He held the strawberry out to me and I opened my mouth. He traced my parted lips with the tip of it, his eyes following the berry's path before he popped it inside. Feeling a warm flush in my cheeks I bit into it chewing while the sweet juice flowed over my tongue.

"How did you know strawberries are my favorite?" I couldn't remember ever having told him.

"I watch. I observe." He stroked my arm softly igniting awareness every time he touched me. "At the restaurant, you never touch the cheesecake. You just eat the berries."

My blush deepened. He noticed a lot. He caressed the round of my cheeks with the pad of his thumb before swiveling to pluck another berry. When he brought it to my lips his gaze was hooded.

"Open again," he ordered his voice low. When I parted my lips this time he teased me tracing the slopes of my breasts with the chilled end then lowered his head to follow the same path with his tongue.

"Oh," I moaned my nipples immediately tightening in

response to the feel of his warm breath and wet tongue and a darker ache began to build much lower.

"Delicious." He lifted his head, popped the berry into his own mouth and gave me a crooked smile before he started to chew. When he withdrew another berry I peeked into the bag. There were at least seven or eight more. I wasn't going to survive it. My heart was already trying to pound its way out of my chest.

"What would I have to do to get you to ditch that towel?" he mused reflectively while tracing his sexy lips with the strawberry.

"Just ask." I met his hot stare boldly. "Nicely."

"Please." How was it that he could make that one word sound like a command?

Head down I untucked my towel. It dropped to the floor at my feet. Cold air licked my skin. My rapid breaths made my breasts rise and fall. I raised my eyes to look at him. His eyes were midnight dark, pupils enlarged, barely any blue showing. I stood before him wanting his touch and waiting once again as his gaze leisurely traveled over my naked form. I was just about to speak when he reached for me drawing me closer, a warm rush of heat piercing me where his hands gripped my ass to that part of me that ached to be filled by him. I could tell that he was thinking along the same lines as me by the size of the erection tenting his towel.

"Open your lips," he commanded. I leaned forward and nipped his fingers surprising him as I took a big bite out of the strawberry he seemed to have forgotten he'd been holding. His expression grew hungry as he watched me consume it.

"Now," I said when I was finished. "What about that towel of yours?"

"Kiss me." Eyes getting even darker he popped the remaining part of the berry between his lips and waited. Feeling the heat and the power of him through the thick Egyptian cotton I drew closer, touching my lips to his then suddenly sweeping the berry from his mouth into my own. I started to pull back as I chewed and swallowed my prize but he easily caught me. "Tricky minx." He straightened, his eyes shining with mirth and the extra something that I now recognized was love. He grabbed me by the shoulders and hauled me forward bringing our mouths together firm lips melding to mine. Mint and strawberry flavors burst from his tongue as he swept it between them. Insistent swipes. Deep bone melting licks. I trembled and burned in his embrace realizing as I pressed closer to him that his towel had vanished. Only his hot hard body and my melting one remained.

"Linc," I begged when we both paused, lips hovering close enough to still touch but far enough apart to suck in needed air. "No more. I can't. I need you. Please."

"You don't have to beg, babe." His expression was tight, his eyes glowing dark with the heat of desire that ruled us both. "Your every wish is my command." His hands went to my ass, strong fingers kneading the sensitive cheeks making the fire between my legs blaze even hotter. "Wrap your legs around my waist, gorgeous." He hefted me and I complied eagerly grinding my aching need against the hot, perfectly formed length of him.

He groaned and tossed me back on the bed so hard I bounced. His hot possessive gaze captured me when I came up on my elbows tossing my hair out of the way. Our heated eyes melded together. A warm shiver of anticipation made me tremble as he tore open a condom packet and rolled it on. Hands to the mattress he put a knee down and stalked toward me his gaze filled with wicked intentions.

Yes, please.

I licked my lips as he moved between my legs and moaned long and low because the instant his lips fastened on mine his hot cock surged inside me. The perfect fit. The wet heat inside me burned hotter with each deep purposeful stoke of his hardness and matching glide of his slick tongue into my panting mouth.

The ache within me grew unbearable. Every time he withdrew he surged back inside even harder. Thrust after thrust I arched to meet him, fingers flexing into his tight ass to help him go deeper, growing more and more desperate with each perfect glide over my sensitive swollen flesh.

"Now, Mona." He plunged inside, delectably deep, grinding his hips and touching that perfect spot.

"Yes, Linc. Yes!" I reached the starry pinnacle, pulsing around him, moaning his name over and over, the sound of my passion and the rhythm of my pleasure propelling him into the blissed out stratosphere with me where he let out a long deeply satisfied male groan.

"I love you," he declared in my ear as he collapsed his passion slickened weight on top of me.

I love you, too, I thought wrapping my arms and legs fiercely around him.

Chapter 40

Linc

We dressed slowly on separate sides of the bed after bathing again. Head bowed as she drew on her dress, I could feel her withdrawing from me the way she had after we had made love the first time.

I didn't like it and it wasn't acceptable.

"Simone," I called softly.

"Yes." She turned my way and I could see that it was worse that I'd thought. Something had snuffed out that inner light of hers. I didn't understand it. Not after the incredible night we just shared. The most incredible of my entire life.

"What's wrong? And don't tell me you're tired." I finished buttoning my shirt and moved behind her brushing her hair to the front so I could draw up the zipper for her. Grasping her shoulders I turned her to face me. "There's more to it than that."

"This was incredible, Linc." Her eyes filled. "You're

214

so incredible. But I'm scared. The things Ash said…they're legitimate concerns." She dropped her chin to her chest. "I don't want to lose you," she mumbled.

"You won't, Mona." Damn, Ash. I lifted her head and brushed a soft kiss across her trembling lips. "You're not going to. I swear it. But…"

"Linc." Ash's voice startled both of us. I glanced at the clock and cursed under my breath.

We were out of time.

"I waited for you at the dock like you told me to," Ash called from the other room. "But when you didn't show…" He trailed off and cleared his throat. "You two need to hurry. I don't know if I we can get Simone home in time. I don't want to get caught speeding at this hour of the night. It's hard enough to get Dad to lend me the van."

"We'll be right out," I shouted over my shoulder then had to grab her as she scooted toward the door eyes wide in her pale face. "Mona, stop." She jumped as I put my hands on her shoulders. "We have to talk. About your dad. About us. About the future. I'm not hiding anymore and I'm not letting you go. Ever." My fingers tightened to emphasis my point.

"I've got to go, Linc." She twisted away from me. "We can't tell my father. You don't understand."

Ash's brows lifted as we both emerged into the central hall where he was waiting jiggling a large ring of keys in his hand.

"Give us a minute," I growled before he could interrupt. I grabbed Simone's arm, her long hair swirling around her slim shoulders as I brought her back to face me. Her hands fluttered along my forearms. "Why not, Simone?"

My eyes drilled unrelentingly into hers. "Why can't we tell him? What does your father have against me?"

Her fingers dug into my arms. "It's because of my mom. She had an affair with a surfer before I was born. She ran off with him but then he abandoned her. My dad took her back but he'll never let her live it down." Tears streamed from her eyes. She swallowed hard before continuing her voice barely audible. "I used to pray that I wasn't his, but the math doesn't add up for me to belong to a stranger." Another tear slid down her cheek and I captured it with my thumb. "I think my mom thought a child would help him forgive her but he never has. I hate living in that house, Linc." My eyes were soft on hers. I hated that she hurt like this but I was glad she had finally told me so I could understand. And understanding the problem was the first stop toward a solution. But I needed to find an answer soon.

Chapter 41

Simone

Tucked into Linc's side my arms were tightly wrapped around his lean waist and my cheek was pressed to his solid chest. The wind whistling through the split side windows of the '63 Volkswagen camper van lifted strands of my hair as Ash drove the vintage vehicle with its whirring engine at a steady pace of forty five miles per hour. Squished together on the bench seat that really was only large enough for two, the three of us were trying to ignore the tension that was building. There was no way we were going to make it to my house on time.

My thoughts pinged around inside my head. I knew how much trouble I was going to be in. But I was beginning to grasp why my mom had done what she had all those years ago. If she had felt for her surfer even a tenth of what I felt for mine...

I peered up at him. His jaw was set and his thick hair

was stirred by the breeze. He was so handsome it hurt my heart to look at him. I was so tempted to trust him, to believe it would all work out the way he had asserted it would back on the yacht after I had told him the truth about my parents.

"You ok, Mona?" His troubled gaze dipped to mine as he sifted through my hair.

"I'm alright." I hugged him tighter breathing in his ocean scent but tensing inwardly the closer we got to the spot where Ash and I would get out and walk to my house as if we had been together all this time.

Linc shifted in my embrace and I felt him press his warm lips into my hair as Ash slowed the van and pulled over to the curb.

"C'mon, fake girlfriend." Ash turned off the ignition and popped open the door on his side. "Let's go." His tone was light but forced. I scooted over and took the hand he offered me to help me out.

"Be careful with the Bug." Ash told Lincoln as he slid over to take his cousin's place at the wheel. "You know how my dad feels about it."

Standing on the curb beneath the street light my gaze met Lincoln's. I desperately wanted him to stay with me. Tonight had changed everything. I had never been in love before, never really understood the intensity of the emotion until he came along. No wonder my mom had been willing to give up everything just for a chance to make something real and lasting. But was I brave enough to do the same thing?

With my father involved I knew it very well might come to that kind of choice.

"Simone, wait. Hold up." Linc ripped off his seat belt and climbed out of the camper as if reading my thoughts. He tossed Ash the key ring on his way toward me. "Wait for me in the van. I'm walking Mona home."

In my heart I was absolutely thrilled to extend my time with Linc. He opened his arms and I ducked into them nearly shuddering with relief when he folded them around me and held me tight. "But we can't let my father see you." My brain forced me to voice that concern even though I was right where I wanted to be, where I always wanted to be no matter what.

"I told you I'm not hiding anymore, gorgeous." He sifted through my hair with gentle fingers. "You're mine now. There's no going back. I'm not letting you face him alone knowing how he's going to react." His tone was as firmly unyielding as his embrace.

I squeezed my eyes shut laying my cheek to his solid chest, willing his strength to become my own and wishing his warmth would take away the chill in my bones. I knew he was right. There was no doubt that my dad would be pissed. I didn't want this nearly perfect night to end in an ugly confrontation.

"We'd better go then," I mumbled against his shirt sucking in a deep bracing breath of soul settling Lincoln scent.

"It'll be ok." He pressed a kiss into my hair and rearranged us so that I was tucked into his side for the short walk home. The birds of paradise and the violet blossomed Jacaranda trees were just shadows in the yards along the way, but the sixty foot tall palms lining both sides of the street loomed like sentinels. The comforting whir of the camper soon faded beneath the growing roar of the ocean, but the sound of the waves didn't sooth me. Even with Linc beside me I grew tenser the closer we got to our destination.

When we were just twenty yards away, my fears grew. Every single light inside and outside blazed, moths circling them seeking their fiery doom. My heart started slamming against my ribs.

Linc placed his hands on my shoulders and gently turned me to face him, his expression resolute in the shadows. He leaned down and brushed his warm lips against my cold parted ones. "I'm walking you all the way to the front door. I'm not leaving till I see for myself that you're ok."

"No, Linc." I put my hands on his sinewy forearms and squeezed. "If he sees you it'll just make things worse. Let's ease into telling him about us. Please. I know how to handle him."

"I know you do." He smoothed the pad of his thumb down my cheek. "But it's not right." He took my hands. "I'm not budging on this, Simone. C'mon. Start walking." His fingers tightened around mine as he led me up the front walk lined with oleander. "The sooner he knows about us the sooner he can start getting used to the idea."

Beneath the porch lights I stared into his sincere eyes and nodded. He was right of course, but my father was unyielding and this was happening so fast that I hadn't had time to prepare. I had lived my entire life bowing to the dictates of my father. In a battle of wills he was used to coming out on top.

The front door suddenly popped open making me jump. The brighter lights of the interior blinded me for a

Outside

moment but I heard his voice loud and clear.

"Simone Bianchi. Get inside this house." His voice was a solid steel hammer and his frame filled the doorway. I felt my resolve automatically buckling and started to comply but Linc stopped me, his grip tightening and tethering me in place like the cord on his surfboard.

"Now, Simone." My father's furious gaze dipped to where Linc and I were connected.

"Daddy, don't be mad. Let me explain. Please. I want you to understand."

"I don't need any explanations. I understand perfectly well." He raked his salt and pepper hair back from his creased forehead. "You've been lying to me. It's been this boy all along."

"Yes, Daddy. I'm sorry I hid the truth from you." His censuring glare and his words rocked me but I held firm because of Lincoln. He was what mattered more than anything. It all became startlingly clear in that moment. I just needed Linc. The rest I would figure out somehow. "If I had told you from the beginning I never would have gotten a chance to get to know Linc. He's not what you think. He's good to me." My chin lifted belying my inner distress.

He made a disapproving sound. "He's nothing but trouble." He moved closer. I could feel the heat of his displeasure. "We've had this discussion before but apparently you weren't paying attention."

"I was only…"

"Mona." My protest was cut off by Lincoln. He squeezed my hand. I turned to look at him. His hard gaze was fixed on my father and his jaw was clenched. "Go on inside. Your father and I need to talk. It'll be alright. I'll see you tomorrow." He leaned in and brushed a tight kiss across my lips, a proprietary gesture his meaning clear. I might be my father's little girl but I was Linc's woman now.

"You arrogant whelp." My dad received the message for sure. Anger rolled off of him and crashed over me like a ten foot wave. "She'll do no such thing." My dad's eyes narrowed to slits and his voice lowered to that ominous level I knew always meant bad things. "This ends tonight. I'll not have my daughter's reputation sullied by a no account beach bum like you."

Linc and my dad faced off, both men drawing themselves up to their full heights. Linc was several inches taller but both men were equally incensed. I was so focused on them I barely noticed my mother. She swayed in the doorway my father had vacated a half empty glass of wine in one hand.

"Daddy, don't." I grabbed for him just as he lunged for Linc. He yanked away so fast I didn't have time to dodge it. His elbow connected with my jaw with a crack and a blinding flash. I flew backward and landed on my ass so hard I bit my tongue.

"Simone!" My mother cried stumbling toward me.

I tasted coppery blood in my mouth and my vision went hazy but not so hazy that I didn't see the mask of rage that replaced the handsome features on Lincoln's face.

"You asshole!" He slammed his hands to my father's chest and shoved him backward into the wall rattling the plaque with the house number. "You ever lay a hand on her again and I'll fuckin' end you." Linc pinned my dad to the wall with a forearm to his windpipe. "You got that?"

Outside

"I'm ok, Linc." I assured him tears clogging my throat as much from the breach of trust as the physical pain.

"You're damn lucky that she is." Linc turned back to my father. "I might be worthless in your eyes but that's not the way she sees me. And her opinion is the only one that really matters."

Chapter 42

Linc

I gave her no good father one more shove to make my point. Simone wasn't alone anymore. She had me to protect her.

Her old man just glared at me. He got the message alright.

I moved to Simone lifting her carefully and pulling her into me. I needed her close. I'd seen enough. Her old man was just like mine.

Her mom remained on the ground where Simone had fallen, like some rag doll so sloshed I doubted she could stand again without help.

"C'mon, babe." I draped my arm around Simone's shoulder and led her from the porch. No way was I ever letting her go back into that messed up house. She stumbled alongside me still in a haze.

"Simone!"

She froze, instant tension breaking her from her spell.

"Stop right now!" The old man's voice sounded strangled.

Good, I thought. He deserved worse than I had given him.

"You go off with that boy and you are completely on your own. Don't bother coming back. I won't be wasting any more money on you."

She dropped her chin to her chest. She was silent for a couple of beats. Slowly with her arms straight at her sides and her finger curled into her palms she turned to face him. "That's ok, Daddy. I don't want your money. I don't want anything from you. You're pathetic. To raise your hand to your own daughter? How could you think that I would stay here after that?" Her voice cracked. "Mom's right. You'll never be satisfied. You'll never accept me no matter how perfect I try to be. And I'm done trying." Years of suppressed feelings expelled, she sagged backward into me and turned her gaze my way. Her eyes were still sparking with leftover ire. "Take me away from here, Linc. Please."

"Absolutely, gorgeous." I tightened my arm around her slim shoulders to silently give her my support and to express how proud I was of her for standing up to him, then steered us back toward Ash and the van. She didn't speak on the way and given recent circumstances I let her have that time to assimilate, but we were going to have to talk and make decisions soon.

"What the hell?" Ash jumped out of the vehicle his look of concern quickly passing back and forth between her and me.

"She's not going back," I explained preemptively noticing his eyes narrowing on her already darkening and swelling bruise.

"Of course she's not." His expression turned as grim as my own. He helped me get Simone into the van. She had settled into an almost catatonic state since her impassioned speech.

After we were situated, Ash rounded the hood and got back behind the wheel. He glanced at me over Simone. "Where to?"

"Your house, I guess." The adrenaline from watching Simone stand up to her tyrannical father was waning. The reality of the situation began to sink in on me.

What were we going to do now? And just how was I going to take care of her?

Short term I didn't think my aunt and uncle would mind her staying with us. Long term required more deep thinking and neither of us were up to that tonight.

"No." Simone straightened in her seat moving away from me. Her voice was raspy as if she had awoken from a dream. A nightmare more likely. "Take me to Karen's house. I'll stay with her."

I didn't like that idea. I wanted her with me. Right now and forever if she would have me.

"My mom won't mind the extra company." Ash came to my rescue as he braked the van at a stop sign.

"But I'd mind," Simone said firmly. "I appreciate the offer, Ash. But Karen has plenty of room and I'll think better there."

What the hell did that mean?

I was still processing that statement by the time Ash pulled to the curb in front of Karen's a two story New England style house with weathered clapboard siding. He called her on the cell while I helped Simone out of the van. My gaze remained on her as I escorted her up the walk. Hers remained straight ahead. I wanted to ask her a hundred different things but she seemed so unreachable, so distant.

"Karen's coming to the door," Ash explained.

I waved a hand over my shoulder to acknowledge that I had heard him, but inside my guts were churning. My girl looked so lost and forlorn. Damn her worthless father to hell.

"Oh my God!" Karen exclaimed as soon as she saw Simone's face. Simone stepped forward and buried her face into her friend's chest. "You poor baby," she soothed as Simone's body started to shake. "I hate that man." Karen shot me a look over Simone's shoulder and I nodded my agreement. I hated him, too. The list of haters for that asshole was growing by the minute.

Karen pulled Simone into the house. "It'll be ok, Linc." She must have noticed the devastation in my eyes. I hated to leave Simone, but if this was where she needed to be tonight then I would go along. "I'll get her to bed. She'll call you in the morning."

I could see why Patch was so taken by Karen, and I was glad Simone had such a good friend. But I still lingered on the doorstep until Ash came to retrieve me.

"Dude, let's go home. Everyone needs some rest. We'll figure it out in the morning."

I nodded numbly and followed him back to the van. The outlines of the houses along the route we took through the hills of OB to Ash's seemed to mock me. Homes filled with happy families. Something neither Simone nor I had now. And maybe never would.

"Don't worry so much," Ash said after he parked the van in the driveway. I guess my trepidation was pretty transparent. "Simone loves you. It will work itself out in the end."

"But that's just it, Ash. She never really said she did." My voice was as raw as my heart admitting that. I had replayed the entire night and that omission on her part weighed heavily on my psyche.

Ash's gaze narrowed. "Well, you can talk to her about that when she gets up. You'll straighten it out." He unlatched his seatbelt and I did the same. My shoulders were bowed. My limbs felt sluggish and heavy.

"I know this isn't a great time." Ash's hands were deep in his pockets as he moved alongside me to the front door. "But I was wondering. What exactly did that Morris say to you before he handed you his business card?"

I glanced up sharply. The performance at the Deck Bar seemed as though it had occurred a lifetime ago. "He told me I should call him when…" I trailed off casting my mind back trying to recollect his exact words.

"When we've got a couple of original tunes and a proven following beyond just the local area. That sound about right?" Ash prompted as he pulled open the door to the house.

I nodded.

"Mom's not likely to be very supportive of that plan." He frowned. "She wants me to finish another year at the junior college and you're going off to do your thing. Bummer. I think we might've had a chance with you fronting us."

Outside

I shook my head in denial as we entered our room. We both knew the music thing was a pipe dream. He went to his bed but I went to my dresser, opened a drawer and pulled out my swim trunks.

He raised a brow. "You going out?"

"Yeah. I'm too wired to sleep and I think better at the beach anyway."

He nodded. He was a surfer, too. He didn't need any more explanation than that.

All the heavy worries, all the concern, everything faded into background noise once my feet finally hit the sand and my body entered the surf, the ocean raging powerfully all around me. The sun hadn't come up yet and I had the entire beach to myself for as far as I could see. That was good. I needed to be alone on my board. Everything seemed clearer out on the waves.

I paddled out past where the they were breaking, scooted to the back of my board, straddled it and waited getting acclimated to the current set pattern. I noticed that the waves were breaking fast and hard just like things in my life right now.

Everything depended on me catching the perfect one and riding it all the way to the end.

I just had to win Fiji.

Chapter 43

Simone

The lights in the guest bedroom were still out but I hadn't slept. I lay in the bed in borrowed pajamas staring at the lace framed window until the soft light of the dawn seeped through it.

The over the counter pain reliever Karen had given me had reduced the pain in my jaw to a bearable throb but the hurt inside my heart was still ardent.

I couldn't stay with Karen forever. I knew that in spite of the sleepy welcome I had received from her parents even their generous goodwill would have its limits.

But what other options did I have?

I could never go home. Not that it had been a real one for a long time I realized, just walls around me and a roof over my head. The ache in my jaw was a grim reminder of the true nature of dysfunction that resided there.

I felt trapped inside my own thoughts, the sea foam walls of the bedroom a poor substitute for the real thing.

Outside

I threw back the covers.

I would think better at the beach.

I got dressed in the clothes Karen had laid out for the morning. The jean shorts were a little too snug on my hips and the off the shoulder sweatshirt top was a little too tight over my chest but they would do. I was grateful to have them.

Starting my life all over again with nothing but the clothes on my back was a daunting task but I could it if I had Lincoln by my side. Oh, and there were the funds in my savings account, if I could get to them before my father did.

I left a note for Karen and slipped quietly from the house starting to feel better as soon as I turned the corner and headed downhill toward the pier, filling my lungs as I went with humid briny air.

Niagra Avenue opened up onto the pier at its end and as soon as I passed through the open metal 'Ocean Beach' gate I saw the black spot of a lone surfer bobbing on the waves and knew it was him.

Lincoln.

I leaned over the rail to watch him. He was facing away from me toward the open ocean, his hands on the rails of his board, looking for the perfect wave.

I wondered what he was thinking about out there as he waited. Was he thinking about me? Were they happy thoughts or troubled ones like mine?

I'm not letting you go. Ever.

Had he meant those words?

At the boat he had mentioned the future, too.

But was he ready to face it with me in tow?

A wave rose behind him and he turned the nose of his board toward the beach paddling hard to gain momentum, hopping into his riding stance and trimming the wave with his hand. He was so fluid he seemed to become a part of it.

I scooted back from the rail when his ride brought him close to the pier. I didn't want him to see me and feel pressured to come out any more than I wanted him to give up his ambitions just because of my predicament.

"Simone."

I whirled around hand to my throat. "Ash, you scared me. I didn't hear you come up."

"Sorry. I could tell you were deep in your thoughts." He raised his chin in Linc's direction. "He's pretty hard to take your eyes off?"

I nodded.

"You ok?" He sounded concerned and his brow creased as he studied me. "You look like you didn't get any sleep."

"I didn't," I admitted. I had a lot on my mind. I shrugged as if it weren't a big deal. But it was actually colossal. My entire focus was Lincoln now and his was centered on that board.

"He didn't, either." He moved to look over the rail and I followed. Linc was paddling back out to his original position again. "He came straight here after we dropped you off."

"But that was hours ago. It was still dark."

"Mostly, yeah. He's very determined about you and about Fiji." Linc charged another wave, popping up immediately and Ash took my arm pulling me further back from the rail and both of us out of sight. "He's gonna be out here a lot longer I'm certain." He rubbed my arms. "You're shivering. Why don't you come with me? I was on my way over to Patch's house. The band's gonna practice early before Patch has to go into work. We'll grab some churros on the way. You can listen to our new set. Tell us what you think with your educated ear."

"I mostly know show tunes so I don't really know that I'll be much help." I glanced back over my shoulder. I just wanted to watch Lincoln. I could watch him surf all day.

"Simone," Ash called squeezing my arms to get my attention. I refocused on him "Leave him be. He's not going anywhere. You can see him when he comes out. Yeah?"

Linc

My muscles burned with exhaustion by the time I called it quits. Back to the house, I stowed my board and gear and hopped into the shower. I was happy with what I had accomplished surfing today and was at peace with the decision I had come to out there. But I was admittedly worried about what Simone's answer might be. She had defended me, sure, but I knew that she could do so much better than an unemployed surfer who had gotten her kicked out of her own house.

I saw Ash's note when I went to the dresser. I pulled on a pair of khaki shorts and a grey and black Volcom emblazoned t-shirt. I traced her name on the paper with my finger. Thoughts and emotions made my chest tight. I loved her. I knew I would never love anyone more. She was it for me, but was I the one for her?

Eager to see her, adrenaline propelled my rubbery legs forward. I headed downhill along Bacon until I got to Patch's street then turned right and trudged uphill to the small cottage he shared with only his dad. The windows were thrown open and I heard her voice as soon as I reached the oleander lined walk.

It wasn't a song I recognized and Ash was fumbling to establish a beat to support her lyrics but she sounded absolutely perfect.

When I entered I registered the darkening purple bruise marring her jaw right away. She was standing too close to Ash for my liking with her hand on his shoulder but her eyes lit up the moment she saw me. I waved to Ramon and Patch who had a handful of tools laid out on the worn couch and were working on the sound equipment in the corner of the living room. I also acknowledged Ash with a chin lift but my focus was mostly on her.

I watched relief transform to something more guarded as she held my gaze, not the look of love that I hoped to see.

Had I been wrong about us?

No. I gave myself an internal shake remembering our night together and all that we had shared. I was just mentally and physically exhausted. She had to be too, for sure.

"Babe," I called. "I missed you. Come here."

Maybe I was overanalyzing things. Her eyes even had a little sparkle as she moved around Ash's drum kit and launched herself into my open arms. I folded her to my chest, held her tightly and breathed her in wishing she could be mine forever and wishing we didn't have an audience so I could have her right that moment.

"I missed you too, Linc. I saw you at the beach but Ash said it would be better if I waited here."

"Oh he did, did he?" I lifted a brow and glanced at my cousin over her shoulder.

Still on his stool behind his drums he rolled his eyes. "It's three in the afternoon, Linc."

Shit. I hadn't realized it was that late. The waves had been so good and I had desperately needed the practice. Placing wasn't an option anymore. The real money and endorsements went mostly to the few at the top of the sport. I had to win Fiji outright. Not just for myself but for both of us now.

"Ash is right." I eased back so I could look at her instead of at the smug expression on my cousin's face. "Did you eat lunch yet?"

She shook her head, her silky hair brushing over the tops of my hands.

"Then come with me. I'll take care of you." My words were for her but for Ash also, a thinly veiled warning as my gaze hit his and I steered her toward the door. I appreciated him looking out for her but she was my girl not his.

Chapter 44

Simone

I sat across the kitchen table from Linc at his aunt and uncle's house and tried to swallow a bite of the turkey sandwich he had made for me, finding it difficult because my mouth was so dry. I was worried. More than I had been when I had left Karen's house this morning. He seemed so out of sorts.

Was it the bruise on my jaw?

He seemed fixated on it even though I had insisted it didn't hurt very much.

Or had he heard the lyrics Ash and I had worked on together?

Had I given away too much of what I was feeling too soon?

Was he having regrets already?

"Babe." He covered my hand with his own. The look of concern in his clear blue eyes and the sizzle of instant awareness from the touch of his warm fingers pulled me from the mental quagmire I had fallen into. "What's going on with you? You seem a million miles away."

"What do you mean?" I asked carefully after taking a sip from my glass of water to moisten my throat.

"I've been thinking about us." His expression turned stony. "Since that's at the forefront of my mind I figured it might be on yours, too."

"I don't know, Linc," I said honestly my chest burning as I opened myself up to the very real possibility of a rejection. His eyes narrowed but I forged bravely on. *No more deflecting, Simone.* Delaying wasn't going to make things any easier. "I want to be with you but after last night I don't know if that's the best thing. I don't want to be a burden to you."

"You're not a burden. You're a prize. God, Simone." His eyes flared as he rose from his side of the table and pulled me up into his arms. I closed my eyes for a moment enjoying his warmth, his strength, the sheer pleasure of being within his embrace again. "I want you with me. All the time." He smoothed a strand of my hair behind my ear. "I'm so sorry about what happened with your father and every time I see that bruise on your pretty face I get angry all over again. It's going to be tough no doubt but I won't let your old man ruin us. Ok?"

"Ok," I agreed dropping my forehead to his chest. "But..."

"Let's just take it a day at a time right now." He lifted my chin with a curled finger, looked intently into my eyes and then pressed a soft kiss to my lips. It felt so good, the affection so welcome from him that I sighed.

I think he felt the same. He groaned his pleasure into

my mouth.

My lids fluttered closed and my hands drifted up the strong hard planes of his back, inviting him closer. I was surprised when he pulled back. I opened my eyes to find his gaze heated, hungry and possessive but he hooked his head over his shoulder and then I heard his aunt and his uncle talking as they came through the front door.

"Later," he whispered touching my nose lightly with the tip of his finger.

Linc

The later I had promised never came. Not that day or the next.

With her at Karen's and her father out of the picture I thought us being together would be easier but it got harder instead.

I had too little time to prepare for Fiji and therefore even less time to spend alone with her. At home my aunt and uncle seemed ever-present watching us with caution in their eyes. And though Karen's parents insisted Simone could stay with them for as long as she needed to, they were as restrictive with her curfew as they were with their own daughter's.

I knew Simone needed my support in the present and I did the best I could but I needed to be out on the ocean securing our future.

We had settled into a routine the past several days. I woke up before sunrise and stayed out on my board most of the day while she hung out with the guys. Then we ate dinner together at Ash's but by that time I was so spent that I usually crashed on her as we watched television on the couch. Last night she hadn't even bothered to wake me to walk her back to Karen's. Ash had taken her.

She was quietly disappointed and I was finding myself increasingly jealous of Ash. The stress of it all was creating strain between us.

Vowing to work harder so I could spend extra time with her tonight, I jogged out into the chaotic surf, tossed my board on it and paddled out. The waves were massive today. A low pressure system was stirring them up. Many were topping the top of the thirty foot tall pilings. Even as early as I had come I had tons of company. Everyone who surfed was eager to get out and attempt the waves.

I was the most accomplished surfer and had the priority so I got my choice of waves and I took them over and over again until no one was left besides me. It was thrilling to take on the ocean when it was angry and more of an opponent than an ally but it was extra exhausting, too.

White water all around me, the waves were so powerful now and setting up so fast that I barely had time to take on one before another one was upon me. I saw Ash on the pier but ignored him. He looked worried and I could tell that he thought I should come in. My girl was by his side looking just as concerned wearing a hoodie and a beach towel that whipped around her shapely form in the gale force winds.

Seeing her spurred me to press on. Time was running out to prepare for an event I was determined to win. Coming in early would feel like an admission of defeat. When I competed the waves might be small or they might be big like today. I had to be ready to put together a perfect ride whatever the conditions. Speed, power and flow. Commitment, innovation and variety. The judges would need to see all of that from me. That's why I had to keep pressing.

Feeling frustrated by my rides thus far, I chose a wave that maybe I shouldn't have. It turned into a monster rising faster and steeper than I had anticipated. I went straight up and over the top of it free falling through the air on the other side my board flying away from me. I felt the cord attached to my ankle snapping tight before I crashed into the ocean. Water surged all around me as I sank beneath it. I clawed to the surface but another wave slammed over me. I tried not to panic even though my lungs were burning for air.

I felt the tug on my ankle from my leash and was grateful it had stayed attached. I used it to follow my board to the surface. I threw my arms around it when I got there and ducked my head into the next wave that crashed over me. That was when I felt the sharp burn in my lower leg and realized one of my fins must have sliced me. I pulled my leg out of the water and lifted it to take a look. What I saw made my veins turn as cold as the water. There was a deep gash in my wet suit and blood was pouring from it.

I immediately turned the nose of my board to the shore and used the power of the waves to take me toward it praying Ash had seen what had happened and would be there. I didn't know if I would be able to stand on my own once I got there.

Simone kept a stoic face until they closed the door to the ambulance and it was just us and the EMT who was on the radio giving the hospital my status. Only one could ride with me to Hillcrest and Ash had insisted that it be her.

Her lips started to quiver and she turned her head to the side but I saw the tears that rolled down her cheeks.

"I'm ok," I told her mumbling a bit. My tongue felt thick and fuzzy after the shot of morphine they had given me. "I'm not going to die." I hoped my attempt at levity might distract her.

"Oh, Linc." She threw her body over me and wrapped her arms around me. She shook and I could feel her hot tears on my cool skin. They had cut away my wetsuit before strapping me to the stretcher and sliding me into the ambulance. "I was so scared. When you came out of the water and there was all that blood." She lifted her head to look at me. Her golden eyes were watery and her face was tear splotched but she had never seemed more beautiful to me. All that emotion for me. I couldn't remember anyone ever crying for me. "You're so good at surfing. I never realized how dangerous it could be. You could have drowned today. You went down for so long I thought you had." She dropped her head again and hugged me even tighter than before.

I stroked her hair with my non-IV hand.

"I'm going to be scared every time you get back on that board," she whispered.

So was I. If I got back on it. But it wasn't the psychological aspect of it that worried me. Lots of guys got sliced by their board. I'd even seen one get knocked unconscious when his board conked him in the head. They usually returned to surf again. But I had seen the look that had passed between the paramedics. I heard the one with us give his report to the hospital. My fin had cut through some serious muscle. They were going to take me to the operating room as soon as we arrived. That wasn't the type of injury that would allow me to go back out to the beach the next day.

Fiji was out of the question. Taking care of her, too. Everything was up in the air now.

Those thoughts made me panic worse than when I'd had an ocean's worth of water crushing me. I ground my teeth together so hard my eyes watered. "If it's gonna scare you, maybe you shouldn't watch," I chastened.

"What do you mean?" She lifted her head looking uncertain in response to the harshness in my tone.

"It's a dangerous sport, Simone." I forced my arms to drop to my sides letting go of her and tightening my fingers into fists as if I could recapture what I felt slipping away from me. "But it's part of who I am. You can't expect me to quit just because of one injury."

"I don't." Her eyes grew wide. "I just wanted you to know how frightened I was."

"I've got enough pressure on me. I don't need more to worry about." It was the truth but I felt wretched for saying it. She flinched but I knew she needed to get me. "*When* I get back on my board." I refused to accept the *if* that kept popping back into my mind. "I don't want you on the beach. I have to focus. Understand?"

Chapter 45

Linc

"She's still out there in the waiting room, Linc."

"Tell her to go back to Karen's."

"No, Linc. I won't. You need to see her. I don't get what's up with you."

"This is what's up with me," I gestured at my heavily bandaged leg. "What's the point, Ash? What do I have to offer her now that I'm like this?"

I squeezed my eyes tightly shut as if that would make the events of the past couple of days go away. We had both lost. *Everything.* All my hopes and dreams gone because of my stubbornness. If only I had gotten her home in time. If only I'd shown some sense out there in the surf.

"Things are hopeless for us now." My throat closed but I powered through it. "She needs to realize that so she can go on with her life." Even as I said the words I knew I could *never* go on without her.

Ash gave me a pitying look but I couldn't summon the

anger to rebuke him. "Talk to her for me." I turned away and looked out a window that had no view.

He put his hand on my shoulder and my eyes burned with the emotion swirling around inside of me. "You tell her that yourself if that's really what you believe. But I think she deserves to see for herself that you're ok."

"But I'm not ok." I spit the bitter words out. "I'm never going to be ok, Ash. You know how it is. You're just like me. Surfing is in our blood. And now I don't have that anymore." I crushed the crisp white hospital sheets between my clenched fists. "You talk to her. I can't. Not right now." It would weaken in my resolve to do the right thing by her if I looked at her pretty face. "Tell her whatever you have to. Just make her go away. Tell her I reached too high. Tell her she's too good for me. Just make her go away."

"No, Linc. I'm not telling her any of that." Ash moved toward the door but turned back to look at me and his eyes narrowed. "I'll tell her you need some more time. That you'll talk to her soon as soon as you're feeling like yourself again."

Simone

Feeling eerily numb I sat on the park bench by the ocean, listening to the roar of the surf and the piercing cry of the seagulls as they passed overhead. But the sun didn't warm my chilled skin and the sparkling surface of the Pacific didn't brighten my dark thoughts as I had hoped.

He's ok," I repeated to myself the lie Ash had told me after Linc came out of surgery. I knew the positive words about Linc's prognosis were meant to placate me but I'd seen the terrible truth in the starkness of Ash's expression. The doctors weren't giving any assurances and there weren't any between Linc and me, either. Not really.

"Why, Ash?" I had pressed a few moments ago in the doorway of his home. "Why won't he talk to me?"

"Give him time to process. Maybe by tomorrow, Simone." He looked more bleary eyed and tired today than he had the day before. I tried to peer past him into the house desperate to catch even a glimpse of Linc.

Tears sprang into my eyes as I voiced the horrible thought that had been rambling through my brain ever since the accident. "Does he blame me for what happened?"

"What?" Ash's gaze sharpened. "What on earth gave you that idea?"

I've got enough pressure on me.

"I don't know." I wrapped a strand of hair around my finger. "Maybe because he was tired. Maybe he was working too hard and staying too long for my sake."

"That's crazy, Simone."

"If it's crazy then why won't he talk to me?"

"Because he's had a traumatic injury. Because he's still recuperating and coming to terms with it."

"Are you sure that's all? I feel like there's something you're not telling me. I told you how I feel about him. Has he changed his mind about me?"

"No, baby." Ash had pulled me into his strong arms and I had wrapped mine around his trim waist clinging desperately to him, not wanting to acknowledge how hollow his denial rang.

I twisted my hands together in my lap so they wouldn't shake. Every time I closed my eyes memories of Lincoln flashed through my mind. On the beach. On his board. In his room. On the boat. My heart ached, a happy ending for us becoming more improbable with each passing day. I wished I had a rope to tie my scattered thoughts together so I could make sense of them or a sudden epiphany that would show the way forward.

I couldn't stay with Karen forever. I needed her advice but she seemed so happy with Dominic. I didn't want to wreck that by confessing how bad things had gotten between Linc and me.

I was tired of everyone walking on eggshells around me as if they all knew something terrible I didn't.

I pulled in an unsteady breath. I couldn't just sit around and keep waiting. It was time to stop thinking and start doing. Linc had worked so hard to try to secure our future. I needed to have the same mindset. I would take that open position at Schooner's. One good thing about all those years of working at Napoli's, I certainly had the qualifications.

Thanks, Dad, I thought with bitter sarcasm. I tried not to think about my mother and the fact she hadn't even tried to contact me.

Chapter 46

Linc

"That's the last time I'm making excuses and sending her away for you. You've been sitting back here in this room avoiding her, avoiding the guys and avoiding going on with your life." The mattress springs on his bed squeaked as he flopped onto it and dropped his head into his hands. "It's bad. I get that. But it's not the end of everything." He dropped his hands and lifted his gaze. "You're already walking pretty good. In a couple of months if you continue rehab you could be right back on your board. You have the injury exemption for a year. You could try to qualify again next season."

"No." My voice was gravelly from lack of use but my denial was firm. "You and I both know how competitive the circuit is. If I'm out that long the odds against me qualifying again are astronomical." My expression was as bleak as my words.

"Ok," he admitted his voice low. "You're probably

right. But competitive surfing is not the entire world, even though you've lived your life to this point as if it is." He hit me with a look. "I know why. I understand. Each time my dad brought you back here after your old man laid into you, you made excuses for him. Eye swelled shut. You said you ran into a door. Ribs bruised. You said you fell down the stairs. Until that last time. Do you remember?"

I nodded wishing I could forget. I had been thirteen but I'd hit my growth spurt early. Thank God since that time he'd come at me wielding a broken beer bottle.

"You had a competition that weekend. We were all there to see you win it. But there you were. Even after all he did to you. Even after all of the horrible untrue things he said. Up on that podium scanning the crowd looking for him. Still hoping for his approval.

I looked away. Ash was right. He didn't miss anything.

"No matter what you do or don't do, he's not going to change, Linc. My family and I, we're always going to be here for you. You know that right?"

Eyes burning I looked back at him, swallowing hard and nodded.

"Right." His voice sounded thick as if he had a bunch of emotional stuff stuck in his throat, too. "So we just need to rethink things." He ran a hand through his hair. "I want to give this Morris thing a go. I talked to the guys already. They're all on board."

"What?" I rubbed a hand over my eyes. The pain meds made my thoughts a little foggy. "I'm not following."

"Mom and Dad have come around, too." He leaned forward. "I think in large part because of you. Dad's going to lend us the van. We'll have to cover our own expenses.

Gas. Food. Lodging. But we'll split it four ways. It won't be that bad." His eyes glittered with excitement. "Why don't you give it a try? We're really good together, the four of us. A few weeks of road trippin' might be just the tonic you need. It'll get your mind off things and we might have more than just Morris offering us a deal by the end. C'mon, it'll be an adventure." He reached across the space that separated our beds and grasped my shoulder. "Hell, it might even turn out to be something big."

Simone

Sweeping the floor beneath the last table at the end of my shift, I saw him pass by the plate glass windows facing the street. I ducked my chin and spun away my heart thumping hard inside my chest despite the arrow of bittersweet longing that had pierced it all the way through.

Still so hopelessly in love with him. Even though I hadn't heard anything but second hand reports about him since the accident.

The bell jingled a couple of moments later. *Shit.* I'd forgotten to lock up after the last customer left. I turned but whatever words I had thought to speak died within my throat, the way my hopes had faded without him to nurture them.

Outside

"Mona." My chest burned hearing him speak the name that only he and Ash used for me.

"We're closed." I turned away. My throat was so tight I could barely swallow.

I heard his footsteps noticing a little hitch in it as he approached. It hurt me to be reminded of the injury and all that it had cost us. I desperately wished I could turn back time and undo it. But that wasn't possible. Instead I whirled around to find him closer than I could bear.

"I'm sorry. I had to see you. Patch told me that you were working here." His gaze narrowed lingering on the bruise that wasn't fading well. If anything the multicolored hue of it made it look worse. I'd been using makeup to hide it but apparently most of that had rubbed off during my double shift.

"Go away, Lincoln." His heat and his unique scent shattered my fragile equilibrium in a torrent of memories. The sweet slide of his skin against mine. His smooth caresses on my body. His words that had tempted me to believe in impossible things.

"I can't. I wish I could...for your sake, but I can't." He touched me. His strong capable fingers felt warm and heavy on my shoulders. A touch at once familiar and forlorn.

"You have to." I shrugged away from him, my husky voice betraying my need for him. Why was he here? Why had he only come to see me now?

"It's been ten days, Lincoln. Ten days without a single word." Frustrated tears stung my eyes. "Pardon me if I don't fall right back into your arms."

His eyes were hooded and seemed to swirl with emotions as tumultuous as my own.

"We don't have to do this," I whispered to fill the tense silence while his hands opened and closed as if he were wrestling with himself about something. "We had a good run. It was fun while it lasted." I backed away from him sticking my hands deep inside my apron pocket so I wouldn't reach for him, for a last touch. "Mr. Brighton will be back soon to close out the books. I've got to finish up here. Goodbye, Lincoln."

He blinked rapidly his brilliant blues suddenly sparkling with an intensity that I hadn't seen since before the accident. I wondered if he had been just going through the motions of living the same way I was. He closed the distance between us and grabbed me by the shoulders, his fingers digging in deep. "I screwed up, Mona. Bad. I felt like my world came crashing down and I was afraid. I lashed out and cut you off when I should've pulled you closer. I should've been strong like you. I should have shared my burdens and assured you we'd make it through them. I'm so sorry. I have no excuse." His expression was heartfelt but his voice dropped so low I had to lean in to make out the next words. "It's just that surfing was my only chance. My one shot to prove I was more than the worthless piece of shit my father always said I was. Plus it was my way to provide for myself...for us."

I shook my head denying what my heart wanted to believe his words meant.

"When I was out on my board the day of the accident, you were all I could think about. All I've thought about since I met you really." His fingers bit into my flesh. "I was going to ask you to marry me, Mona." His eyes took on a faraway glow. "I didn't have all the logistics worked out. I just knew I wanted you with me."

"Linc." I reached for him, greedy fingers clinging to his strong arms even as my desperate heart clung to the lifeline his words represented.

He refocused on me and there was something primal in his gaze, something I responded to because when it came to him my feelings were just as elemental. "Everything's changed now. I should be unselfish and just let you go. But how can I when every time I close my eyes I fuckin' see you, touch you, taste you and take you over and over again." He pressed his forehead to mine. "I can't do it, Mona. I can't let you go. Don't say goodbye. Not yet. Give me one more chance to prove myself to you."

Chapter 47

Linc

"We gotta go," Ash said. "We can't wait anymore. We've got to be on time for the show tonight in San Clemente." He slapped my shoulder before moving to the driver's side of the packed to the gills van. "I'm sorry, man. I know how much you wanted her to come."

I nodded once and moved to the passenger side. Just then I saw the car pull up in front of the house. Simone hopped out and leaned in the open window to pull out a green and blue striped backpack from the seat.

My heart went nuts but I schooled my features to neutral. But that was difficult to do when she was here and looked so hot in cutoffs and a midriff baring light green tank top. She hurried up the driveway toward me hitching the strap of her bag further up her shoulder.

"You came," I said lamely, moving to intercept her, sliding the backpack off her shoulder. I threw it at Dominic who protested loudly before tossing it into the back with the instruments and other luggage. The boards were on the roof. Only three of them. I had been trying to avoid thinking about that.

"Are you surprised?" Her voice was lightly teasing. I wanted to kiss her right then. Desperately.

"How come Linc gets to bring his girl with him?" Dominic complained.

"Cuz his said yes when asked, Loser," Ramon quipped. Apparently Karen had turned down a similar offer from Dominic because she had to get ready for school.

I took Mona's hand, my heart stumbling the instant I touched her. So did my stupid feet as my bad leg caught on the uneven pavement. I helped her up onto the front seat then I got in slamming the half wood paneled door a little harder than necessary. I despised my physical infirmity and the emotional insecurity that went along with it.

My confidence had taken a hit since the accident. I didn't want her coming along just because she felt sorry for me. The certainty that I had once felt about us had faded into haze.

Ash's route for our impromptu tour had us going up the coast all the way, the ocean almost always in view, in case the surf looked good. The path of my relationship with Simone was much more obscure.

We got up on the Five for a little jog but got off at La Jolla Parkway rolling through hills of pines and expensive houses. Ramon opened a bag of chips and passed around some sodas. Everyone munched noisily until the SDSU campus came into view. The interior of the van fell into an uncomfortable silence. Feeling Simone's tension, I reached for her hand and squeezed it.

My stomach roiled as chaotically as the surface of the ocean had on the day that changed everything.

I should have told her I was sorry for all she had given up. I should have said that I understood her loss. But Ash broke the tension with a loud belch and of course Patch had to one up him.

The awkward moment passed.

But I wondered if the feeling that I represented a consolation prize to her forfeited college dreams ever would.

After a brief bathroom break at the beach facilities at Torrey Pines State Park we entered the historic 101 with its charming string of beachside communities. Solana. Cardiff by the Sea. Encinitas. Carlsbad with its arch and Oceanside with its patriotic banners. Then a really long section away from the ocean through Camp Pendleton's undulating hills where Patch had lived for a long time when his dad had been a staff sergeant.

Finally we reached San Clemente with its iconic red roofed white washed buildings spilling down the hillside to the Pacific. Even though the trip had taken longer than we had anticipated we still made it to the rooftop club in the postage stamp downtown in plenty of time. Patch and Ash went inside the building to finalize the financial arrangements with the club's owner and Ramon took off mumbling something about printing off handbills for the show. I turned to Simone and proposed that we find something to eat.

She agreed. We took the downhill path from the public parking lot, her stride graceful while I struggled not to limp. We passed consciously by the surf shop peering inside the other window displays but nothing caught her eye. I resisted the urge to take her hand. I wasn't sure if she would allow it.

We found a burger joint at the end of the block. I needed to rest my leg. It was just about to give out.

"Will this do for dinner?" I asked. The wind had blown her hair into her face. I wanted to brush the satiny locks over her shoulder so I could see her lovely features better.

"Sure. It's perfect." I put my hand on her arm and curled my fingers into her soft skin trying not to think about how all the rest of her might feel as I escorted her to the counter. I gave several interested guys looking her way the proprietary glare while she perused the chalkboard menu.

We both ordered malts and burgers hers with extra jalapenos. I located an empty booth in the back and steered her toward it. She scooted in moving to make space for me on her side, peering up at me expectantly. No way was I going to pass up the invitation to sit beside her again, my thigh touching hers like it had on the drive from OB.

I folded in and she touched my thigh seeming hesitant. "Why don't you put your leg up on the bench on the other side?" Obviously she was nervous about my response to her suggestion. "If you want to, that is...I mean...it's got to hurt, right?"

Yeah, she had probably noticed my grimacing and was feeling sorry for me. Thus the invitation to sit on her side. Hot bitterness churned in my gut. Who the hell was I anymore? What good was I to her? And how long could we go on pretending that things hadn't changed?"

When our food arrived, I took a couple of bites but

mainly just moved my food around. I had lost my appetite. I noticed she had, too.

"Mona, you should eat more." I touched her hand. She looked down at where my hand rested on hers and covered my fingers with her own before looking up at me.

"So should you, Linc." Hope unfurled inside me like a ray of light breaking through the clouds. I didn't fail to notice this was the first time she'd called me that since I had screwed everything up for us.

"Fair enough." The knot in my gut loosened. She was cute as hell being stubborn on my behalf and I so liked my hands folded in hers. I pointed to her plate with my chin. "You eat half of yours and I'll do the same. Deal?"

She nodded. I slid out my hands and we both began to eat in earnest. As I finished a bite I worked up the nerve to ask something that had been bothering me. "What did your mom say when you told her you were leaving with us?"

She tensed. "I didn't tell her. I haven't spoken to her since..." She trailed off and I filled in. "Since your old man clocked you?"

She dumped her half eaten burger in her basket and nodded.

"You haven't had any contact with her at all?" I pressed.

"No I haven't." She dipped her chin, her hair sliding forward shielding her face. "Why should I? She was there, too. You saw her. She didn't do anything."

She was right. At least with my dad it was pretty straightforward, just him being a drunken asshole loser and me. She'd been betrayed by *two* parents.

"I'm sorry, Simone." I located her clenched fist in her

lap and brought it to my lips brushing a kiss across her delicate knuckles, keeping her hand in mine and forcing her fingers open so I could thread our fingers together. She didn't lift her head for a long moment. She seemed to be staring at our hands again. When she finally looked at me her eyes were brimming.

"Where do we stand, Mona?" I found myself asking though I feared the answer. "I love you, but I've ruined everything for us, haven't I?"

She pulled in a sharp breath.

To work up the courage to tell the truth or to formulate a lie, I wondered.

"I love you, too, Linc." Her eyes were steady on mine but she blinked a couple of times as though something had gotten caught in her eyes.

I knew she was waiting for me to say something in return. I should have. I so wanted to believe her but I couldn't. Not really. In life and surfing timing is everything. Those beautiful words came too late to control the current that was already carrying her away from me.

Chapter 48

Simone

L ater at the motel after the Dirt Dogs inaugural road performance, I was the last one to get the shower. I washed my hair using the dregs of the complimentary shampoo provided by the single room that the five of us shared and reflected on the evening.

The show had been a rousing success. The band had been tight. The guys had obviously been practicing a lot before leaving OB. But Lincoln had stolen the show sitting with a hip hitched on a stool crooning into the mic, his effortless charm winning over the standing room only crowd. The flirty half smiles and winks he cast made the women in it go crazy.

I had stood off stage in the shadows nursing a diet coke throughout the hour and a half long set. I had to be careful with my funds. Though he'd invited me, though I'd come, there had been no talk about the future and after his silence at dinner when I'd made my feelings clear I was more uncertain than ever that his future would include me at all.

Stepping out of the shower onto the sodden bathmat, I dried off and slipped on my pajama set, a new one with ties on each shoulder and ruffles on the short hem. I'd never gone back to my house. The few clothes I had now were either hand me downs from Karen or those I had purchased from the clearance rack at Walmart.

When I left the bathroom, switching off the light behind me, the room was nearly pitch black. Someone was already snoring softly. A swath of light from the crack in the curtain pointed the way to the pallet I had made on the floor. The guys had been so hyped up rehashing the highlights of the show and counting the two hundred dollars they'd cleared that they almost completely forgot me.

I glanced at the dark lumps in the double beds. Patch and Ramon occupied the one by the bathroom. Ash and Linc were on the other, but I couldn't tell which side Linc was sleeping on. If I could have I might have said something to him, might have put myself out there, touched his strong shoulder, whispered in his ear and maybe even invited him to join me on the floor.

Feeling alone, I bit my lip to hold back the sting of tears. This wasn't at all how I had imagined things would be. I moved toward the window and peeked out through the slit in the curtains at the ocean and the moonlight sparkling on its surface. I heard someone stirring beside me.

"Mona." Warm hands squeezed my shoulders. Firm lips pressed a kiss to my temple. "Come to the beach with me."

His statement came off more like a question.

I nodded my agreement. Linc reached for my hand

shifting a blanket into the other one as he led me toward the door sliding a key card into the pocket of his cargo shorts along the way.

I wrapped my arms around his waist. He wasn't wearing a shirt and his skin was deliciously warm in contrast to the cool night air. We tiptoed across the parking lot together. Ash had mentioned that our route would take up the scenic coast all the way to San Francisco and that the motels he had booked were all within walking distance of the ocean.

The guys might be testing out this rocker thing but they were still surfers at heart…especially Lincoln. My heart had squeezed painfully when I had noticed his board missing from the roof of the van.

I sighed as soon as the bottom of my feet touched the soft sand and I snuggled tighter into Lincoln's side pulling in deep breaths of ocean and him, the first easy breaths I had managed since we had parted ways after dinner.

He spread out the blanket between two dunes that provided a modicum of privacy shielding us from view. I immediately plopped down brushing off my feet before scooting to the middle, my gaze to the ocean as I pulled my knees to my chest and rested my chin on them.

"Babe," he called softly as he dropped down beside me. "I'm sorry for the way I acted earlier, all evening really." He sighed and ran a hand through his mop of hair. "This is really tough for me, finding who I am again, who I want to be for myself and for you. It's harder than I thought it would be finding my footing. Pun intended." He chuckled wryly. Surfers were very particular about foot placement on their boards, but even in the moonlight I could see that the laughter didn't reach his eyes.

"I understand, Linc. Really." I swiveled to more fully face him touching his bristly cheek, running my fingers reverentially over the masculine planes of his face, stopping at his lips as he stared into my eyes. "It's hard for me, too for a lot of reasons. But please can we work through things together? It hurts when you shut me out."

"I'm sorry, Simone. My sweet Simone." He leaned closer his breath warm on my lips before he touched his to mine. I nearly shuddered from the ecstasy of having his mouth on mine once more. It had been too long. My hands plunged into the thick strands of his hair and wrapped around the base of his skull to bring him more fully into me, telling him, begging him to deepen the kiss.

His strong hands on my nearly bare shoulders, he pushed me back onto the blanket granting my request, slanting his mouth over mine, licking the seam between my lips, slipping his tongue between and sliding it seductively along mine. Arousal bloomed immediately, hot, heavy and undeniable.

When he lifted his head several long breathtaking moments later, my lips felt deliciously sensitive and swollen. "Don't stop." My fingers tightened on the taut muscles of his shoulders.

"Not planning on it, babe. I just didn't plan on this. Not really. I hoped. God I hoped, but I didn't bring protection." His blue eyes glowed with regret in the moonlight.

"It's ok." I reached up and skimmed my fingertips across his gorgeous sculpted lips, silky soft but firm, the full bottom one still wet from our kiss and dipped my forefinger into the masculine v of the top one. "I'm on the pill."

"And I'm clean." His gaze brightened. "Totally. They ran ever single test known to man at the hospital. I even had a tetanus booster. His gaze dipped to my mouth, his lips following, he brushed them firmly over mine. Once and I sighed. Twice and my lips parted. On the third I met him halfway taking his tongue while my fingers greedily glided over the contours I had been dreaming of exploring. The strong lines of his wide shoulders. The corded biceps. The wall of his solid chest. I dreamed no longer.

He inhaled sharply when my fingers skimmed over his flat nipples. Everywhere I went his warm flesh seemed to leap to my command. "Enough." His breath coming out in rapid bursts he leaned his forehead into me. "Enough, Simone. Lay back," he ordered and I smiled hearing the confidence in his cocky tone.

"Ok." I shimmied purposefully, my breasts bouncing as I leaned back on my elbows.

"You're so beautiful." Walking on his knees he opened my legs and moved between them, kneeling reverentially before me. My chest and throat grew tight just from looking at him.

He reached for the ties on my top undoing them slowly his eyes growing heavy lidded as he slid the cotton covering off my breasts. "My goddess," he breathed as he traced them. I arched my back off the blanket to bring them more fully into his skilled hands. Warm thumbs flicked and plucked the aching tips. My pulse pounded through my veins and restless desire pooled hot between my thighs.

His gaze darkening even more, he dropped one hand placing it low and purposefully over my center resting it there while he watched me. The message was clear though unspoken. I knew he needed to hear the words from me, words I had withheld that night that seemed so long ago.

"Yes," I whispered. "Make love to me. Yes I love you." I reached for him bringing his face to mine. His lips scalded me in their fervor like an answering brand, each stroke of his hot tongue claiming me as his own.

His cargo shorts came off with just the quick downward rasp of his lowered zipper. He was gloriously naked and aroused beneath them. When I touched him velvety crown to base he groaned and the low purely masculine sound sent a heat rush of desire through me so strong that it dampened my inner thighs.

Lips hard on mine, fingers frantic to remove all the barriers that separated my heated skin from his, he ripped my shorts down my legs and his mouth briefly lifted from mine to do the same with my top. He tossed it aside as soon as he had it over my head. Then his hungry mouth was back devouring my neck, sucking my nipples deep, tongue swirling my navel while I writhed beneath him skimming my hands over the width of his shoulders, dipping them into his spine and finally grabbing his sexy ass. His skin was slick with passion. So was mine.

"Linc," I praised. "Linc. I love you." I pressed soft kisses to his flesh everywhere my mouth could reach. Inside my head I chanted the same refrain over and over. *Don't leave me. Don't ever leave me.*

"Mona." His eyes black with desire, he eased back on one arm his muscles taut and brought my hand to his cock so we could stroke its hard length together. So hot. Especially with his eyes locked on mine so I could see the pleasure in them and he could see the same in mine. He groaned approvingly then took my hand and brought it to his lips placing a hot open mouthed kiss in the center of my palm.

Before I could recover from that sweet gesture, he lifted my arms and trapped both of my hands above my head. Slowly he moved into position. Slowly inch by delicious hot inch he slid inside my slick heat. Slowly he started to stroke inside me.

Deeper and deeper. Higher and higher my passion spiraled. Closer and closer I got, we both got, to the crest of the wave.

"Mona," he groaned.

"Linc," I moaned lifting my hips to meet each hard thrust, desperate to take him with me to the top and then I was there. The summit. The consuming heat. The perfect ecstasy. I shook with the sheer dark pleasure of it. The joy prolonged as he shuddered his release within me filling me with his essence as I pulled him even deeper into me until he collapsed heavily on me whispering my name one final time.

Chapter 49

Linc

S tanding behind her I helped her retie the straps on her pajama top, fingers lingering on her soft skin. Something tightened beneath my rib cage when I realized she didn't smell the way she usually did. No more sweet gardenia scented lotion. She'd left it all behind along with her clothes, college and everything else. For what? For me. The guy with the messed up leg and a messed up future dragging her into who knew what because he was still too selfish to let her go. I didn't want to ever let her go.

I lifted my glistening gaze to the ocean breeze avoiding her eyes as I shook out and refolded the blanket.

I wanted her again even though I had just had her.

Would this need for her ever lessen?

She bumped my shoulder as we started back toward the motel. I was so busy staring at her that I failed to register the extra set of large footprints in the sand or the faint scent of cigarette smoke lingering in the air. I was completely unaware of his presence until he was suddenly right there in front of me.

"Ash!" Mona exclaimed hand to her throat looking back at the dunes where we had just made passionate love to each other moments earlier. "I didn't see you." Why hadn't either one of us seen him? "How long have you been standing there?" I very much wanted to know the answer to that question as well.

"A while." Ash flicked the cigarette he'd been smoking aside and lifted his chin. "The door's open. Why don't you go on inside, Mona? I wanna have a word with my cousin."

Uncertain she looked to me. "It's ok. I'll be inside in a minute," I reassured her leaning in to brush her sweet lips and then watching her sexy hips sway as she moved away before turning back to Ash.

"What the hell, Ash? Were you watching us?"

"You're not very discrete." His jaw hardening he reached inside his half buttoned shorts, pulled out a crumpled pack of cigarettes, withdrew another smoke and offered me one. I refused it.

"And since when did you start smoking?" I added waving away the puff of smoke that drifted into my face.

"There's a lot of things you don't know about me, dude," he stated enigmatically. "But back to Simone."

"Yeah. What about her? If you have a problem with her being here you should have told me upfront," I guessed.

"That's not it at all. Where else is she gonna go?" His gaze narrowed. "You do realize she gave up everything for you."

I nodded once. Yeah I realized that alright. It was prac-

268

tically all I thought about. How could I ever even out the
tally so heavily weighted on her side?

"And so you're back together now? She's giving you
another chance?

"Yeah." Not that I deserved it. "What's your point?
What's got you in such a confrontational mood?" I asked.

"You." He poked me in the chest hard enough to hurt.
"You didn't see her at the hospital and then at our house
after that. Dammit, Linc. She's totally gone for you and
she's one of the sweetest girls I've ever known. You can't
keep jerking her around." Was Ash in love with her, too? It
certainly seemed that way. "You almost broke her once.
You step out of line with her again and I'm telling you right
now, cousin or no, I'm not covering for you." He took a
long drag from the half smoked cigarette and his tone
though still angry seemed more reflective when he continued. "You're a smart guy, Linc but a lot of the time you
have your head up your ass and don't see what's standing
right in front of you. Open your eyes. Get your shit together. You love her. Be the type of guy she needs you to be.
I'm not asking you, I'm telling you."

Ash's words ringing in my ears, I climbed back into
bed and insisted Simone join me there. Grumpy Ash could
sleep on the floor if he came back inside. Even though my
leg throbbed I was exhausted and immediately fell into a
hard sleep, until Dominic tossed a cold glass of water on
me jarring me awake.

"What the hell?" I sputtered clearing the water from
my eyes and noted immediately that the bed was empty on
Simone's side. "What time is it?"

"Frickin' noon, man." He threw a McDonald's takeaway sack on the bed answering the question before I could ask it. "She's out on the beach with Ash taking a bunch of pictures to chronicle the tour."

My stomach grumbled and I dug into the bag even as my brow creased in confusion.

"He thinks she needs something to do, to feel useful, part of the band so to speak." He ticked off on his fingers. "Ash is on logistics. Ramon's our PR man. You're a lazy piece of shit." He grinned. "And I've got transportation covered. Got the van gassed and rinsed the undercarriage so the fan will cool the engine more efficiently."

"Fair enough." I finished the egg, sausage and cheese biscuit and cracked open the orange juice.

"We're all packed up, too. Ash says you've got fifteen minutes to shower before they kick us out." I raised a brow. Ash was getting awfully bossy. "Some girl from the local radio station saw us at the club last night. Called Ramon. Told him she wants to do a live interview. Seemed particularly interested in you."

"That's cool." I'd done interviews before on the surfing circuit so I wasn't nervous or anything. Mostly just stoked. This had to be good for the band. I drained the juice and climbed out of bed heading to the shower.

"Linc," Dominic called before I shut the door.

"Yeah?"

"Listen." He rubbed a hand over his short black hair. "This isn't my place but Simone is Karen's friend and well …I like her a lot, too. We all do." Fuck. Was everyone half in love with her and going to ride my case? "She told Karen a lot of shit about the way she feels about you." My stomach clenched. "My dad says there's a good woman behind

Outside

every good man. I know she's been through a lot, so have
you. Seriously, just don't tool her around, alright?"

Chapter 50

Simone

We listened to the broadcast Linc and Ramon had taped on KLOS during our short hour drive on the Pacific Coast Highway. The Rock of Southern California's segment had been picked up and re-broadcast on the Newport Beach station and several others in the surrounding area apparently. The evidence that it had been heard was currently all around me in the red brick wall to wall, completely packed, sold out historic club located in an alley off of McFadden Square. All three dramatic sprawling levels of the Blue Beet were filled from the ground floor where the band was set up, to the rooftop bar with a romantic view of the ocean.

And it was only our second stop.

"My sister's best friend said she caught their show in San Clemente." Club lights flashing in her short brunette hair the woman swaying to the recorded music beside me in the high heels and fishnet stockings swirled the straw in her tumbler before adding, "She also said the lead singer is smoking hot."

That he was for sure. I tried not to let it bother me that they were talking about my boyfriend with me standing right there sipping on my diet coke. Listening.

"Yeah, he *sounds* hot, too. Did you hear the interview?" The blonde with her nodded vigorously like a bobble head doll while rearranging her bustier to show more cleavage. "He's totally unattached. Said so. Several times."

My heart stopped. He did what? Surely she had gotten something wrong. Maybe she had gotten Linc confused with Ramon.

"I just talked to one of the guys in the band." Another brunette pushed into the group dressed sluttier than the other two. The alcohol fumes coming off her nearly made me gag into my diet coke. "Hispanic guy. Pretty cute. Said he'd let us backstage to hang with them if I show him my tits."

I closed my eyes. *Holy shit.*

"I got dibs on the lead singer," Blonde Cleavage Girl insisted.

I started to shake and was leaning in so far to hear them that I lost my balance and one of their drinks slopped all over my only pair of high heels, my fake silk blouse and studded shorts.

"You ok?" the brunette in the fishnet asked me.

I nodded numbly backing away, pushing through the crowd and not breathing easily again until I reached the bathroom. I locked myself in a stall.

Calm down, Simone. It's just typical rock band stuff. You wanna be with a guy as handsome as Lincoln? Then you're just gonna have to get used to the lifestyle. Besides you can't always believe everything you hear.

After my internal pep talk, I splashed water on my face in an effort to regain my composure and went back outside pushing to get close to the corner stage again so I could re-sume taking pictures of the guys with the camera Ash had taught me to operate. Linc smiled at me when he saw one of the flashes. I smiled back burying the trepidation the girls had caused until it resurfaced again backstage after the concert.

Scantily dressed girls draped themselves over the guys who were left looking a little befuddled by all the attention. A local television station was talking to Linc about the ra-dio segment and his surfing career. The bright video cam-era spotlight made his handsome blue eyes shine. I tensed when the blonde from earlier crawled into his lap and passed him a beer like she had a right to. I waited and wait-ed and watched but he didn't push her aside, as the pretty red headed professionally dressed reporter continued to pepper him with questions.

When Linc flashed her his flirty smile, the one that showed off his dimple, my stomach didn't flip the way it usually did, it churned on the diet coke within it.

I tried to remind myself that Lincoln had made love to me just last night. That I had woken up to his arms around me just this morning. But it didn't help. I still felt sick. I had to leave. *Now.* I spun around and ran straight into Ash.

"Whoa," he said stopping me, his platinum hair still damp with sweat from the stage, fingers calloused from years of drumming curling around my upper arms. "Where are you going? It's not safe for you to wander around by yourself in all this craziness." He frowned as he continued to study me. "What's wrong? Why are you so upset?"

My eyes drifted back across the room. His followed. His lips formed an 'o' of surprise before he tried to placate me. "He's just playing up the sex appeal for show, Simone. The seductive angle is part of the sales pitch. He's with you. As soon as the interview is through I'm sure he'll take you back to the motel himself."

"Take me now, Ash. *Please*," I pleaded. "I hear what you're saying but I don't feel good. For real."

"Sure. Ok." His face softened. "This all kind of just blew up overnight, didn't it? I'm sure we'll all get acclimated. It's just going to take a little time." Putting his hand on the small of my back he moved in close behind me and led me from the room. "It's kind of exciting though, don't you think? In my wildest imagination I never dreamed we would get attention like this."

Exciting was not the word I would have used. More like bad or really horrible.

But I kept silent and was grateful for Ash, grateful for the ride he gave me back to the motel.

After some crackers and a Sprite from the vending machine, a lot of fretting and a couple of hours of bad sitcoms, I eventually fell asleep. I startled awake when the bed dipped and I heard a vaguely familiar feminine voice.

"Hey there's somebody already in your bed," Blonde Cleavage Girl whined as I opened my eyes.

I moved my hair out of my face and scooted toward the middle of the mattress.

"Yeah, it's my girlfriend," Linc slurred sitting down beside me and patting my head like I was his puppy. My entire body went tense but he didn't seem to notice.

"I thought *I* was your girlfriend." Boobs bouncing that I wondered if Linc had already seen, she put her hands on her overly ample hips.

"Nope." His hair messy and his eyes glazed Linc shook his head. "Never. I just needed the ride to the hotel since my cousin took off with the van and some guy to..." Expression blanking he trailed off. "I don't remember." His level of intoxication reminded me of my mother after she had chugged down a bottle of wine. I had never seen him this drunk. Never seen him drunk at all actually. What was going on with him?

"Get out of my room." I climbed out of the bed and took control of the situation grabbing the skank's arm and dragging her to the door.

"Hey." She dug in her stilettoes trying to stop me. "Aren't you going to tell her to let me stay...Mr., um..." She was having as many memory problems as he was.

"Nope," Linc said swaying as he got to his feet. "Thanks for the booze, Sugar. But," he smiled and it was a sad pale imitation of the real thing, "this is the only woman for me. My Simone. My sweet, sweet Simone. Oh, shit." He added reaching up to cover his mouth a split second too late. He emptied the entire contents of his stomach all over the floor.

After I kicked the skank out, cleaned up the mess, got Linc to bed and myself a shower, the guys stumbled in looking only slightly better than Linc had.

"Oh hell no," I said shaking my finger at them. "Don't you dare. If you're gonna be sick go in the bathroom and sleep in the tub. I'm not cleaning up after anybody else."

Outside

I don't know if Dominic and Ramon actually heard me. They were leaning heavily on each other and their eyes were unfocused. I gave it less than two minutes before they both passed out. Ash heard me though and he was the only one who had the decency to look embarrassed. So I laid into him. "You guys are gonna self-destruct before you ever get a chance to make it if you act like this after only putting together two decent shows. No one wants to pay good money to see a bunch of losers stumble around on stage drunk or hungover no matter how good looking they are."

"You're right, Simone. Absolutely right." He crooked his finger. "We're all lucky to have you looking after us. Come here." He reminded me of Lincoln for a moment even though they didn't look at all alike. I crossed to his side of the room and he pulled me into him hugging me tight. He glanced at Linc who was totally out of it sprawled perpendicular across the bed. "I'm sorry you had a tough night. You can sleep in my bed. I'll take the floor.

Chapter 51

Linc

We were all moving like sunglass wearing slugs the next morning except for Simone who incidentally was still not speaking to me. Not that I blamed her.

My perfect goddess. I'd screwed up majorly with her last night. I told her repeatedly that I hadn't slept with that girl. Why would I want to sleep with anyone else when I had her?

I had just taken the celebration a little too far. We had made over five hundred dollars to add to the two hundred from the previous gig. And after the television thing aired we might make even more at the next stop. The money and all the attention was validation to me that I desperately needed. That the band really might make it and that my worries about taking care of Simone might be over.

I hadn't told her or anyone else also about the pain in my leg after the performance, an infirmity I despised and a reminder of everything I had lost. It had been throbbing like hell by the time we had exited the stage. I had no more pain pills so when the blonde had passed me the booze I had chugged it looking for relief.

I was paying for my ill-advised self-medication.

In more ways than one.

I had learned my lesson. I would sit on the stool tonight and I would keep Simone close as soon as I got her to speak to me again.

I put my aching head in my hands. "Got any Advil?" I asked Dominic.

On the bench seat beside me he focused his polarized lenses my way but hooked a thumb over his shoulder. "Ask Ramon. I gave him the bottle before we checked out of the motel this morning."

Turning my head gingerly, I looked in the back. Ramon was with the gear leaning against Ash's snare case and was holding a chilled water bottle to his pain creased forehead. He looked as bad as I felt. Without me having to ask he tossed me the bottle. I caught it, shook out a few caplets and choked them down.

I leaned my head against the window trying not to wince as the van lurched at each stop light. Simone and Ash were in the front and I heard them singing the lyrics to the tune the two of them had been working on at Patch's house back in OB. I certainly didn't like it that they were harmonizing together but I didn't have the energy or the right to complain after the way I had acted last night.

Feeling raw and regretful I zoned out for a bit. When I finally started to get some relief from the pounding inside my brain I refocused on my cousin and my girl just in time to hear her sweet laughter. I cracked open my red rimmed eyes only to immediately narrow them.

Simone giggled again turning her head giving me a glimpse of her pretty profile and gifted a smile to Ash. Feelings of insecurity resurfaced and my guts churned, not from nausea now but from red hot jealousy. She was sitting entirely too close to him and they had been way too chummy all morning, the entire trip even.

"Yes he did." Ash flashed her a grin paying too little attention to the road and too much attention to her. "Looked like a lovelorn little puppy. I think he fell for you after that first time you met him on the beach."

Was he sharing confidences with Simone? I hadn't been paying enough attention to their conversation. I gritted my teeth trying not to rise to the bait I think he was purposefully dangling. "Ok you guys. Yuck it up. Go ahead and have fun at my expense while I'm dying back here."

"Serves you right," Ash said soberly. I knew he was saying a lot of things with just those three words. Our sunglassed gazes clashed in the rearview mirror.

"I am aware." I would have given him the one fingered salute but it would still hurt too much to move. After a lingering glance at Simone's stiff shoulders and pretty profile annoyingly tipped toward Ash, I closed my eyes. I vowed once more to steer clear of Jim Beam and all his kin while determining to have another talk with Simone as soon as we reached the next stop.

We arrived at the Best Western in Huntington Beach just after taking lunch at a diner back up the road. Simone's orgasmic sounding moans as she'd eaten the deliciously crispy fries and slurped on her shake while sitting too far across the table from me had nearly driven me insane.

The guys grabbed their boards to go to the beach across the street as soon as we parked. The fact that I couldn't join them didn't really bother me as much as it had previously. Right now I had a more pressing concern. I needed to make things right with her.

"Simone." I touched her arm softly and she jumped. Why was she so keyed up? What had she been thinking about standing beside the van with that faraway almost lost look in her eyes? "Stay at the motel. Talk to me." Looking like that was the last thing she wanted to do, which hurt my heart, she glanced in the guys' direction one more time before nodding.

I could feel Ash's gaze lingering on us but at the moment I didn't care. She was my priority but later he and I were going to have words. He was getting entirely too friendly with *my* girl.

Inside the indoor outdoor green carpeted motel room Simone flopped into the desk chair and fiddled with a laminated pizza takeout menu while continuing to avoid my gaze.

"What can I do to make things right between us?" I asked kneeling in front of her and peering up at her. "Name it, babe, and I'll do it."

"It's not that simple, Linc." Her hurt filled eyes focused on me. "I'm wondering now if I should have ever come on this trip in the first place. Since the boat everything seems to keep going wrong for us." Her lips trembled and I felt regret churning in my gut even worse than it had before. "Maybe we should take the hint and call it quits before we hurt each other any worse than we already have."

She meant before I hurt her any more than I already had. When had she ever done anything wrong?

But I was done screwing things up with her. I wanted to run away with her and our problems leaving the past and all its problems. But I knew I needed to stay and fix things in the here and now. So I compromised with myself, scooped her out of the chair and carried her to the bed pinning her beneath my body instead.

"Linc, don't," she protested though her eyes darkened the way I was sure my own had as soon as I had her soft curves beneath me.

"Yes, Mona." I smoothed her silky hair back from her pretty face. "This. You and me. This is right. Perfect in fact. You just need a reminder."

"Not perfect. No relationship is perfect. You put me too high on a pedestal." She looked away. "Sometimes I don't think you keep things in perspective. And then we get into trouble because you think you don't measure up. It's just me, Linc. Accept my love. Leave the rest of the world and their expectations outside. Let's just be together. Like it was before everything went wrong." Her eyes when she slid them back to me held a glassy sheen and were no longer filled with passion the way I wanted them to be.

"I love you, Linc. I really do. I wish you would take it to heart." She framed my face with both hands fingers gliding over my features as if memorizing them…as if she were saying goodbye.

I didn't heed the subtle warnings. I didn't hear the deeper meaning in her words though I remembered everything later when I had nothing left but time to analyze my mistakes. I just wanted to make her mine again and immediately set out to do just that.

Peeling her tank over her head, asking her to lift up so I could unclasp her bra, tracing her breasts and teasing her by not touching the nipples until she begged me to, then sucking on them so hard she gasped and arched her back off the bed.

"Yeah, babe. Just like that," I praised, rewarding her and myself with languid swirls around her rosy nipples and harder licks across the peaks that made her moan and me groan as my dick jumped in approval.

She was wrong. She was perfect. An erotic goddess. I couldn't look at her let alone touch her without falling under her spell.

Eyes heavy lidded, her hands under my shirt, her soft fingers sliding over my skin. I wiggled to help her remove it.

Lowering my head I feasted on her lush cherry glossed mouth licking between the seam and plunging my tongue between to take possession slanting my head one way and then the other until she writhed beneath me.

"Linc," she whispered when I switched angles her fingers laced deeply within my hair. "Linc. I love you."

I showed her I loved her too by sucking on her tits again. Hard and deep. No more gentleness. Just raw and rough passion until her breasts were completely red and her body was shuddering with the force of her need.

Perfect, I decided though she denied it.

"Shorts and everything off," I ordered easing off the bed to quickly remove and fling aside my shorts and boxers. She had the comforter kicked aside, was naked and reaching for me with her shapely arms before I could get my knee back to the mattress.

I complied with her beautiful unspoken request eagerly taking her lips again fusing my mouth to hers coaxing her to open wider and take my tongue deeper the way I planned to give her my cock soon.

"Mona," I bathed her kiss swollen parted lips with her name then the column of her neck as I moved down it. Her hands moved restlessly across my shoulders and kneaded muscles that bunched beneath the strain of holding back. I desperately wanted to be inside her, the two of us moving together in unison.

But not yet. My goal was to make this perfect for her.

I went back to her tits lapping the breast bone in between and nipping the puckered peaks until she reached down between our slickened bodies and grabbed my cock.

"You ready for me, babe?" I queried in a low more beast than man rumble.

"Yes." She peered up at me from beneath her lowered lashes. So seductive.

"Good. I'm ready for you, too, gorgeous." I was always ready for her.

Her hands covered mine as I caressed the soft skin of her inner thighs and gently parted them wider. She kept her heavy lidded eyes on mine as I positioned. She moaned as I sank my cock inside her until I was buried to the hilt.

"You feel so good," I told her. "So right. No place in the entire world I would rather be than here with you like this."

Her hands moved to my ass. Her eyes fluttered closed as I started to move but even without the visual reference within them her ecstatic expression confirmed that she felt exactly the same way as I did.

There was no denying anything. No mistakes. No past. Just the present reality as we moved together. Her hips lifting to deepen my thrusts. Her moans making my rhythm even more frenzied. Her fingernails scoring my ass to urge me on.

And then the hot implosion that started at the base of my spine. My cock stiffened and sublime pleasure hit me greater than any other high I had ever experienced. She made me feel better than anything in the world. Worthy. Valued. Loved. Better than I used to feel when on my board maxing out on a tube in a competition. Insecurities. Shortcomings. Doubts. They were silenced when I had her in my arms, when we were joined together like this. She was it. She was the one. She would always be the one.

Chapter 52

Simone

I hid my tear soaked cheeks in his neck. It had been so beautiful, every caress, every heated glance, each touch until the culmination proving his love.

Hair hiding my face and skimming my breasts, I scurried off to the bathroom mumbling about getting cleaned up fast so he could have his turn.

When I was done and we switched places he stopped me to brush a soft kiss across my still stubble abraded sensitive lips. I told him I loved him. Again. He didn't need to tell me. He'd shown me. Thoroughly and completely.

I located my discarded clothing and put it back on smoothing my hair and draping my towel over the chair to dry, before running my fingers reverentially over the spot on the bed that was still warm from our lovemaking. But even with all that evidence of how right things could be between us there were still those parts that felt wrong. Things I had tried to explain to him. Things I still thought he didn't really understand. Things I had been ignoring for too long because I was so far gone for him.

"Let's go grab something to eat." He emerged from the shower in a cloud of steam drying his hair on a towel that he tossed over mine when he was through.

"Sure," I agreed watching appreciatively as he bent to retrieve his clothing and also noting the red jagged scar on his leg. A grim reminder he would always carry, as if he could ever forget all that he had lost. To me it represented the beginning of the unraveling between us.

Almost losing him.

Getting him back.

But not all of him I was coming to realize.

Only the parts he allowed me to have.

Not the lows he had fallen into after the accident.

And not the highs of success either.

Would he ever share the whole of him again?

I took the hand he offered me trying not to cling too desperately to his fingers as he pulled the door closed and we hit the palm lined sidewalk above the beach toward town. There were a few vendors set up on the plaza in front of the pier when we got there. I bought him a skull ring from one insisting it was a necessity for his new rocker image. And he bought me a silver curb chain with our initials so I could be just as cool, his rocker chick.

My eyes were misty by the time we got a couple of hot dogs and sat on a bench to eat them with the ocean laid out before us like a dispassionate void. The vast expanse of the Pacific once used to settle me and make my thoughts hopeful. Now it seemed capricious and untrustworthy like some aloof entity unmoved by our plight.

I started to turn away from it when I noticed a couple of surfers bobbing side by side on their boards in the waves. They reminded me of Linc and Ash. Linc visibly stiffened when he noticed them and he tried to disguise the longing he felt, but it was obvious and my heart ached right along with him.

"Outside," the one on the right yelled to the other as a steep wave rose and curled over him.

"What does that mean?" I asked Linc. I had heard the term before and wondered but had never had the opportunity to ask.

"That there's a good wave, a surf-able wave coming up behind you," he answered his eyes still trained on the ocean. "Up to you to turn around and take it or get out of the way before it crashes over you."

I popped the last bite of hot dog in my mouth, chewed reflectively and mulled it over watching the surfers. When he finished eating he tossed our cardboard containers and the napkins we had used into the trash bin. I leaned my head against his shoulder as we headed back to the hotel trying to put aside my morose musings and allow the soothing ocean sounds to put my mind at ease.

I frowned when Linc's cell suddenly rang bursting our brief bubble of solitude.

"Yeah," Linc answered…Shit! You're kidding?…No way…Ok…A block once we hit Main Street past the fountain…I got it. We'll meet you there."

"Who was it?" I queried as soon as he hung up. "What's going on?"

"That was Ash. He said they're surrounded by a group of fans at the motel. Apparently they saw the KABC feature and recognized our van. Kind of a unique vehicle. It sticks out if you're looking for it. Guests at the hotel complained about the crowd. The cops are escorting the guys to the club. He said if we're close it'll be easier for us to meet them there."

"Ok." I couldn't quite believe it, but the evidence was hard to ignore. The power of the media had definitely taken our little known local band from OB and turned them into an overnight sensation.

"That's not all."

"Seriously?" I raised my brows.

"Morris apparently is aware of all the coverage we're getting. He told Ash he's sent one of his AR guys to check us out. He's bringing a video crew with him. They're going to record us. If he likes what he sees and hears and if we can keep the momentum going Morris might come talk to us personally when we reach San Fran."

"Congratulations, Linc. That's awesome news." I was so happy for him. He'd been through so much bad. We both had. We were due a break. Tears sprang into my eyes and I launched myself at him throwing my arms around his neck as he spun us both around in a celebratory circle.

Chapter 53

Linc

*H*untington Beach. We crossed the multilane Pacific Coast Highway at a stoplight holding hands. The self-proclaimed Surf City USA had huge two story surf shops at the beginning of its main drag and images of famous surfers stamped into the sidewalk we followed on the way to the club.

I immediately understood why Ash had sounded freaked on the phone when the neon marquee of the Main Street Club came into view. Two news vans waited out front with their crews rolling footage of a crowd of fans holding handwritten Dirt Dogs signs. Mostly girls.

I glanced at Simone to gauge her reaction. She glanced back at me just as stunned. "You think anyone will recognize me?" I posed the question but I didn't get a chance to hear her answer. The video crew had spotted us and the screaming girls drowned out whatever she said.

I wrapped my arm protectively around her shoulder as

the crowd surrounded us pulling her close feeling her unease as were jostled, pinched and prodded under a near blinding light shining down on us from a handheld pole. I continued to press forward in the direction I hoped was the entrance to the club.

When we made it to a velvet rope, the stern faced club bouncer stepped around us and glared at the crowd while opening the glass door for us. I grabbed Simone's ice cold hand and pulled her inside.

"Holy shit!" I exclaimed while looking at her. "Can you believe this?"

Eyes wide she shook her head.

"He's here." A girl with a French braid and wire rimmed glasses spoke into a hand held walkie talkie then motioned for us to follow her. Down a long ramp and through a narrow corridor we went until we reached a door with the club's name on it. She knocked on it twice before pushing it open. The guys were all inside looking excited rather than shaken like we were.

"You guys alright?" Ash immediately came toward us and tagged Simone's free hand pissing me off.

"We're good." I pulled her closer into me. "What the hell's going on? It's pandemonium out there."

"That's what is known as success." Ramon was smiling as he joined us, Dominic, too. "Freakin' unbelievable success," he added unnecessarily. "It must be all those fliers I handed out." His grin widened.

"My transportation skills you mean," Dominic teased playing along.

"My logistics," Ash announced folded his arms over his chest.

"It's all of us." I smiled, too feeling the burden I had been shouldering since the accident easing somewhat. "It's pretty incredible." I kissed the top of Mona's head. "Has anyone talked to the Morris rep yet?"

"No." Ash shook his head. "We were waiting for you. But we saw the cameras being set up all over the joint near the stage and in the audience."

"What's up with all of that?" I asked brows pulling together. "I thought it was just going to be a one camera one angle low cash outlay kind of thing."

"I think Zenith must've decided since they're already out here making sure the Dogs aren't a fluke they might as well get some useful video they can use later if we're not. Hard to fake the kind of energy that's out there right now," Ramon explained. "PR for the group is moving to the next level *vatos*. It's above my pay grade now."

"Yeah free will only get you so far," Dominic joked.

I toned down my smile and turned to the woman with the hand held. "You with the club or Zenith?" I queried.

"Zenith," she confirmed what I suspected.

"Good. I want to talk to Morris right away. Before the show," I clarified.

She moved a couple of steps away and before Ash and I had time to agree on the set list, she swept back and offered me her cell with Morris on the line.

"You wanted to speak to me," he cut straight to the point sounding intimidating as hell.

"Yeah," I pulled in a breath and my grip tightened on Simone's hand. "It's cool that you're interested in the Dirt Dogs." Zenith obviously had the resources to make us a big hit if we could impress them. "But I have a stipulation before we agree to be recorded."

"And that is?" he sounded irritated and my palms got sweaty, but I wasn't going to back down. I had to do this for my girl.

"My girl gets to go out first. She's got a song of her own." She glanced at me sharply. I guess she didn't think I had noticed. I noticed *everything* about her. "I want her to get recorded same as us and then for you guys to take a look when you get around to watching the video of us. That's all." There was no way anyone hearing her sweet voice singing those words wouldn't fall for her and her talent the way I had from the first.

"Fine," Morris agreed quickly, too quickly in my opinion, making me doubt my negotiation prowess. Though the guys beamed proudly I got the impression I probably should have asked for more.

Simone

"I can't do it." I gulped down oxygen in slow shallow sips trying not to hurl at just the thought of going out there and singing in front of all those people. Important people, media and industry types.

"You've got this, Mona. It's nothing you haven't done before."

"At school. In musicals. That one time at the Deck Bar.

But never when it counted so much."

"Relax, babe." He pulled me into his strong capable arms, his warm hands settling on the curve of my hips, his talented fingers rubbing tempting soothing circles into my skin. I drew in his familiar scent, the ocean and sunshine embedded in his skin from all of the hours he spent on his surfboard. Totally and uniquely him. "Listen to me. No one has a voice like you do. I get chills every time I hear it. There's no way they aren't going to fall in love with you the way I have." He eased back his clear blue eyes traveling the length of me, his lip curling in appreciation at what he saw. There wasn't much he couldn't see with my borrowed slinky dress revealing too much thigh and cleavage.

"I'm gonna be sick." I tried to shrug out of his grasp but he held me tightly. "Please, Linc. Let me go." I dropped my chin staring at the silver heart pendent that contained our initials. "I just can't do it. I'm sorry."

"You can." He gently lifted my chin with his curled forefinger. The inexpensive silver skull ring I had bought for him from the vendor on the beach felt cold against my clammy skin. "I'll walk with you right to the stage."

I stilled taking a couple of deep breaths wanting to make him proud. Always wanting to please him. Loving him so desperately with every fiber of my being. Never coming close to imagining how badly he would break me at the end.

I acquiesced to him as easily as Morris apparently had. Who could withstand the power of Linc's personality?

I went out on the stage, Ash accompanying me on keyboard, sang my heart out in my borrowed dress and the audience politely applauded when I was done a scant few but terrifying minutes later.

Linc kissed my head when I exited the stage then he, Ramon and Dominic joined Ash on the stage. I quickly discovered how much louder, rowdier and enthusiastic the crowd could get.

The walls vibrated as soon as the spotlights hit them. Feet stomped. Fans yelled. Some even stood on their chairs. Camera lights clicked on and so did Lincoln. Brightly. He strode to the center of the stage moving without any noticeable limp. Confident. Compelling. Controlled. A cosmic force.

He plucked the mic from the stand glared at the audience daring them to come along with him or get the hell out of the way, before he and the guys launched into a cover of 'Satisfaction' that kicked ass as righteously as the original.

It went uphill from there. Ramon on guitar flashing his flirt. Ash slamming sexy on his drums. Patch firm and steady on bass. And Linc my gorgeous wounded warrior with depths of worth that he still failed to recognize eclipsing them all. The Dirt Dogs might still a bit rough around the edges but they were undeniably on the ascent. What had started out as something to occupy their time when the surf wasn't up had transformed into a magical mélange of Pacific saltwater, California sun and hard rocking in your face attitude.

Sweat plastered Linc's hair to his skull by the time he ended their set with a rousing version of 'Better When Bad', a brand new original Dirt Dog's tune. Confidently. Arrogantly like it didn't matter to him what the audience thought, he carefully returned the mic back to the stand. But they loved him and I think he knew it. They went bonkers as he exited the stage. The noise they generated rang in my ears every bit as loudly as the band's sound had. Beaming Linc came straight to me immediately hoisting me up in a triumphant hug.

"You did it!" He told me as I smiled back into his sparkling clear blue eyes.

"I did ok. You guys were off the charts. Phenomenal." Before he could reply, Dominic called my name moving towards us with an ominous look on his face that made my stomach tighten immediately.

"Your mom's on the phone." She must have gotten his number from Karen. I squeezed Linc's hand and I took the cell Dominic stretched toward me. "It's ok. I'm sure." I gestured toward the rest of the group hovering nearby waiting on him. "Go on start the celebration. I'll just talk to her and come find you in a minute." The guys slapped each other on the back and were talking loudly to each other as they took off.

I covered one ear and pressed the cell to the other so I could hear better. "Hello."

"Simone." Hearing her voice after all this time, after all that had happened made conflicting emotions vie for position within my heart. Anger grappled with a lingering desperation for her approval that made me feel small again. "Baby, I want you to know that I've sobered up. I got a lawyer after your father hit you. I've left him. I moved out. And I'm asking for half of everything."

I felt dizzy. I looked for a chair but not finding one I just sagged into the cold surface of the cinderblock wall. "I need you to come home, Honey. Right away." No inquiry about how I was doing. No apology for anything. "The attorney needs to talk to you. He wants to get your statement about the way your father treated us."

Chapter 54

Linc

sensed something was dreadfully wrong the moment she rejoined us and I saw her drawn features. I set aside the champagne, excused myself from the reporter from KABC and moved across the room taking her hand and pulling her out into the hall. It seemed pretty obvious to me that she was about to break down. Screams from a crowd of restrained fans erupted in the corridor as soon as we emerged.

"Shit!" I cursed and took her directly into a janitor's closet across the hall telling the bouncer guarding the backstage door to keep everyone away.

"What's going on?" I asked pulling a dangling string to illuminate the tiny space. Her grip tightened.

"I've got to go home, Linc. Back to Ocean Beach." She was leaving me? Now? The strong smell of bleach made my eyes burn. "My mom filed for divorce. The lawyer needs my testimony."

Outside

"No," I stated, the denial emphatic instantly angry on her behalf. "Why should you go, Simone? When did she ever stick her neck out for you?"

"But..." she sputtered blinking at me her expression revealing that she hadn't expected those words or the vehement tone I had used when delivering them. "I..."

"But nothing, babe. You're my girlfriend. You don't go traipsing off just 'cause your mommy calls, who I'll remind you did absolutely nothing when your father clocked you. You saw how it was out there tonight. We have to keep that kind of energy up all the way to San Fran to keep Morris interested. I don't know if I can do that without you. I'm not out there for my ego. I'm out there for us. It's our future I'm building. I thought you got that."

She was quiet for a long moment, emotions flickering within her gaze too fast and complex for me to read them. "But she's my mom, Linc," she whispered eventually. "She needs me."

"I need you, too." I told her the honest truth while grasping her by the shoulders to emphasize my point. "And I love you." My voice went raw. "Doesn't that mean anything?"

"Yes of course it does." Her eyes filled. "It means everything. But you have Ash and the guys. She has no one." Her voice was steady but she looked uncertain. So I laid things out more to clarify.

"You are mine, Simone. Dammit. You aren't her little girl anymore. She needs to stand up for herself. Take care of herself."

The way she never took care of you, I thought. *Fuck her.*

Simone dipped her head and an icy trickle of trepidation tiptoed its way down my spine. "She's all I have, Linc. Please understand."

"Fuck that," I said bitterly. I didn't see the big picture in that moment only that she was thinking about leaving me in the here and now. In my mind that slumbering dragon of insecurity awoke and lifted up its fiery red head.

"I'll just be gone for a couple of days, maybe a week and then I'll come right back." Her voice got smaller and smaller. "Don't be mad at me, please."

"No." I released her and took a step back my ass rattling the cleaning supplies on the steel shelves behind me. "I'm not bending on this, Simone. If you go out that door it means you're choosing her over me."

She looked at me with a wounded expression and gathered tears spilled from her pretty honey colored eyes. "You're acting just like my father." Her chin came up to a stubborn angle but I was too full of my own righteous indignation to back down much less admit that she was right.

"And you're acting just like your mother." I lashed right back. "Running away back to what's safe and familiar the moment there's an opportunity to." If she returned to OB I was afraid she would forget us and remember the things she had given up for me, things that I couldn't offer her. A home. College. Her dream. How could I compete with that? All I had to offer her right now were nebulous hopes for an uncertain future.

"You're the one who shut me out," she said bowing her head in defeat.

"Maybe I did. Maybe I have. But maybe that was because I knew where you and I were headed all along." Not true, but once the words were out I couldn't take them back. Old habits of self-preservation had risen to the forefront because I knew she had the power to utterly destroy me. I knew if I let her walk out that door that she wasn't coming back. Away from me she would come to her senses. She would realize what a poor choice I was.

She froze as solid as the ice sculpture on the buffet table in the other room. She didn't speak for several moments. I hated myself in those moments because I could see that I had hurt her, because I knew what was going to happen and because I was no hero after all, just a sorry bastard who couldn't stop the inevitable conclusion to us.

Fucking fake arrogance that was too ingrained to be exorcised.

"The man who took a job at my dad's restaurant just to look out for me. The man who sent his cousin in his place when he couldn't be there. The man who sent me all those notes and pictures. The man who spent all that time on that set up on the boat. The man who pursued me with all of his passion and made love to me with all of his emotion like you have doesn't believe that." Her words sounded certain but she wasn't I could tell. She was unsteady on her feet as she turned slowly away from me and put her hand on the door knob. "I'm going, but I'll be back for that man. For that man I would do anything. For that man I'd risk it all."

Part Three
Present

Chapter 55

Simone

My eyes filled just like they had back then all those years ago when I had walked back to the motel by myself, grabbed what little money I had left, my backpack and the camera Ash had given me and had taken the Coaster back to OB.

Alone.

Losing a little bit of myself with each mile that I had traveled because I had left it with him.

I traced the last picture in the photo album that had started my journey back into the past. My mind wary of reliving any more. Even now after all this time the pain of that loss still threatened to consume me.

Seeming to sense my distress my little Havanese padded into the room and jumped onto the bed beside me pressing his warm body against my leg. I petted him absently while staring at the picture of Linc. So handsome and so young flashing the skull ring I had given him along with his killer smile.

The pages were empty of mementos after that much the way my heart had become. Without its anchor now just like back then my mind slid right back into the past and the events of that fateful day…

"Hey you going in?"

"Huh?" I blinked at the blonde with the heavy makeup. I had been stalled in front of the door to their hotel room too afraid to go in. I could hear the loud music and the laughter inside. Lots of feminine laughter. It sounded like the guys were having a party. It had been a little less than two weeks since I had left him. Two weeks since we had fought at Huntington Beach. Two weeks since he had spoken those harsh words. Two weeks of stress and doubt. It didn't help that I was never able to get a hold of Linc when I called. I had been communicating with Ash instead and received only vague replies to the direct questions I asked about Linc.

My heart thundered in my chest. The courage to come seemed to have abandoned me once I had deplaned in San Francisco.

"The door's open. They always leave it open." The blonde gave me a funny look as she twisted the handle a six pack in her other hand. "As long as you have beer, and… well…you know."

Numbly I followed her flouncing form inside. Typical hotel suite. Definitely larger than the ones I had shared with them. The band had done well. Ash had been forthcoming about that at least, spouting club attendance, receipt tallies, and miles logged on the camper van but never any news about Lincoln. Seems he hadn't needed me all that much after all.

I glanced around the room. At least thirty or forty people were crammed inside. Mostly women. Beautiful women. Some dancing. More than a few not fully dressed. Some talking in groups. Some moving toward the back where I guessed the bedrooms were. Booming bass slammed my chest and I waved a hand in front of my face to dispel a dense cloud of smoke that made my eyes water and that definitely was *not* cigarettes.

I didn't see any of the guys. I felt out of place and my stomach was so knotted I wished I hadn't eaten the doughnut at the airport. That had been a big mistake. Then the group of girls beside me moved away and I was confronted with an even bigger one. Lincoln sprawled out on the couch, his shorts down around his ankles, his eyes closed, his head thrown back, one girl between his legs working him with her hand while two other ones played with the rest of him.

The blood drained from my face. My heart broke. My soul ripped into two separate parts.

Apparently he had never been expecting me to return.

My breath abandoned me. A last tiny flutter of hope extinguished inside my chest and then the partially digested doughnut resurfaced in the back of my throat to gag me.

"Simone. Shit!"

I heard Ash call me but I didn't stop. I couldn't stop. I spun, dodged more incoming girls and reached the railing outside their room just in time to hurl over the side, scalding hot tears blurring my view of the mess I made in the monkey grass down below.

Familiar hands landed on my shoulders and my stomach lurched again. "Why, Ash? Why?" I rasped before heaving once more. When I was certain there was nothing left, I wiped my mouth on my sleeve and curled my fingers around the cold railing. Cold like my heart now, like my body, like my devastated soul.

"I don't know. Because he's an asshole and an idiot I guess. I'm so sorry, Simone. You never said you were coming back whenever we spoke. I didn't expect that you would, neither did he. Maybe before the accident he would've believed you would, but not after. I told you once that Linc's childhood was tougher than he let on and I wasn't lying. The accident ripped more than just his flesh, Mona. It ripped right through his self-confidence. And it was already flimsy after all the years of listening to his old man tell him he wasn't worth anything. I honestly think he's convinced himself that you made the right decision leaving." He gently turned me to face him, sympathy filling his eyes as he attempted to stem the flow of tears that were coming too fast. He smoothed my hair behind my ears. "He went nuts after you left and it got even worse after your mother told him that you had reenrolled at SDSU."

"What?" My pale face went paler and my knees went out from under me.

"Is that not true?" Ash steadied me.

I shook my head a deep sadness and body numbing regret robbing me of speech.

"But when we spoke the first time you told me you

were in the registrar's office."

"I withdrew from the fall semester and was setting up an escrow account with them in case I ever got the chance to attend in the future." My voice was a low rasp.

I knew she probably thought she was protecting me but I couldn't believe my mother had betrayed me with a half-truth.

But then how much of it was really her fault? I should have stayed. And Lincoln should have trusted me to return.

"Maybe you should talk to Linc," Ash said softly.

Too late. It was far too late for that. The inevitable end had come and it was far worse than I could ever have imagined.

"No." I lifted my hand and covered his mouth with my fingers. Something unidentifiable flared in his dark sapphire eyes. "Don't say his name. Don't talk about him." My raw voice hitched. "Don't. Just don't." I started to shake uncontrollably and felt weary to my bones as though I had aged a lifetime in a few moments. I dropped my pounding head to Ash's chest.

A roar suddenly sounded from within the hotel that gave me a chill. My name immediately followed. Someone must have told Lincoln I had come and gone. I started to shake harder.

"Get me out of here, Ash. Please. Please. *Please* get me out of here. I don't want to see him." My chest burned as if it had been set on fire.

"Ok, Mona. Ok," he soothed sweeping me up into his arms just before my wobbly legs went completely out from under me. I clung to him, not registering anything clearly. Him settling me into the van. Me crying even harder. A very short drive to another part of the hotel. Him carrying me across the pavement, producing a key to another room.

"Is this your room?" My teeth started to chatter.

"A friend's."

"But…"

He cut off my protest. "He's a flight attendant. He's gone until tomorrow. It's the only place I could think of on such short notice. You can stay here tonight." He set me down inside a cramped bathroom but I clung to his lavender polo shirt. "Don't leave me alone, Ash."

"I wasn't even thinking about it. Only Simone, I'm afraid you might be going into shock. You need to get out of those clothes and into a hot shower."

"Oh…kkk." I lowered my chin my fingers trembling so bad I couldn't undo the buttons.

Firmly gripping my shoulders Ash peered down at me his sapphire eyes somber. "Will you allow me to help you get undressed? I'll try," he swallowed as if his throat had suddenly gone dry, "I'll try not to look any more than I have to."

"It's ok, Ash. I d.d…don't care." I covered his hands with my own. *He was familiar*, I told myself. *He was safe.* "I understand…"

"I don't think you do," he interrupted. "But we'll talk later when you feel better."

He turned on the water to get it warm and then he undressed me more gently than I would've thought a guy as big as Ash could. Not just the outer layers but my sexy see through bra and my matching panties, too. He avoided eye contact and I started crying again when he laid the expensive lingerie carefully on the vanity counter.

Outside

"It's ok, Simone. It's ok." It wasn't and it would never be but his voice and his manner soothed me. In the end I was too shaken to take care of myself. He had to take off his clothes, too. He held me close to his strong body in the shower under the warm spray until my skin turned red and I stopped shivering.

One muscular masculine arm around my shoulders, he leaned out, popped open the medicine cabinet and withdrew a new toothbrush and toothpaste. I took the brush and unwrapped it from the plastic while he uncapped the toothpaste squeezing a generous amount onto the bristles for me. Attending to me so tenderly.

"Brush," he ordered and I did. I was so grateful to remove the horrible taste from my mouth. I tipped my face up to the spray to rinse and spit into the drain below my feet. "Good girl." He reached over my shoulder to lay the brush and tube on the counter beside my underwear.

I noticed two things. My nipples puckering in response to the inadvertent glide of his forearm against them and the rock hard erection that was pressed against my rear. "Ash." I turned around in his embrace, hand curling around his arm, fingers stroking the fine platinum hairs that covered his tan skin.

"Simone I'm sorry. You're a beautiful woman and I care for you deeply. I can't help my body's response. You're safe. I would never take advantage of you."

"Even if I want you to?" I whispered loud enough to be heard over the running water while peering up at him through my lashes. I needed to be affirmed as a woman and I needed to forever purge the image of Lincoln and his betrayal from my brain.

He squeezed his eyes tightly shut as if he had to close them to resist me. "You don't know what you're asking." His voice was strained and when he reopened his eyes there was a depth of pain within them that didn't make sense to me.

I moved closer pressing my nipples to his chest and reaching up my hand to stroke his face. "It's ok, Ash. I know what I'm doing. I want you. Do you not want me, too? Just a little?" I thought back to all the times he'd been around watching me and Lincoln. The longing looks I had intercepted but pretended not to see.

"I do." He groaned. "But you're too vulnerable right now. And I don't want you to get the wrong idea about what this is, either. I don't want to hurt you anymore than you've already been hurt." He took my hands from his face and gathered them to his chest. "I love you, Simone." My breath caught. "I was jealous at first but then I think I fell for you right along with him. But you need to know that I love him more." His eyes were deep sapphire pools that I had to focus on to maintain my bearings within a world that he'd just completely rearranged with those words.

"You...you love Lincoln?" Saying his name made sharp pain slice through my heart. "Like you want to be with him...physically?"

"Yes." His answer was immediate and sincere.

"But you're his cousin."

"His mother and mine were adopted. We're not really related but we've grown up together so I would never betray that trust or his friendship by crossing any line. I just told you because I want you to understand why we can't be together. It just wouldn't be right. Not when I can't love you fully the way you deserve."

"Oh, Ash." I framed his conflict ravaged face with both my hands finally understanding the sadness that always clung to him while the warm water continued to rain down on us hitting my back, cascading around my shoulders and sluicing down my legs. "I'm so sorry. I never knew."

"No one does. You can't tell anyone."

"I won't. I promise, but…" I was just about to tell him that I still wanted him to make love to me. That we could proceed as friends who understood each other's pain and could give each other the mutual pleasure and comfort that I think we both needed, when there was a loud crash and the sound of splintering wood from the other room.

"What the fuck?" Ash grabbed two towels from the rack throwing one back at me while moving protectively in front of me. He had barely gotten the towel around his waist when Lincoln appeared in the doorway. Hair standing up all over the place eyes wild as they moved back and forth between Ash and me.

"You son of a bitch! I knew there was something going on between you two!" He slapped his hands against Ash's chest shoving him hard. Ash rocked back on his heels but stood firm holding his ground.

"Stop!" I protested hating that I felt guilty as I held the towel in a desperate grip in front of my body. "It's not what you think." I didn't want Ash to get hurt on my account. Lincoln looked like he wanted to murder him. His dark wrathful gaze sliced to me.

He made a hateful sound of disbelief in response to my clichéd excuse before he turned back to his cousin. "How could you do this to me?" The sting of betrayal brightened his eyes and fury mottled his face.

"You did it to yourself. After witnessing that scene in your room, what did you expect? You should be glad it was me and not someone else," Ash said harshly. "Now turn around and get out."

Lost within those memories from the past, in the present my heart raced and my stomach churned anew as I reprocessed the final events that had ruined everything for all three of us.

I didn't even register my cell ringing next to Chulo until the missed call lit up the display.

Then my eyes glazed over one final time and I remembered the rest. How Ash had forced Lincoln into the other room and how their voices had risen in anger then fallen right before Ash had returned and pulled me into his arms.

"He's gone," he had intoned the words like whatever had gone down in the other room had broken him. We were both broken by our love for Lincoln. I threaded my arms around his waist and we clung to each other. "He hates both of us now. But he's gone."

Chapter 56

Simone

My hands shook as I redialed the missed call. The emotions I had relived felt as raw and as incapacitating today as they had been all those years ago. Everything had ended that day. Not just for me and Lincoln but for me and Ash.

Ash and I still only spoke on the phone, brief conversations where we talked about things that didn't really matter. I would often wonder if Lincoln was around listening. Ash invariably stumbled on his words, avoiding painful topics.

"Hey," I greeted when Karen answered rubbing Chulo's soft pink belly as he rolled over in his sleep as limp as a puppet. I had to steer my way clear of the past if only so I could be functional for him. At least somebody needed me, though if he could talk I think Chulo would have insisted that I needed him more. "What's up?"

"Nothing much. I just got in." *Holy shit.* It was late here. She was on the east coast. It was the wee hours of the morning there. "I thought I'd check up on you. We haven't spoken for a week. How are things at the shop?"

"They're ok." I hadn't admitted yet how tight finances were. She had run the surf shop so much more efficiently than I did when she had owned it. "Any extra overstock from last year's line you can send my way?" I inquired.

When Karen left OB she had become a public relations rep for Roxy. She was a senior VP now, traveling all the time and was rarely home in her apartment in New York City anymore. I think she needed to stay that busy. Whereas she had run away from OB and her heartache, I'd run back toward it. But through the highs and lows in both our lives we had remained friends.

"Yeah I've got some good stuff. Backpacks. Jackets. A couple of dresses I think will move well there." She paused and it sounded like she was taking a sip of something. "What's new with you?"

"Lincoln's back in town." I dropped the news without any build up. She reacted much as I expected.

"What?" she screeched. "Back in OB?"

"Yeah." I nodded my head even though she couldn't see me. I was still off kilter and had been since he stepped out of the corner at the Tiki Bar and back into my life requesting the tune I'd been singing when we had met at the beach that first time. "He wants to record 'Save Me' for the next Donovan Blaine film. He's going to produce it and split the royalties with me fifty-fifty."

"That's awesome I think. Sounds like you've already decided to do it. But how do you feel about it?"

"You sound like a shrink." I felt my brows pull together.

"And that I do surprises you, why?"

It didn't. She had spent a lot of time over the years with different ones trying to get the nightmares to go away so she could move on and let go of the past. Our circumstances were certainly entirely different but we both carried our share of pain.

"Is that all he wants..." She let her question hang meaningfully.

"Um, no." My cheeks warmed. Remembering what had almost happened with Lincoln and me in the middle of the day at the shop where anyone could have seen us...*Shit.* I needed to clear the video on the security cameras. "He definitely wants a lot more." And beyond the physical too if I could believe him. Which I wouldn't. That would be crazy. Given our history, I needed to be solidly determined to avoid his advances.

"He still as good looking?" Oh yeah. More so. More confident. More cocky. More mature. Dangerously irresistible.

"Yeah," I understated. Majorly.

"Then I say go for it."

"What?" It was my turn to screech. "Are you insane! You're supposed to be my bestie. You're supposed to look out for me. Tell me to guard my heart and that kind of stuff."

"You two had something incredible," she stated softly, nostalgically in a way that made me think she wasn't just remembering Lincoln and me.

"Yeah something that went incredibly wrong. You of all people know how badly he hurt me and how long it's taken me to move on."

"I do. You're absolutely right." I was a little surprised she pivoted to agree with me so quickly. "Though you really haven't gone on have you, Simone?" That sounded like an admonition. "Listen," she exhaled heavily, "if I could have one more day with Patch, even just one more hour, don't you think I would take it?"

Shit. Shit. Shit.

"Yeah, Karen of course you would. I'm sorry." My heart twisted for her. It always did and I was only a bystander to her pain. She had lived it and survived it. Just barely. "But you know it's not the same. Patch didn't fool around on you after letting you believe he was committed to you." And after marking me so indelibly that now every time another man touched me, I thought of Linc instead and felt unfaithful to him.

"No. But what if he's changed? What if he has regrets? Wouldn't you want to hear about them? It was a crazy time. You were so young and had so much going against you. If your mother hadn't interfered. If you hadn't left. Mistakes were made on both sides. You said so yourself. Don't you think you owe it to yourself to see if there's still something there, if maybe the love you once shared could be rekindled?"

Chapter 57

Linc

S tanding on her porch early the next morning after I had kissed her before she kicked me out of her shop, I was as nervous about how she would receive me now as I had been fifteen years ago when I had entered Napoli's after our chance meeting on the beach.

I waited a beat and knocked again hearing the sound of scrabbling nails on hardwood. Then the sound of snuffling leaked through the crack below the door followed by a squeaky bark. And then her beautiful voice.

"Who is it, Chulo?" she asked flipping on the outside light. The gauzy curtain on the window beside the door fluttered and went back in place. "Go away, Lincoln," she ordered through the door.

"Not happening, Simone," I said firmly dropping my forehead to the wood wishing it was her instead. I used to press my forehead to hers when I had something important to say and wanted her to listen closely. I had been up all night thinking about her and remembering important details like that. Details I had never forgotten.

The dog barked again and scratched the door from their side. At least someone seemed eager to see me. "Open the door, gorgeous." There was no answer for a long protracted moment so I threw down my trump card. "I've got churros in the jeep."

The lock popped instantly, a flood of brighter light from inside blinding me for a minute. No that was a lie. It was she who blinded me standing there in an oversized surf shirt that gave an enticing hint of those luscious tits that I longed to rediscover and capri sweats that sat low on her shapely hips exposing a compelling swath of tanned midriff. My mouth went 'I've been out surfing until midday in the sun without drinking anything but salt water' dry.

A beach ball covered in white and black fur bounced nearly three feet in the air beside me, tongue hanging out, demanding to be noticed.

"Down, Chulo, baby," she scolded her voice sounding husky. Things came together in a rush. That phone call that made me jealous. Had she been talking to the dog the other night and not a boyfriend? I tried to peer beyond her to see if there was any trace of a man in the house.

She scooped the dog up and put him under her arm like an accessory. He relaxed into her as if boneless. She giggled when he licked her and snuggled into her chest.

Lucky damn dog and apparently serious competition for her affection.

"You said something about churros," she reminded me, eyes narrowing as she looked at my empty hands.

"Yeah in the car. Coffee, too. I thought we might go to

Sunset Cliffs. Have a picnic breakfast together. Watch the sunrise. Talk before you go to work."

Several emotions passed through her eyes. Hurt. Longing. Desire. Hunger. For me or the damn churros I wasn't entirely sure but I'd take whatever I could get at this point. I just wanted to spend time with her again.

"Alright," she agreed. "But I need to get a jacket and put Chulo up. He does fine at the beach by the pier but Sunset has too many crumbly cliffs and he has a tendency to wander off."

"Ok." Elation spiked within my heart that she was agreeing to come. I tried not to read too much into it but I failed abominably.

"Stay here," she ordered her expression stern before she shifted and pointed to the pale blue couch in the living room just behind her. "Don't wander." She hurried off, dog in tow his plume like tail wagging. I watched her cute ass sway until she disappeared into what appeared to be a kitchen on the other side of the room.

Before I had time to scoot back and get comfortable she reappeared sans Chulo. She glanced at me nervously before moving past. Her bare feet padded on the hardwood surface of the stairs as she flew up them.

Needing to distract myself from thoughts about Simone disrobing without me, I looked around for something to read. The coffee table was empty except for one thick photo album. Curious I picked it up.

My sudden intake of air did nothing to relieve the tight pressure inside my chest. With shaking hands and burning eyes I flipped rapidly through the pages that contained images of her, of us and the band on our SoCal mini tour back when she had still been mine. The sweetest of sorrows pierced my heart.

I didn't hear her return at first. I had frozen on a picture of her. The one at San Clemente the morning after we had made love on the beach, the same day Ash had given her the camera. Her eyes sparkled, her face was lit from within. Pure captivating beautiful Mona fire. I remembered it had been Ash and not me who had taken the picture.

"So beautiful." I ran my fingers reverentially over the image knowing she was watching silently, caressing the one dimensional image before I looked up to acknowledge the real beauty. I knew my eyes were burning with an emotion she wasn't ready to receive from me yet but I didn't care.

"I loved you so much," she whispered emphasis on the past tense. The sweet sorrow began to blaze painfully within my chest. I closed the book carefully and set it back on the table.

"Interesting reading you were doing last night," I guessed. I hoped. How could she look at those pictures and only remember the bad? "I thought you told me yesterday that you had put them all away."

She opened her mouth maybe to deny it but she snapped it shut. A wry 'I've been caught and I might as well own up to it' look filled her gaze instead.

"Busted," I said.

She nodded.

Seemed she was still quick to let things go that were minor. Could we get beyond the major?

"C'mon, gorgeous." I stood and slipped my arm around her. "You look cute as hell in that hoodie and it would be a shame not to get your churro before it gets cold."

After I helped her into the passenger side of the jeep, rounded the hood, fired up the engine and maneuvered onto Sunset Cliffs Boulevard, she proceeded to rock my world some more by giving me an opening I'd never in my wildest dreams imagined receiving.

Maybe it was the Broadway music flooding the interior. The same music we had made love to that unforgettable first time.

Or maybe she noticed how hard I had to grip the steering wheel to keep from touching her after inhaling her familiar sweet gardenia scent.

Or maybe it was just the churros.

"You were the best thing that ever happened to me, Lincoln Savage. And the worst." I turned my head to look at her. The surface of her eyes was glassy. I would be lying if her confession didn't make mine sting just as sharply. She turned away after detonating that bomb, dropping her chin to her chest and twisting her hands together.

The center of my chest was raw as if her words had been shrapnel but I managed to get the jeep down the road and through the couple of stop signs necessary to get us to the cliffs. I slid the jeep into a parallel parking space, flipped the ignition off and rolled the power windows down. I needed to hear the thunderous roar of the waves below us and I needed to feel the soothing ocean breeze on my skin. Formulating my thoughts I stared at the blue water of the Pacific and watched an arc of spray blast into the air when a stubborn wave smashed into the craggy rocks below. I felt like those damn rocks, ravaged by the years apart from her.

"You were my shield, Mona. My buffer from the hell my life was before you. The hell it turned into after you left."

"Do you really expect me to believe that? You're a rock star now, Linc. You have tons of money. You can have anything you want, any woman you want whenever you want, however you want."

"The rock star part is debatable. For a while we were maybe. But you were there in the beginning. You know it's all marketing, logistics and a lot of fuckin' luck. I have some money now, sure. I can buy things. And there were other women. But none of them were you. They didn't care about me. They just wanted to sleep with someone famous. That's not a life. That's purgatory. But the real reason my life has been hell is because I've had to live it without you."

She inhaled sharply but I didn't turn to look into her eyes. Gaze straight ahead I laid it bare.

"Ash told me everything."

"Meaning what exactly?" she asked slowly and carefully.

Yeah she, Ash and I were a minefield that needed to be carefully negotiated.

"Everything," I said turning my head to finally look at her. She had her seatbelt off and her legs folded to her chest. Her eyes widened.

"But only just recently, Mona. I don't think he ever would have told me if not for…" I pressed my lips together. That part wasn't for me to share. I returned my gaze to the ocean, fingers tightening around the steering wheel. I worried about Ash. "We have an outdoor concert Friday night at Humphrey's by the Bay. Ash wants me to bring you so he can talk to you himself. I told him I didn't know if you would come."

"I'll come." She covered one of my hands with one of her own. The elation that surged through me from just that one meaningful touch, a sign that she still cared was crazy, but that was her. Still the tenderhearted girl I had fallen in love with back then and that I had never gotten over. She was still there behind the beauty of the grown woman who sat beside me. The turbulence that had raged within me since I set out to win her back settled like a wave coming home to a welcoming shore.

Keeping my gaze forward, I plunged into deeper, potentially more treacherous water.

"When you left me at Huntington Beach I didn't believe you'd ever come back. Why would you after we fought and I said such horrible things to you?" I blew out a ragged breath remembering how quickly I had unraveled without her to hold the seams of my life together. "Your love, Mona and the kind of loyalty you showed me all along, defying your father, leaving your home and your dreams behind for me..." My heart swelled and my throat closed. There weren't words to do her justice. I still had difficulty fathoming the depths of her. "You were too perfect for the boy I was. Too unbelievable a gift for someone so broken and confused."

"I'm not perfect, Linc. I wasn't. I told you so. I should have stayed with you. I should have tried harder to find a compromise."

I shook my head. "It was all on me, babe." I turned to

look deep into her beautiful golden eyes and saw that the light wasn't completely out, just dimmed. There were embers that I could stoke to a flame if she would let me. "You were right about everything you told me back then. I was holding back. I was afraid. I was so busy trying to find myself that I lost track of you in the process. You were like the perfect wave but instead of turning around and swimming toward you with all I had in me I went the opposite way, the wrong way."

Any direction that took me away from her was the wrong way.

I took her hand that still covered mine and brought it to my face brushing my nose to her wrist inhaling deeply, filling my lungs with her sweet fragrance and pressing my lips to the pulse point that was as close as I could get to her precious heart...for now.

"I'm sorry, so sorry that I didn't believe in you or in us enough. When your mother told me you had re-enrolled it was confirmation that one of my biggest fears had come true. I went completely insane after that. Full on self-destruct mode. Booze and drugs. I tried everything to drown the memories. None of it worked, though. Nothing was right after you left. Not a fucking thing." I looked into her eyes and saw the corresponding darkness and desperation that had burdened us both since San Francisco.

"I should have called you at the very least no matter what your mother said, no matter what Ash believed, but I wasn't capable of rational thinking at that time. I just kept telling myself that you had made the right choice, the best choice, that if I loved you I had to let you go. And then it was too late for us. I'm sorry I hurt you. You were my hope. The light that made every bit of misery I had before you burn away. You are a fire in my blood that can't be put out. My life has been empty since I lost you. I've just been treading water ever since. On the outside of my own life watching it pass me by." I brought her hand to my cheek and peered deeply into her eyes vowing. "But now I've found you again, Mona and this time I'm here to stay."

Chapter 58

Simone

I pondered Linc's words munching a sweet cinnamon churro as he drove us downtown and parked in front of my shop.

On the way he had mostly talked about inconsequential things telling me about some of the places he had been on tour and how he wanted to go back to his favorites with me. He also told me more about Diesel the guy who had replaced Patch on bass. He was an old buddy of Linc's from the qualifying circuit. He had quit competitive surfing over some kind of domestic dispute. And apparently he hated women. *All* women. I found that intriguing and wondered what had happened to make him so bitter.

But Linc's words were what I thought about most, his apology and the declaration that had followed, affirming that our love had been true and meaningful to him, too. Those words seeped through the cracks that time and doubt had left behind and went a long way toward initiating the process of healing.

"Let me stay with you today." Linc turned off the ignition and turned to face me.

"Pfft. Lincoln Savage stocking shelves and ringing up sales? Don't be ridiculous."

"I'm not Lincoln Savage when I'm with you. Just Linc. I had an identity crisis back then. I thought what was important was what I did or what I accomplished. It's not. It's more simple and yet much more profound. What's important is who I am when I'm with you. The man who makes you light up. That's the real me. The man I always want to be. You saw it in me back then. It took me a lot longer to see it myself, but that guy is still here, Mona. I'm sitting right beside you. I never went away. I just went into hibernation for far too fucking long."

I was captured by his gorgeous eyes, the blue sparkling with sincerity. I knew he was telling the truth. I felt it. I saw it. And deep down I responded to it just the same as I had before. He was still the man I had loved and yet he was also more. I wanted to learn about that more. I wanted him to share that with me along with everything else he had done since we had parted. And even deeper down I realized that it wouldn't be hard for me to fall for him again. It would be easy. Frighteningly effortlessly easy.

"Ok, Linc." His eyes widened. He was obviously surprised I had agreed. "Come with me. You can help me reach the tall shelves. I'm sure you'll charm the customers and heaven knows you certainly know more about surfing than I do."

He got out of the jeep and came around to open my door his loose limbed stride confident and sexy. My gaze slowly meandered upward over the dark denim that encased his long legs, the worn belt around his trim waist and the heather grey Hurley t-shirt that clung to his chiseled chest in all the right places. I licked my lips and stepped out onto the pavement forcing myself to look away from all of that masculine perfection. My shoulder brushed into his side as he shut the door. Just the light touch was enough to make my legs shaky with desire.

I hurried to the shop hearing the beep of the locks acutely aware of his enticing heat the minute he moved in behind me. Heat that had recently felt so good pressed against me just skin to skin. He and I together had always been so incredibly good. No other man compared ever since that first gentle kiss at the Deck Bar when he had re-arranged my world.

A fine tremor shook my hand as I popped on the lights. He scanned the interior much like he had the first time then his gaze returned to me. "What should I do first, boss lady?"

His words were teasing but his voice was noticeably thick, perhaps remembering the passionate tangle from the other day. Hmm, I needed to keep him busy and myself out of that kind of trouble. I smiled, a little wickedness rising up within me.

"Well…" I paused for effect. "I usually start by cleaning the restroom."

Outside

After tackling that chore without any complaint beyond rolling his eyes Linc had followed me around the shop as though he were my shadow. A gorgeous nearly six foot two shadow whose scent gave me palpitations.

The dozen customers who came in gravitated toward him and he won them over effortlessly just as I had predicted. I was pretty sure they had all purchased more than they'd planned just to see him flash his dimpled smile.

I understood the allure. Completely.

"Hey, gorgeous." His shirt settled back into place and the tantalizing glimpse of skin disappeared as he popped the last box of Roxy flip flops into position on the top shelf. He had organized them all for me by sizes. I never seemed to have enough time to do that. "It's noon. You want me to run over to the Mexican place and grab us a couple of take-out burritos?"

"Yeah, sure." My mouth watered. Churro power could only take a person so far. "That would be great."

He moved toward the door but I stopped him just as he put his hand on the glass.

"Linc," I called.

"Yeah?" His sandy brown hair brushed over his shoulder as he looked back at me.

"Thanks for helping out today." I swallowed powering through to say the rest. "It's been really nice having you around actually."

"You sound surprised."

"I am a little, I guess."

He looked a little sad for a moment then smiled the Linc dimpled special. My heart summersaulted just like it used to way back when.

"We were always good together, Mona. Better together than apart. It will be my pleasure to help you remember."

The shop bell jingled just as I was putting away some of the winter things in the back. I was trying to be productive while I waited for Linc to return with our lunch. I climbed down from my ladder and dusted off my cutoffs, a smile accompanying my greeting when I peeked at the camera and saw who it was.

"Hey," I began.

"Where the hell have you been?" Patrick's voice echoed off the shop walls as he came barreling toward me in his Hodad's t-shirt and jeans.

"You mean this morning?"

"Yeah this morning." He stomped toward me limbs noticeably stiff and the closer he got the more I realized how worked up he really was. Waves of intensity rolled off his tall frame. "A guy tells a girl things like I told you and they share a kiss like the one we did and that guy has certain expectations, Simone." Grey eyes stormy he grasped my shoulders and pulled me close removing all the distance between us. "You're always at the beach. Every morning." He stroked my cheek with a finger. "I was worried."

I thought there had been a choice between him and Lincoln but I'd been deceiving myself. What man could ever compete? The only choice really was whether or not I was going to risk my heart being broken a second time.

Outside

"I had breakfast with Lincoln." I pulled in a fortifying breath. "And he's been here at the shop helping out today. You're a terrific friend, Patrick. One of the few I'm lucky enough to have. One of the few people I trust."

"Oh, hell no," he muttered gaze sliding away. "Do *not* give me the I want to be just friends speech." His smoldering grey gaze drifted across my features and lower before it came back up darker than before. "You seem...different," he decided. "What's happened?" He frowned. "Don't tell me you slept with him?"

I brought my hands up to Patrick's forearms. He was such a large guy my fingers looked puny resting on top of them and when I flexed my fingers I realized how rigid his corded muscles were. "That isn't any of your business." I kept my gaze level with his by craning my neck back.

"Not true." His raven black brows came together over sexy eyes almost as mesmerizing in their uniqueness as Linc's. "And I already laid out the reasons why beneath the pier the other day. What's going on Simone? You're not the type to get her head turned around just because a guy's famous and some of his music videos have near a hundred million hits on YouTube. Something's changed with you and with us. I can tell, and I wanna know what and why."

"Nothing's changed. Not really." I pulled in a deep breath for courage before saying the words aloud. "But you were right. I *am* still in love with Lincoln."

"Ridiculous, Simone. No way. How can you be? That all was so long ago."

"I know it's hard to understand but Linc and I are like two halves that make up one whole. We don't work right apart. I think we were always meant to be from the very beginning. Even with so much against us." Still against us. Unless I put myself out there again, came to terms with the past and gave us another chance to move forward. "You deserve to know the truth. That I wake up missing the comfort of his arms around me. That I go the beach every morning because that's where I feel the closest to him." Where the memories were the strongest. Where we made love so many incredible times. "And that I go to sleep…"

"Enough." He shrugged away from my touch, his eyes hooded but not so much that I didn't see the flash of hurt within their grey depths. "That's enough. I get the picture." His voice was deeper than I had ever heard it and I realized in that moment as we held each other's gazes that I'd been deluding myself in another way. Patrick Donegal wasn't a boy. He was a man, all man and at the moment he was a heartbroken one.

"I've been patient with you. Too patient it seems. No more. I'm not the kind of guy to give a woman ultimatums but in this case I think it's my only recourse." He reached for my hand, lifted it to his mouth and ran my fingertips across his firm lips while watching me with heated eyes. I felt a warm shiver roll through me. Patrick was an intense good looking guy no doubt. I cared about him deeply and he cared about and had looked after me for a while now. But he wasn't Linc the boy who had rearranged my world fifteen years ago and the man who had returned apparently determine to do it once more. Permanently.

The scales didn't weigh in Patrick's favor that when he brought my hand to his lips it reminded me of when Linc had done something similar only hours ago. Only with Linc I hadn't just felt a body shiver, it had been my heart that felt his passion and my soul that had been stirred by his words.

"Patrick, I..."

"Two years," he cut me off. "He's been back less than a week. Don't throw us away and the potential we have to be so much more. Don't decide now. Think about it. Come to our show. Tell me your answer then. Choose me, Simone." He gently framed my face with his strong hands. "The more I could give you if you'd only let me," he whispered low and passionately, "would rock your world Simone Bianchi. Guaranteed."

Chapter 59

Linc

Simone was strangely distant when I returned with lunch. I didn't have time to question her or to push to get us back to the easiness we'd found earlier because we got too busy. A bus full of women from an intramural softball team descended on the shop. It took the two of us working nonstop together till closing snagging bites of cooling food between turns at the register to take care of all of them.

"We did it." She gave me an exhausted smile after escorting the last customer out the door and flipping the 'closed' sign over.

"You did it," I clarified. "You're really good with the customers."

She shrugged seeming uneasy with my praise.

"You barely ate anything." No wonder she wasn't eating right. She really needed two people at the shop. "Why don't we go to dinner together?"

Outside

Her lush lips flattened. "I don't think that would be a good idea."

I didn't even attempt to hide my disappointment, though I was grateful for the day with her. Every minute I spent with her was a gift.

"I'm really tired." Her expression was gentle, her eyes full of the sparkle I had missed. Another bittersweet arrow to the heart. How had I ever let her get away from me?

"I understand." I did for sure, I just didn't like it. "Would you let me walk you home past the pier? I'd like to show you something."

She raised a brow.

I laughed. "Nothing like that. Something I've been working on. Something Ash and I have been working on together. I think you'll like it."

"Ok," she agreed and we set off together after she powered off the POS system, turned off the lights and locked up the shop.

Downtown was busier than it had been in the morning. A line stretched down the sidewalk to get into Hodad's so we moved to the other side of the street. When we reached the public parking lot by the beach I steered her to the left placing my hand in the small of her back. I was extremely pleased when she let me keep it there. I kept glancing at her. She was so beautiful with wisps of her sun burnished cinnamon hair floating around her face. I couldn't get over the fact that I was with her again.

"What?" she queried noticing my interest. "Do I have burrito in my teeth or churro sugar in my hair?"

"No. You're just so damn beautiful you take my breath away."

She stumbled a step and I helped right her. "I'm just wearing the sweats I slept in last night and flip flops, Linc," she muttered.

"Doesn't matter. Beauty like yours doesn't need outer trappings. Hey, hold up. We're here." I pulled out my keys and took her hand to stop her.

She looked up at the door to the dilapidated building Ash and I had purchased at a bargain price. "Why are we stopping at Patrick's apartment building?"

I frowned. "He lives on the third floor?"

She nodded looking perplexed so I clarified by opening the door and flipping on the lights.

"Whoa," she said glancing around at the interior and I imagined seeing it for the first time. Wires hanging from the ceiling. The soundproof floors covered with protective paper. The wood frames where the walls for the individual recording rooms would be. "What is this? A studio?"

"Yeah." I tried not to look too proud but I was. Excited, too.

"You and Ash are putting together a recording studio here in OB? Right by the pier?"

"Yeah, gorgeous. I told you. OB is home and where you are is where I want to be."

"Ash, I don't know alright? I brought her the churros. You were right she still loves them. I showed her the studio. I laid everything out for her." Even so I didn't see a whole lot of evidence that she was softening. I ran a frustrated hand through my hair and looked around at my empty hotel room. "She's definitely listening though. It's just…"

"You giving up already?" He sounded irritated. "You gonna run away from her again just because it might be hard to win her back? We talked about this. You knew going in the tide was going to be against you. That you were going to have to be patient. That it was going to take time and more than just words. You just need to keep showing her that you two belong together."

"I know, asshole," I grumbled without any heat. He and I were at a real good place. Had been for a while but even more so since he had come clean about everything with her. Knowing the truth, knowing the man I loved like a brother and the woman I loved with all my heart had never slept together helped make things a lot less complicated between the three of us. "But you know how I feel about her. I've waited so long and she's right here." Where the memories were so strong. With her, her tempting bright smile, her intoxicating scent. With all that she meant to me.

"Yeah, then what's the real problem? I get the idea there's something else."

Someone else. "There's another guy," I admitted. Younger. Good looking. Kind to her. Serious competition.

"They exclusive?"

"Hell, no." She hadn't even realized he was into her until I had pointed it out. "Just another interested party."

"Surprised there's just one," he muttered.

"Not helping, brother," I grumbled.

"Sorry, dude. Just keeping it real. Listen you just need to be honest. Tell her that letting her go was the biggest mistake you ever made and keep reminding her every chance you get how well you guys work together. What? Ok." I heard another voice. "Hey Linc, hold on for just a minute. One of the contractors needs to ask me something." There was a pause on his end and the sound of a buzz saw and hammering got louder. I heard him speaking to someone else before he spoke to me again. "Simone still as pretty as she was back then?"

"Even more beautiful."

"Damn."

My cell beeped in with someone on the other line. "I've got another call. I better take it." In case it was Simone. Ash clicked off and the other call came on. I froze solid knowing something was wrong the instant I heard her panicked voice.

"Linc, I need your help."

"Absolutely. You've got it. What's going on?"

"It's Chulo. I need to get him to the emergency clinic but my car won't start." Her heavy breath puffed into my ear. "He chews everything. Paper especially. I can't even put toilet paper on the holder or he gets it, shreds it and strews it all over the house."

She was so nervous and talking so fast that her words were running together. "Slow down, babe. I don't get why that's relevant. Did he get into something dangerous?"

"Yes, I think. A gag gift Karen sent me. She knows how much I liked the *Fifty Shades of Grey* movie." She did? That was news to me. Very interesting news. But I set that aside for future reference focusing on the rest of what she was saying. "The Christian Grey figurine inside was one of those sponge type things that swells up to twenty-five times its original size when you put it in water."

I barked a laugh imagining it.

"Yeah, I thought it was funny, too. Karen's got a quirky sense of humor. And at first I was amused when I saw Christian's little orange arm hanging out of Chulo's mouth, but then I got to thinking. What if Chulo actually swallowed one of the pieces? What if it swells up in his stomach, Linc? Won't that hurt him?" Her breath hitched.

"Don't think like that," I said firmly swiping the jeep keys from the hotel dresser in my room. "I'm on my way to the car to come get you. Check the house. Try to round up all the pieces that you can. Maybe he didn't eat any of them. Try to see if you can put Christian back together. But we'll take him to get an x-ray just to make sure."

"Ok." She was quiet for a moment. Looking for parts of the Grey doll, maybe? "Thank you, Linc."

"No problem. Hold tight, gorgeous. I'll be there in a couple of minutes."

Simone

/ clung to Linc's hand while we waited in uncomfortable plastic chairs at the emergency veterinary clinic.
I had found a lot of the pieces. Enough to reassemble most of the doll on the kitchen counter but there were still enough pieces missing to give me cause to worry.

MICHELLE MANKIN

"What time is it?" I asked Linc again.

"Five minutes since the last time you asked," he said gently.

"Ok." My fingers flexed in his while my stomach rolled. "I love him so much."

"I know you do, babe." He swiveled, the motion stretching the black Henley he wore tighter across his chest. His jean clad thigh pressed into my bare skin. I had been at home in my cut offs and a Roxy t-shirt planning dinner when I discovered what Chulo had done. "You dote on him and he adores you. Anyone can see that." Studying me closely as he spoke Linc took both of my hands and tucked them into his. "How long have you had him?"

"Since he was a puppy. After my mom died, I was lonely." Lonelier would be more accurate. I'd been missing my other half, lost and adrift from the moment he and I separated. "Karen suggested I get a dog or a man."

"Gotta say I'm glad you chose the dog." His ocean blue eyes were soft, his hair a wild halo around his head that I wanted to run my fingers through. He smiled his dimpled smile, familiar and comforting and I was distracted enough by its appearance to forget my present worries if just for a moment.

"Yeah, me, too," I said offhandedly without even realizing how much those words gave away. Linc squeezed my hands and I cast my glance back to the door they had taken Chulo through.

"Was he cute as a puppy?"

I nodded, my gaze returning to Lincoln's handsome face. "He was so tiny he fit inside my hand. He used to lie on his back and sleep on my lap while I worked on the

342

computer. He follows me everywhere…" I trailed off as the door to the back suddenly popped open. I jumped to my feet and Lincoln stood with me, steadying me with his strong arm around my shoulder.

"The x-rays were completely negative." The lab tech emerged with Chulo in her arms. Lincoln gave me a celebratory hug and pressed a firm kiss onto the top of my head. Chulo squirmed in the tech's arms and I reached for him taking him from her and then sagging into Lincoln's side. He turned so he could wrap his arms around both Chulo and me. Warm, protected, held in his familiar embrace I felt something settle into place inside of me, a piece that I had been missing for a long time.

Chapter 60

Linc

I pulled the jeep into her driveway and parked right alongside her marooned Accord. Seven thirty exactly. I killed the ignition and stared up at the brightly illuminated porch. I recalled another night, one when she had snuck out and come to me and slept in my arms for the first time.

I closed my eyes trying to slow my hammering heart. This was so important. *She* was so important. I still was having trouble believing that she had agreed to go out with me. But then again, maybe some of those old feeling were beginning to awaken in her.

I wiped my sweaty palms on my dark jeans and got out pocketing the keys, slamming the car door closed and raking my hair from my eyes as I turned.

She must have heard me pull up. She was already on the front porch seeming frozen in place as she returned my perusal. Was that sparkle in her eyes because she was just as eager as I was to go out on this date together or just a reflection of the porch lights?

"I just need to lock up." She waved her ring of keys in the air. I nodded while leaning against the door of the jeep greedily taking her in with my gaze.

The white dress she wore clung to her delectable body. It accentuated her awesome tits, dipped in at her waist and flared out just a bit around her fabulous hips.

My mouth went dry.

I needed some water.

My lungs were tight.

I needed some air.

She turned around and smiled hesitantly at me.

My heart leapt in my chest.

I was going to need a doctor.

No.

I just needed her.

I pushed away from the jeep meeting her halfway, sliding my hand to her lower back as I walked her to the passenger side.

"You look fantastic," I said leaning over her door and looking down at her as she fastened her seatbelt, my gaze lingering on her shapely calves where her golden skin was all shiny and glossy. Had she just slathered lotion on them?

My cock got even stiffer in my jeans imagining her standing naked to perform the task with one leg on the bed and her slippery fingers gliding over that sexy body of hers, or better yet my slippery fingers gliding all over her sexy body.

"Did you say something?" She peered up at me through thick lashes. Had I groaned out loud?

"Um, no, gorgeous. Just waiting for you to get buckled in." I carefully closed her door and rounded the hood telling myself to keep a lid on my fantasies or I was never going to make it through the evening without putting them into action in the first private spot I could find.

Somehow I got us backed out of the driveway on the pavement without sideswiping her car or popping up on the curb. My meandering thoughts about the goddess by my side left little room for mundane concerns such as driving.

"How is Chulo?" I asked.

"He's doing great, thanks to you."

"How about work?" I had thought about her all day hating that contractor woes had kept me from helping her again at the surf shop. I drank in her delicious profile before reluctantly setting my gaze back to the road and turning left on Point Loma.

"I had a couple of tourist groups come in. I topped a thousand in sales."

"Another strong day. That's great. Anything else interesting happen?" I flipped on the indicator and steered us south onto Nimitz Boulevard grateful to discover the traffic was light on the busy north south thoroughfare.

She paused so long before answering that I risked another longer glance at her at the stoplight. "Nothing really." She twirled a long caramel lock around her finger. Her nervous tell.

"I'm thinking maybe that's not the truth, babe." She turned to look at me her eyes hooded, betraying that whatever had occurred wasn't trivial. I suspected it involved me in some way. An idea came to mind that had me tightening my grip on the wheel. I stiffly steered the jeep left onto

Harbor Island Drive. "This 'nothing' have anything to do with Patrick?"

Biting her lip and staring at the silver masts and glowing blue outlines of sails on the Shelter Island welcome sculpture as if it were somehow fascinating, she nodded.

"He know you and I were going out tonight?" *He know you belong to me and that if he touches you I'll break every one of his fingers? Simmer down, Savage. She's here with you now. Not him.*

I parked the car in front of the Old Venice awning and unbuckled my belt before I swiveled in my seat to face her. "What exactly *does* he know about you and me?"

"He knows we had a serious past." She held my gaze. "And that you're back now and…" She hesitated then pressed on. "I told him how I feel about you."

"And how do you feel about me, Mona?"

Eyes brightening, she shook her head refusing to share.

She had given me an opening the other morning. I decided to return the favor now untangling her clasped hands, taking one and threading my fingers between hers before recapturing her gaze. "If I could have anything I wanted in the entire world it would be you. And you telling him you still have feelings for me and that you've never been able to forget me because that's exactly how I feel about you."

"Linc," she whispered her golden eyes flaring and her fingers tightening on mine. "I don't understand if that's how you feel, how you've felt all along, why did you wait so long to come back?"

"Because I'm an idiot, Simone. Because it took me this long to get my shit together well enough that I felt I legitimately had something to offer you."

"But…"

"That's the short answer. We'll talk more over a nice meal together."

Chapter 61

Simone

Linc let my hand go but only for the amount of time it took him to come around to open my door for me. After that his grip on me remained firm, his hand warm, familiar and proprietary as we checked in with the hostess. We then passed through the driftwood paneled restaurant on our way outside to a walled off courtyard with a single table beside a romantic tinkling fountain.

"This is lovely," I commented appreciatively taking the chair he pulled out for me and leaning forward across the red and white checkered table cloth as he took his own seat. "But it smelled even better in there. The garlic. The fresh baked bread. The tomato sauce and basil." My stomach grumbled its approval.

"Yeah but it's more private out here and the view is definitely better." He trailed off fingers soft across the round of my cheek before he leaned back into his chair straightening the cuffs on his black linen shirt.

"I couldn't agree more." I stared into his clear blue eyes meaningfully, completely captivated by the way they captured the glow of the tiny lights twinkling in the tropical foliage all around us.

He grinned approvingly and I was dazzled anew by how handsome he was with his tousled sandy brown high-lighted hair and his half dimpled smile. I also had to admit to myself how much I had missed seeing him after he had come to my rescue the other night. My day had been dull in his absence.

A waiter suddenly appeared. Linc ordered a water for himself and a Longfin Lager for me after receiving my nod of approval. I continued to bask in the compelling aura of the powerful man before me who was at once comfortably familiar and yet mysterious and new owing to the years the two of us had weathered apart.

Once we had our drinks and had settled on a pepperoni white pizza to share, he lounged in his chair the backs of his masculine hands sprinkled with fine hair folded together under his strong chin as he regarded me. "Tell me what you've been up to these past years. Did you ever go back to college?"

"Yes." I was surprised Ash hadn't told him. "I used what was left in the escrow fund from the semester I sat out and some of my own savings for the first two years. Then my mom paid for the rest after the divorce was finalized."

"It seemed from the way you spoke of her the other day that you two had made amends."

"Yes. My mother had herself been so cowed and abused by my father that she had no self-esteem to stand up to him. That is why she drowned herself in alcohol. Miraculously something awakened in her the night you rescued me from him. She found an inner strength that propelled her to break free. She stopped drinking. She apologized as only a mother can, for allowing me to be ensnared in the cycle of abuse. We cried and then we held onto each other. Love melted all the bad memories away. She flourished and we found we totally enjoyed each other's company. After I finished school she was the one who encouraged me to move to New York."

He suddenly looked a little wistful as though lamenting those lost years. Maybe he was. I had been able to follow his career easily enough through the media. My career had never gotten big or bright enough to draw that kind of attention.

"How did that go?" he asked. "I bet you dazzled them all."

"Not so much." I tried to downplay the disappointment I'd felt when I remembered that time in my life. It had never been what I had thought it would be.

"Then they must have been complete idiots." He leaned forward and took my hands. "It's not too late to try again if that kind of thing still interests you. After this Blaine thing debuts I have a feeling you're going to get lots of calls."

"Maybe," I allowed pasting on a weak smile.

"How long were you out there?"

"Three years. I gave it a good go." One attempt at a relationship that ended up going absolutely nowhere. Lots of off, off, off Broadway performances. We both leaned back when the pizza arrived and he served us pieces with the spatula on the smaller plates that the waiter had provided.

"What did you think about the city?" he asked after taking a bite and dripping a small spot of sauce outside the outline of his chiseled lips. I gestured toward it by pointing toward my own chin but really wishing I would have been brave enough to remove it myself, but not with a napkin, with my lips or my tongue.

"It was exciting, loud, vibrant and overwhelming at times," I admitted. "I'm glad I did it but I missed the sound of the ocean." And the connection I felt to him at home in OB.

"What brought you back?" he inquired after serving me my second and himself a third slice.

"Karen and I kind of switched places. She sold me the shop after Patch died and..." I trailed off noticing the flash of strong emotion in his eyes.

"I'm sorry." My throat tightened and my voice reflected the strain. "I didn't realize you two had remained close. You weren't at the wedding or the funeral. I just assumed that..."

"That I was a heartless bastard too self-absorbed to attend?"

That was exactly what I had thought. I looked down at the napkin in my lap. The beer and the pizza with the garlic, Alfredo sauce, mozzarella, fontina, ricotta and parmesan that had tasted so delicious a moment before now sloshed together in my unsettled stomach.

"He invited me to the wedding but the Dogs were so big by then I knew that my appearance would just have made it into a circus." I looked up to find myself immediately ensnared by his intense gaze. His voice was much lower when he continued. "Plus I knew you would be there and that I wouldn't have been able to handle seeing you."

"It was a beautiful wedding," I whispered with tears filling my eyes. "They were so in love." I shut my eyes briefly against the onslaught of images that came into my mind of the two of them together. When I reopened them he was still gazing at me just as intently as before. "Did you not go to the funeral for the same reason?"

"No." His eyes brightened and his tone turned self-condemning. "For that one I was too fuckin' blitzed to clear customs out of Japan." He glanced away looking embarrassed. "I don't know how much of my life you might have seen played out over the years in the media but if you saw much of it you'd know it wasn't pretty."

I knew. I'd seen. But I hated that every single muscle in his body appeared to be strained from his jaw to thighs where his long fingers were curled into fists. Expecting me to condemn him. I stood and tossed my napkin into my chair and moved to kneel in front of him gathering his hands in my own.

"What happened to you, Linc? You were so strong. So determined to prove your father wrong."

"Turns out the old man was a prophet," he spit out bitterly. "In my genes, I guess." He lowered his head. "Anyway I wasn't strong enough at the time to find the right path." He lifted his gaze and stared into my eyes. "The one that would have led me back to you sooner." He stood and pulled me up to my feet gathering me close. "One of the first things I did after I got out of rehab was apologize to Patch's family and to Karen." She never told me that. I guess maybe it was too sore of a subject for either of us to handle. "Patch's dad was so incredibly cool about it. He accepted my apology like it meant something. He told me a man's worth isn't based on his missteps but on the steps he takes to rectify them. I made a promise to myself after that. If I could stay clean for a year then I would come see you again. Just see you. Not to reinsert myself because after all hadn't I caused you enough grief already? But then my old man died."

"I'm so sorry, Linc." I touched his face wishing I could smooth away the pain contorting his features but realizing he needed to get it all out. I could feel the physical and emotional space between us dwindling the more we continued to share with each other. Life had taught us both how little individual accolades end up mattering over time. Rather it's the memories we create together that truly sustain us.

"Yeah," he said bleakly. "They found him under some bridge. His body had been there for weeks, Mona."

"His death made me see things even more clearly." He turned his face to press a firm kiss into my palm. He shifted to bring our bodies more closely together and gathered both my hands and brought them to the center of his chest. I could feel every taut line of his. "He was wrong, you know. His was the real worthless life. Not mine. Not because of any success I had or didn't have on my board, not because I had a couple of hit records, but because of the people I've had love me. You. Ash. My Aunt and Uncle. If I hadn't spent so much time at the bottom of a whiskey bottle I would've saved everyone a lot of grief and reached that conclusion a lot sooner." I felt his grip tighten. "I was serious when I said I was here to stay. The band is finished or at least my part in it is. I want you to be mine again, Mona. You have my heart. You took it with you when you left all those years ago. The Blaine thing is just a reason to be near you, and an attempt to give you back at least part of the dream you sacrificed for me. I came back not to ask for anything but to offer you everything. All that I have, all that I am, I give to you." His voice was low and his eyes burned bright with the sincerity of his words. "Will you take it? Will you have me?" His plea resonated somewhere deep within me. Somewhere that had remained empty and dark since the day I had departed from his side. "No more talk of yesterdays. Right now. Tonight. This very moment let's start a future together. What do you say?"

Chapter 62

Linc

She was so incredibly beautiful, so alluringly feminine both of her hands small enough to nestle within one of own. My other hand was low on her back holding her to me so firmly that I could feel the eyelet pattern of her dress imprinted upon the surface of my palm. But no matter how tightly I held her, no matter how much I wanted to keep her, she was the one in control. She was the one who held all the cards. She was the queen of my heart and it was completely hers to do with whatever she decreed.

"Are you sure you don't want dessert?" the waiter asked as he stacked our empty dishes together. I wanted to growl my frustration. I'd already declined and requested the check. Could he not read the situation? I had my girl in my arms. *Finally.* He had to be completely clueless.

"No thank you. I couldn't possibly eat another thing," Simone politely chimed in, her cheeks becomingly flushed seemingly from embarrassment which was adorably refreshing to me after the type of woman I had been around during far too many drunken backstage parties.

Gaze tucked to the center of my chest her voice a little breathy she tried to struggle free but I didn't let her. I was perfectly happy with the current scenario sans waiter. I loved having her sexy curves pressed against me. Her tits to my chest. Her shapely thighs to mine. There was no place else I would rather be though of course my cock had other plans.

"I wanna be yours," she whispered lifting her pretty head and peering up at me through her sooty lashes the moment the waiter disappeared from view. "How soon do you think you can get the check paid and us out of here so we can make that a reality?"

My heart took a leap like my board when it picked up big air and went nearly completely vertical in steep water. "So fast I can make your head spin." I tucked her under my arm and headed back into the main part of the restaurant withdrawing my wallet and shoving a wad of way too many twenties into our surprised waiter's hands.

Outside I pressed her up against the side of the jeep. My body was vibrating with more tension than it had a moment earlier when I'd been waiting on her answer. I gave her a hard hungry possessive stare gazing down into her lovely eyes. "My hotel...your house...do you..." I swallowed to gather my fractured thoughts and to moisten my parched throat. Hell, my whole body felt parched and desperate with the need to reclaim her and make her mine again.

"Are you trying to ask me if we should go to your

place or mine?" she purred in her sexiest voice, the one she used all those years ago when she used to chant my name as she unraveled around me. My cock got even harder and I answered for her.

"Mine. It's closer," I growled leaning back putting some space between our bodies but only so I could help her into the car.

As soon as I had my seatbelt on, I threw my arm over her seatback, glanced behind to check that the way was clear and got the hell out of there.

My hotel was only five minutes away, a simple matter of negotiating a couple of blocks down closer to the waterfront. I got us there in half that amount of time.

She smiled softly when I ripped open her door and grabbed her hand before she could even offer it to me. "Wouldn't it be easier to just throw me over your shoulder?" she quipped hurrying to keep up with me as I strode toward the South Pacific longhouse style building with her in tow.

"That sounds like an excellent idea." My mouth curved into a dark grin. "Why don't you sashay your sexy body a little closer so I can?"

"Why don't you make me?" Her tone was teasing.

"Are you flirting with me, Mona?" I stopped outside my door so abruptly she ran into me.

"That depends." She blinked her dark framed eyes at me. "Is it working?"

"Hell yes." I leaned in to try to capture her lips, but she took a slight step to the side thwarting me. "Then how come I'm still standing out here outside your door?"

She didn't escape my second attempt. Not that I think

she intended to. In perfect sync with me she went up onto the toes of her ballet flats tipping her face to my lowering head as I plunged my hands into her silky hair. The instant my hard mouth met her soft one her lips parted and I thrust my tongue inside, the sweet distinctive taste of her blending with the Italian spices we'd both partaken of at dinner. Her hands curled around my forearms as if her knees had given out and she was depending on me for balance. Her tongue met my own. I felt the slick slide of them rubbing together all the way down in my dick.

"Linc." Her golden eyes looking slumberous she clung to me, her body trembling when I lifted my head.

"Simone." I brushed a softer kiss across her lush mouth. "My sweet Simone." Somehow I got the key card in on the first attempt. Once inside I spun her around lifting her arms over her head as I pressed her body against the door. "Need your lips again, babe. It's been too damn long."

"Yes," she agreed and I took her mouth again. Hard like I used to and she was with me all the way, her body restlessly moving against mine, her lips bearing the brunt of my assault, our tongues dueling wildly.

I couldn't get enough of her.

My fingertips burned with the need to ravish every single inch of her. I slanted my mouth one way and then the other while combing through the long strands of her hair scalp to ends tangling it in my haste to relearn its silky texture.

I broke the kiss but only so we could both catch our breath. Her breasts lifted and fell with each ragged one she took. The sound of hard breathing punctuated the heated space between us.

"My goddess," I praised, pressing her hands further into the wood, brushing her hair aside then lowering my head, letting my humid breath bathe her sensitive skin before my hot tongue followed. She shivered and I nearly did too imagining her rosy nipples hard and puckered beneath her dress.

She arched her neck to give my mouth more territory to conquer. I traced the stately column she offered me from just below her ear to just above where her neck met her shoulder. She tasted sweet like the summer we had once shared. Only better. Infinitely better. Because I knew now the priceless value of the woman I held in my arms.

I ran my parted mouth across the smooth round of her cheek and took her delectable mouth deeply again, and then with shallow sips of the nectar inside, over and over again before I soothed the plump abused flesh that framed it with soft back and forth passes of my parted lips to hers.

Her eyes fluttered open, the depths black revealing need that matched my own. My entire body was misted with a sheen of passion, my clothes stuck to my damp skin.

"Mona." I dropped my forehead to hers. "I'm barely holding onto my control by a thread. I'm too shaky to attempt all those buttons on this dress." I drew my palm down between her breasts and laid it over the tiny fastenings that held her dress together from the scooped neckline to the hem. Her breath hitched. I wanted to touch her. I suspected she wanted that nearly as badly as I did. "I'm gonna rip it. My hands all over your skin. It's gotta go. Now."

She nodded and I didn't hesitate. I released her hands,

grasped the bodice with both of mine and tore the fabric apart. Buttons flew everywhere but I didn't care. I was too busy staring at her gorgeous body, the white cotton hanging from her tanned arms like a curtain over an illicit view. I eased back to enjoy it.

I thought my memory had exaggerated her perfection. It hadn't. Her tits were pushed up and outlined in nude lace that had a flowery pattern and delicate pearl beading. Her rosy nipples were beautifully budded beneath and lower, her thatch of curls was barely covered by a matching triangle of the same lace.

"Perfect," I whispered, eyes making another appreciative pass before I lifted my gaze. I hadn't allowed myself to remember her predilection for wearing sexy lingerie.

"Not perfect," she protested.

"Perfect for me." *You were always perfect for me*, I thought. *Perfect for any man.* But that was irrelevant. She was mine from here on out. Only I was allowed to gaze on that perfection. I took a step toward her and she moved toward me at the same time reaching for the buttons on my shirt.

She showed me her hands. They trembled. "I seem to be having the same problem." She moved her hands lower to the hem of my shirt. "Do you mind?" she asked in a teasing tone.

"Not at all, babe." I captured her hands and helped her tear my dark linen shirt asunder. Her lips curled into a slow smile as if she appreciated the view of me as much as I had of her. Not likely. But her hands on me I *loved*.

I groaned when I felt her soft fingers gliding slowly over the contours of my skin, my shoulders, down both my arms to my hands where for a brief moment she connected our fingertips before she tossed aside what was left of my shirt.

"I'm about at the end of my control, babe," I warned stepping out of my Vans and kicking them aside starting right to work on my belt and jeans. She took off her flats and shrugged out of the remnants of her dress. We watched each other while undressing our movements seeming synchronized and our mutual need making our lingering gazes heated.

Her mouth parted when my cock sprang free. I hauled her hot sexy body into me shuddering when my erection came into contact with her warm beckoning heat. Her hands latched onto my arms and I lifted her chin to reclaim her lips, needing to taste her again, needing to show her with my mouth what I was getting ready to do to her with my dick lest she had forgotten.

Slanting my head immediately to deepen the angle, I glided my tongue between her sexy lips making love to her mouth with it not letting up on a single stroke, until she whimpered and I felt the dampness of her arousal through the wet lace she slid back and forth over my hard cock.

"On the bed," I ordered. "Now." I slapped her sexy heart shaped ass as soon as she turned the pink mark proof of my ownership. "Ditch the bra and thong, babe." My voice was low, vibrating with the weight of my need. "Or I'm gonna rip it, too, and it looks expensive." I stalked after her. She turned around at the bed.

"Linc." Her eyes widened as she took me in, my darkened gaze, my features and muscles taut, my cock completely vertical a full frontal turned on male poised to take her.

"I can't get it." She dropped her arms frustrated with the clasp behind her back. Were here hands shaking because she was as nervous as me? Probably not. The last time I had truly made love to someone it had been her.

"It's ok, babe. I'll help." I soothed brushing her hair over her shoulder, noting the chill bumps on her skin as I unclasped it, slid it from her body and tossed it aside. I located a condom while she shimmied out of her panties.

When she was beautifully perfectly nude she turned around lifting her gaze. "The lingerie is a hit, huh?" she whispered skimming her soft fingers over the stubble roughened line of my tight jaw.

"No your body is a hit," I clarified. "The lingerie was just a bonus." I took her freed breasts in my hands weighing and shaping them, stroking the taut peaks with my thumbs before lowering my head and feasting, swirling my tongue around the pebbled areolas and lathing the tips until she started to moan, then sucking each one in deep.

When she began to pant between moans that was my cue to lift her by the arms and toss her into the bed. Before she could recover I had a knee to the mattress and followed her down.

I traced my hands upward parting her legs as I went, ankles to calves until I opened her lovely thighs and settled between them. Tossing her hair out of her eyes she came up on an elbow and skimmed her palm down the center of my chest until she had the hard hot length of me in her grip.

"Mona. Holy fuck." I shuddered.

Eyes on her task lip between her teeth she swirled a thumb around the velvety tip.

"Enough of your teasing, goddess." I captured her skillful hands, kissed the palm tasting the saltiness of my own desire on her skin before I ripped open and rolled on the condom. I drew both of her hands up over her head and pressed them into the mattress, positioned myself between her warm thighs and glided inside of her in one long languid luxurious stroke.

She moaned and her lids closed. "So good, Linc. That feels so good," she praised as I started to move.

So beautiful, I would have told her but I was too far gone to speak anymore. Every time I stroked inside I squeezed my hand around her hands and felt her tightening around me lower, squeezing my cock. As close as two people could get, yet it still wasn't enough. It would never be enough with her. I had to show her that. I had to make her mine again. Need riding me hard, I rode her even harder until she started chanting my name and I felt her body shuddering. Her pleasure was the fiery spark that ignited my own.

"Oh, Mona. My Mona." I groaned my release sliding over the edge plunging into her heat again and again, our pleasure linking our hearts intrinsically together. She took what I gave her hips up to meet each thrust taking me deeper and better than ever before until I collapsed on top of her, my face buried in her neck.

"I love you, Linc," she whispered stroking her fingers up and down my perspiration slicked spine while I stroked in and out of her a couple of more times just for pure enjoyment. I knew from the roughened tone to her words that her eyes were as wet as my own.

Together again. She mine and I hers. *Finally.*

Outside

"I love *you*," I told her pressing my lips into her damp hair.

Chapter 63

Simone

I ran my fingers up and down the perspiration slick skin over his spine as he languidly stroked in and out a couple of more times. I knew my tears betrayed everything. How good it was. How much I had missed him…this…us.

He pulled out and I stretched out on the soft luxurious sheets basking in the view of the perfectly formed naked man before me as he peeled off the condom, tied it off and tossed it into a nearby bin. "Babe," he offered me his hand to help me off the bed, "come take a shower with me."

"Ok," I agreed not caring that I sounded overly eager to have his soapy hands all over me and mine on him.

Yes, please.

He tugged me into the opulent bathroom that looked as if it had been recently renovated. Neutral stone walls, pewter fixtures and a shower big enough for two.

While he turned on the water and checked the temperature I admired him. How was it possible that he had gotten sexier over the years?

His body more chiseled.

His muscles more firm.

His cock…

"Babe."

I looked up into dark eyes that glittered dangerously. "But we just…"

"I'll never get enough of you, Mona." His voice was gruff, his gaze intense and I believed him because that was exactly how I felt, too. He pulled me into the shower and positioned me under the water, its warmth drenching my hair and skin as he caressed me with his strong talented hands. A swipe of his thumb across my cheekbone. Smoothing both over my shoulders. His expression one of extreme concentration as he touched my breasts, circling the nipples over and over again until they were hard and achy for his mouth all over again before he lifted his darkened gaze to regard me.

"Let's get you cleaned up. Then I want to try something new."

What did he want to try?

My heart stumbled but I nodded my head and reached for the hotel shampoo. He snatched it from my fingers.

"Let me."

"Only if you let me first," I bargained.

"Alright," he agreed with a slow smile and we switched places beneath the water.

I ran my gaze over him as he dipped his head back to wet his hair. He had to bend at the knees to get his height low enough to get under it. When he reopened his eyes I gazed back up to his handsome face. "You'll have to bring yourself down to my level." My voice was husky with need. Tone, lean, aroused Linc had that kind of predictable effect on me.

"Sure, babe." He did as I requested, but it was acquiescence on his part. Linc was a powerful male. We both knew who was really in charge. I filled my palm with melon scented shampoo, lathering his hair first then running my fingers through the thick strands, kneading his scalp until he groaned in pleasure. Every single time he groaned like that my body responded. Nipples hardening, heat pooling between my legs, deep places becoming darkly needy. It was embarrassing how easily he affected me.

"Rinse," I said.

"Ok, boss lady." He grinned mischievously complying with my order but in a cocky way that made me wonder yet again just what he had planned for later after the shower.

When it was my turn he lingered over my hair until the lather was thick and my limbs pliable from his ministrations. His strong masculine hands had been so unbelievably gentle. He seemed just as affected by my moans, his cock hot and hard between us.

"You go first with the soap." He handed it to me and I took it wondering about his choice of order, but only later. In the moment I enjoyed the way it felt to have a powerfully beautifully built man like Linc beneath my fingers. My soap slippery hands made my fingers glide smoothly over every hard contour and chiseled plane. I ran flattened palms across the width of his shoulders. I slid them over his pecs. His nipples were hard and he drew in a sharp intake of breath when I passed over them purposefully slow.

I moved my hands nearly everywhere, down his lean torso, over his hard ass and even between but avoided his cock until he took my hands and guided me to it. Over the velvety tip down the long hard length, not a single inch of him did I leave unexplored.

I was trembling and incredibly turned on when we finished. That was when I realized why he had let me go first. I was wound so tightly I was probably going to come the minute he touched me.

"Linc," I said breathily as I watched him lather the soap for his turn on me. "I'm...what I mean is..." My voice shook. "I don't think I can..."

"Oh, yes you can and you will, gorgeous. I took what you gave. You take while I have my fun. You'll come only when I say."

"Ok, I guess." What was he up to?

He was up to driving me totally and completely insane.

He did my lower half first. Legs, ass, brisk and efficient, between my legs only briefly with just a few swipes but enough to make me arch into his caress before he moved up to my breasts. Then he acted like he had all the time in the world. The only evidence that he didn't were his heavy breaths through parted lips and his cock that kept leaping between our bodies every time he ran his palm over my hardened nipples.

The earlier trembling was only a precursor. Now my fingers curled into my palms and my muscles locked tight. If he just kissed me deeply I knew I might come.

"Rinse off, babe. Then get out."

In a sensual daze I nodded. The water cascading over my body felt deliciously erotic. So did the plush towel that

I used to dry off after he shoved it at me giving me a gruff order to be quick as he exited the bathroom.

When I came out his surfboard was on the bed, the orange and turquoise colorful against the stark white rumpled sheets.

"What did you have in mind, Linc?" I asked as he withdrew his leash from the side pocket of a silver nine and half foot long insulated case that I knew was his travel bag for his board.

"I've seen that movie too, gorgeous." He stepped over his black guitar case and turned around to face me. "I want to fulfill your every fantasy." His voice went lower as his eyes scanned me head to toe evoking a visceral response. "Because you certainly fulfill every single one of mine."

He wound the leash cord around and around his hand as he regarded me steadily with eyes that looked like they were on fire. I licked my dry lips. "Get on the bed, Simone," he ordered. "On my board. On your back. Arms above your head hands together."

Wet heat flashed between my legs. "I don't know." My words belied my body's response.

"You afraid?"

I shook my head. I was never afraid of him. Never.

He studied me a beat seeming to notice my parted lips, heavy breathing, hard nipples and trembling.

"Turned on?" he guessed.

I nodded.

"Get on my board then, babe. I aim to please if you'll let me."

I scurried to the bed and climbed in, but not quickly enough to avoid a smart smack on my ass.

Outside

"Owed you that one," he explained when I snapped my neck around to glare at him. "You might want to stow the sass."

I pressed my lips together, lying on the board, the plastic cold and hard against my naked skin. He moved closer studying me so long I started to squirm. Just having him look at me at this point turned me on. How could he wait? I could see that he was just as aroused as I was.

Nostrils flaring he unwound the leash from his hands and rewound it around my clasped hands instead. He smiled slowly and brushed the length of my hair back over each shoulder. "Like you like this, babe. You're fucking gorgeous." His dimple seemed to be mocking me. "I can't wait to be inside you. *Again.*" A warm shiver rolled through me from the smolder in his tone.

Then he climbed onto the bed from the foot of it where he parted my legs slowly. Firm warm hands still gripping my thighs he looked up at me when he saw the evidence of just how turned on I was. "Mona. Babe." My cheeks warmed but I held his gaze not regretting being aroused by him. He leaned in and I pulled in a quick breath when I felt his warm exhalation. No one had ever done this before. Touched me so intimately, but...

He answered the question I didn't voice. "I'm clean, Simone. Been tested every six weeks since I got out of rehab. If you want me to stop, I won't go any further, but I want to. I want to taste you and touch every part of you. If you'll let me."

I nodded and he did.

And it was *glorious.*

Being restrained and unable to do anything but experi-

371

ence was freeing. It heightened the effect of everything he did. I felt every wet swipe of his tongue, every swirl, every purposeful thrust.

Only…

"Linc!" I was too close. I started to sit up trying to pull my legs together only he didn't let me. He kissed each thigh with lips wet from me. Then he lifted his head his eyes nearly black with passion. More heat pulsed through me. I wanted to run my fingers through his tousled hair. I wanted to smash my mouth to his to taste myself on his firm lips. I wanted him inside me.

"Not yet," he warned climbing up over me and shaking his head when I started to lower my arms. I wanted to wind them around his neck and bring his mouth to mine. "I'm not finished yet."

Before I could tell him I was, he lowered his head and brushed the damp ends of his hair over my taut nipples, then his whisker roughened cheeks, then his warm lips, then his wet tongue.

"I can't, Linc." Wet gathered in my eyes from the strain of holding back. "I can't anymore. *Please.*"

"Yes, sweet Mona." He slid his deliciously tight hot body down and parted my legs again, settling between them and thrusting his hard length inside me in one smooth decisive motion that felt so good I let out a long broken moan. He smiled darkly then immediately withdrew and did it over again nearly coming out then going all the way back in so hard this time that my body slid up the board.

"Sorry, babe." His voice was deeper than I'd ever heard it and his face was drawn tight with need.

"Don't be. Do it again," I begged. "Harder."

His dark grin widened. "My pleasure." He grabbed my hips and did.

"No mine," I managed through a broken breath.

"Ours," he groaned. "Always ours." Then he started pounding into me and I raised my hips to meet each thrust.

Everything else faded away except his delectable hardness filling me over and over again, each angled stroke measured and purposeful, until my thoughts completely scattered and the world as I had known it unraveled and came back together in a way totally unlike it had been before.

Better.

"Mona," he rasped my name and stiffened inside of me. I felt the wet heat of his release filling me but he kept going powering through his climax and extending my own taking us both higher than we had ever been before, beyond anything we had ever known.

Chapter 64

Simone

The night ended and the dawn came bringing with it cold clarity beyond the neutral botanical comforter and the glossy rosewood furniture within the South Seas inspired hotel room. I was fully dressed and sitting on the edge of the bed wearing a borrowed shirt from his closet since my dress was in tatters. Tears burned the back of my throat as I stared at a dream that was too good to be true. I stroked softly over his thick wavy hair the way I had in the past. The fine lines around his mouth and eyes disappeared as he slumbered peacefully.

Unaware.

"I love you," I whispered wanting to press one more kiss to his chiseled lips, but too afraid if I did it would wake him.

Why was I lingering?

Why make this harder than it already was?

I told myself that I was doing what had to be done.

Make the break now before things got even more compli-cated.

Safer, easier, better to just put all those memories back into the album and the album back into the box and my life back to the way it had been before he'd returned and turned everything completely upside down.

The man at the front desk was helpful, though he raised a brow at my attire. The taxi he summoned came quickly, and in a shorter amount of time than it had taken Lincoln to drive us out to Shelter Island, I was dropped off back in front of my house.

My disabled Accord was still in the driveway as I walked up the front sidewalk. Everything looked the same and in order as if the incredible night before had never oc-curred. But inside I couldn't deny that it had. Inside I was afraid. Afraid he had stirred up feelings, longings and dreams that once awakened would never go back into stasis mode again. Not easily. Not ever if I was being honest with myself, which I was having trouble doing at the moment.

I let myself in and went straight to the utility room. Chulo was ecstatic to see me. I fed him and let him out be-fore I went upstairs to take my shower trying to avoid no-ticing the marks on my body from my night with Lincoln, trying not to hyperventilate when I stepped out of the tub and slathered on lotion and realized that most of them had already faded.

I made coffee and poured it into a thermos but didn't bother to eat anything. I didn't think I could hold it down anyway.

"Chulo, c'mon on," I called into the backyard and he came running curly white tail plume wagging. I clipped on his leash for the walk to the beach but even when he put the end of the leash into his mouth and pranced to the door as if ready to walk himself, it didn't elicit a smile.

The familiar route passed by in a blur, down the stairs, over the sandstone path, under the pier. But my mind wasn't on my surroundings. It was on him.

"You're wrong. I haven't forgotten. I can't forget any of it."

"...the real reason my life has been hell is because I've had to live it without you."

"You have my heart. You took it with you when you left all those years ago."

Though beautiful, both he and his words, the same conundrum existed between us that had always been there. What place did he really have in my life or I in his after all the years and heartbreak?

"Hey, Simone." Vassel greeted from the back of Tasha's Outback, the scene familiar but not comforting to me today. None of my routine was. Something was off. Something was missing. *Someone,* my heart practically shouted in order to be heard over the din of my fears.

Vassel stuffed his mouth with his last bite of English muffin, chewing and swallowing while watching me closely. "I heard you were finally coming to hear us play."

"Oh." I had forgotten about that. "I don't know," I hedged. "Maybe. I'm not sure. My car isn't working." I glanced around. "Where's Patrick and the others?"

"Tasha and Dylan are finalizing things for our gig." He hooked a thumb over his shoulder. "Pat's out in the surf already. He and a new guy are hitting some beautiful sets right now but they exchanged some heated words involving you before they went out."

It couldn't be. Could it?

I moved quickly across the parking lot shielding my eyes from the glare when I reached the sand. The tension inside my stomach instantly ratcheted tighter. I recognized Lincoln right away. Even in his wet suit the way he moved across the surface of the ocean on his board was as unique as he was.

Under the curtain unleashing his fins.

Maxing out of the tube.

Finding steep wall and going nearly vertical.

Those were the maneuvers I knew, the others I didn't but that didn't make them any less awe inspiring.

Linc took one wave, rode it, dry docked it halfway in, then immediately paddled out to catch another. Patrick sort of held his own for a couple of rounds then gave out, wading out of the surf with his lime colored board under his arm, collapsing in the wet sand on his back.

Chulo squeaked happily and bounded over to lick his face then went back to dashing back and forth along the beach demanding attention from everyone who had gathered to watch the two accomplished surfers compete.

Why was Lincoln doing this?

What was he trying to prove?

"I was wrong."

I stopped twisting my hands together and glanced down at Patrick. He was still breathing hard.

"About what?" I asked.

"The guy's crazy about you. Totally insane. He bought out the entire apartment complex where I live. He's repurposing it as a studio. Repurposing his whole life he told me just to be near you, Simone."

"I know." I nodded absently, heart in my throat as I watched Linc enter the barrel of a huge wave. It collapsed on him and my breath caught. When he didn't immediately pop back up I'd had enough. I wasn't going to lose him again. No way in hell.

I kicked out of my flip flops and ran into the water ignoring Patrick's call to come back. I swam when wading was no longer an option and was halfway to where Linc had gone down when he resurfaced.

But instead of paddling back in like a sane person, he hopped right back onto his board again and paddled back out toward the big waves.

"Damn you, Lincoln!" I shouted but there was no way he heard me over the roar of the surf. He probably couldn't see me over the height of the crashing waves. I swam harder trying to reach him but got caught in the current. Even though I was a strong swimmer, without a board, without a wet suit, my limbs started to get cold and I started to get into trouble.

I went under and came back up sputtering salt water. Remembering that awful day with Linc, when he disappeared then reemerged with all of that blood on his board I panicked in the here and now. There was a reason I hadn't been back in the ocean since that day. I still admired the beauty of the waves and the men who attempted to tame them but not for myself, not after I'd seen what they had done to my champion.

My eyes burning with fearful tears, muscles cramped on one side, I started to sink beneath the surface when I was suddenly snatched up and out of the water to the safety of Lincoln's board.

"Dammit, Simone! What the hell do you think you're doing?" He looked furious.

I clung tighter to the turquoise and orange hibiscus striped surfboard but didn't answer. It took me a couple of breaths before I could even attempt one. "Coming out to tell *you* to get the hell back to shore," I finally croaked my voice raspy from all the salt water I'd swallowed.

"I will." His jaw tightened. "After a while."

"When?" I pressed. "You've got to be exhausted. It's dangerous to be out here without any reserve, without an extra set of eyes to watch your back."

"You're absolutely right. My point exactly." His blazing eyes narrowed. "But that's what we've both been doing for the past fifteen years. Drifting alone. Barely staying afloat."

He was right that was exactly what I'd been doing. I'd gotten stalled out inside my own life without the man who was as vital as the ocean to me, the one who helped me believe in limitless possibilities.

"I'm not doing it anymore," he continued. "I came back for you and I'm staying."

"Out here in the water?" I grumbled finding my sass and brandishing it as I pulled myself up onto his board. The ocean suddenly didn't seem so ominous anymore. Not with him there to protect me.

Had he been out in the surf all this time waiting for me so he could show me that he could take care of himself and me, too?

"No." He gave me a half-smile with that damned dimple. "Although it's a great place to get your mind straight.

Your buddy Patrick and I had a long interesting chat out here. I think we understand each other now. I told him we were together and that he needed to stand down." He studied me a moment and his expression softened. "Why don't you come out here anymore, Mona?"

"How did you know that?"

"Patrick mentioned it. Is it because of my accident?" he guessed.

I looked down and gripped the rails tighter.

"Because if that's the reason, it's a shame." He covered my hands with his own and squeezed. "Shame to give up something you loved so much, something that brought you so much joy and gave you so much peace just because you're afraid." I got the distinct impression that he was talking about more than just the ocean.

"Not *so* afraid," I lifted my chin casting my gaze to the gently rolling surface of the Pacific around us to make my point.

"No, I guess you're not," he decided after studying me with that unnerving intensity of his. "Good." He nodded his approval then leaned forward and the line of his jaw tightened once more. "I didn't like the note you left me, Mona. In fact it pissed me the hell off. Didn't believe a word of it by the way. I had plans for the morning. Plans for you and me in the plunge pool with my surfboard. You kinda ruined them though and I expect you to make it up to me later." He leaned even closer, so close I could see the flecks of gold within his mostly clear blue eyes. "Everything I've told you since I came back is the truth. I failed at being your hero in the past, but I've learned from my mistakes and I promise you I won't fail you in the future. Whatever

the conditions, whatever comes our way, we can take it."
He stroked my cheek and I nuzzled into his touch. "All I
ever really wanted was this. You on my board. You in my
life. Us together. What we started last night I plan to repeat
and repeat and repeat." His gaze positively smoldered.
"I've got a lot of stamina for an older guy and a lot of years
with you to make up for. It's time for you to take that first
step and start believing me. For us both to start living life
again. Together."

"I have. I mean I just did," I grumbled, flinging wet
hair from my eyes and starting to wring the water out of the
ends. "It wasn't a step by the way. It was more of a dive
and a near drowning. But I'm here now. On your board.
With you." My solace in the storm. Always him. Forever
him. I pulled in a breath and took the plunge that I wanted
to, that I needed to, the one that was vital to me. "You're
right, Linc. I do care. I never *stopped* caring." It wasn't that
I didn't believe in love anymore. It was just that I didn't
believe in it for me with anyone but him. "I love you. I'm
sorry I got scared this morning. But I'm ready now, ready
to begin again with you." I peered up at him through my
wet lashes staring into eyes as crystalline blue as the ocean
and saw my reflection, the reflection of the woman I was
with him. His goddess. Far from perfect but perfect for
him. "If you're gonna be out in the deep water then I am,
too," I stated firmly then lightened my tone. "So…since
you're sticking around for a while…why don't you teach
me how to do that vertical maneuver?"

Chapter 65

Simone

"I'm coming. I'm coming," I shouted while hopping on one shoe and cursing under my breath when I glanced and saw the time on my cell. The driver that was supposed to take me to the Dirt Dog's concert was fifteen minutes early and I wasn't ready yet.

Mostly that was my own fault since I had tried on a half dozen dresses before settling on a powder blue strapless Roxy with an asymmetrical mid-calf length hem. Classy yet casual. Not as expensive as the Lilly Pulitzer ones I liked to wear when performing but I thought more practical just in case Linc wanted to play rip the clothes off of each other again.

His mood had still been a little edgy when he had walked me home from the beach. I didn't know if that was because of residual emotion or because of the impending Dirt Dog's performance tonight.

I scooped Chulo under my arm and opened the door.

Outside

My jaw immediately unhinged.

"Ash!" I exclaimed. "I can't believe it." Handsome as ever he filled out a long sleeve pewter silk shirt and black tropical blend wool pants. His clothes were as tasteful as the silver linked TAG Heuer sports watch around his wrist. "What are you doing here?"

A subtle smile on his tan face, his sapphire eyes sparkling, he tucked a straight strand of his platinum hair behind his ear. "Aren't you gonna let me in, Mona?"

"Oh, yes. Yes of course. I just wasn't expecting you."

"I know but Linc is busy doing interviews. The drummer is always an afterthought in those kinds of things. He was just going to send the driver alone, but I came with. I thought it would be a good time for us to talk privately." His gaze dipped to Chulo. "What kind of dog is that?"

"A Havanese from Havana," I explained. "They're the national breed of Cuba."

"Oh. He's cute." He stroked Chulo's fluffy head and Chulo squirmed in my arms. Spoiled baby that he was he had to be adored by his latest fan.

"Can I hold him?" Ash asked while giving me a head to toe scan. "You look beautiful, Cinderella, but you seem to be missing a shoe."

"Very observant," I quipped and thrust Chulo at him. "I need my bag, too, but I'll grab my shoe and be right back." I started to go then whirled back to throw my arms around him. Chulo got squished between us but he didn't seem to mind. He liked group hugs. "I missed you, Ash. It's been too long."

"Since the funeral," he mused. "I agree. It's been far too long for *all* of us." His eyes were penetratingly intense.

After I slipped on my other sandal, dressier than my usual flip flops because of the shiny glittery thong, I took Chulo back from Ash. Both seemed reluctant to be parted from each other even though they had just met. My fluff ball knew no strangers only new best friends.

I closed the door to his crate giving him a treat and warning him that I might not see him till much later. I was hoping maybe Linc still wanted me to make up for my mad panicked dash this morning. I was a big fan of his creativity.

When I grabbed my purse and returned to the living room, I noticed Ash had picked up the photo album I hadn't moved since Linc had flipped through its pages. Ash extended it toward me pointing out the same picture that Linc had seemed to stall on, too.

"I remember that day," he said lifting his gaze. "That was when you and Linc got back together. The day I gave you the camera."

I nodded.

"You were so happy."

I nodded again eyes filling as I recalled how beautifully Linc had made love to me on the beach.

"Are you happy now, Mona?" Ash put down the album and picked up my hand his eyes searching.

"Yes." The edges of my mouth curved up softly as I studied him in return. "How about you, Ash? Lincoln said you told him everything."

"I did. It was time. I think he already knew how I felt but I was glad I said the words out loud. I think we both were relieved to get it out in the open. About me not sleeping with you, too. Having honesty between us has allowed us to grow close again when we both really needed each other. We've got no secrets anymore." He tucked a strand of platinum behind his other ear suddenly looking a little tired. "We don't have much time. Traffic's probably not going to cooperate. Let's talk some more in the car."

After I locked the front door I noticed the stretch limo waiting for us at the curb. A couple of the neighborhood kids on their bikes were gawking at it. It felt a little extravagant for just Ash and me but this was all part of their rock star world now.

Gathering my skirt for modesty, I slid inside while the driver held the door and Ash followed sitting beside me on the bench seat that faced forward. The driver closed the door before making the long trek to the front. Once we were underway, Ash pressed a button letting the driver know he was putting up the privacy partition and not to disturb us. Then he shifted to face me and gathered my hands into his.

"Did Linc tell you tonight is the Dog's final performance?"

I shook my head. "No, not tonight specifically."

He nodded reflectively. "Well it is. With the current line up at least." His eyes grew unfocused for a moment. "It was a dream for me at one time but we're both really tired of it. It has taken on a life of its own and become more of a nightmare to tell you the truth." His gaze refocused and settled on mine. I squeezed his fingers encouraging him to continue while shadows of hazy scenery passed us by in the heavily tinted windows. "Linc wasn't the only one who struggled with the alcohol and drugs. One by one we all inevitably succumbed and it got worse after Patch. Except for the new guy. Diesel's a bit of a self-disciplined zealot." He stopped and pulled in a shaky breath.

"I know. I understand. Patch's death hasn't been easy for any of us to come to terms with."

He nodded once. "Linc got clean before me. It's only been a little over six months for me, and I was doing worse things than him. Shooting up."

"I'm sorry, Ash. I didn't know."

"Yeah." He snorted. "The media's not as interested in the supporting cast of the band. Ramon didn't care too much about me by the time I hit bottom. I'd burned too many bridges with him, borrowing money for dope, being strung out and wasted one to many times at one too many venues making us all look bad. But Linc stood by me through it all. Best cousin. Best friend a guy could ever have."

I just nodded, my throat and lungs were too clogged with emotion to speak. Being a celebrity apparently wasn't the dream it appeared to be to the rest of us on the outside looking in.

"These past several years have been hell for both of us." His brow creased into a deep v. "He told you about his father?"

I nodded.

"That really hit him hard, but I think it's also helped him in a lot of ways, too."

I nodded remembering Linc's words about how his father's death made him see things more clearly.

"It made him even more motivated to change and more open to my advice." His fingers flexed in mine. "I'm the one who convinced him to return. He was never happy without you, Mona. Not a single day."

My eyes filled. "Neither was I," I admitted.

He nodded. "That's as I suspected. Linc. Me. You. None of us were really happy after you left. We all learned too late that it's better to have nothing and the right person to hold onto than anything else in the entire world. But sometimes the only way you can move forward is to come to terms with the past. In your case, with the three of us, I'm hoping we can merge the past and the present into a better future for all of us. Sweet, Mona." He brushed my cheek softly with his knuckles. "It's good timing then for the Dirt Dogs to hang it up. I'm planning on sticking around to make sure you two do right by each other. There are no two people in the world I care for more except for my parents. They're the only other ones besides Linc and me who know the other reason we're calling it quits." He pulled in a breath gaze turning stormy sapphire. "I'm HIV positive, Mona."

"No!" Eyes widening, I sucked in a shocked breath.

"Don't know whether I got it from sharing a dirty needle when shooting up or from unprotected sex. Doesn't really matter at this point."

I unbuckled my seat belt belatedly realizing we had stopped. I threw my arms around his neck. I wasn't prepared to lose someone else I loved. "I'm sorry, Ash. So sorry. Whatever I can, I'll do. I'll be here for you, too. Just like Linc. All the way. I love you."

"I love you, too, baby. But hey," he unpeeled my arms from around his neck and smiled softly, "it's not a death sentence anymore. As long as I take the antiviral drugs, I can live a long time just like other people with a chronic illness."

"On a happier note, Linc and I have a project together that we're very excited about. One that involves you. You're actually the first artist we're signing."

"The Blaine deal. I know. Linc mentioned they want to use our song." The one about our feelings for Lincoln and the love for him we had in common.

"I actually approached their people under the label Lincoln and I formed a month ago. You probably remember I'm pretty good at the negotiation side of the business."

I remembered. He was the one who had put together the mini tour. He was the one who always talked dollars and cents with the club owners. "I think that's so incredibly cool. What are you calling it?"

"The label? Outside. It's a surfing term and..."

"I'm familiar with it," I interjected.

"Yes. Well, it kind of summarizes a lot of things for us. Catching the big wave when it comes along. Finding a place in life where we can see the whole picture and the things that are really important. Family. Friends. Each other." He flashed me a smile. "Speaking of things that are important. We have a little surprise for you during the performance. Afterward we're hoping the term means even more to you."

Chapter 66

Simone

*A*sh and I had talked for so long I didn't get to see Linc before the show. I was treated like a VIP though and escorted through the tropical foliage that surrounded the venue to a front row center seat in a comfortable folding chair on the artificial turf that sloped toward the raised stage.

Everything was in position on it. The mics. The speakers. The drum kit on risers sporting the Dirt Dog's logo, a tough looking bulldog on a surfboard. The only thing missing was the band.

In the marina on my left the masts of the boats seemed to lean expectantly toward the stage, the Dirt Dog fans on them holding their breath as they awaited the show from their prime position on the water. To my right several Half Moon hotel longhouses with balconies provided those facing the stage a free bonus of a kick ass rock concert included in their nightly rate.

The restive crowd volume increased as the sun disappeared over the horizon. I moved forward in my seat as anxious for the show to begin as everyone else was, probably more so. I hadn't seen the guys performing live since Huntington Beach.

I smoothed my skirt around my legs and rubbed my arms to warm them. I wished I had thought to bring a sweater. The breeze off of the water right now was a little chilly.

From the chair beside me a distinguished Hispanic man with a liberal amount of grey intermingled in his black hair leaned toward me and asked for the time. I slipped my cell from my bag to check. A message from Linc came up on the display.

Linc: Love you, gorgeous. Nice dress.

I grinned and glanced up at the stage but I couldn't see him. I turned to tell the man the time and I think he caught a glimpse of the message on my phone over my shoulder.

"You a friend of Linc's?" he asked.

I pulled in a breath and said the words. "His girlfriend," I clarified and stuck out my hand. "Simone Bianchi."

His eyes brightened as if he knew me. "Your father used to own Napoli's." He squeezed my hand and released it. "I'm Enrique Martinez. Ramon is my son. It's a pleasure to meet you. I hear it's going to be a great show. I hope you enjoy it."

I didn't get a chance to reply or to speak further to Enrique because the show had begun, a heavy bass beat and a blindingly bright flash of lights heralding the arrival of the first Dirt Dog to the stage.

Outside

The new bassist was an imposing figure, built and tall, maybe taller than Lincoln. Diesel had harsh features or maybe just harsh thoughts that made them seem that way. His darker skin tone hinted at what I guessed might be Polynesian ancestry. He was a very accomplished musician but seeing him on bass made me miss Patch. I wondered if it was that way for the others, too.

My wondering ended as the rest of the guys strutted out.

Ramon's black curls were shorter than they had been the last time I had seen him, the fine lines on his face noticeably deeper. I knew Patch's death had hit Ramon harder than any of us. They had been best friends before the rest. I remembered how he had been at the funeral. He had barely held it together and now he seemed even more troubled.

He stomped on his floorboard and let loose on his ebony Les Paul with a volley of complicated chords that erupted out of the speakers sounding as angry as the new bassist looked.

Ash had already taken a seat behind his drum kit when I slid my gaze to look at him. I was a little surprised to see that he had changed. No more fancy clothes. I guessed those had been for my benefit or for smoozing in the back with the VIP's. Now he had on shorts and a Dirt Dog's t-shirt that appeared to be more than a little faded and worn.

And then my gaze found its happy place at center stage. There it lingered through the entire opening song when his sandy brown locks were still dry and curled around his ears and swayed against his neck. There it remained for ninety minutes as he prowled the stage, his exertions drenching his hair and making his toned body gleam with perspiration.

I thought it was a good thing Linc had gone for the board shorts and a t-shirt with cut off sleeves. Besides the fact that the wet dry surfer apparel made it easier for him to cool off with an upended water bottle between numbers, he looked handsome in the orange and turquoise colors. Maybe an intentional choice, I hoped. Perhaps a subliminal cue to let me know he still had plans for us and his similarly hued surfboard later.

I could only imagine how much hotter it must be for him and the rest of the band underneath all those blazing lights. The heat from them actually radiated to the front row making me change my mind about the sweater.

As the applause died down, Lincoln turned to look at Ash. He got a thumbs up from the Dirt Dog's handsome equally perspiration soaked drummer.

"Our last one tonight is a brand new tune," Linc announced. "It's our best work yet but it's the final one for us as the Dirt Dogs." He had to speak louder to be heard over the protests in the audience. "It's a song for best friends you'll always have. It's for bandmates who are more like brothers. And it's for the girl you loved who you never got over." He looked at me directly and I readily returned the love I saw within his eyes. "It's called 'Outside'."

Outside breathe in the salty air
Murky thoughts become clear
Courage comes in many forms
Now you fall to stand once more.

Outside

Charge the wave
Don't be afraid
Tack the power
Make it your own
Trim the wave
Don't let it beat you
Link the flats
Home to your shore.

Outside another world awaits
Well beyond your comfort zone
Set aside your inhibitions
What lies ahead is worth the cost.

Charge the wave
Don't be afraid
Tack the power
Make it your own
Trim the wave
Don't let it beat you
Link the flats
Home to your shore.

Outside is everything you need
Family, friends, the one you love
Treasure all you've been given
Don't let it slip away from you.

Charge the wave
Don't be afraid
Tack the power
Make it your own

Trim the wave
Don't let it beat you
Link the flats
Home to your shore.

Epilogue

Linc

I bent over Ash's shoulder sliding up the treble on the soundboard. It had been too low during our first run though.

"She looks good," Ash said and I glanced through the soundproof glass to follow the direction of his gaze.

"She does," I agreed. Simone still had her headphones on and her silky caramel hair was loose around her bare shoulders. She was wearing a sleeveless dress like she had worn at the Dog's last concert along with the silver necklace I had bought her in Huntington Beach. The one with our initials. It was back around her neck where it belonged and I had on the skull ring she had purchased for me.

Her hair was lighter than it had been when I first came back to OB and her skin was darker. We had been spending *a lot* of time at the beach on my board.

We had a lot of time to make up for.

My pulse kicked up just looking at her and remembering the way she'd come apart in my arms this morning. She had been on top and I had gotten to play with her tits the entire time the way she liked, the way I loved, the way it had been in that private plunge pool the night of the concert, my board floating on the surface, me lying on it and her doing most but not all of the work. What would be the fun in that?

My mouth went dry remembering. Then she looked up and caught me staring at her. Heat blazed through me, the awareness between us sizzling even through the glass, even though I had just had her this morning. Even fifteen years apart hadn't been able to put out that flame. Mona plus me equaled a fiery love that endured and couldn't be extinguished or contained.

I clicked the switch to open up the two way mic connection between the sound booth and the recording room at Outside Records. "Let's get Chulo back in here with Uncle Ash so we can get this duet recorded. Your buddy Patrick and his band are coming to the studio, and we need to get ourselves back outside in the surf." I glanced out the window where the OB pier and the ocean beckoned. "The surf looks almost as good as you do, babe."

She smiled and kissed that spoiled rotten dog one more time.

Spoiled rock and roll Chulo, I should have clarified.

I thought he looked ridiculous with all that fluff stuffed into a black leather jacket with his name embroidered on it. But his Uncle Ash had bought it and Mona liked it. Whatever Mona liked I eventually came to love because whatever made my sweet Simone happy made me happy.

Each and every single day.

Outside

Sound board finally adjusted to the way I wanted it, I returned to the studio with Simone. Back in the booth Ash put Chulo under his arm and gave us the count down with his fingers. Five. Four. Three. Two. One.

Headset on, I settled into place beside my girl and we joined our hands, melding our fingers, hearts and our voices together as we sang the story about how we really saved each other.

Believe in the promise of us
Hearts as one love's guarantee
A bond so strong we both can trust
To draw us close whatever may be

I just want you to
Take me
And shape me
Remake me
Baby, come on and
Save me.

Lies between us in the dark
Hearts divided you and me
Ties all broken we're apart
Drifting on an empty sea

Why can't you just
Take me
And shape me
Remake me
Baby, reach out and
Save me.

I don't need some perfect hero
All I really want is you
By my side today tomorrow
Tell me that you want me, too

Please come back and
Take me
And shape me
Remake me
I'm begging you to
Save me.

I know I'm no perfect hero
But I've come to claim my prize
Got you now won't ever let go
Cause who I am is in your eyes

I'm right here to
Take you
And shape you
Remake you
Baby, I'm gonna
Save you.

Please leave a review to help other readers know about *Outside*. Copy and paste your review from your favorite book retailer site to my email foofighterfanatic@gmail.com and I will personally email you back to express my gratitude.

Rock Stars, Surf and Second Chances series continues with
Riptide
Knowledge is power. Don't miss out. Hot rock stars. Up and coming. First to know. Guaranteed.
Black Cat Records sign up at:
http://eepurl.com/Lvgzf

Acknowledgements

*I*t really does take a village of supporters and countless hours and hours of time.

Thank you to my husband and boys for allowing me my obsession with fictional characters.

Forever indebted to my copy editor Dr. Diane Klein who makes my words shiny and cool

Thank you to the most talented dual narration team in the business. Kai Kennicott. Your beautiful voice and spirit is the inspiration for Simone. Wen Ross your sexy smolder makes me want to write every love scene from the male point of view just to hear you read it.

My best friend and loyal champion: Lisa Anthony

My Chicago best friend and always encourager: Michelle Warren

My research PA: Chantelle Stx who said never again after our SoCal trip. She told my hubby she really does work on these 'research trips'.

My first surfing lesson by Maverick mastering surfer: Conor Beatty. I could have talked to you for more hours than we did and I can't wait to hit the Gulf to continue putting into practice what you taught me. Keep shining your light and surfing, *dude*!

My test readers who persevered with a two inch thick paper copy of the manuscript and time constraints to help put the final polish on Simone and Lincoln's story: Brandee Price from Bookworm Brandee. Anthony Dupuis. Sarah Haugh.

My formatting goddess and forever friend: Julie Titus

My talented Star Angel of everything cool. This lady rocks graphics on teasers. Carol Allen of Star Angels Reviews & Promo Stars Services.

The rock star of book bloggers: TRSOR, The Rock Stars of Romance's own Lisa Schilling Hintz

Black Cat Divas: April Merriman, Rita Jinkins Post, Wendy Neuman Wilken, Harvey Gaudun-Stables, MJ Fryer, MandyIreadindieAnderson, Alyssa Williams, Lisa Pantano Kane from Three Chicks and Their Books, Peggy Warren, and Teresa Marsh-Jensen.

About the Author

Michelle Mankin is the Amazon bestselling author of the Black Cat Records series of novels.

Romance with subtext.

Reimagining classic stories with sexy rock stars and thought provoking issues.

Love Evolution, Love Revolution, and Love Resolution are a BRUTAL STRENGTH centered trilogy, combining the plot underpinnings of Shakespeare with the drama, excitement, and indisputable sexiness of the rock 'n roll industry.

Things take a bit of an edgier, once upon a time turn with the TEMPEST series. These pierced, tatted, and troubled Seattle rockers are young and on the cusp of making it big, but with serious obstacles to overcome that may prevent them from ever getting there.

Rock stars, myths, and legends collide with paranormal romance in a totally mesmerizing way in the MAGIC series.

Catch the perfect wave with irresistible surfers in the ROCK STARS, SURF AND SECOND CHANCES series.

When Michelle is not prowling the streets of her Texas town listening to her rock music much too loud, she is putting her daydreams down on paper or traveling the world with her family and friends, sometimes for real, and sometimes just for pretend as she takes the children to school and back.

Connect with Michelle Mankin on Facebook:
https://www.facebook.com/pages/Author-Michelle-Mankin/233503403414065

On Twitter: https://twitter.com/MichelleMankin

On tsu: https://www.tsu.co/AuthorMichelleMankin

On her website: http://www.michellemankin.com/

Receive the Black Cat Records newsletter:
http://eepurl.com/Lvgzf

BRUTAL STRENGTH series:

Love Evolution
Love Revolution
Love Resolution
Love Rock'ollection

TEMPEST series:

Irresistible Refrain
Enticing Interlude
Captivating Bridge
Relentless Rhythm
Tempest Raging
Riveting Remix. A Tempest Brutal Strength Mashup. Summer 2015
Tempting Tempo
Scandalous Beat

The MAGIC Series:

STRANGE MAGIC:
Part One
Part Two
DREAM MAGIC: November 2015
TWISTED MAGIC: coming soon

ROCK STARS, SURF AND SECOND CHANCES series:

Outside
Riptide
Oceanside

50403890R00229

Made in the USA
Charleston, SC
24 December 2015